THE PAIN COLONY

THE COLONY BOOK 1

THE PAIN COLONY

SHANON HUNT

NARROW LEDGE
PUBLISHING

First published by Narrow Ledge Publishing 2019

First edition

ISBNs
978-1-7338212-2-3 (Hardback)
978-1-7338212-0-9 (Paperback)
978-1-7338212-1-6 (Ebook)

Preface

We live in an age where scientific and technical advances can, and frequently do, outpace our ability as a society to fully understand their future implications. What follows is a work of fiction, though if I have done my storytelling job well it will feel disturbingly real at times. This book pushes not only the boundaries of what's technically possible in the very near future, but also what's ethically and morally acceptable. Lean in to the adventure and remember: With pain comes peace.

col·o·ny
/ˈkälənē/

noun

1. A group of individuals with common characteristics or interests situated in close association

   // an artist *colony*
   // a nudist *colony*

2. A group of persons institutionalized away from others

   // a leper *colony*
   // a penal *colony*

3. An experimental unit of animals, typically housed together for the purpose of selective breeding

   // a C57BL/6J mouse *colony*
   // a MCH class 1 rhesus monkey breeding *colony*

1

Layla scurried down the path to the community building, eager for today's caning. Morning devotions began promptly at five-thirty, and inductees would be scolded for showing up late. She pulled her white wool poncho tighter around her and stepped up her pace, barely able to see the cracks in the river stone in the predawn darkness. It wasn't easy jogging in the sandals she'd been given. Back in her impure life, she could full-out sprint in six-inch heels. She was sure of this, even though she couldn't remember ever having done it. But these standard-issue thong sandals, known among the inductees as "slides," required her to shuffle to keep them from sliding right off.

The morning bell bonged as she trotted through the wooden double doors into the great room. She exhaled with relief, found a spot in the back of the room, and knelt on the unforgiving cement floor. She carefully folded her poncho and glanced at Isaac in the next space over. He gave her a terse nod. Sweat beaded on his forehead as he panted, unable to get control of his breathing. His face contorted as he shifted to one side and rubbed his bruised shins. She offered a sympathetic smile. Not everyone had the same tolerance for pain or devotion to purification.

She carefully removed her sandals and rolled her pant legs just past her knees. She paused to collect her inner strength and then rolled onto her swollen, knotted shins, leaning back onto her heels in the heel-sit position. Then just as she'd been taught, she closed her eyes and exhaled into a whisper. "Thank you, Father."

All around her, she heard the same breathy whisper from her fellow inductees. "Thank you, Father."

She imagined a blue sky. *With pain comes peace. With gratitude comes the Father's love.* She selfishly stole a moment to reprimand herself for being late. Even after months at the Colony, she still struggled with the sleep schedule. *Father, please help me adjust.* The Father was testing her resolve. He needed her strong in mind, body, and spirit before she would be allowed to begin purification. Until then, she would dazedly crawl through her daily schedule on the six hours of sleep inductees were allowed each night.

Her legs throbbed as she offered one last whispered "Thank you, Father." The front door opened, and she smiled, thrilled to see that Brother James would be leading the devotions today.

At six foot four, Brother James towered over the inductees in their heel-sits. Layla dropped her gaze as she always did when he was in the room. She feared he would read her mind, see her attraction to him. Her chances for purification would be ruined.

"Good morning, everyone," he said softly. "Let's start today's devotions with five minutes of meditation to release the pain."

The meditation eased the throbbing in her legs, melting it away into the numbness she'd grown to love—to need—in order to reach a state of physico-mental openness. She took a deep breath and exhaled to the count of four, visualizing pain dissipating into the air along with the poison she'd built up over the years of her impure life.

Brother James walked among the inductees, gently touching their shoulders as he passed, and Layla smiled at this obvious gesture of love and support. Many of them were sweating or shaking from the weight on their painful bruises. Like her, they were finding their own methods of reaching a higher state.

Her mind wandered back to the day she decided nothing could be more important than being pure like Brother James. It had been months ago, after she was promoted from the recruiting program, and she'd been excited for her cleanse. She arrived at the purge room a full two hours early. Olivia, who'd been inducted before her, had told her that the Father would be pleased by her eagerness and would bless her with a deeper cleanse. She'd tingled with excitement and fear as she ducked into the small candle-lit chamber. The drab cement room felt like a tomb, and the flickering light of six candles barely illuminated its only feature, a long, narrow stone bench with leather harnesses anchored into the floor at each end, one for each wrist and one for each ankle. *Make sure the harnesses are tight*, Olivia had said. *You don't want to reflexively pull out of them. The whip hurts a lot more than the cane. Even the Princess of Pain will jump on that first lash.*

Layla felt a squeeze on her shoulder. "Layla, love, are you with us this morning?"

She opened her eyes, startled, and glanced around the cavernous community room, her head cloudy. Brother James rested his hand on her back and smiled down at her tenderly. Others around the room eyed her.

"Out partying too late last night?" he asked with good-natured suspicion.

The others giggled at the ludicrous suggestion. There was no partying during induction. No drugs, no alcohol, and no sex.

Her face turned beet red and she lowered her eyes to her legs. "I'm so sorry, Brother James."

His soft voice didn't falter. She'd never heard him speak anything but kind words. "No need to be sorry, beautiful girl. I can only assume you were with the Father."

He glided to the lectern, where he picked up a heavy wooden rod and addressed the whole room. "Shall we begin? Today is Tuesday, and you know what that means. Let's line up."

Layla hopped up, ignoring the pins and needles that stung the soles of her feet, and shuffled toward the front of the room, intent on being first to show her commitment to devotions after that shameful daydream.

Brother James gave her a crisp nod as he gestured for her to sit on the austere wrought iron stool. "Layla, the Father is very pleased with you today. I've witnessed a warmth from him this morning. Today's caning will bring you closer to him."

It was a great commendation coming from Brother James. He was pure, and as such, he had the immense privilege of communicating directly with the Father.

"I am at his will." She inhaled deeply and aligned her toes at the edge of the black rubber mat. Brother James liked precision.

The inductees chanted in unison. "With pain comes peace."

She exhaled to the count of four and looked Brother James in the eye. She steeled herself.

He lifted the cane over his head and brought it down hard across her shins. She winced ever so slightly.

"Thank you, Layla, for your devotion to purification." He gave her a satisfied smile.

"With gratitude comes the Father's love."

Layla rose with a respectful nod and returned to her spot without limping as the canings continued.

"Crystal, welcome. The Father is with you."

"I am at his will," Crystal croaked. Her head was lowered, and Layla assumed her eyes were squeezed shut. Most new inductees had trouble with their first few canings.

Layla couldn't suppress a grin as she rolled onto her newly inflamed shins. She breathed deeply to release the pain and closed her eyes.

Her day was off to an outstanding start.

2

Allison Stevens stood beside the stage, hands clasped tightly as her boss clicked to the summary slide for his presentation. Every seat was full, and conference attendees lined the back wall of the auditorium. All eyes were trained on Dr. Harris, CEO of Quandary Therapeutics, enchanted by him. No one even glanced down at their iPhone.

She wondered if they would all leave when she stepped up to the lectern. Austin was a hard act to follow. He moved so easily across the stage, spoke with such confidence and conviction. He wasn't just a great presenter; he was a passionate artiste.

"Just think how far science has come." His voice boomed over the speakers with a dramatic flair. "Two centuries ago, patients depended on magic potions and local plants to heal life-threatening diseases. And the first antibiotic, penicillin, isn't even a hundred years old yet—I have a grandma older than penicillin." He grinned. "Granny smells a little like mold herself, but don't tell her I said that." He winked at the audience.

The crowd laughed. Allison laughed too, even though she'd heard about Austin's moldy granny a dozen times before. He loved that line, and it worked every time.

"In the last hundred years, we've developed thousands of drugs for hundreds of diseases. In the last thirty, we've moved to new approaches for reaching even more targets and curing more diseases using more complex molecules like proteins and monoclonal antibodies. And now in the twenty-first century, with the surge in biotechnology and a better understanding of immunology, we can design and build compounds with multiple objectives—bispecific antibodies with one leg that finds a cancer tumor and another that calls in the body's own killer T-cells."

Her heart jumped as he neared his final point. She was up. Her mouth filled with cotton. She glanced at the lectern for the third time to ensure that her bottle of water hadn't disappeared.

"We can remove specific cells that aren't doing their job, reprogram them, and put them back into a patient's body, curing cancers and diseases that can't be treated with conventional medications. What would Granny have thought if she'd heard this outlandish science fiction when she was a child?"

Again, another round of laughter.

He lost his smile and put on his serious scientist face. "But where we are today with gene editing is a whole new level addressing the very foundations of what makes us human. It's truly remarkable to live in these times, and I'm so privileged to work with a team of brilliant scientists and clinicians who've taken the next step with me in this journey into gene therapy."

As Austin pivoted, a surge of adrenaline raced into her legs. She stood tall, trying to look worthy of the crowd's attention. Despite the over-air-conditioned room, her armpits felt damp.

"One of my brilliant scientists happens to be here with me today. Allison Stevens is my right-hand man at Quandary, and she also leads our most advanced clinical program, Enigmax." He held his hand out to her as if asking her to dance. "Allison?"

Smiling, she stepped onto the stage and gracefully took his hand. He dropped her hand and put an arm around her shoulder. It was a move they'd rehearsed many times to make it look natural. He'd seen a TV evangelist use this move to give the audience a feeling of wholesomeness, and he thought it might dissuade the skeptics from believing the work they were doing was ungodly. It wasn't easy being a trendsetter in medical advances.

"Allison is going to show you what you've all come here for today, the astounding early clinical results of Enigmax gene therapy in young patients with Duchenne muscular dystrophy."

The audience applauded as Austin stepped off the stage, allowing her one quick second to take a sip of water, a feeble attempt at replacing the saliva that just wouldn't come. She picked up the slide advancer, reluctantly stepped out from the lectern, and peered into the audience. Unable to see a single face beyond the blazing stage lights, she tried to focus on the small red dots of phones and recording devices.

"Ladies and gentlemen, thank you so much for the opportunity to share with you the important work we've been doing in Duchenne muscular dystrophy, or DMD. And thank you, Austin, for the introduction.

"DMD is a genetic disorder characterized by muscle degeneration and weakness that begins at a very young age in some children."

She kicked off a video of a young boy playing on the grass in a sprinkler with other children. He was limping and listing to one side. "This is one of our patients from Norway, Jakob. At three years old, he's struggling to walk and can't run like the other children."

Jakob, now a bit older, walked across a doctor's office. His legs moved slowly, his knees buckled inward, and he moved with an unnatural waddle. "And here is Jakob at age five. His large-motor control had become worse, and he was diagnosed with DMD by a genetic test. By the time Jakob joined our study a year ago, he was confined to a wheelchair."

Her voice cracked. She sidled to the lectern for another sip of water, glancing back at a still photo of Jakob sitting awkwardly in his small wheelchair. He was smiling, though, and his eyes twinkled with the energy and optimism of youth. Smiling Jakob had had no quality of life the day Allison had met him, but he'd smiled because he had hope. This was why she loved her job.

"There is currently no effective medicinal therapy for DMD, and unfortunately, Jakob did not respond to the only available gene therapy at the time, Exondys 51. This isn't entirely surprising since Exondys works in only thirteen percent of DMD patients. So Jakob joined our clinical trial and was treated with Enigmax eight months ago."

She clicked the slide advancer, and a new video of Jakob began. He stood up from a chair and walked down a long hall toward his mother. He didn't limp or waddle; he walked like a perfectly normal child. His mother got down on one knee and opened her arms, and he broke into a weak jog and fell into his mother's embrace.

The audience murmured in approval.

Allison smiled back. "Jakob gets stronger every day. He goes to school, plays on the playground with the other kids, and has a very bright future. In fact, I received a call from his physician just yesterday. He told me Jakob can now do a somersault."

Scattered applause gathered momentum quickly, and Allison blinked from the eruption of a hundred camera flashes. Damn, Austin was right. *Start with Jakob,* he'd told her. *Trust me. Jakob will take away your stage fright. He brings out the best in you.* At that moment, her mouth remembered how to salivate, her hands stopped shaking, and her smile came naturally.

She strode toward the edge of the stage. "Now let me tell you about Quandary Therapeutics' amazing new gene editing technology and our future plans for Enigmax."

***

"Bartender, bring this incredible woman a beer."

Austin's voice was boisterous as if he were announcing the winner of the World Cup. Despite the tavern's proximity to the conference center, they sat alone at the bar. Apparently, Boston didn't start drinking before eleven in the morning, despite the city's reputation. Good. Allison settled back on her stool. She was thrilled to have some time alone with Austin, a rare moment when he was neither presenting nor managing an important stakeholder meeting.

He raised his beer in the air. "To a well-deserved celebration."

She beamed and clinked his glass.

He moved closer, swept her hair off her neck, and punctuated each of his next words with a sensual kiss. "You. Were. Perfect."

"Austin? I'm phasing you out." She'd read enough self-help books to know that threatening a man wouldn't make him leave his wife, but she at least wanted him to think she wasn't the spineless gull she knew she was.

He sat up slightly and smirked. "Are you, now?"

"I've decided you're not my type."

"I believe I'm exactly your type." His grin widened.

Cocky bastard.

"No, it's become clear to me by your actions—or inaction, as the case may be—that you're not as serious about our relationship as I am, so I'm going to look for someone more—"

He booped her nose. "Insecure?"

"Funny."

"Beer-gutted?" He moved in on her again, playing with her hair, then tracing his fingers down the inside of her bare arm.

"No." She set her beer down, slightly shaky.

"Unemployed, living with his mother?" His eyes glistened with lust, following his hand as it wandered down her side and across her thigh.

God, he was irresistible. But she wasn't going to wane. She removed his hand. "Someone more *unmarried.*"

Whoops. The last word came out with a bit too much emphasis.

"Ah, baby, you're such a perfectionist. And I love that about you." He pulled her off the bar stool, spun her around, and pressed her back against the wall, kissing her hard on the mouth.

She folded instantly. Another failed attempt to regain her dignity. Maybe dignity was overrated.

"Austin Harris?" A deep voice came from behind them.

Mortified, Allison wriggled out from his grasp and turned away to put some space between them.

"Yes?" Austin asked. "What can I do—"

"Dr. Harris, you're under arrest for identity fraud and conspiracy to commit securities fraud. You have the right to remain silent."

She spun around. "What?"

The deep voice had come from a stocky man with a cleanly shaved head. He wore a sensible gray suit and red tie, and he held out a badge prominently identifying him as FBI. His dry, croaky voice reminded Allison of Vin Diesel's portrayal of the human-alien Riddick, and his monotone delivery of Austin's Miranda rights made him seem just as intimidating. Standing beside Agent Riddick was another suit, much taller and sporting a thick blond 1970s mustache. He eyed Allison briefly before scanning the empty bar, stopping at the bartender, who busied himself organizing clean glasses in an obvious attempt to avoid the confrontation.

The whole scene was a cliché straight from a CSI episode; it had to be a joke. She examined Agent Riddick's badge, searching for a tell, before realizing she had no idea what a real badge looked like.

Austin stoically listened to his rights, nodding slightly. She desperately searched his face, but it held no readable expression. She instinctively backed up, not daring to utter a word, fearful that whatever this was would be made worse by drawing attention to herself.

"Do you understand these rights?" Agent Riddick concluded.

Austin nodded. His face still showed no sign of emotion, fear or otherwise.

Agent Mustache stepped forward, pulling handcuffs from his pocket.

"I don't think that'll be necessary, will it, Dr. Harris?"

Austin's expression finally changed to a brief, sad smile. "No, of course not."

He followed them to the door.

"Austin!" She couldn't let him go like this, with no explanation. What was she supposed to do?

But he didn't turn back.

Instead, Agent Riddick turned and acknowledged her with a slight nod. "Ms. Stevens."

She stood alone next to the bar, her heart still drumming between her ears, and stared as the door banged closed, the dangling COME AGAIN! sign swaying back and forth.

3

"Layla, you can come in now," Dr. Jeannette called from her office.

Layla put down her copy of *Little House on the Prairie* and walked carefully but with purpose into Dr. Jeannette's office. She took a seat on the soft brown leather sofa, straining to sit upright. She really didn't like the cushy, pillowy sofa. It was impossible to make a good impression half reclined, and her legs were too sore to cross.

Dr. Jeannette noticed her discomfort. "How about we sit at the table."

She offered a hand to help Layla up, but Layla pushed herself out of the sofa and moved to the rigid armchair angled next to a small round pedestal table that held only a small box of tissues.

"You're my best adapter to pain, Layla. You should hear the others complain about the soreness and bruises."

She knew this to be true already. She could hear their suffering during devotions. She eased into the chair while Dr. Jeannette poured two cups of green tea. She admired her therapist's grace as she moved across the office. Dr. Jeannette was fit, not thin and frail like Layla, and she appeared strong, healthy, and worry-free. But most important, she knew that Dr. Jeannette genuinely wanted to help her.

"Thank you." She graciously accepted her teacup.

"Of course, my dear. How are you doing this week?"

"I think very well. I've been spending extra time in meditation group and yoga. I'm getting stronger. My weight is up to one sixteen now. That's almost a whole pound this week, and I got my period."

"That's excellent! Congratulations. Dr. Jeremy must be thrilled."

She slid forward on her chair. "Oh, and remember that cooking contest I was going to enter, over in the rec center? Well, I did enter, thanks to you not letting me back out, and I won third place. It was the curry. Curry's such an intense flavor. Hard to beat."

Dr. Jeannette beamed. "And how have you been progressing with your past memories?"

"Um, okay, I guess." She picked at a hangnail on her thumb.

"Can we talk a little about your father today?"

"Um, sure." Her eyes remained fixed on her hands. She'd practiced several ways of describing the beatings, but none of them sounded convincing. "Um, my father was a mean, horrible, abusive man. He, um, used to come home drunk and he would, um, you know, hit me."

Dr. Jeannette sighed and removed her glasses, setting them gently on the table. Layla had seen this nonverbal response many times before, and her eyes filled with tears. It was the wrong answer. Dr. Jeannette wasn't happy with her progress.

"Layla, let's do the chant together."

She reluctantly lifted her eyes, willing the tears back. "A poisoned life cannot be purified until it is fully understood. As an impure, I must acknowledge, accept, and despise the poison inside of me so that I can be free of it."

She dropped her eyes back to her lap. She felt Dr. Jeannette staring at her, pitying her.

"I know how difficult this is. I do. I've seen so many before you struggle to accept their pasts, unable to learn how to despise them. I promise you'll get there—but you have to work harder, Layla. You have to listen to what I've told you about your poisoned life. You have to feel the pain he caused you. This isn't just an exercise in telling me what you think I want to hear.

You need to feel it. Believe it, down to your core."

Layla's nose ran, and she plucked a tissue from the box on the table. She knew her inability to remember her childhood trauma was holding her back from progressing.

"Let's talk about something else. This will make you happy."

Layla searched her face hopefully.

"Last week during your hypnosis, you told me a fun story. You were maybe eight years old, or at least that's how old your voice sounded to me." Dr. Jeannette let out a small chuckle.

"Really? What was it?"

"Well, okay, let's see. How did it start? You were at a birthday party for one of your classmates. It was at a roller skating rink. You were holding hands with a friend, skating around the rink, when your friend fell down. She pulled you down too, and you both giggled madly. Do you remember?"

She squeezed her eyes shut as tightly as she could, hoping the memory would pop right out of her unconscious mind and project itself onto the backs of her eyelids like a movie. But all she could picture was a large oval cement floor with kids smiling as they skated around the circle, as though she were looking at a picture in a book.

"It's okay, my dear. So then neither of you could stand up. Your skates kept rolling out from under you every time you tried to stand, and that made you laugh even harder. What happened next is the best part. Another group of girls who were also holding hands tripped over you while you were trying to get up, and they fell on the floor with you."

Layla giggled. Just the idea that she might have been part of this silly group, invited to a roller skating birthday party, made her feel so normal, so human.

"And all of you just gave up trying to get up and just lay on the floor and laughed and laughed. All the other kids had to skate around you."

She wanted to hear more. She wanted the story to go on forever.

"See?" Dr. Jeannette put a hand over hers and gave it a squeeze. "I told you not every moment in a poisoned life is bad. There are happy moments, too. And this is why I think you're special, my dear. You have all this beauty inside you. Your foundation is rich and complex. And when you've released the poison during your purification, you'll be able to help so many others become pure just like you."

The words gave Layla chills, and her resolve returned. She would work harder. She would do whatever it took.

Dr. Jeannette stood up and held out her hand. In her palm was a small white tablet. "Now take your pill and finish your tea so we can begin today's hypnosis."

She swallowed the pill with the last gulp of the now lukewarm tea. She got up and took a step toward the sofa. Then, changing her mind, she turned back to Dr. Jeannette and hugged her tightly.

Dr. Jeannette laughed and hugged her in return. "Hey, what was that for?"

She bounced on her tiptoes. "I'm just feeling really optimistic about my future."

***

Layla left Dr. Jeannette's office feeling refreshed. The weather had grown quite a bit cooler, so she slowed to a stroll toward the yoga studio, enjoying the light, arid breeze carrying the peppery smell of sagebrush. She hummed a tune. She wasn't sure if it was a song, but it didn't matter. She felt better than she had all week. Dr. Jeannette's sessions had a way of giving her a new outlook.

She swerved over to the fruit stand, where her slightly pudgy friend Nicole hovered over the snacks. Layla selected a pear as Nicole grabbed her arm and pulled her to the side.

"Layla! Oh my god, I have to tell you something—two things, actually. Are you ready? One, I've been selected for purification. I'm. Starting. Purification!" She danced an excited jig. "And two, I'm being considered for a position outside the Colony with a sponsor, and it might be New York. A sponsor in New York!"

Nicole had always dreamed of going to New York and living among its tall buildings and flashing neon billboards. This was the perfect outcome for Nicole.

"Wow, that's amazing," Layla said, trying hard to sound as enthusiastic as she should have felt. But in truth, she was crushed. Nicole had been at the Colony only a few months. She'd completed the same inductee program Layla had. But it wasn't right that she should get her call to purification first. Layla was a model inductee. She was completely engaged in her daily schedule, she lived and breathed by the Colony's code of ethics, and she was so ready for purification.

"I know. And Brother James told me I'm like one of the fastest inductees to progress through the program."

Layla stepped back, wanting to escape this conversation.

"Anyway, I have to run now. Dr. Jeremy says I need to have a physical before I can start." Nicole rolled her eyes. "Like I could be any healthier."

She grabbed Layla in a hug, then skittered off without a goodbye.

Layla looked around to make sure no one was watching, then tossed her unbitten pear in the trash can.

***

Layla lay unmoving in the sensory deprivation tank for what must have been hours. Long durations in the tank were forbidden, but the staff trusted her after all these months, and they turned a blind eye to her extended sessions. She'd hoped that the isolation might help, but her poisoned life would simply not come to her. She tried to focus on the individual features of her dad's appearance, as she'd been told to do. *He had dark blond hair, Layla, a bit darker than yours, but thinning on top. He had a bald spot.* No good. Nothing. *He had a small gap between his front teeth, and you told me he had bad breath.* Still nothing.

Why was this so hard? What was wrong with her?

Anger got the better of her and her muscles involuntarily contracted, disrupting her motionless state. Irritated, she dipped her towel into the salt water and spread it across her face, reveling in the sting of the salt in her eyes and the bitter taste in her mouth. *Release the pain.*

After what felt like another hour, she finally knew what she must do. She left the new recruit center and headed uphill toward the administrative building, where she hoped she would find Brother James.

***

Brother James looked up from his journal with his customary warm smile when Layla knocked. He swept his hair to one side and pulled on his black-rimmed glasses over eyes that appeared impossibly blue. She blushed and dropped her gaze, but only for a second before she remembered her newfound resolve. She lifted her chin and took one step toward his desk, then stopped, second-guessing herself. She stepped back just a bit and began picking a new hangnail.

Maybe she should just accept that she wasn't meant to be pure. She should just leave the Colony and go back to her poisoned life, whatever that was.

She frowned. Dr. Jeannette would scold her for being self-critical. She gathered her strength again and stepped forward, holding her arms stiffly at her sides.

Brother James still hadn't spoken. He waited patiently.

"Brother James?"

"Hello, Layla. To what do I owe this lovely visit?"

She blushed again and glanced away. She hadn't stepped into Brother James's office in a long time, and it felt smaller. His shelves were lined with medical books and journals and stacks of folders. More books and journals were stacked on the floor around the perimeter.

Brother James was obviously an extremely busy and important man and certainly had no time for her. Her confidence waned again, and she stalled.

"Um, are you, um, working?" It was the dumbest question she could have asked, and she grimaced in disgust.

"Yeah, a little. I'm just reviewing the profile of a new recruit. Come here, let me show you."

She took one step closer. Why was she so terrified to be close to him?

Brother James got up with his folder and walked in front of his desk. He stood next to her, holding the folder open. "This is Kelly. She arrived yesterday. Here, take a look." He held up the file with a photo so she could get a good look.

She gasped. The girl in the picture was only about twelve years old but so emaciated that Layla couldn't believe she was able to stand up on her own. Her face, turned upward and directly into the camera, was gaunt and ashen, her eyes sunken. She appeared mournful. She looked like she might be dying.

"What happened to her?" she breathed, unable to turn from the image.

"She was found on a busy city street, staggering around aimlessly in only a long shirt with no identification or money. Our recruiters saw her and offered to help. They had fruit and sandwiches in the truck and a warm blanket. She accepted, and we brought her here."

"Is she sick?" The emptiness in Kelly's eyes unsettled her.

"Sort of. Kelly's a drug addict. She's in the infirmary now, getting treatment for her addiction. Our doctors are trying to remove the poison from her." He gave her an encouraging smile. "When she's able to join the group, I hope you'll befriend her. You have so much love to give, and you could really be a good mentor for her."

"But what about her parents?"

"She's nineteen, so she can make her own decisions."

She leaned in closer to the picture, incredulous. Kelly looked like a child.

Brother James closed the folder and lifted her chin so she would meet his eyes. He spoke to her in a serious tone. "Do you see how important our work is here at the Colony?"

She nodded.

"All your friends and all these people who live and work here are here on their own accord, to try to make a better world for you and Kelly and everyone else who had a poisoned life. We have doctors and therapists and nutritionists and exercise instructors, and they're all here because they believe in making a pure society."

"I understand."

"And you have an important role in that."

"Purification."

"Exactly." He smiled, and her courage returned.

She cleared her throat, even though she didn't need to. "I came here to ask for your help. Dr. Jeannette says the Father will not allow my purification until I can remember my poisoned life. Will you perform another cleanse? I think it might help me release my memories from my unconscious mind."

"Of course, beautiful girl." Brother James enfolded her in his arms, and for just a moment she indulged the warmth. The comfort. The faintly musky smell of his linen shirt.

Then she pulled away, embarrassed and ashamed. *Please forgive me, Father.*

4

Allison glanced at the clock: 4:22 a.m. She rolled over in bed and opened her laptop—she'd slept with it again—and scanned her emails, desperately looking for Austin's name. Nothing. She snatched up her phone. No messages. It was Thursday morning, a full forty-one hours since she'd watched Austin escorted out of the tavern, and she hadn't heard a word from him. The arrest hadn't made the local news, and apparently no one at the office had even heard. She'd come home yesterday before lunch to wallow in self-indulgent misery. How could he do this to her?

She scrolled through her texts. She'd sent him twelve texts since Tuesday, not one of them answered, not even the embarrassingly truthful one from last night at 10:42 that read, "Austin, please, PLEASE! I haven't slept. I haven't eaten. I can't stop crying. I don't know what to do. PLEASE!"

God, she sounded like a pathetic jilted girlfriend.

She hurled her phone across her bed. Was it really possible he'd had no opportunity whatsoever to contact her? She was certain he wasn't sitting in a jail cell somewhere. People like Austin Harris didn't do time, not even overnight time.

Her swollen eyes stung as she rubbed them, and her stomach churned with dread. She pulled the blanket over her head and tried to sleep.

***

The phone was vibrating. Allison jerked awake and dug frantically through the blankets, her heart hammering. There it was—on the floor. She grabbed it and instinctively swiped to accept the call before she noticed the caller ID.

"Al, where the fuck are you?" Ryan. Damn it. Ryan Garner, Quandary's chief business officer, was barely thirty with all the maturity of a frat boy. He was likable but not nearly experienced enough for his position, as evidenced by his greeting.

"I, uh … What time is it?" She rolled over to look at the clock. 9:20 a.m. Christ.

"Kiran's on his way over for a major announcement at ten. Do you not read your goddamn email?"

Shit. Why hadn't she thought to contact Quandary's legal counsel herself? Obviously, that's what a chief of staff would have done. She felt like such an idiot.

"Um, right. Okay. I was, uh, just finishing up something. I'll be there in thirty."

She dropped the phone and flew out of bed. She was never going to have any credibility with these guys if she didn't start acting like a professional. She grabbed her jeans, thought again, and tossed them aside. Kiran would expect her in business attire. And, damn it, Austin had trusted her to take on this role. He believed she could do it. She found one pair of unwrinkled dress pants and pulled on a shirt and sports jacket.

She looked in the full-length mirror. Good enough—for someone who was the last to know about an announcement she herself should have initiated.

***

"I'm so sorry about all this, Allison." Kiran Parsons was waiting in her office when she arrived.

"Thank you so much for coming." She leaned in for the loathsome East Coast cheek kiss. "I'm sorry, I should've called you. I just wasn't sure how to proceed in a situation like this." She'd practiced several excuses during her drive into the office. This one was the best she could do.

"Of course. Listen. Austin was released on bail yesterday, and he's staying home today to be with his family. He's asked me to make an announcement to the whole team, but I thought I should share it with you first. We should be on the same page."

She knew it. He wasn't holed up in some jail cell. She couldn't decide if she was hurt or angry that he hadn't called. She smiled to try to be polite, but she was sure Kiran could see how distressed she was. She closed her office door and turned to face him.

Kiran leaned back to half sit on her desk. "Austin was arrested for illegal insider trading and fraud. He's allegedly been trading call and put options on Quandary, then leaking information to investors to manipulate the stock price in his favor."

She stared at him, unable to speak.

"The SEC was alerted of suspicious trading activity on Quandary's stock by an anonymous tip about a month ago. The FBI and SEC followed the money coming in and out of Austin's various accounts and discovered a trading account and a trust had been set up using the identity of his wife's deceased brother, a guy by the name of William Chase Stetson. Does that name ring a bell to you?"

The phrase "insider trading and fraud" looped through her head like a stuck record.

"Anyway, allegedly Austin has been trading with this account. The SEC is focused on the insider trading, hundreds of thousands of dollars, but the FBI has built a case for identity fraud." He offered a sympathetic smile. "It's a white-collar crime. Unfortunate, but it does happen more than you think."

She felt like a house had fallen from the sky and landed on her. Or maybe she just wished one would.

He stood up and gazed out her office window into the lobby, as if this was just a routine legal status report. "Not gonna lie, the SEC has a strong case. The penalties for this kind of fraud are a bitch. If Austin's convicted, he'll be on the line for stiff fines and even jail time—usually only Club Fed, but a felony's still serious business."

A wave of nausea ran through her, and she leaned on her desk to keep from fainting. She sucked in air, hard.

"Are you all right?" He sounded concerned but he didn't move to help.

"Fine." She squeaked out the next question, not wanting to hear the answer. "And Quandary?"

"I don't know that yet. Quandary stock will fall when this gets out. You could be a target for acquisition. Plenty of sharks out there who will smell blood."

She clenched her jaw, grinding her teeth together so hard they hurt.

Kiran said gently, "We need to get out there, get this over with."

She envisioned the lecture room filled with all eighty-two Quandary employees. They would feel angry, betrayed. How could this man they'd trusted for years have deceived investors? They would ask about their jobs, remind her that they had families to support. They would need answers and emotional support she was unable to give.

Allison felt as though she was shrinking.

"Are you ready?"

They already hated her. She was sure of it. They believed she was too inexperienced for her job. And as soon as she stepped out there with Kiran, she would prove them right.

She glanced at the clock: 10:10.

She scooped the pen and notepad tidily left on the corner of her desk and followed him down the hall. What would she jot down? *How do you spell "fraud," Kiran? Do you happen to know the visiting hours at Club Fed for homewrecking girlfriends?*

The air seemed thick and hot, as if she were breathing in a steam room. All her strength left her body, and she felt simultaneously sweaty and cold.

"Kiran."

He glanced back questioningly.

"I'm sorry. I can't do this. I can't go out there."

His piteous look at her—Allison Stevens, Quandary's chief of staff and program leader for the life-changing DMD drug—validated what she'd always known deep down. She was an imposter, an unworthy fake who'd built a career by fucking the boss.

Without a word, he hurried onward to the lecture room alone.

5

Six weeks into this damn case, and he'd gotten nowhere. DEA Special Agent Peter Malloy eyed the stack of folders in the tray labeled DEA-994. He'd combed through the case files day after day, looking for connections between the six victims he'd identified so far. Nothing. It didn't help that four of the vics were Does, three Johns and a Jane, and their case files were little more than an autopsy report and a few postmortem pictures.

As he waited the usual ten minutes for his computer to boot, courtesy of the agency's excessive IT policies, he got up and stood at his window, sipping his urn coffee and admiring his view of the parking lot. The sun was already beating down at ninety-three degrees, and he could see heat haze coming off the asphalt. Ironically, the day would be significantly less gloomy if it would just fucking rain. But this was the desert southwest, not known for moisture.

He polished off his coffee and sat down again when his DEA login page appeared. The machine whirred loudly like it might die at any moment. Goddamn government-issue technology. How could they be expected to keep up with the bad guys with bullshit tools more than a decade old?

His brain seemed to be spinning in the same hateful blue cursor of death. He'd gone over these cases a dozen times. Six bodies across Nevada, Arizona, and Southern Utah. His team had interviewed the families and friends of their two identified victims. The case profiles were damn robust.

What frustrated him the most, however, was that this case was like nothing he'd ever seen—and he was certain that over the course of twenty-five years with the DEA, he'd seen everything. Two months ago, when Cramer had approached him, he'd tried to avoid taking this case. Opioid pumps were rising in popularity but still within the purview of physician practice, and this didn't feel like an illegal drug case. Pumps certainly weren't being implanted at the local opioid den, not to mention that he was short-staffed and had his hands full with the meth problem. But he'd lost the fight, and the files had landed in his lap. It hadn't taken long to figure out that opioids weren't the problem. Whatever was going on didn't involve any known controlled substance, narcotic, stimulant, depressant, or performance drug.

He poured another cup of coffee and pulled the two identified victims' folders from the stack. He rubbed his tired, gritty eyes and scratched at his beard stubble before pulling on his reading glasses.

Eric Sparks, age twenty-one, African American, played football for UNLV, wide receiver. Died of traumatic brain injury after six days in a coma, and his autopsy revealed multiple recent severe skull fractures for which he hadn't received medical care. In fact, his medical records showed he hadn't visited the team's physician at all since his physical exam at the start of the school year. The autopsy report also mentioned Eric had three broken ribs and a broken clavicle, which his brother had said probably occurred when he jumped out of his second-floor dorm room window a month ago and landed on a cement stair rail below his room. Yet Eric hadn't missed a game or even a practice.

Why hadn't Eric seen a doctor after a stupid stunt like that? Improperly healed injuries might've cost him his scholarship, not to mention his future if he planned to go pro. Malloy made a note to have his guys talk to the team physician about the injuries.

He tossed his reading glasses back onto his desk and sat back in his chair. He wasn't doing his best work. And dammit, he owed it to these families to try harder. He put his glasses back on and picked up the second folder, then stood up and paced while he reviewed it.

Karen Richmond, twenty-three-year-old Caucasian woman, living with her father and three younger siblings in Tempe, Arizona. Karen was a long-distance runner who'd completed most of an ultramarathon in the Yukon Arctic before collapsing and dying of hypothermia. According to other competitors, she'd shown signs of hypothermia at mile 148 but refused help from the support crew, insisting she was fine. They'd allowed her to continue to the mandatory checkpoint at mile 156, eight miles ahead. Her body was found on the course at mile 180. There was no record of her stopping at the mandatory checkpoint, and given the distance and her time of death, she couldn't have stopped, slept, or eaten. That would have been nearly twenty-four hours of continuous running in subfreezing temperatures and a foot of icy snow.

"The most she'd ever run without resting was thirty-eight miles, which took her six hours," reported her father, Lyle Richmond. "She'd been excited about this race because the longest leg was only thirty-four miles. She ran these races for the social part, makin' friends and talkin' about running with other like-minded folks."

Malloy tried to put himself in her head. Even if she'd taken a drug that made her feel—what? elated? superpowered?—why would she have attempted such an absurd distance? What told her she should just keep going? Based on her psychological profile, which admittedly came from anecdotal reports from friends and family, her behavior didn't fit the kind of person she was.

He closed her file and opened her online file, scrolling through the images until he found the one he was looking for. He enlarged it on the screen and focused on the subcutaneous port surgically implanted at the base of her spine—the one and only physical feature that linked all six victims.

"Talk to me," he growled. "What are you hiding?"

Barely the size of a quarter, the port would probably have been overlooked on anyone not lying on an autopsy table. The small, round chamber with a silicone center had been found embedded under the skin between the L2 and L3 vertebrae on every victim, next to a two-inch incision scar. In both the Richmond and Sparks cases, not a single friend or family member had ever seen the port or knew anything about it. It was the best-kept secret he'd ever encountered in a case, confirmed by the fact that no one else had come forward either with a port or knowing someone who had a port, despite widespread communications to local hospitals and clinics.

He'd spent an entire day with his team researching the device and discussing how such an apparatus might be used. An opioid pump was the obvious first idea. Pain pumps were available for patients with terminal illnesses, and perhaps they'd made their way to the street by some ethically challenged or disgruntled jackass doctor who didn't like his cut from the HMOs. But the autopsies showed no implanted intrathecal pumps. The ports appeared to be nothing more than a simple way to inject a drug directly into the spinal cord in a precise location.

That led the team to their second idea, injectable morphine. To their astonishment, not one of the victims had even a trace of morphine or any opioid or analgesic drug in their bodies. No performance enhancers. Not even goddamn Tylenol. The labs had been such a shock that he'd ordered a second report for every victim from a different lab. The results had been the same.

Someone suggested that perhaps the victims were on an experimental medication. He consulted colleagues in the Diversion Investigations to see if any pharmaceutical companies might be conducting ongoing clinical studies in the US or Mexico requiring a spinal fluid port. No luck.

He groped for his phone without looking and speed-dialed.

Danny Garcia picked up at one ring. "Yeah."

Garcia was his youngest but best agent, well trained in Malloy's no-nonsense work style. Malloy appreciated that Garcia didn't wear him down with unnecessary greetings.

"Did we ever find a manufacturer of the spinal ports?"

"Nope. Called every supplier I could find and showed 'em the pictures. All legit suppliers have product numbers imprinted on their devices."

"What about residue? Did Forensics find anything?"

"Nah. Nothin', boss. The ports were clean."

"Shit."

Malloy hung up. This case was nothing but dead ends, and it was only a matter of time before the media got ahold of it and turned his case into a goddamn circus.

**

Malloy glanced up from his lunch as Garcia entered his office without knocking. Even though Garcia was over six feet tall, Malloy figured he must weigh maybe a hundred forty soaking wet. He kept his jet-black hair in a ponytail most days, but today it hung over his shoulders. If he'd been wearing some eye makeup and bell bottoms, he could have doubled for a young Cher.

Garcia dropped a folder onto his desk. "Latest vic."

Victim number seven.

Malloy glanced down at the file, labeled with a name and the picture of a teenage boy. He tossed the rest of his sandwich in the trash. "All right. Spill it."

"Mark Vespe, a freshman at ASU, living in a frat house. His body was found in the basement after a party early this morning at"—he opened the folder—"3:24 a.m. One of the kids called the police saying Vespe had cut his wrists, so the university police show up expecting a suicide scene. But you're not gonna fuckin' believe this—it was a five-finger fillet game that ended badly."

Garcia pulled out two enlarged photos of Vespe's hand, one taken before it had been cleaned of the blood. His hand was in fact completely filleted. Although the fingers were still intact, it looked like the hand had been pushed through a material shredder.

Jesus. He didn't have the stomach for that kind of thing, despite working in crime so many years.

The cleaned photo showed much more detail: inch-long cuts, maybe fifty or a hundred even, from each fingertip to his wrist. In some places, the flesh was missing and the thin metacarpal bones were visible.

He turned away.

"I haven't even gotten to the fun part yet." Garcia pulled out a flash drive, his expression saying *You ain't gonna like this, boss.*

Malloy plugged the drive into his USB port and sat back in his chair, as if distancing himself from the screen might make it less horrifying. It was a video clip, apparently taken by another student at the party. It was shaky and often bounced around the room, but it was good enough to clearly depict what had happened. The screaming and yelling in the video were so loud he lowered the volume on his speaker.

Vespe stood in front of a poker table with his left hand flat on the table, fingers spread wide. In his right hand, he held a long-bladed kitchen utility knife, which he stabbed madly into his left hand. He alternated between singing the five-finger fillet song and laughing maniacally, his eyes wide with excitement. Or delirium. He wasn't watching his precision, as the game's supposed to be played; instead, he was watching the crowd and looking into the camera. It was eerie; it reminded Malloy of a guy on PCP. Then a loud male voice shouted *Stop it!* Vespe startled, and his stabbing hand shifted. The next plunge of the knife went straight through his forearm.

The video ended.

"Holy fucking mother of god," Malloy said in one long exhalation.

Garcia seemed unfazed by the horror. "The cops questioned everyone at the party, though a lot of them had already taken off. Supposedly Vespe stopped the game and walked casually to the bathroom. They said he sounded completely lucid, assuring everyone it was just a cut, and he wasn't hurt, and he was just gonna go wash it up. Then he locked the door to the bathroom, and someone called university police. By the time they arrived on the scene, Vespe had bled to death sitting with his back against the locked door."

Garcia stopped talking and sat down in the chair opposite Malloy.

"And the kid has a port?" Malloy didn't know why he asked such an obvious question.

"Yepper." Garcia pulled out the picture taken by the medical examiner.

"I need those labs. Let me know when the autopsy report comes in. And can we please send our forensics guys over there immediately? Those mall cops will just fuck everything up."

"Got it." Garcia stood up and walked out.

"And get interviews from everyone in that video!" he yelled after Garcia.

He clicked Play to watch the video again. The senseless stabbing had continued for twenty-two seconds before the scream. Twenty-two long seconds—Vespe had stabbed himself repeatedly for the same amount of time his own son ran the two hundred meter. His stomach churned, and he mindlessly reached for his bottle of Tums, shaking a couple directly into his mouth.

His runner was now in graduate school. How many times over the past twenty-four years had he tormented Robbie with his nuggets of parental wisdom? *You know marijuana is a gateway drug, don't you?* Robbie'd always had a smart retort. *Really? Wow! That's news to me! Guess the son of a DEA agent is always the last to know,* followed by a smile and an eye-roll. *Dad, come on. Seriously?* And somehow, he felt sure that Vespe's parents were no different than he was. They'd brought up a fine young man, prepared him for the road ahead, made sure he had pizza money. They probably couldn't wait for him to come home for Christmas. A tragic, drug-related death wasn't in the cards for their little boy; illicit drugs killed addicts with unfortunate upbringings or who made too many bad choices, not college students with loving parents and bright futures.

That's what everyone thought.

***

Malloy stood outside his car, waiting for the AC to cool it down to something that wouldn't melt his skin. Even though the sun was nearly setting, the temperature hadn't dropped one degree. He hated Phoenix in the summer.

The image of Mark Vespe played back in his head as he waited. That freakish look on Vespe's face, the PCP look. Why? Why'd the kid do that? What was he thinking? For that matter, what had Karen Richmond been thinking? Whatever they'd been pumping through that port had to be a psychoactive. Maybe a hallucinogen. A new type of LSD?

He got into his car, checked the rearview mirror, and put the car in reverse. As he took his foot off the brake, he was startled by a loud knuckle rap on his window.

He rolled down the window. "Christ, Garcia. What the hell?"

"They found vials and a syringe."

6

Allison pulled out a Chinese food container that boasted of "Northern NJ's best Chinese take-out." She sniffed it, grabbed a fork, and padded back to her sofa. She'd stayed home from work the next day. She knew it was unprofessional, and she did, of course, feel guilty about not being in the office to support the staff. Not that she was any real support.

"I haven't called in sick for over a year," she said to her television, in a vain attempt to justify herself.

Ryan was no doubt holding it all together anyway. Ryan Garner was an Austin in the making. He'd been working for Austin for just two years, and it was clear that Austin was having a huge influence on him. Ryan had begun shadowing Austin around the office, adopting his mannerisms and expressions. He'd even started attending important meetings with him. Austin treated Ryan with a different level of respect and professionalism. Ryan got to be part of the good ol' boys club with cigars and scotch and all that went with it. Allison was just the after-party.

She hit Play on the Roku remote and started the next episode of *Sex and the City*. She'd binged most of season 2 in the last twenty-four hours, which of course she'd already seen years ago. She hadn't showered in two days and she felt grimy, but she had no intention of showering today either.

As the opening credits rolled, she wished she were more like Carrie, with close, lifelong girlfriends. But the truth was she didn't have any friends. She'd never been good at connecting with people, and her job had always seemed a higher priority than socializing. Perhaps she could've led a happy life as a loner or maybe even developed some friendships if she hadn't fallen completely in love with a white-collar criminal. A white-collar criminal with a wife and two kids who apparently didn't care for her enough to let her know he was okay.

She lay back on the sofa and pulled the pillow down under her head. Her thoughts drifted to the first time she met Austin. She'd been standing around the obligatory graduate student reception, waiting for ten minutes to tick by so she could shake hands with her advisor and excuse herself. She loved neuropsychology, and she was particularly proud of her research in pain psychology, but she despised the politicking and posturing that went on at these events. But before she had a chance to steal away, she was approached by a man whose name tag read "Austin"—no last name, no affiliation. He slipped a glass of champagne into her left hand and removed the Diet Coke from her right with a flirty smile, and she was immediately attracted.

"We have a lot to talk about," he'd whispered in her ear. Just the way he'd leaned in had sent shivers through her. She would fall in love with that confidence and assertiveness before that night was over.

The phone rang, and she picked it up to look at the caller ID.

She flew off the sofa. "Austin, oh my god, I've been so worried. Where've you been? Why haven't you called?"

Her voice sounded shrill, and she hated it.

"I'm sorry, honey. I know you're really disappointed in me right now. It's extremely complicated, and I can't explain my actions now on the phone."

She said nothing, afraid she'd cry.

"Listen, Al, some agents from the SEC or FBI will be coming into the office to review the finances of Quandary. We both know that there's nothing to find there. You've been keeping all our business records, and you're neurotically detailed." He chuckled awkwardly. "But they need to complete their investigation on all my business dealings, so they'll want to review your records and documents. Please just cooperate and give them everything they ask for. Don't give 'em any reason to question you. You're not involved in this, and I don't want them to suspect otherwise."

"Austin, I don't—" She stopped, unsure how to finish. She wanted to appear strong, even though she was crumbling inside.

"Kiran'll be there as well. He'll review the warrants and set them up in a conference room. Then he'll help you gather whatever materials are necessary. They may ask you questions, or they may ask you to sit with them and review your spreadsheets. Please just do as they ask, and they'll be done soon enough."

She kept her voice even, trying to sound professional. "So when do you think you'll be back in the office? The staff needs to see you, to hear your side of this."

God, she needed to see him, needed him to hold her and tell her everything was going to be fine.

"I know. I'll be back soon. They've requested I stay away from the office until the investigation is complete. And I have a lot of things to take care of at home. My family needs me right now."

It was a dagger through her heart, and she started crying.

His voice softened. "Honey, oh baby, I'm sorry. I'm so sorry. I know this has been hard on you. But please promise me this. Please go back to work. Ryan needs your help managing the team. You can't keep hiding out in your apartment."

She clamped her mouth shut. He'd called Ryan before her. God, this couldn't get any worse.

"Go back to work, keep the projects moving, keep everything on track," he continued. "Show the team that Quandary is operating normally. Focus on our very important work in DMD. We can't lose our work, Al. Think of the kids who need this drug. Make it about them. I'll be back to work really soon. My legal team is top-notch, and they'll make sure this gets resolved quickly."

"Okay." She sounded like a dejected little girl, and she knew it. "So you'll be back next week, you think?"

Please, please, please.

"Maybe another week, ten days. We'll schedule a town hall meeting with the whole group, okay?"

"Austin." She collapsed onto the sofa. "I miss you so much, I—"

"I can't talk any longer, Al. I'm sorry, I have to go. I'll see you soon."

The call disconnected.

7

ustin stared at his phone for a few minutes, wondering how Allison would fare. There was nothing to find in the Quandary records, and although he could have used a few more days to tidy things up, he'd always been careful to separate the various arms of his business ventures. Still, she was young and naive. The feds would push her around and intimidate her. She wasn't built for this kind of crisis.

"That's why I picked you, Al," he whispered.

In a way, he was relieved to be at his home in Darien. Allison was a hard worker, but she didn't adapt to change easily. She needed time and space from him to toughen up.

He took a sip of bourbon and stood up from his mahogany desk to survey the floor-to-ceiling mahogany bookshelves filled with everything from genetics to sports cars to literary fiction of the 1800s. He loved his books. And his glass-encased pen collection. Each pen had been bought at auction; the cheapest one was valued at $30,000. He admired his beautifully framed educational credentials: the doctoral diploma in molecular biology from UCLA, the master's degree in business administration from Columbia University. He'd built it all from nothing. Every accomplishment, every penny invested into this $3.7 million Connecticut home.

He would be genuinely sad to see it all go away.

Finishing his bourbon in a large swallow, he closed his brand-new Apple iMac Pro and loaded it into the sleeve. He carried it out of his office, closing the door behind him.

As he stepped onto the Italian marble in the foyer, Jackie appeared from the dining room. His wife was stunning. There was simply no other way to describe her. She was tall and lean, and she dressed in expensive but sensible beige business suits and stiletto heels. But today, her full, lustrous hair was tightly pulled back away from an expressionless face, and he realized he couldn't remember the last time he'd seen her famously radiant smile.

"You'll be gone two or three days?" she asked.

"Three days at the most." He glanced at his packed suitcase.

"Where did you say?" It was a test, and he knew it.

"California, remember?"

"Right."

She knew he was lying. They'd lived together too many years for her not to see that, even if their relationship had become so strained they rarely spoke anymore beyond polite conversation or logistics for the boys. But she could still practically read his mind through body language and tone.

She called over her shoulder. "Boys, your dad's getting ready to leave."

He wondered again if she'd call the police. Her look held neither fondness nor resentment. The sooner he was out of her life, the better. She probably didn't think he was worth the effort to dial 911.

"Bye, Dad!" He heard in stereo from two ends of the massive colonial house.

"Be good for your mom," he yelled out, aiming nowhere. Whatever he said would fall on deaf ears, anyway.

He picked up his suitcase and stepped toward her, giving her a polite kiss on the cheek. She stiffened, which didn't surprise him. He turned and walked out the front door, where a chauffeured town car awaited him.

As the car pulled out of the driveway, he took one last glance at his beautiful home. He turned to hold onto the image as long as he could, to burn it into his mind, knowing he would never see it again.

***

Austin sat silently in the back seat of the Lincoln sedan, staring out the window as his driver sped down the turnpike toward New York. A few minutes into the ride, he leaned forward.

"Sebastian, would you mind pulling off at that truck stop? I'm really sorry. Seems I had one too many bourbons tonight."

"Of course, Dr. Harris," Sebastian replied. "What are you doing these days? Eagle Rare?"

"Knob Creek. A bit nuttier than Eagle. Got it from a colleague, and I've really warmed up to it. Let me send you home with a bottle when I get back."

"Very good, sir. I wouldn't say no to that."

Austin really liked Sebastian. He'd been Austin's driver for several years, and in all that time he'd remained professional but friendly, with very little chit-chat.

Sebastian pulled into a parking spot in front of the service area and hopped out to open the door.

"I'll be right back." Austin swung himself out of the car.

"Take your time, sir."

Austin whisked through the front door, past the restrooms, past the Subway and the Dunkin' Donuts, and out the back to the patio tables. He moved with purpose but not fast enough to attract attention, which made it simple to drop his iPhone into the trash container on the way out.

He pulled a key from his coat pocket, pressed the unlock button, and scanned the parking lot for the blinking taillights. A white Ford Explorer. He hurried to the vehicle and settled inside. A brown leather computer bag was placed neatly on the seat beside him, just as planned, and behind him, a small suitcase lay flat on the back seat. So far, so good.

He looked back through the rearview mirror. The area was quiet. He started the car and backed out of the parking lot.

The truck rumbled across the warning strip on the onramp as he dug through the bag for the new Tracfone. He powered it on and held down the number one key to dial the preset number.

The phone rang once. "Yes."

"I'm rolling."

"Yes."

He disconnected the call and tossed the phone back into the bag. His stomach fluttered, and he smiled. His new adventure had begun.

8

Malloy sat opposite the newest member of his team, Agent Vincent Wang, on temporary assignment from New Jersey. Wang brought experience from pharmaceutical drug development, which is what they thought they were dealing with now that the DEA Forensic team had recovered two empty vials, a half-empty vial, and a syringe from Vespe's trunk.

Wang was not what Malloy had been expecting. Barely five feet tall and considerably overweight, he waddled into the conference room with confidence, and when he smiled, his eyes all but disappeared. He reminded Malloy of a fat, happy Buddha statue, and he seemed just as likable.

Malloy refocused on the close-up image of the vial. "So what do you make of the label?"

The printed label reading LXR102016 was the only remarkable feature of the otherwise unexceptional glass vials. The vials themselves were standard lab equipment, the number one–selling vial on Amazon. It would be nearly impossible to trace where they'd been purchased. Better to focus their resources on the label.

A loud knock on his office door interrupted them.

"Yeah."

Garcia opened the door and stuck his head in. "Nothing definitive from Chemlab." He nodded toward Wang and then did a horrified double-take at Malloy. "Jesus, what the fuck is that? Easter came and went, boss."

Malloy glanced down at his light pink dress shirt, a gift from Darcy. *Pete, you have such nice skin. I'm not going to let you wear these dull colors every single day.* His ears grew warm, and he decided not to engage.

"What do you mean, nothing from Chemlab?" he asked.

Garcia stepped in and closed the door, then read from a paper he was holding. "One unidentified high molecular weight peak on HPLC trace, but substance unidentified."

Malloy stared at him, uncomprehending.

Garcia shrugged. "Chem sent it to Bio."

"What? Why?"

His DEA analytical chemistry lab team was top notch. Not only could they determine the composition of practically any substance, but because they maintained a cataloged library of every substance they'd ever analyzed, they could usually pinpoint where it had come from as well. He'd been expecting them to wrap this case up with a bow so he could get back to his opioid and meth work. The bioanalytics team would surely take forever.

"It means whatever's in the vial is something we haven't seen before," Wang said. "Since this is an injectable and showed up by HPLC with a high molecular weight, it's most likely a biological substance. They're bigger and heavier."

Impressive. "I want high priority with Bio."

"You got it, boss."

"It's a compound name," Wang said.

Malloy and Garcia swiveled their heads in unison.

Wang crossed one short leg over the other, sat back in his chair, and laced his fingers together across his ample belly. "The label. It's a research drug name."

"Isn't that usually a really long word that no one can pronounce?" Garcia asked.

"Huh-uh, that's a generic name. Before a drug gets a generic name, it has a research compound name, usually some letters representing the company and numbers representing the compound. Like that." He pointed at the label on the enlarged image of the vials.

Malloy studied the image. The printed label seemed pretty low budget: plain black Arial type on white, with no logo and no image. "You really think this comes from a legitimate drug company?"

"Maybe, but it certainly isn't from a hospital or a clinic. Experimental drugs used in human studies always include a lot more information on the label. The FDA's pretty strict about that kind of thing. But when it's just being used in a lab, like with animals, they usually keep it pretty simple like this."

Or they could've been filled in Walter White's RV out in the middle of the damn desert and distributed behind a Walmart. Malloy grabbed his bottle of Tums. "All right. See if you can find anything that might match those initials."

He glared at the nondescript image as if forcing it to give up more information. LXR. El-ex-ar. Elixir. Jesus Christ, if the media got hold of this, they'd turn it into the latest cure-all—"the magic elixir that makes you invincible." Or at least makes you think so.

9

The purge room appeared darker, more ominous, than Layla remembered. A chill went through her as she removed her sandals and neatly lined them up in the corner of the chamber. She carefully smoothed the fabric of her white cotton tunic, making sure there were no wrinkles or folds. The Father would be unhappy with her if she appeared disheveled during this important event. She licked her palms and smoothed her hair. Satisfied that she was as pleasing as she could be, she sat down on the cold sandstone bench and lifted one leg to the other side to straddle it.

She reached back and strapped her ankles into the harnesses. It was a bit awkward, and she buckled them loosely. She wouldn't be trying to escape. She smoothed her tunic one last time, lay flat on her stomach, and wrapped her arms around the bench. Unable to harness her wrists, she clasped her hands together underneath. The insides of her thighs burned against the edge of the stone. She exhaled, closed her eyes, and began her meditation chants.

By the time the door opened, her legs were numb. She relished the pins and needles.

Brother James belted her hands underneath the bench.

"Layla, I know you've been preparing for today, and I know you'll have a successful cleanse. Remember to focus on your breathing, in and out to the count of four. Don't cry out in distress. The Father loves you very much and wants you to be cleansed of the poison that consumed you during your life as an impure. He needs you strong in body, mind, and spirit. Do you understand?"

"Yes." Exultation fluttered in her stomach.

"Then let's begin," he whispered.

The first crack of the whip landed hard across her back. Her body jerked and she gasped, eyes wide. *With pain comes peace.* She must release the pain.

Crack!

The second lash whipped across her lower back and buttocks. She bit her lip to avoid screaming, then remembered to breathe slowly to the count of four. She squeezed her eyes shut and focused hard on one spot in the middle of her forehead. Her face contorted as she tried to push the images from her unconscious mind into that spot. She needed to see her impure life. The poison.

She listened for a signal, expecting some sort of pop in her head, followed by a stream of images scrolling right across her eyelids. The spot remained maddeningly black and empty.

Crack!

An inhuman, guttural growl escaped her as the whip came down again, less due to physical pain than frustration. Why couldn't she see it? She breathed in slowly and breathed out, releasing her anger, unwittingly taking control, guiding a picture that just needed a little coercion. She drew a small bedroom in that spot between her eyes. She made the walls cement gray, much like the room she lay in now. On top of a small dresser in the corner stood a pair of roller skates. On the wall was a poster of—

Crack!

—a poster of, well, she couldn't make out the image on the poster just yet. She shifted her gaze to the door and saw a man materialize there. He was tall, his head nearly touching the frame. He had dark blond hair. Thin. No, even thinner. The image wavered like a mirage, and she concentrated hard to keep it from fading. He smiled at her, and she focused on his mouth, stared at it until she saw a gap between his teeth.

Crack!

This time, the lash of the whip completely overwhelmed her, snapping the image right from her mind. Her eyes flew wide in shock as the physical world engulfed her. Her senses had intensified a hundredfold. Pain surged through her entire body in waves and she convulsed once, then completely stiffened. She lost focus and her mind seemed to liquefy, spreading to her aching thighs, the unbearable pins and needles making her legs quiver, then to her wrists, raw beneath the savage leather wraps. A whimper escaped her lips. Her calves cramped, curling her feet and toes into grotesque, spasmodic shapes she couldn't relieve. And her back felt as if she'd been branded with a cattle iron. Her head exploded into fireworks and she tasted bile as her vision narrowed until—

Crack!

The stars faded, and Layla was no longer spread across a stone bench.

***

I'm standing with a group of people in a park. The sweetness of freshly cut grass combines with the scent of roses. Lots of roses. I'm hot and sticky, and the sun is beating down on me. I hear bees nearby. I hate bees. I look down at my black patent leather sandals with a strap. My big girl shoes. They're covered in blades of wet grass, and I want to clean them off so they'll be shiny again.

"Can we go?" I whisper and look up at the woman holding my hand.

Mom looks down at me with sad eyes. "Soon."

My gaze falls to the Bible in her other hand, which she grips so tightly her fingers are white. In the corner of the Bible, the letters RLC are printed in gold letters. It was a gift. From him.

I face forward again and look at the fancy rose-covered casket raised above the hole in the earth. I know who's inside. I saw him in there just an hour ago when I snuck up to the open casket in the big red room. He looked different, like a plastic doll, and I was too afraid to kiss him goodbye. But now I wish I had. He'll go into the ground thinking I don't love him.

***

Crack!

Layla struggled to hold onto the scene, but the vision was gone. Her body slackened against the bench, depleted. She no longer cared about the whip walloping her. She no longer noticed the pain rippling through her body.

Because something had happened. A perfect truth from her unconscious mind had just stormed into her memory, as real as the very blood that coursed through her veins. Her impure life. It was real.

Her hair matted around her face and filled her mouth as tears dripped from her eyes and nose.

"Daddy," she whispered. "Daddy. He was real."

"Yes! I knew you could do it. Yes." Brother James tenderly untied her bindings and knelt beside her with a small cloth. He wiped her face gently and pulled her hair back. "You did it, Layla. You did it, my girl."

"Thank you." Her sobs shook her entire body.

"Oh, beautiful girl, don't thank me. I'm just a servant for the Father." Brother James's voice was so calm, so soothing.

"Thank you, Father. Thank you so much."

Brother James stayed by her side for—how long? thirty minutes? an hour?—as she released the pain and cleansed her mind and spirit for the Father who loved her.

***

Layla awakened in her room. Her comforter was pulled over her head. The welts on her back stung, and she felt the bandage under her tunic. She shifted to try to relieve the pain. Her head felt hazy, and she was so sleepy. She carefully rolled to the other side and closed her eyes to drift back to sleep.

Daddy.

She bolted upright in bed. Her cleanse. The vision. Her real dad and her real mom. The funeral—her dad's funeral when she was a young girl.

How had he died? She concentrated, but she couldn't pull up the facts. What had happened after the funeral? Again, she couldn't picture anything. Her unconscious mind would only allow her this one elusive scene, this one memory. But it was so vivid. She knew now that she'd loved her father more than anyone. She'd felt it, standing there on the grass watching him leave her forever. She was sure this image had stuck with her through her poisoned life—well, until the accident and being saved by the Colony.

She closed her eyes and tried to envision her mother looking down at her. Her mother had short dark brown hair. Did she look like her mother? For the first time, she wished she had a mirror. *Mirrors are a tool of vanity not to be abused by inductees*, Dr. Jeannette had explained when Layla had asked.

She gingerly repositioned herself under the covers and tried to sleep, but all she saw on the backs of her eyelids was the funeral, replaying in an endless loop in her conscious mind. Even though it was only a few minutes from her entire poisoned life, she felt whole for the first time since she'd arrived at the Colony. She had been a real person. She was one right now.

She couldn't wait to tell Dr. Jeannette.

10

Malloy stared intently at the YouTube video on his computer screen. KTVX, the local NBC news station out of Provo, Utah, was reporting the death of victim number eight. Barely four days since the Vespe kid was found. At this rate, his case would fill the morgue by the end of the month.

The all-too-cheery reporter tried her best to sound somber as she read the teleprompter. "Today, the entire BASE jumping community is mourning the loss of world-class BASE jumper Jake Graventoll. BASE jumping, the extreme sport involving parachuting off large structures, is illegal in most towns and parks but has grown in popularity nonetheless. After successfully completing over seven hundred jumps, Jake lost his life yesterday on a particularly difficult cliff in Springdale, Utah, within the boundaries of Zion National Park."

The scene turned to a live reporter interviewing a young man outside Eddie McStiff's bar in Moab. The young man's eyes were downcast. "Jake was our idol. He'd been in this sport longer than any of us. Everyone called him Dad, not because he was older but because he was always ragging on us about every little safety measure. He was completely anal-retentive. Triple-check your *(bleep)* chutes, no booze twelve hours before a jump, that kinda *(bleep)*." The young man shook his head in disbelief. "The whole world out there thinks BASE jumping is just a suicide mission, but Jake was always trying to prove that it's safe if you're well trained and smart. He was so (*bleep*) conservative. And he hated flyers, hated 'em. Jesus. He was never supposed to die. (*Bleep*)."

He stalked away.

The reporter faced the camera. "We've learned from many of his friends and family here in Moab that Jake was not only an outspoken advocate for the sport and a strong proponent for extended safety measures, but he actively campaigned against the more extreme and deadlier version of jumping called wingsuit BASE jumping, which has been growing in popularity across Utah. That's what makes Jake's death particularly surprising. He was wearing a wingsuit when he died, and he did not deploy his parachute. Kirsten, back to you."

Malloy stopped the video as Kirsten cheerfully transitioned to "In other news …"

"Well, at least the autopsy report hasn't leaked." Malloy opened the file and skimmed for confirmation. "He was really wearing a wingsuit? A guy who's been so vocal against them?"

Garcia's lanky body flopped into the chair in front of the desk. "Not only that, he launched off Angel's Landing, which is about a fifteen-hundred-foot cliff. It's a pretty normal height for a BASE jumper, but that height for a flyer in those narrow canyons? Suicide."

"Flyer?" Malloy picked up a tennis ball and rolled it between his palms.

"Yeah, a wingsuiter. Just the slightest change in wind conditions can really throw off your flight plan. If you don't have enough space to adjust, you'll crash. That's what happened to Jake, presumably. Report says he slammed into the Streaked Wall on the west side of the main canyon. Caught a gust of wind going the wrong direction, and bam." Garcia clapped once.

"How do you know so much about this?"

Garcia raised his eyebrows. "I wasn't always an agent."

He was about to ask what that meant but was interrupted by the phone. He hit the speaker button. "Malloy."

"Uh, yeah. Uh, is this Peter Malloy?" The caller sounded like a twenty-something. His twenty-something, in fact.

"Robbie?"

"Uh, no. This is, uh, Jordan Jennings. I'm looking for Special Agent Peter Malloy. Is that you? I wanted to talk about your drug."

Damn Dispatch was paid to screen these idiot calls. Malloy's tone sharpened. "Hang on, let me transfer you to Dispatch."

"Wait, no. Are you Peter Malloy? Sorry. My name's Jordan. I have some information about your drug, and I wanted to talk to you about it."

"What drug is that?" His patience was waning.

Garcia sauntered to the door.

"Uh, hang on."

There was heavy breathing on the phone and a rustling of papers, and then something hit the floor with a muffled thud. This kid had about three more seconds of his attention before he hung up.

"Uh, LXR102016. Are you the agent in charge of this one?"

He jerked to attention. Garcia stopped midstep and whipped around, eyebrows raised.

"I'm sorry, what did you say your name was?"

Garcia flicked open his notebook.

"Jordan Jennings."

"Uh-huh. And what do you know about this case?"

"Uh, yeah. I was hired by your Biologics team to analyze the substance?" His voice rose as if asking for confirmation.

Malloy looked quizzically at Garcia. Garcia shrugged.

"I was wondering if you could send me some samples from your patients so I can validate my theory."

"Mr. Jennings, is it? You need to back up—"

"It's Dr. Jennings, actually. But really, I prefer just Jordan."

"—a moment. We sent our drug sample to our internal DEA Biological Analytics team, and we're awaiting a report from them. Can you tell me again exactly who you are and how you think you are connected to this case?" He stood up and leaned over his desk resting on his knuckles. What the hell was going on?

"Yeah. They couldn't identify the substance, so they sent it to me. Thought it might be genetic rather than a small molecule or protein that they could pick up in chromatography."

"Excuse me?" He looked at Garcia for clarification.

"I'm sorry. I'm not very good on the phone. Let me start over. My name is Dr. Jordan Jennings. I run a genetics lab at the Broad Institute in Cambridge. I was hired by your Bio team to analyze LXR102016, and what I've found is extremely interesting—so interesting, in fact, that I reanalyzed it. I sent a report back to your Bio team, but to be honest, I don't think they'll understand it."

Malloy no longer cared about the backstory. "What did you find?"

"Well, it's a bit difficult to explain, and I really need the tissue samples before—"

"This is an extremely urgent case. Tell me what you found."

"Well okay, but the details are pretty technical. I'm not a hundred percent on our conclusions just yet. I need to confirm my analysis of the contents of the vial against your actual patient tissue samples."

"Victim samples." He looked to Garcia again for help and got only a shrug in response. "Our victims are dead."

"Yeah, right. Sorry. Victims. Anyway, if we see that the substance we isolated from the vial has actually produced corresponding genetic changes in the genomes of your victims, then we'll have confirmation that we know what we're looking at."

"What does that mean exactly?"

"I need a biopsy sample. Brain or spinal tissue. If my theory is correct, your drug is a gene editing technology that has modified the patient's—I mean victim's—DNA."

Garcia moved toward the phone speaker with purpose. "Listen, kid, what the fuck are you talking about? This drug is killing people. It's already killed eight people. If you know something that can stop people from dying, tell us—but for fuck's sake, speak in English."

Malloy would have to speak with Garcia about his diplomacy skills, but he did have a way of getting the job done.

Jordan replied in a low voice. "Okay, it appears from our genetic databases that this drug is capable of silencing a gene associated with the brain's ability to perceive pain. The thing is, whoever made this drug is ... Well, I don't know who did it, because no lab's ever produced anything like what I'm looking at here."

"It could have come from another country," Malloy said.

"You're not getting me. What I'm trying to say is, this gene is ... It doesn't have any naturally occurring polymorph. I mean, it's not ... it's not really human."

11

Allison typed "Asics women trail runners" into the search bar of Amazon.com and scrolled through the styles. She glanced up just to be sure no one was looking in through her window, judging her personal use of company time. This was the third day she'd been enslaved in her own office while the SEC auditors carried out their orders, deeply navel-gazing on the financial state of Quandary Therapeutics. She couldn't wait for this damn audit to be over, and she was growing more and more irritated at Austin for selfishly creating this problem in the first place. He'd been allowed to stay home and play the loving husband and father while she sat in the office each day and cleaned up his mess.

A rap came on her open door.

"Quick question." Craig Rooney, the lead auditor, was what Allison thought of as the front man.

"Sure." She waved him over.

"We found this invoice for some research." He slid it across her desk. "It appears the payment was made from Quandary's accounts payable system, but the transaction isn't recorded in your spreadsheet. Do you have any documentation on the scope of work? The invoice is pretty vague, and we can't find the final report for the work either."

She picked up the paper: Spiragene Inc. Never heard of them. "Doesn't look familiar. Must've been before my time."

"But that's your signature on the bottom, isn't it?"

She looked again. Damn if he wasn't right—her flowing *Allison C. Stevens* signed on the line with her name typed beneath it. Another name and signature accompanied hers, a Bradley Elliott. She'd never heard of him.

"I'm sorry, I don't remember this one, but let me look through my files. I sign a lot of invoices, it's just hard to keep track of all of them in my head." She regretted her words immediately. They sounded like an excuse for incompetence.

"Okay. Let me know what you find." He regarded her with a hint of concern. "It's important, though. It's an awfully large payment."

She stared at the invoice after he left: $180,000. She was sure she'd have remembered such a large payment. Most of her invoices were in the $30,000 to $50,000 range. How could she have forgotten this?

She walked into Ryan's office without knocking.

"I have to go, Cruella needs me." He hung up the phone.

She scowled. One of his barely legal girlfriends, no doubt.

He gestured toward her. "Door. Noun. A swinging barrier often used to provide privacy from others."

"Ry, have you heard of a company called Spiragene? Looks like they're in Jersey City?" His blank stare irritated her. She handed him the invoice. "We paid one-eighty for some research with these guys, and the invoice has practically no information on it."

He scrutinized the paper for a long time, squinting as if trying to remember through a hangover, which she was sure he probably had. "Nope." He handed it back.

"Nothing? What about this name, Bradley Elliott? Do you know him?"

"Doesn't ring a bell."

"And the Spiragene research lead who signed? Chung-Hee Hwong?"

He shook his head.

She grabbed the paper back from his hand and flapped it at him. "But look at the date. This was dated fourteen months ago. Wouldn't you have been the one to do the deal?"

He clasped his hands together in a gesture that seemed condescending and spoke slowly and calmly. "Allison, I know every collaborator I've ever dealt with by heart, as well as their email addresses, phone numbers, and favorite brands of scotch. I can dictate the contracts I've executed by memory. I'm telling you, I didn't write this deal. I don't know what it's for, but it's not for anything during my tenure. Maybe the date's wrong."

"It's signed and dated by three people."

"I see that. Apparently, you were one of them. I wasn't."

He had a point.

She sighed and stomped back to her office, where she dialed Austin's phone for the twentieth time. As expected, she received no answer except a female robot reminding her that his voicemail box was full. Her frustration with Austin and this audit crept into apprehension. Something felt wrong.

She got up and closed her door before dialing the number on the invoice.

"Spiragene, how can I direct your call?"

"Hi there. I'm looking for Chung-Hee Hwong?" She hoped she was pronouncing the name correctly.

"One moment." The receptionist put her on hold briefly, then returned. "Dr. Hwong is out for lunch. Would you like his voicemail?"

Allison looked through her office window at the team of auditors still fervently reviewing documents and cross-checking them against her financial tracking files. Rooney glanced up and noticed her eying them. He smiled, but the attention made her feel unsettled. Did he know something?

"Hello, ma'am? Are you still there?"

"Uh, sorry. Yes."

She looked down at the invoice again. Bradley Elliott, signing on behalf of Quandary Therapeutics, $180,000, cosigned by Allison Stevens just over a year ago. She traced her finger over the signature. It was perfect. She would have to answer for this, and quickly.

"Ma'am?"

She snapped to attention. "Yes, I'm sorry. My name is Allison Stevens with Quandary Therapeutics. Dr. Hwong has been doing some important research work for us, and I'd like to meet with him to get a report on the status. This is quite urgent, as we have a meeting with the board of directors first thing Monday morning, so do you think it would it be okay if I came by this afternoon to speak with him?"

She had no idea where this lie had come from. She cringed, waiting for the receptionist to call her bluff.

"Oh, Ms. Stevens! Please accept my apologies. I didn't recognize your voice. Please hold on for just one minute, and I'll connect you with Barbara."

The adrenaline rush made her queasy, much like her stage fright. She paced in front of her desk to calm her nerves. She was a terrible liar.

"Ms. Stevens, this is Barbara Gilbert. It's so nice to hear from you! I understand you'd like to come over for a project update?"

Jesus, this woman knew her. Allison was aghast. She held her composure, now fully committed to her story. "I'm so sorry for this last-minute request. The week just got away from me. Do you think Dr. Hwong would be available?"

"Of course. What time will you arrive? Is three o'clock okay?"

Allison glanced at her watch. "Yes, that would be perfect. Thank you so much. I really appreciate your flexibility."

"Of course. And will Brad be joining you? We haven't seen him in months."

Brad? Shit. Now what? "Uh, n-no. I mean, I wish he were joining me. I know Brad's far more familiar with the project than I am, but unfortunately he's … he's out of the country. A family emergency."

"Oh, I'm so sorry. Please give him our very best. And we'll all look forward to finally meeting you this afternoon."

"Thanks again." She hung up.

She had to urinate in the worst way; she was hopping back and forth like a little girl. What the hell was she doing?

***

"Here goes nothing," Allison murmured as she stepped through the revolving door into the building's lobby. The company was located in one of the nicest skyscrapers in the coveted Journal Square district of Jersey City. Very posh. It was one of those places where jeans would have looked out of place, and she was glad she'd dressed up today. The lobby must have been three stories tall inside, with floor-to-ceiling white marble walls and an enormous crystal chandelier. Her heels clanked on the shiny marble floors as she made her way to the elevators. This didn't make sense. Every research lab she'd ever visited looked like it could've doubled as a college dormitory.

She stepped into the elevator and pressed button twenty-two, next to the Spiragene Inc. logo and the slogan Global Leader in DNA Origami. Nervous knots coiled in her belly. What on earth was DNA origami? It wasn't like her to be unprepared for a meeting, but the auditors had kept her captive until she had to excuse herself at two o'clock. She knew nothing about Spiragene, and she had no idea who Bradley Elliott was or how he represented Quandary in this collaboration.

"Hello, Dr. Hwong," she rehearsed under her breath. "Thank you so much for your time, and I do apologize for the urgency. I can't seem to locate the documentation—" No. That would make her look sloppy. "We have an urgent meeting with the board—and ugh, bad timing, Brad had to leave the country for a family emergency. I thought perhaps I should check in with you about the project."

Her phone rang, and she glanced down at the caller ID. Kiran. No doubt he was calling to scold her for leaving early. That weasel auditor had probably thrown her under the bus. She pressed the decline button and continued with her rehearsal.

"I'm kind of embarrassed. I should probably know more about this project, but we tend to divide and conquer over at Quandary. This has really been Brad's baby."

That would have to do. The elevator opened into an elegant reception area. Fresh flowers were arranged in vases on the end tables next to a plush sofa. A stand with complimentary herbal tea stood in the corner.

"Ms. Stevens!" The receptionist greeted her enthusiastically and grabbed Allison's hand to lead her across the room. "It's very nice to meet you. The team is already gathered and waiting."

Allison's mouth turned to cotton at the sight of the cherrywood conference doors across the lobby. "Thank you. But before we begin, I was wondering if you could direct me to a water fountain?"

"Oh, don't worry, I've ordered refreshments for the meeting. Everything's inside. Right this way."

The receptionist ushered her through the double doors. "Ms. Stevens has arrived." She left quickly, closing the door behind her.

Around a stunning cherrywood boardroom table sat fifteen people in formal business attire, all staring back at her. A slide displaying the Spiragene logo was projected on a large screen behind the woman at the head of the table. A lone empty chair waited before a pad and pen at the opposite end of the long table. Allison assumed that was for her. Along the wall, a long, slender table was staged with a tower display of small finger cakes, a large antique silver coffee urn, and lines of perfectly arranged bottles of Evian and Pellegrino. Her eyes lingered on the Evian and she licked her dry lips, but she didn't move.

This was a really bad idea.

The woman at the head of the table stood up and walked over to her, smiling. "Ms. Stevens. I'm Barbara Gilbert, CEO of Spiragene. We're so glad you're able to visit." She held out a stiff arm.

"Please call me Allison." Her mouth was so dry it came out as a croaky whisper. She tried to smile, but it felt more like a grimace.

She groped for Gilbert's hand, wondering if she'd just committed career suicide.

12

Malloy glided past the dozen or so agents seated at the three briefing room tables, buried in their phones. He nodded at Garcia, who stood leaning against the wall with a cup of coffee in one hand and a glazed doughnut in the other. All systems normal. The Skype logo was splashed across the top of the video screen at the front of the room above a view of what appeared to be an empty dorm room. The bed was piled high with laundry, and several posters of Kiss circa 1980 hung from the unpainted cinderblock walls.

Malloy addressed the room. "Thank you all for joining us. Most of you aren't working on the LXR case, but I thought we'd all benefit from a bit of education on a new type of drug problem we might be dealing with in the near future."

On the video screen, a lanky teenager sat down in front of a camera. He wore an unbuttoned blue shirt over a T-shirt of what appeared to be an image of Bugs Bunny sitting on a toilet. He pulled a leather cross-body messenger bag over his head, causing his bushy hair to flop down over his eyes, and dropped it next to him.

"Perfect." Malloy struggled to keep a straight face. "I'd like to introduce Dr. Jordan Jennings."

The hostility in the room was palpable. His seasoned old-timers sat back in their chairs and crossed their arms over their chests, a clear message.

If they only knew what was coming.

"Dr. Jennings is a consultant working with us from the East Coast," he continued. "He's here to help us understand what we're dealing with. As all of you know, Forensics discovered three vials, two empty and one half-full, in Mark Vespe's possession. Analytics was unable to identify the substance, and they recruited Dr. Jennings and his genetics lab to help."

He took a seat in the corner.

"Hey. Thanks for inviting me. Please call me Jordan." Jordan waved a hand so close to his camera that it took up the entire screen. Illegible notes had been scribbled across his palm in blue ink. "Just real quick on my background. I'll start with your obvious question. I'm twenty-one years old." He glanced down at his watch. "Actually, I'm twenty-one and a quarter."

That elicited a chuckle.

"I was one of those nerdy kids who graduated from high school early—at fifteen, actually—and then went straight to college. I graduated with a bachelor's in biology and computer science from MIT in three years and went on for a PhD from Harvard. I finished my thesis this year in epigenetics, and I've been doing postdoc research for the Broad Institute in Cambridge, Massachusetts." He paused to catch his breath. "And as I'm sure you've all figured out, I've never been laid."

Another chuckle from the group. Malloy grinned. His agents now sat forward, interested. Poor kid must have to go through this song and dance every time he met someone new.

"Now, on to the good stuff," Jordan said. "Your lab sent me a sample from the vial labeled LXR102016, and I had my own team analyze the substance. We didn't believe what we were seeing, so we reanalyzed it. What we found was pretty shocking. Then Agent Malloy was kind enough to procure a tissue sample from two victims, which we also analyzed, and they confirmed my theory."

Jordan took a long pull from a bottle of Tazo iced green tea.

"What we're looking at is nothing we've ever seen before in humans. We did an extensive search through the literature, looking for a successful implementation of this drug—or rather, this new technology—in any lab, and we can't find anything. Not in the US or anywhere else in the world. This drug you're trying to find isn't a chemical drug like meth or coke. This is a gene-altering drug. And the genes that it's targeting are newly discovered, so this is brand-new territory."

Jordan leaned off-camera and reappeared holding a colorful, corkscrew-shaped object about eighteen inches long. The agents nodded, clearly recognizing the double helix model of a DNA strand. It emitted a soft, glowing light.

"I could bore you to tears with a mindless PowerPoint presentation, but I thought I'd play with toys instead. I understand that's what a kid my age is supposed to be doing."

Malloy smirked. The kid probably got a lot of mileage out of that one.

"You all probably remember from Bio 101 that all the cells in our body contain DNA, which is the genetic code of all living things. DNA is made up of four types of nucleotide bases, the building blocks of DNA, and every characteristic in every individual is defined by some sequence of these four bases, which attach as pairs, creating the rungs of the ladder here." He pointed at the crossbars between the helix strands. "With me so far?"

Nods came from everyone in the room.

"Okay, so this DNA strand, which lives in all cells in your body, is wicked long, all coiled up in the nucleus of every cell. Three billion base pairs. Fun fact: If you were to scale up a single strand to the width of a human hair and stretch it out, it would be sixty-two miles long."

He took another swig of tea, then pulled a hairband off his wrist and tied his around his hair to create a man bun on top of his head. Malloy recognized the pauses and fidgeting as nervous behavior and felt a pang of sympathy. Despite his accomplishments, Jordan was just a kid. Younger than Robbie, even.

"Yeah. So all along this strand of DNA are small sections—sequences, we call them—of bases that instruct proteins in our bodies to do different jobs. These small sequences are genes. And genes, you all remember, are what determine every characteristic about humans, and about you as an individual, including some diseases. Only just recently, with a greater understanding of the human genetic code and advances in biotechnology, are we now able to manipulate genes, giving us more ways to cure genetic diseases. Lots of biotech and pharma companies out there are working on gene therapeutics for diseases. That's all good, wholesome work."

"You're talking about CRISPR," Miles Deleon called out. Malloy wasn't surprised. Deleon was well-read and wanted everyone to know it.

"Yeah, exactly!" Jordan nodded. "Right. So remember that your genes are also responsible for normal functions of your bodies: eye color, allergies, athletic performance, food cravings. Every aspect of your being is controlled by specific genes. Including your ability to feel pain."

The room perked up at the word *pain*.

"Your victims here are just like the Joker in Batman. This drug has made them immune to pain."

13

The room erupted in whispered conversations. Malloy put a stop to it when he heard someone mention a "goddamn superhero drug."

"Let him continue."

Jordan reangled his camera and stood up, as if too nervous to sit any longer. "Only in the last couple of years have scientists discovered these pain genes and their functions, primarily by sequencing the genomes of families who curiously have a very low sensitivity to pain—street performers who walk on fiery coals, kids who break bones but never notice. You've seen stories in the news. Anyway, in studying these families, they've learned of a handful of these genes so far that when they're missing or turned off in these special people don't send pain signals to the brain. What's in your vial is a gene editing drug for one of these pain genes. It's called SCN9A."

"So ... what?" Garcia asked. "You're saying what's in this vial is destroying these pain genes?"

"Not destroying it, per se. What's in the vial has altered the gene in a way that's made it no longer able to do its job." He moved off-screen and returned with a smaller DNA toy, which he snapped into a middle section of the larger DNA strand. The snapped section went dark. "Silenced it. Turned it off like a light switch."

"Get the fuck outta here!" Garcia edged closer to the video screen, like a moth drawn to the light. "You can do that?"

"Yeah, but here's the thing. Silencing a gene is pretty simple, and we've been doing that for years. You don't need complicated gene therapy just to silence a gene." Jordan leaned over his desk and peered into the camera. His voice took on a conspiratorial tone. "So this is the part that gets spooky— and I'm talking mad scientist creepy. Let's say Dr. Frankenstein wanted to create a drug that silenced a pain gene so that someone wouldn't feel pain. All he'd need to do is send out a very small RNA—think of it as a little Smart car—that instructs the gene to stop doing its job. Simple. The gene would turn off like a switch, just like we talked about."

Garcia's expression of childlike wonder made Malloy uneasy. There was nothing wondrous about a mad scientist creating a superhero drug.

"But what Dr. Frankenstein has done here is he's taken a super-huge megagene related to pain perception, and he's removed and replaced sections—a little snip here, a little addition there—to create a modified gene. He's added in some mutations and taken out sequences. He created a little nano-size Frankenstein's monster that's very different from the original gene. It's no longer anything we'd recognize in a normal human."

"Jesus," Garcia breathed.

"And here's the important part: It's huge, like a freight train. This new Frankengene—let's call it gene Z, since it no longer looks anything like the original SCN9A gene—this gene Z exists in perfect formation in both victims whose tissue I analyzed."

"So that's it? The victims can't feel any pain at all?" Rachel Simcoe asked. Rachel was newest to his team, and Malloy liked her go-getter attitude.

"Impossible to know for sure since they can't tell us, but that's my theory, just reading the profiles of the victims. One of your John Does practically carved up his entire body with messages from aliens, right?"

Malloy had wanted to forget that particular image. The homeless man had spent hours with a dull knife carving his legs and torso, even his face. It was only a matter of days before infection spread through his body and killed him.

"Why would someone want to create a drug like this?" Malloy asked.

Something else was bothering him. Mark Vespe's expression had haunted him since he'd first seen the kid's video, a delirious PCP look that lingered even as junkies jumped from a skyscraper or took a dozen bullets. Vespe's face wasn't the face of someone high on a painkiller.

"I have an idea, but it's just a guess," Jordan said, holding up a finger. "Stay with me. Something's been nagging at me. Why would someone go through all the trouble of creating a complicated Frankengene? In science, we always look for the simplest approach to solving a problem. In this case of trying to eliminate pain, you don't need to replace a whole gene with a mutated gene or use complex gene editing technologies like CRISPR for that. Why create the freight train–sized gene Z when all they needed was to silence it with a little Smart car–sized strand of RNA?"

"And so?" Malloy barked. Get to the point, Jordan.

"I'm no mad scientist, but the only thing I can think of is that they weren't trying to silence the pain gene entirely. They were trying to modulate it."

"What does that mean?" Garcia asked.

"The RNA silencing is like an on–off light switch, right? Maybe instead they're trying to create a dimmer switch. That might give them a new approach to pain management."

"Is that possible?" Christ. All this science was so far beyond Malloy's expertise, he was losing confidence in his ability to effectively manage this case, let alone solve it.

"Well, that's the thing. The technology to engineer a new gene like gene Z is already known and available, though in all honesty I've never seen anything like this before. But what we can't do yet—what no one in the whole world has been able to do yet—is to precisely deliver a megagene like gene Z into the DNA of a human. From the injection, the gene has to first find the right tissue. Then it has to find the right cells. Specific targeting like that is extremely difficult. But even if it manages to accomplish getting to the right place, it still has to cross the cell membrane into the nucleus." Jordan stared into the screen. "It would be like trying to drive a freight train through a keyhole. It's impossible. But if that's not impressive enough, get this. In both victims, more than ninety-five percent of the target cells expressed the modified gene Z. It's the most effective gene delivery system I've ever seen." He looked down at his DNA toy and spoke in a low voice, as if only to himself. "How the hell did Dr. Frankenstein do that?"

Spooky as hell.

From across the room, Wang spoke for the first time. "Do the spinal ports have anything to do with it?"

"Kinda," Jordan replied, standing up straight. "The drug is targeting neurons. Brain cells. And the easiest way to get a drug to a brain cell is intrathecally, through the cerebrospinal fluid. Great big genes like this wouldn't be able to cross the blood–brain barrier to get to the right cells. But again, a port is just another overcomplication. You don't even need it. You could easily just stick a needle directly into the spine."

Several people groaned.

"So why have the port at all?" Wang asked.

"Two reasons I can think of. One, if the patient is getting a lot of injections or infusions over time, a port reduces infections and injection site reactions. But this is usually for inpatient care, like at cancer centers. The other reason is if the patient is self-injecting. A port provides a precise point for the needle when the drug's being delivered by someone without medical training. But obviously it'd be pretty hard to self-inject at that angle. In this case, they'd probably need a friend or family member to inject them."

Jordan sat back down and again reangled his camera.

"Jordan, this is extremely interesting." Malloy rubbed his temples. "But we have eight people dead, and we need to find the source of this drug before others die. How do we begin?"

The question was really more to himself. He wasn't expecting the boy to produce an answer.

"I don't know, but this guy had to come from somewhere with money. This is cutting-edge biotech, not cheap and not widely available. It had to come from a biotech or university with a huge grant or some kind of special funding that could build a super-high-tech lab. This wasn't developed in some lunatic biohacker's garage, that's for sure."

A lunatic biohacker. Malloy snapped his fingers. "Exactly. That's exactly who we're looking for—a lunatic biohacker. A do-it-yourself biology lab built by someone with money." Some shop set up in the middle of nowhere. Hiding.

14

Allison felt the weight of the Spiragene team's stares as she stepped over to select an Evian from the untouched refreshment table. She picked up a napkin imprinted with the Spiragene logo. Austin never would have approved such a ridiculously ornamental expense for Quandary. She was out of her league.

Hiding a grimace, she took her seat at the end of the table.

Barbara Gilbert shot her a winning smile. "After Chung-Hee has reviewed the Quandary portfolio, we hope you'll indulge us for just a couple minutes to tell you a little about our latest design ideas. We haven't had a chance to discuss some of our new technologies with Austin or Brad, so perhaps you could relay our excellent progress to them when you see them."

Allison clutched the Evian bottle in both hands, wondering how long she'd be able to pull off this charade. "Of course. And how long has it been since Austin has visited?"

Gilbert looked at Hwong. "Has he even been to our new location?" She looked back at Allison. "Austin and Quandary are the reason we have this beautiful new building, and he hasn't even been here to appreciate it. It's been over a year, I think. Maybe you can drag him over some time."

Her coquettish smile made Allison wonder if Austin had slept with her, and she tried to suppress a flash of jealousy. She willed her tense shoulders to relax, hoping Gilbert wouldn't notice her uneasiness. How had Austin become such a mystery?

Hwong stepped up to the front of the room. "We currently have three ongoing projects for Quandary, so I thought I'd review them in order. We've finished the work on the other five projects. You don't want to hear about those, do you?"

Allison relaxed her grip on her bottle and sat up taller. "I won't need an update, but I was wondering if you could provide me with reports? I couldn't find them on our server."

"Oh yes, that's probably because we don't send the reports to Quandary. Brad requested that we only load them onto the secure shared drive, due to the stringent nondisclosure agreement with Quandary."

She forced a snicker. "Boy, don't I know it. Austin's very concerned about data leaks. We've had some issues in the past."

She was getting better at this.

"When we're done here, we can go over to my office and I'll give you access to the drive," he said. "Okay, so we have two constructs for your chronic pain program."

Funny, they didn't have a chronic pain program. Despite her frequent reminder to Austin that initiating a pain program was the reason he hired her, Austin hadn't taken an interest in chronic pain. It'd always frustrated her.

"They're both delivered via the spinal fluid, but one targets nociceptors and the other targets neurons. I'll start with the SCN9A mutant gene. This is just one of a handful of genes responsible for pain perception, and it's the first one we've ever been able to target."

Gilbert was watching her closely. Allison dropped her hands onto her lap, afraid her nervousness would be obvious.

"The SCN9A gene, when it's functioning properly, opens ion channels that send pain signals to the brain. If you have a mutated 9A gene, those channels don't work properly. One of two things can happen. They don't open, resulting in no pain sensation, or they open too often, resulting in an oversensation of pain. You might have heard of Man on Fire Syndrome."

She nodded. It seemed pretty self-explanatory.

"What Brad wanted us to do was see if we could deliver two edited fragments of the 9A gene to the cell—not replace the entire gene, just make a small modification to the gene in two locations to mutate it so that the ion channel gates wouldn't open quite so frequently and the patient would feel less pain. It's the effect you'd expect from a painkiller. Make sense so far?"

She nodded again.

Hwong displayed an image on the screen, which looked like a clamshell made of honeycomb. Sitting inside the clamshell were several spirals that looked like short DNA strands standing up. "So we designed a DNA scaffold that looks like this. This is literally just a 3-D nanoscale object built with short DNA strands that lock together like Legos. The idea is that we can enclose our nanorobots and cargo within this shell and send the whole package to the target cell."

"I'm sorry, did you say nanorobots?"

"Yeah, that's right. This is very new technology. We can design and string together DNA strands with a specific set of instructions or purpose. We can make them walk, we can make them pick up items, sort them, or move them around the scaffold."

Hwong clicked a button, and the clamshell came alive. The small DNA strands moved across the honeycomb grid. "See the blue one? That's a nanobot whose task is to pick up the red cargo and move it to a different location. We can even make bots that are instructed to assemble DNA or RNA ..."

She couldn't hide her awe. It looked like science fiction, and Austin and Quandary were on the forefront of it. But her awe turned to resentment. Why hadn't Austin told her about this? She'd begged him to consider starting a program in chronic pain. Pain was her area of expertise; she'd hoped to run a program like this someday. Why would he have given it to a consultant?

" ... whole package, the clamshell, gets locked with the nanobots, gene fragments, and viral vectors inside." Hwong pointed his laser to a small floppy DNA strand outside the shell. "This strand here is looking for the target cells. In this case, it's looking for nociceptors that run from the spinal cord all the way to the skin." He clicked the Play arrow again. "The package gets injected into the spinal cord, seeks out the nociceptor, and attaches outside the cell membrane. Then the shell opens. The red cargo is the 9A fragment, encased in a gene editing platform—your CRISPR platform, actually. A nanobot attaches the cargo to a viral vector that will transport the whole package—we call it the payload—into the cell." He pointed the laser at one of the DNA strands. "This bot here moves the payload to the cell surface. Then another bot transfers these gene fragments, one by one by means of this virus, into the nucleus of the cell and then builds the gene on the inside. Once the job is finished, the DNA scaffold self-destructs."

Gilbert leaned forward to meet Allison's eyes, sliding her slender hands along the gleaming cherrywood surface. "You can see why we're so excited to move our work into animal models. This is cutting-edge technology. Spiragene is on the cusp of a breakthrough with gene delivery. No one in the world has been able to modify a gene so precisely. We could cure so many incurable diseases with these nanoscale DNA robots. In time, they'll be able to do anything we can think of."

"So this one, this SCN9A mutation robot—does it work?" Allison couldn't wait to hear more.

"That's the part that's frustrating us," Hwong answered. "By contract with Quandary, we're not allowed to publish our work until the proof of concept. We haven't yet actually seen if it works in cells or in an animal model, and we can't even tell the world about this new platform."

Allison frowned. "But I thought you'd built the construct already."

"Oh, no. We're not a wet lab. We don't do any in vitro work. We're an in-silico lab. We only design the constructs on the computer. It has to be synthesized in a gene synthesis lab, and then it can be cloned and screened for lab experiments."

That explained the fancy high-rise office. It was just a computer lab. "Who's doing the synthesis?"

Hwong exchanged a curious glance with Gilbert.

"Um, we thought you're the one managing that. Brad said you were researching and had a shortlist of labs?"

Shit. Shit. Shit.

Gilbert frowned at her, leaning in a little closer.

She couldn't come up with something to save herself. She stammered, "oh, yeah, right. I'm, uh, still working on that. Sorry. I've been really stressed lately. A lot of balls in the air."

Gilbert's eyes narrowed, then she forced a smile. "Of course."

15

Allison stepped into the lobby of Quandary and paused, listening. It was 7:10 p.m., thanks to New Jersey rush-hour traffic, and the office had to be empty. But she didn't want to answer questions about her whereabouts over the last five hours, least of all from the auditors. The floor seemed quiet as she moved down the hall toward her office. She peeked into the conference room. Rooney and his team were gone. Thank god.

Her head was spinning from everything she'd seen and heard at Spiragene. The pain research project appeared promising, especially given Austin's commitment to supporting diseases that currently had no treatments. So why had he kept her in the dark about this? Worse, he had to have lied to her all those times she'd brought up moving into chronic pain.

None of this explained why her signature was on this invoice without her knowledge, and she still owed an explanation to the auditors about the scope of the work.

As she waited for her computer to boot, she twisted the ring on her right ring finger. A gift from Austin, it was cubic zirconia, but it sparkled like diamonds. He'd told her he would buy her the real deal when he finally left Jackie. Allison sighed. She wasn't dumb. It would be years before he left his wife. But she loved the ring and wore it every day, and Austin smiled every time he saw it on her finger. It was their special secret.

Of course, that was before all this weirdness started.

She felt a flush of anger creep up to her face. She reflexively pulled out her phone but only scowled at it. Trying to get answers from Austin was a waste of time. He hadn't taken her calls in a week.

She checked her notebook from the Spiragene meeting and logged in to the shared drive. Eight file folders. She drew a deep breath and opened the first, LXR101008—the Elixir portfolio, Hwong had said, the name being Bradley Elliott's big contribution to the program. The boss had apparently thought it was a clever naming convention. *Brilliant, Brad. Well done, sir.* She despised that guy, and she hadn't even met him.

"Hey, Cruella, wanna grab a beer?"

She yelped. "Jesus, Ryan! You scared the shit out of me."

Ryan leaned casually against her door as if he were modeling his three-piece suit. He fancied himself a ladies' man, but he tried way too hard. He had the pretty-boy, clean-cut look of Neil Patrick Harris—and the Barney Stinson attitude to go with it.

"Thanks for the visual," he said. "Pack up. Let's go to the bar."

She narrowed her eyes. He'd never asked her for drinks before. "Can't. My day isn't over yet. Still have some things to do."

"Really? What's so important that needs to be done at 7:00 p.m. on a Wednesday?" He moved into her office and peered over her shoulder. "Since when did you have that kind of work ethic?"

Shit. She slammed her laptop closed, the only thing she could think of to keep him from seeing the Spiragene shared drive. "You know what? You're right, I do deserve a beer. We both do. It's been an incredibly lousy week. Let's go. You're buying." She swiftly closed her notebook and swept the stack of Spiragene business cards into the trash can.

She could keep secrets, too.

***

"Cheers."

She'd planned to make this a very quick happy hour so she could get back to the Spiragene–Quandary drive, but Ryan wasn't drinking his beer. He sat next to her, looking at her suspiciously.

"What?" she snapped. She was in no mood for a long night of slow sipping and stories of Ryan's Tinder dates. She had stuff to do.

"I'm just a little surprised you're not taking this harder."

She tilted her head. "What do you mean?"

"Listen, Al, I know you and Austin were bangin' boots. I'm not an idiot." He laughed. "Though even an idiot wouldn't have missed it. Subtlety is not your greatest attribute."

She opened her mouth for an indignant denial but gave up. "That obvious?"

He took a long drink. "So how are you doing with the news?"

"What news?"

"You didn't talk to Kiran?"

She broke out in a cold sweat. Dammit, another Kiran announcement, and she'd missed it. No wonder Ryan was Austin's golden boy; he was the one actually showing up and answering his phone.

She dropped her gaze back to her beer. "I saw his call, but I was in a meeting. I couldn't pick up."

"You don't know."

"Know what? For the love of god, just spit it out. What happened?"

Quandary was being acquired. That had to be it.

He kept his eye on the bartender as if he were too nervous to look her in the eye. "Austin's AWOL. He didn't show up for a deposition yesterday, so the feds stopped by his house. Jackie said he told her he was going to California on business, which was illegal in the first place. But there was no record of him getting on a flight. His limo driver confessed that he disappeared at a truck stop somewhere on the way to the airport, but the chicken-shit didn't call the police. Now he's busted for aiding and abetting. Dumbass."

She gaped at him as she struggled to piece his words together. AWOL. Austin was running away. He was leaving Quandary and everything they'd worked for.

"Ryan, are you messing with me? Because if you are, that's a really shitty joke."

He still didn't look up. "Sorry. I thought you'd talked to Kiran. And then I thought you might need a beer. Even Cruella de Vil needs a friend every now and then."

Austin was leaving her.

She took a pull from her beer to hide her expression. She didn't want to appear fragile in front of Ryan. Sleeping with the boss somehow carried a slightly higher dignity score than admitting that she was in love with a coward.

She changed tacks, hoping she could hold it together. "So what does this mean for Quandary?" Her voice shook.

Ryan perked up, and she could tell he was surprised she hadn't crumbled into sobs. Relieved that he didn't have to pretend to be compassionate. "Business as usual, Kiran says. He's going to call a meeting with the board, but it's not easy to get those dolts together, as you well know. It could be a couple weeks."

He signaled the bartender for another round.

"Oh, I can't—"

"And they've put a hold on the SEC audit. I know that'll disappoint you, given how much you're into that sweetheart of a guy, Craig." He smirked. "So that means you can sleep in tomorrow and stroll into the office at your usual ten o'clock."

"They're not coming back to finish up?" She tried to sound casual. *Please, please, please.*

"Nope. You're free to go back to online shopping at your desk."

"Thank you, God." She pressed her palms together. Now she could dig deeper into Austin's work with Spiragene. "I guess another beer won't kill me."

"Atta girl. Now, let me tell you my problem. You're not the only one smoochin' ass with the boss. I was going to go along with him to a meeting with Jonathan Chambers—you know, the head of the Pain Institute? He recently made the Forbes 2019 Top Physicians List, by the way. Bet you didn't know that. Figured maybe I could talk him into a letter of recommendation into the Sterling Club. But now that's shot to shit."

Allison spun on her stool. "Who?" she demanded, even though she heard him clearly. What the hell…the Pain Institute?

"Dr. Chambers? World-famous pain doctor? Don't tell me you haven't seen him on the news. He's always ranting—"

"But what were you meeting about? What business does Austin have with him?"

"Beats me. Probably just networking. Austin wants me to meet all of his bigwig buddies. It's a guy thing." He waved dismissively and picked up his beer.

She swallowed her jealous rage to question him further. "But why are they buddies? Are they working on something together?"

"No deal that I'm aware of."

Fingers, followed by a small hand and arm emerged from behind Ryan and glided over his torso. He jerked around.

"Well, hello there, sugar." He twisted and put an arm around the shoulder of a gorgeous teenage-looking brunette with breasts far too large for her bony frame.

"You remember me!" She squeaked.

Allison sighed and swung her legs back under the bar. *No, sugar, he doesn't remember you. That's why he called you 'sugar.'*

She chugged her beer in one long gulp, and waved to the bartender. She should have just left, but she wanted to interrogate Ryan some more. Who else had Austin introduced him to?

Sugar wedged herself between her and Ryan, and rested her bangle-adorned wrist on the edge of bar. The message was clear. Fuck off, he's mine.

She ordered a vodka tonic to settle her thoughts and hunched over the bar. She was probably overthinking it. Austin was a powerful CEO in northern New Jersey, and he had lots of friends in high places. Not that she'd met any of them. Still, it wouldn't be so far-fetched to think he and a prominent physician might sip the same scotch at some VIP party.

Sugar moved on, but Ryan didn't turn his attention back to her. He swaggered over to another group of girls, introduced himself with confidence, and in mere seconds was whipping out his phone to take selfies and get phone numbers. She couldn't help admiring his social skills, even if he was an insatiable lecher.

Her vodka seemed to evaporate, and she ordered another. Her apprehension began to loosen as the liquor numbed her body, a bit quicker than usual because she hadn't really eaten anything today. Her thoughts turned to Bradley Elliott. Brad. Who was he? A brief web search earlier had returned hundreds of Bradley Elliotts, but none with a research or biotech background. Was he Austin's first lapdog? And oh my, what would Ryan do if he found out? Cyberbully the man on Instagram?

She giggled at her own joke and swiveled around to see how Ryan was doing.

"Excuse me? This is Brooks Brothers." His indignant tone rang out over the crowd. He removed his jacket and flashed the label for his adoring fans.

The suit was a knock-off. He'd bragged about how cheaply he'd gotten it.

She watched his shameless flirting for a few more minutes, then polished off the rest of her vodka —was that the second or the third? – and left. Ryan could pick up her tab.

16

Layla hoped devotions would be led by Brother James this morning; she hadn't seen him all week. She combed her hair with her fingers and smoothed her white linen tunic as she turned toward the community building. The sun hadn't yet risen, and the sky was darker than usual with patchy clouds overhead. Could it be a monsoon brewing?

She crossed the courtyard past the nursery, where gentle light illuminated a nurse-mother feeding a juvie a bottle. She appeared to be talking or singing to the baby, rocking in a chair, her face serene and smiling. Layla wondered if she would ever be so lucky as to be assigned to the nursery, feeding and playing with the infants, taking the toddlers out to the playground. If the Father found her worthy, of course.

Still, she was grateful for her assignment in the dining center. Each day after devotions, she dashed over to the kitchen to prepare the cold salads for the buffet tables. The recipes were provided, but she often deviated from them to add her own flair. She took great pride in her salads, and she often received praise for how tasty they were. Today, she would finish her assignment by noon and then go to the park to meditate and collect her thoughts for her appointment with Dr. Jeannette.

But first, devotions.

She entered the community building and took her place on the cement floor. She closed her eyes and breathed in and out to the count of four, releasing the pain.

"Thank you, Father."

The side door opened, and Sister Mia entered the room. Layla's heart sank. She hadn't seen Brother James in so long, and she missed him. Maybe she'd visit his office after her appointment with Dr. Jeannette. She could ask about the progress of the new girl with the sad eyes—Kelly, was it? She looked forward to being a mentor.

"Good morning, ladies and gentlemen. How's everyone feeling this morning?" Sister Mia chimed. "Let's take a few moments of meditation to release the pain."

Sister Mia was the most beautiful African American woman Layla had ever met. Her skin was dark and smooth, a stunning contrast to the Colony's mandatory white linen uniform. Her long black hair, which she gathered loosely in a hair tie, reached all the way down her back. Sister Mia was the perfect image of purity to Layla, and she hoped she would have the same glow when she became pure.

Layla breathed deeply, but her mind refused to let go of the news she would share with Dr. Jeannette later that morning. *I had a breakthrough. I saw him. My real dad and my real mother! It wasn't as you described them, though. He died when I was young. He wasn't horrible or abusive at all, let me tell you. It's still fresh in my mind, even now.*

Dr. Jeannette would smile and clap excitedly. *Tell me all about it, my dear.*

"Okay, everyone, let's begin," Sister Mia said. "We will not have a pain ritual today, I'm afraid."

The inductees glanced around the room at each other. Could something be wrong? Was the Father punishing them for something?

"Experiencing pain is not the goal of induction. The reason you're here is to demonstrate your worthiness for purification, physically, mentally, emotionally, and spiritually. The Father knows you can suffer physically, and he sees your commitment every day."

Layla was disheartened. She hoped this wasn't a bad omen for the rest of her day. She didn't feel like herself without her pain rituals.

"This week, we'll dedicate ourselves to a different type of suffering: that

of the poisoned world, from which you are protected here at the Colony."
Sister Mia picked up a remote control and pressed a button. The lights
dimmed, and a large screen descended from the ceiling. "This isn't meant
to make you fearful of what's on the other side of our walls, but instead to
enlighten you to the atrocities of impure human nature. This may be
upsetting. Just as you've been taught to do with the pain rituals, you should
embrace what you see and release it. Allow it to reinforce what you already
know, that being a member of the Colony is a privilege and purification is
an honor."

"Thank you, Father," Layla whispered in unison with the other
inductees.

"We'll begin a new chant today: 'With knowledge comes insight. I cannot
know purity inside until I embrace the poison outside.'"

Still in heel-sit position, Layla repeated the chant. She inhaled to the
count of four and exhaled, chanting and breathing as the horror unfurled
on the screen in front of her. She sat tall on her aching shins, refusing to
turn away, unwilling to give in to the impulse to recoil at scenes of war,
sickness, hunger, and violence.

"With knowledge comes insight," she whispered, inhaling and exhaling
to the perfect count of four.

She forced herself into the scenes in front of her. She wrapped her arms
around a slave who cried out in agony as her child was torn from her and
sold. She hung tied to a stake next to a terrified young woman and watched
her skin melt as flames engulfed her. She sat next to a sixteen-year-old
soldier as he tried to stop the bleeding from his little brother's throat. She
lay next to an old man as he shivered under a wet, musty blanket on the
cold pavement behind a dumpster.

Finally, she extracted herself.

"I'm so sorry for your poisoned life," she whispered. She embraced the
anguish she felt as tears rolled down her cheeks.

Thank you, Father. Thank you for showing me the poison outside.

She rolled off her numb legs and rubbed them to get the blood circulating again. And without a word to Sister Mia or anyone else, she left devotions with a heaviness in her chest.

***

Layla looked at the clock: 10:35, and she was already finished with her salads. She cleaned the knives and dishes, said goodbye to her friends, and left the dining center.

Unable to shake the images of the impure world, she headed toward the flower garden. She wanted to be in a positive frame of mind for her meeting with Dr. Jeannette. Over the past week, she'd visited the garden as often as she could to smell the roses. Each time, her memory was flooded with images of the funeral. The vividness of the scene left her invigorated. The colors and smells and the sound of her mother's voice filled her head and heart. She didn't mourn the loss of her dad; on the contrary, she felt as though she'd gained a family member. She had a mother somewhere out there in the impure world.

She strolled past an indoctrination purity circle engaged in a group chant and couldn't help smiling. The public bloodletting ritual had been one of her favorites, and she was envious of the young inductee lying on the bench in the center of the circle, his arms and legs covered in leeches.

Poison from the impure world runs through our veins. We must release the poison.

His white mesh veil caught a breeze and fluttered up over his head, allowing her a brief glimpse of his face. His jaw was clenched, and he scowled. His look troubled her. Why would he look so anguished when his poison was being pulled right from his veins?

"Layla!"

Nicole waved from a park bench where she sat next to a woman Layla didn't recognize, a tall, older woman wearing a light blue dress and a yellow sweater. Clothing from the impure world. Curious, she smiled and walked over to them.

"This is Mrs. Madeline Barnett." Nicole gestured as though Mrs. Barnett were a piece of fine art displayed at an auction.

The woman smiled up at Layla. She wore a necklace with a large stone surrounded by a ring of diamonds. It was the most beautiful necklace Layla had ever seen, and she couldn't take her eyes off it.

Madeline laughed cordially at Nicole's flamboyant introduction. "Very nice to meet you, Layla. Please call me Madeline. Nicole was just giving me all the gossip of the Colony. I haven't been here for a while, and it seems I've missed some juicy stuff."

She exchanged a glance with Nicole, and they giggled as though they were sharing a secret.

Layla had no idea what she was talking about. She sneaked another look at the necklace, transfixed by the iridescence of large stone in the center.

Madeline traced her finger around the circle. "Opal is a stone of purity, and it sits within a white circle that symbolizes both purity and eternity."

Layla looked down and smoothed her shirt, with a mumbled "Sorry."

"And how long have you been here at the Colony, Layla?"

"A little longer than me," Nicole piped up.

Layla winced. Nicole was just boasting about her fast progress to purification.

"And where did you live before arriving here?"

"She doesn't know. Layla doesn't have any memories. It's like a form of amnesia." Nicole rattled off the response before Layla could come up with a tactful reply.

She smiled weakly.

Madeline turned to Nicole. "How about if we let your friend speak for herself?"

"Okay." Nicole didn't notice the scolding. "Look! The dessert cart is out! I'm going to go grab us a selection before the good stuff is all gone." She bounced up. "Be right back!"

Madeline squinted up at Layla and patted the bench beside her, an invitation. Layla obediently sat, her hands folded in her lap, eyes downcast.

"How do you like it here, Layla?"

She looked up at Madeline with shining eyes. "Oh, I love it here! The Colony is a wonderful place to live. We have a much higher quality of life than the impures in the outside world. We all work together like a family to make this a beautiful place."

"That's wonderful to hear. And how are you progressing to purification?"

She rubbed each finger of her left hand, looking for stray hangnails. "Um, it's going well, I think. I guess."

It was embarrassing that Nicole was so far ahead of her, but she couldn't say that. She looked up and saw Nicole in animated conversation with Sofia. Probably bragging about her purification.

Madeline took Layla's hands into her own.

She stiffened.

"Can I tell you something?" Madeline's voice was solemn.

"Um, yes."

"You are my hero. You and everyone else here working so hard for purification. I know you're told every single day how special you are, but I want you to know that you're so much more than merely special. You're striving to be pure, and as a pure, you will be a higher priority than anyone else in the world. I'm impure, and I'll never have the opportunity to be pure like you. You're superior to me and all the other impures out there."

Layla was taken aback by the conviction in Madeline's voice. Pures were special, of course, but she'd never thought of herself as superior. She looked into Madeline's eyes, trying to discern her message.

"And I'll share a little secret with you. I've been visiting the Colony for many years and seen many inductees who've been unable to attain purification. Not everyone is successful. In fact, most fail. To be pure, you must have the right mindset. You must be able to endure significant physical challenge. You need discipline and focus. Most importantly, you must be willing to unselfishly give of yourself for the greater cause. You must want to be a part of something bigger than you. It's a tremendous purpose and responsibility. The Father can identify the pures—usually from the first day they arrive, if you can believe that."

Layla drew back. "You know him?" She thought only pures like Brother

James could speak to the Father.

"I do. And"—Madeline leaned in closer and whispered—"I've already heard from him that he believes you're an extremely strong candidate, even more so than Nicole."

Her heart nearly exploded with joy.

"You'll do great things, Layla. Amazing things. I'll be very proud to watch you grow and thrive here."

Layla bowed her head humbly. "Thank you. That really means a lot to me."

Madeline dropped her hands and they sat in silence, watching the crowd mill around the dessert cart.

Nicole scampered back, vibrating with energy, although she seemed to have forgotten the desserts. "Madeline! Let's go over to the nursery! The babies are out playing."

"Remember what I said, Layla," Madeline said as Nicole tugged her up by the arm. She reached out as if to shake hands, and Layla felt something drop into her hand. "Good luck, darling."

Layla watched how gracefully Madeline glided across the lawn with Nicole. Madeline may be from the impure world, but there was no way she had any poison running through her veins. She was the perfect picture of elegance.

She opened her hand and couldn't believe what she saw. The sparkling opal necklace.

***

Layla sat in the garden a long time, rubbing her finger over the spectacular opal and the nubbly smaller diamonds surrounding it. It was the only beautiful thing she owned. She wondered if she'd be allowed to keep it. Perhaps it would be best to keep it hidden.

You're superior. You have a tremendous purpose. You're an extremely strong candidate. God, she wanted it so badly. She was aching for purification, for Brother James to call her and tell her it was time. She didn't know why she wanted it, because she didn't know what being pure meant. But she didn't have to know. It was the sole reason for her existence.

She would be pure.

She looked at the sun, now lowering to the west, and bolted off the bench. The time had flown by so quickly. Dr. Jeannette would be waiting.

17

Allison eased into her office and quietly closed the door, hoping Carol wouldn't see that she'd overslept yet again. She'd hoped to get in early enough to have some privacy to research the Spiragene programs, but it was already nearly lunchtime. Maybe the third glass of vodka last night had been a bit too much.

The database opened, revealing eight project folders, each with the same naming convention. She opened the first folder, LXR100101 ZFHX2 Gene Construct—Chronic Pain. It included a request for proposal, a scope of work document, a subfolder titled Raw Data, a final report, and an invoice. She opened the invoice and scrolled to the bottom.

"Oh my god!" She jumped out of her chair, her hand over her mouth. There it was, her own name and signature, right below Bradley Elliott's, exactly like the invoice Craig had presented yesterday.

But this one was for $120,000.

She sat down on the edge of the sofa and hit the back button to open the next folder, LXR100801 KIBRA Gene Construct—Amnesia. Her hand was shaking as she opened the invoice.

Another signed by her. $70,000.

One by one, she opened and printed each invoice and lined them up next to each other, eight different constructs targeting genes for pain, memory, and sleep regulation. Over $1.4 million had been paid to Spiragene for work across these projects, every invoice signed by her and Bradley Elliott.

She had no experience with corrupt business practices, but she'd seen enough legal dramas on TV to know full well that whatever was going on here would be perceived by an auditor as illicit. One forged signature could perhaps be explained, but a string of them implied that Austin and this Bradley guy were trying to hide the payments. Why else would they have kept her in the dark about Spiragene? And if the FBI couldn't find Austin, it would be Allison who'd have to explain who Bradley Elliott was and why she hadn't captured these payments in her financial documents.

Kiran would know what to do. She dialed his number and was sent to voicemail. "Kiran, hi, this is Allison Stevens. I wanted to talk to you about something I found during the audit. If you could ring me back, I'd appreciate it."

She gathered the invoices, put them in an envelope, and resumed her research. Each project was exactly as it'd been described to her. Some of the early research seemed quite simple, just a small origami package to carry a single, small DNA nanorobot to a specific target cell. Over time, the projects became more sophisticated. The most recent program, still ongoing, appeared to be a gene delivery project related to amnesia. The DNA origami contained what appeared to be eight or ten nanobots within an intricately folded scaffold that more closely resembled a wadded piece of paper than a clamshell.

Her phone rang. Kiran?

"Allison Stevens."

"Yes, hi, Ms. Stevens. My name is Vincent Wang, with the Drug Enforcement Agency. I was looking for Dr. Harris, but your receptionist said he's unavailable and referred me to you as the acting CEO?"

Allison sat up, flattered by the title. "Well, yes, I guess I am. What can I do for you?"

"If I could have just a moment of your time, I was hoping you could help us. Our team is investigating an illegal drug found in Arizona, and we'd like to ask you a couple questions."

She already wanted this call to be over. "Oh, we don't do any work out west. I'm sure I can't help you."

"I understand, but we're really desperate for a lead, and perhaps you could help us move in the right direction. Eight people have died on this drug, and the DEA is doing everything it can to find the source so that we can stop the deaths. It's really important."

"I'm really sorry to hear that." She opened her email and began scrolling through the new mail.

"I won't take too much of your time. We've learned that Quandary Therapeutics is doing genetic research and clinical development with gene therapies. Can you tell me, are you doing any research in pain management or chronic pain?"

Apparently, we are. "Our research is primarily in DMD and other degenerative diseases."

She flicked down to an email from Jakob's physician in Norway. Maybe her favorite young patient had advanced from doing somersaults to cartwheels. She opened the email and began skimming it.

"And do you use CRISPR Cas9 gene editing technology?"

"We do. Our DMD drug, Enigmax, which is in the clinic right now, uses our own CRISPR platform. It's a brilliant drug."

Her stomach dropped. Jakob had taken a turn for the worse.

"Ms. Stevens? Did you hear me?"

"Uh, I'm sorry, what?"

"Have you done any research targeting neurons using CRISPR Cas9?"

"No."

But she was only half-listening as she read: *Jakob has regressed in his ability to run. He can still walk but has a slight list to the left.*

"Thank you so much," Wang said. "Just one last question."

She continued reading. *I'd like to set up a call with you to discuss additional dosing. This is quite urgent, as the family is traveling to the site today to meet with me to discuss discontinuing his treatment.*

"Have you ever heard of a drug named LXR102016?" Wang asked.

No, no, no! They couldn't stop the treatment.

"Huh?" was all that came out.

"Lima, X-ray, Romeo, one-oh-two … ?" Agent Wang prodded.

If you could call me at your earliest convenience … the email concluded.

She glanced at the clock. It was already the end of the day in Norway. Shit.

"I'm so sorry, Mr."—Allison looked down at her notebook—"Wang. I just realized I'm very late for something urgent. Could we continue this another time? I'm very sorry. I have to hang up."

She disconnected the call and quickly dialed Dr. Johansen but only got his voicemail. She left a message.

Damn it! He couldn't take Jakob off the study. It was too soon.

She sat back in her chair, her hands clasped tightly, willing her phone to ring.

18

Malloy opened his office door and looked out over the room. Wang and two other agents were on the phone working their way through a list of small biotech companies that had done some early work in gene therapy. Not that a mad scientist would have set up a nice, respectable shop in biotech-land. It was far more likely that they were looking for a disgruntled geneticist who'd left to conduct his own research. Biohackers were the loose cannons of biomedical research, scientists who didn't appreciate the strict regulations of the Food and Drug Administration for testing drugs in humans. He'd seen several documentaries on biohackers who dosed themselves and their friends with untested gene therapies.

They were looking for a needle in a haystack, sure, but he was elated to be working on anything that might produce a lead. They'd been crawling around in the dark since the case had been assigned to him. At least now they finally had a concrete starting point. They had a haystack to start combing through.

"Ms. Stevens? Hello?" Wang was shouting into his phone handset.

Malloy stuck his head out of his office door. "What …?"

"She hung up on me," Wang answered, a look of disbelief on his face. "I haven't been hung up on since my first wife left me in the eighties."

Malloy smirked at his genuinely shocked expression. Apparently, Wang hadn't done much fieldwork. "Why'd she hang up?"

Wang still held the receiver in his hand. "Said she was late for something important. What could be more important than a call from me, Vincent Wang, DEA agent extraordinaire?"

"Oh, that reminds me," Malloy noted, then raised his voice. "Everyone, we're having coffee cake in the kitchen to celebrate Melanie's upcoming wedding. And listen, no making bets this time about how long the marriage will last." He lowered his voice. "And while we're on the subject, Garcia, you still owe me a hundred bucks from last time."

"I'll come in a minute," Wang said, beginning to dial the phone. "I can't let this go. I'm calling her back."

"Not now. Cake first. Melanie needs your blessing and good wishes. Again."

Wang hung up and rubbed his Buddha belly. They exchanged grins.

Malloy's own phone vibrated. Darcy. He stepped back into his office and closed the door behind him.

"Hi, sweetheart." He grimaced. "Sweetheart" had been his name for Suzanne—not that Darcy would know that, but he wanted to preserve his relationship with his late wife. She was the first love of his life and the mother of his son. She deserved to have a part of his heart all to herself, including her own pet name.

"Hey, babe. I just stopped by your house to drop off groceries. You're welcome. While I was there, you got a call from Jessica Heffner."

He racked his brain. "I don't know a Jessica Heffner. What'd she want?"

"She didn't say. She hung up rather abruptly, actually."

Was that a hint of jealousy in her voice? Did she really think he was dating other women? It had taken him over a year to find Darcy, the one woman out of thousands of desperate over-fifties who were looking for a second or third or fourth chance. He had strong feelings for Darcy and he knew, despite Robbie's intentions of setting him up with an online dating profile, that his swipe-right days were over.

"She didn't leave a number, so I just thought I'd let you know." Her voice trailed off.

She seemed to be waiting for him to say something, but he had no idea what. What would he have said to Suzanne? *Well, if she calls back, ask her to meet me at the motel—and bring some blow.* But his days of witty comebacks were also in the past. Deflection was his new MO.

"Thanks. Do you want to go to Joe's Crab Shack for dinner tonight?"

Silence. It wasn't what she'd wanted.

"Sure, Pete," she said with a sigh. "That'd be lovely. And in the meantime, I've packed your fridge with fruits and veggies. If we're going to be together for a while, I'd like to believe you're not on the verge of a triple bypass."

He grinned. "Bye, Darce."

***

Garcia was standing outside smoking when Malloy returned from the deli.

"I've crawled social media for every known fuckwit out there calling himself a biohacker of genetic drugs. Shocking how many people are into this do-it-yourself CRISPR stuff." Garcia stubbed his cigarette out and followed Malloy through the door. "Nothing yet on keywords LXR or elixir or that gene SC9-whatever or chronic pain. It doesn't seem to be in mainstream biohacking. I have a buddy looking into the deep web, but it'll take some time."

Malloy set his ham and Swiss on rye on his desk, fell back into his chair, wrung out from the two-block walk in the ninety-nine-degree heat. His appetite was gone.

"Maybe we're coming at this the wrong way." An idea had struck him on the way back with his lunch.

Garcia raised an eyebrow.

"How do we find the source of a new street drug?"

"We beat the street. Work our way from the bottom up, starting with the users."

"Exactly. We've been approaching this backward, looking for the kingpin. We have to work the layers."

"Last I heard, dead guys don't talk, boss. We've already gotten everything we can from the vics' families."

"We're spending too much time on the victims we know, trying to figure out what links them. Let's focus on the Does. Think distribution. They lived on the street. How did they get access to this drug? Sure as hell wasn't from an encrypted website."

Garcia rubbed the back of his neck. "At a shelter? A soup kitchen?"

He shook his head. "The victims weren't near each other in proximity. Two in Arizona, two in Nevada." He opened his sandwich but didn't pick it up.

Garcia eyed it. "What about a mobile food truck? One of those community trucks that drives around giving out sandwiches? Don't some of them provide first aid and shit?"

Exactly what he'd been thinking. "It's a place to start."

Without another word, Garcia left his office.

Malloy leaned over and picked up the vial found in Vespe's car, holding it between his thumb and index finger, inspecting it carefully. If a mobile unit of some kind was making the rounds, recruiting subjects to participate in a study, they would need to set up a dosing schedule. They'd have to meet up with subjects at specific times to do the injections.

He grabbed the zippered bag that held the other two vials and the syringe and pulled out the syringe, then stood and untucked his shirt. With one hand, he groped around his lower spine while aiming the syringe with the other. Jordan was right. The angle was too awkward for self-dosing. But if Mark Vespe hadn't been dosing himself, then why did he have vials and a syringe in his possession? Maybe there wasn't a mobile clinic making rounds. Maybe the victims had help. Help from a friend.

He shuffled through the files on his desk until he found the file for Karen Richmond, the ultramarathon runner. He thumbed past the interview notes of the family members and friends and stopped when he saw a page titled "Previous Employer, Jane Rocher, Albertson's Grocery Store, Tempe."

Malloy reread the excerpt he'd glossed over before. "Ms. Richmond was terminated upon returning from extended medical leave for sciatica, having failed to provide a note from her physician. Ms. Richmond stated she was in the care of her father. Mr. Richmond confirmed that to be the case, but—"

She'd had help. They'd all had help.

"Garcia," Malloy called out. "Shit." He got up and opened his door. "Garcia!"

Garcia leaned out of the kitchen holding a forkful of this morning's cake. "Yeah, boss?"

"Lyle Richmond lied to us. Get him back in here. Immediately!"

Richmond. That son of a bitch.

19

Layla sat on the leather sofa in Dr. Jeannette's office as the therapist poured the tea. Finally, Dr. Jeannette handed her a cup and sat down opposite her in a rolling desk chair.

Layla was grinning. She couldn't help it. She hadn't stopped grinning since she walked in. Still, she waited to be addressed.

Dr. Jeannette laughed. "Okay, you silly girl. You know Brother James couldn't wait to tell me about your cleanse. But I can see that you're ready to explode. Tell me."

Layla sat forward on the sofa, trying to keep her composure. "Dr. Jeannette, I saw him. I saw him! I couldn't believe how real and vivid it was. But it wasn't like you told me it would be. He was—"

Dr. Jeannette's smile had disappeared. Layla saw disappointment in her face, the look that she'd grown to know so well over her many sessions.

"He was what, Layla?" Dr. Jeannette smiled again, but Layla could see that something was very wrong. Her smile was forced, the corners of her mouth slightly twitching. She had gripped her teacup tighter but wasn't drinking from it.

Something inside Layla told her she was in serious trouble. She was bad. She'd failed again.

She dropped her cup and lurched forward, heaving. "S-sorry."

She coughed and heaved again. Her mouth filled with acidic bile, and she sprang off the couch and ran to the bathroom, slamming the door shut behind her. She dropped to the floor over the toilet, spitting the contents from her mouth. The heaving continued for nearly half a minute until she could sit back and catch her breath. She was sweating and panting. Her hands were shaking. But she wasn't thinking about her physical condition. She was thinking about failure. Dr. Jeannette didn't approve of what she'd just said. It was just like when she'd first started induction.

It's difficult to believe that your poisoned life was filled with trauma and abuse, Dr. Jeannette had told her. *Our minds don't want to believe that, so it creates a better world in our imagination. It's a coping mechanism.*

But Dr. Jeannette, I don't feel abused or traumatized, she'd insisted. *I feel like I was loved.*

Dr. Jeannette returned to her computer, as if Layla were no longer in the room.

Did I say something wrong?

Dr. Jeannette removed her glasses and dropped them back onto her desk. She glared at her.

Layla, I don't know if you're the girl I thought you were. I don't know if you're fit to be pure if you cannot accept the truth about your past. I think we may need to consider terminating your program here at the Colony.

She'd asked Layla to leave her office. Layla had sobbed all night. The next day, she'd visited Dr. Jeannette first thing after devotions and asked forgiveness for her stupidity. After that, she had never denied her poisoned life of abuse again.

Layla gripped the toilet seat. She was so stupid. She was going to lose everything. She'd lose her purification, be expelled from the program. She'd be sent into the impure world, back into her poisoned life. She wouldn't be special. She wouldn't be superior.

She heaved again and coughed, spitting more acid in the toilet. Her tongue tasted dry and sour.

"Layla, honey, are you okay?"

She croaked. "Yes, sorry."

She started crying.

"Are you sick, sweetheart?" Dr. Jeannette was just outside the door, but she didn't enter the bathroom. "Shall I call medical?"

Layla couldn't stand. Her body was shaking, and she felt weak. "Yes, Dr. Jeannette. I'm sorry. I think I'm very sick."

She flattened against the cool ceramic tiled floor. Sweat soaked her hair and clothes. Just the idea of being forced out, stepping outside the Colony walls and taking that first breath of poisoned air, made her shiver with terror. The horrors of the impure world. The hate, and the crime, and the desperation. She would surely die. The poison would fill her lungs, then her veins, and she would rot and die.

She curled into fetal position. *Please, Father, don't make me leave. Please, Father, don't make me leave.* The chant continued even while she was lifted onto a stretcher and taken to the infirmary.

20

Allison waited all afternoon for a call from Jakob's doctor. Disheartened, she finally started packing up her things to go home. Maybe she'd hit the gym after work instead of going for a run outside. New Jersey summer afternoons were like a steam bath.

Her desk phone rang, and she hit the speakerphone button.

"Allison Stevens."

"Allison, it's Kiran. I'm sorry for the delay. It's been a crazy day. What's going on?"

In her concern over Jakob's progression, she'd completely forgot about Kiran, and now she scrambled to decide what to say. "Oh, yeah, right. Thanks for calling me back. What's been so crazy?" She could hear traffic in the background and appreciated that he'd called her back from his car.

"The FBI has been all over me about accessing Austin's personal records and information in hopes of finding him," he said. "They're drowning my team in paperwork. We don't know where he is. Damn him for doing this. He's really gotten himself into a huge mess."

"Yeah." She tried to sound sympathetic, but she had her own problems. "I'm sorry about all that. I'm sure this must be hard on you."

"So what can I do for you?" Kiran obviously didn't need her sympathy. He sounded irritated and impatient.

She decided to stick with the known invoice. "The auditors found an invoice and I was trying to track down some information, but—it's like I'm going crazy. I can't seem to remember it. I was hoping you could jog my memory."

"Shoot."

"Spiragene? It's a company that does DNA origami. It looks like we contracted with them to do some early research work for us."

"DNA origami? That's a new one for me. I don't think I did the contract."

"They have a nondisclosure agreement with us."

"They probably had their own lawyers draft it."

"You don't know them at all?"

"Sorry."

One more approach. "Okay, one more thing. Can you look up the status of a patent that we probably filed?"

Kiran was silent, but Allison could still hear the sounds of his car.

"Kiran? You there?"

"Pick up your handset, will you?"

She picked up the handset, frightened by his change in tone.

"Listen, Allison." His voice was low and quiet. "Things are really unsettled at the moment. I don't know how to say this to you gently, so I'm just going to say it. Do not dig around Quandary's documents looking for anything out of the ordinary. At this point, with the FBI and SEC so ignited over Austin's business dealings, anything that doesn't look like business as usual will set off a lot of fire alarms. We're already buried in trying to figure out where the real fires are. And there are some very real fires, Allison. Do you know what I'm trying to say?"

"Yes." Allison heard the message loud and clear, the gravity driven home by his conspiratorial tone. "Of course. I get it. Thanks. I'll see you soon."

She hung up and sat still. Did Kiran know about Spiragene? Did he know Austin had signed her name? Was he trying to protect Austin?

One thing was certain. She wouldn't be asking for Kiran's help again.

21

Beep ... beep ... beep ... beep. *The machine next to Dad's hospital bed keeps a steady rhythm. I stand next to the bed looking at him. He's half lying, half sitting, smiling at me.*

"It's okay, you can touch them."

I very gently poke the heavy white gauze bandages that cover the two stumps where his legs used to be. He moves them slightly, and I jerk my hand away.

"Gotcha!" *he says, but I'm not in the mood for joking.*

"Does it hurt?" *I look into his eyes.*

"A little. But—come here, Butch—I'll show you."

"Daddy," *I whine with exasperation. I hate it when he calls me Butch.*

"See this?" *He points to a small remote control.* "This little button controls the medicine, up there in that bag. See that?" *He points up at a bag hanging from a large metal pole with wheels at the bottom.*

I nod.

"When I push the button, a little bit of medicine that makes my pain go away trickles down through the tube and right into my hand, here." *He points and follows the tube down to his hand, which is covered with white tape.*

I don't know how it gets into his hand, but I don't ask.

"Once it's in my hand, it moves through my blood to the parts that hurt. I don't use it very often, though, because the medicine also makes me veeery"—*he yawns loudly*— "sleepy." *His head drops to the side, and he snores softly.*

"Daddy?" I ask, concerned.

He opens his eyes. "Gotcha again!"

I give him an eye-roll.

Mom walks into the hospital room carrying a cup of coffee, a bottle of water, and a small can of fruit juice for me.

Dad beams. "Just what I wanted. Did you load that coffee with a shot of Bailey's?"

"No, but if you're a good boy, I'll sneak you in some Taco Bell later. Your favorite …" She opens the bottled water and hands it to him.

"Keeps me regular. What can I say?"

Beep … beep … beep … beep. *The machine continues its rhythm. I step closer to it, watching the pattern on the screen.*

"What does this do?" I ask, taking a sip from my can.

"That's a heart rate monitor. See the little spikes that pop up every time it beeps? That's my heart beating. How does it look, Butch? Am I still alive?"

"I guess so."

Mom drops into a chair across the room and picks up a magazine.

Beep … beep … beep … beep. *I watch the spikes intently. I put my hand on my chest to feel my own heart rate.*

Beep … beep … beep … beep. *The rhythm picks up, the spikes come faster.*

"Mike?" Mom says from her chair.

Beep beep beep beep. *The spikes come even faster now.*

"Mike?" Mom repeats, now sounding concerned. She gets up from her chair.

Beepbeepbeepbeep. *The beeps become a high-pitched alarm. I stare at the monitor as the spikes form into what looks like a mountain covered in trees.*

"Mike!" Mom shrieks.

I finally turn to look. Dad's body is jerking on the bed, flopping around like my goldfish, Honey, when she accidentally jumped out of her bowl and landed on my desk.

***

Layla's eyes flew wide open and contracted painfully as she looked into the bright florescent lights in the ceiling. She closed her eyes and turned toward the beeping.

Beep … beep … beep … beep.

She opened her eyes to a squint. A heart rate monitor stood next to the bed. A hospital bed. She closed her eyes tightly in a desperate attempt to return to her dream, to see what would happen to her dad. But it was over. The memory was already fading. She grasped at whatever images she could. Her mom shrieking. Her dad pretending to fall asleep. The can of fruit juice. She replayed the conversation with her dad, trying to commit it to memory before the dream dissipated forever.

Beep ... beep ... beep ... beep.

"Oh, look who's awake!" A tiny nurse with a squeaky voice arrived with a tray of soup and crackers. She set it down on the table beside the bed and dramatically swooshed back the drapes, letting sunshine pour into the room. "You've been out like a light for nearly three hours. How are you feeling?"

The nurse pressed a button on the side of the bed, and Layla's head began to rise. Once she was mostly upright, the nurse rolled the dinner tray table over her lap.

"Fine." Layla's throat was dry, and the word came out like a scratchy whisper. She took a drink of juice from a box with a thin bendy straw. Her bladder was about to burst. "I have to use the bathroom."

"I'll bet you do! We've been pumping fluids into you all day."

In the bathroom, she refreshed her memory again. Mom yelling "Mike!" over and over. Dad crowing "Gotcha!" It might have manifested as a dream, but Layla knew it wasn't. It was a memory, a real memory from her unconscious mind. Her dad had been a double amputee. How had he lost his legs?

"Layla?" the squeaky voice called from outside the bathroom. "Are you okay, sweetie?"

"Coming."

The nurse helped her crawl back under the blanket. "Dr. Jeremy will be coming to check on you in a few minutes. Meanwhile, eat up. We need to get some meat on those bones of yours."

Layla gave her a weak smile.

"Thank you," she said, lowering her eyes respectfully.

***

The clock beside the bed read 5:25. Dr. Jeremy had been kind enough to remove Layla's IV earlier today, but he hadn't discharged her, much to her dismay. She wanted to go back to the residence hall. She felt captive in the small room. She wasn't ready to face Brother James or Dr. Jeannette, and every time she heard footsteps outside her door, she panicked.

She tried to focus on her book, *Pride and Prejudice*, but her mind wandered constantly. What was purity, anyway? What did the purification process entail? Why hadn't she asked these questions before? Of course, she would never literally ask. Purification and purity were not to be discussed, period. But why hadn't she been curious until now?

Did the pures have special powers? Could they heal sick people? Did they die? Why were the pure superior to the impure, as Madeline had—

The necklace! She shuffled to the closet and rummaged through her pockets. It was gone. She sagged against the wall and clutched her stomach. She'd lost it. Or perhaps the nurse had taken it from her. Inductees were not allowed nice things.

She crawled back into bed and pulled the blanket over her head, beginning to doze, trying to recreate the picture of the hospital room and her mom and dad. But the picture just wasn't coming. All she could see was the backs of her eyelids, dark but with black rectangles the size and shape of the fluorescent lights above her bed.

They started fading.

Don't you quit on me, Butch! You're almost there!

Layla jolted awake and flung the blanket off her head. Daddy?

"Layla, sweetheart. How are you feeling?" Dr. Jeannette sat beside her bed, adjusting a bouquet of flowers in a vase.

Layla's stomach flip-flopped. "I feel much better." Even she could hear the tension in her voice.

Dr. Jeannette looked at her intently.

She tried to relax and sound casual. "I'm sorry for getting sick in your office."

Dr. Jeannette shook her head reproachfully. "Dr. Jeremy says you were severely dehydrated and undernourished. How many times have we talked about this? You'll never be pure if you don't build your strength. Dr. Jeremy is extremely disappointed. It seems you've lost two pounds. You haven't been following your nutritional plan, have you?"

"I'm sorry." She looked down. How many times in a day did she apologize to someone?

A porter strolled into the room.

"Ah, perfect!" Dr. Jeannette said in her animated way. "Please set it right over here."

The porter brought over a steaming teapot and two small teacups with saucers. He removed Layla's tray of uneaten soup and set the tea onto her table.

Dr. Jeannette poured green tea into both cups. "Dr. Jeremy said he wanted to keep you overnight, so I thought we could pass some time by finishing our session." She smiled. "I remember how excited you were to tell me all about your vision."

Her smile spread into a sneer as she leaned closer, so close Layla could see the steam from her tea. Above the cup, Dr. Jeannette's eyes never left Layla's face.

22

Layla diverted her gaze to her own steaming cup of tea. Her stomach lurched.

Don't you quit on me, Butch. You're almost there!

She smiled and drained her cup to the halfway mark, refusing to let her stomach muscles clench in disagreement.

Don't you quit on me, Butch.

"That's my girl," Dr. Jeannette said, still eyeing her. "Green tea has so many health benefits, you know. And a girl like you, so thin and anemic, needs all the help she can get, right?"

Despite the tightly stretched smile, the tone of her voice had become tart, and her eyes bore into Layla's like shards of glass. But Layla didn't shy away. She felt something that wasn't familiar to her. She felt knowledgeable. She felt worldly. Madeline had described her as "superior." Was Dr. Jeannette pure? When Layla was pure, would she be superior to Dr. Jeannette the same way she would be to Madeline?

Don't you quit on me, Butch.

I won't, Daddy. She could do this.

She gently set down her tea.

"Well, Layla, tell me. I can't wait to hear!" Dr. Jeannette crossed her legs and folded her hands in her lap.

Layla threw her hands to her sides, fingers splayed widely, in the kind of dramatic gesture that Nicole would use. She leaned forward in the bed and shifted her weight so that she could cross her legs. "Dr. Jeannette, it was the greatest experience of my life! I can't believe how real the vision was, and I can't stop thinking about it. The images, they're so colorful and ... wow, I couldn't wait to tell you."

"So tell me," Dr. Jeannette said with a hint of impatience.

"Well, what I was going to say yesterday before the, um, accident, is that the vision wasn't exactly like you described."

Dr. Jeannette's smile remained, but Layla saw the tilt of her head change. *Don't you quit on me, Butch. You're almost there!*

She grasped at the first thing she could think of. She knew it was weak, but she spoke with as much enthusiasm and conviction as she could. "My dad. My real dad. He didn't have blond hair. He had light brown hair. He had a giant forehead, with hair only way in the back." She indicated on her own head. "And he didn't have a gap in his teeth, he had a tooth missing. This one." She pointed to her front tooth. "That's a bit different from what you told me."

Dr. Jeannette was a statue in her chair.

She continued quickly. "Anyway, that's not the important part. That's the vision. He had come home drunk, as usual, and he stood in my bedroom doorway. I could smell the alcohol on his breath, and it nearly made me sick. Uh, I feel like I can still smell it, even now." She turned away from the tea, which was now actually making her feel nauseated. Funny how this all seemed to work. "And he said, 'Come here, Layla.' But I could feel deep inside that he was going to hurt me, so I picked up a ..."

Her mind went blank and panic flooded up within her, but she closed her eyes and an image appeared. "A box. It was a lunch box. It had Scooby-Doo on the front, and it was made of metal, and I had loaded it with rocks. It was my weapon. I had built it as a weapon because I feared him so much. And he moved in on me like he was going to grab me. I swung the lunch box at him and hit him in the head." She mimicked the swing from her bed. "He fell back. Then I got up, and I ran. I left the house and ran down the street. I didn't know where I was going, I just kept running. My feet were killing me because I was barefoot, but I couldn't allow the pain to stop me. I just kept running to escape him."

She stopped, panting. Her eyes were focused on the wall, her face flushed. She stared at the wall for another couple of seconds until she had the courage to look at Dr. Jeannette.

Dr. Jeannette was staring at her intently, studying her face. She didn't speak, and her face held no expression that Layla could read. Layla held that piercing gaze as long as she could, then dropped her eyes to her lap and waited.

Dr. Jeannette finally spoke. "Interesting."

Just the one word, slowly and thoughtfully.

Layla sat back against her pillow, wanting to put some distance between the two of them. Dr. Jeannette knew she was lying. She'd failed. Dr. Jeannette wrote something in her notepad, but Layla couldn't read it from her bed.

Dr. Jeannette's eyes narrowed. "You said that in your vision, you'd filled up a lunch box with rocks. Correct?"

She felt herself cower. "Uh-huh."

I failed, Daddy. I didn't make it.

"And what did you say was the image on the box?"

"Scooby-Doo. You know, the cartoon?"

"Right. Yes, I certainly know Scooby-Doo. It was a cartoon on TV when I was young. I used to love that show." Her smile fell away when she looked back at Layla. "What I find surprising is that you know Scooby-Doo. You're a lot younger than me, and it wasn't a popular show when you were growing up."

Layla, too, was completely mystified by where she'd gotten the idea of a Scooby-Doo lunch box. She didn't remember watching the cartoon, and she certainly didn't remember seeing it on a lunch box. Where had that come from?

"Do you remember where you got that lunch box?"

A sour taste filled her mouth. Why was her therapist tormenting her?

"Layla?"

She looked up, steeling herself. "No, Dr. Jeannette, I don't know the cartoon, and I don't know where I got the lunch box. It was just there, and I'd filled it with rocks. It was a weapon. I don't remember where it came from." She couldn't have forced a more genuine answer, because this part was the truth. Yet she knew it would only get her in trouble.

Dr. Jeannette didn't smile, but she didn't look angry or disappointed either. She made more notes. Finally, she closed her notepad and stood up, towering over Layla. The sides of her mouth turned up slightly, but in no way did it look like a smile.

"Well, then. Maybe in our next session, you'll come with a new vision. A vision that includes more information about your surroundings and more details about your past poisoned life." Dr. Jeannette articulated the last words very clearly and slowly. "Remember, Layla, a poisoned life cannot be purified until it is fully understood."

Layla didn't respond.

"Oh, I almost forgot." She reached into her pocket. "I found this on the floor in my office bathroom." She handed Layla a necklace with a large opal in a ring of diamonds. "Secrets like these should be hidden very carefully. You wouldn't want to get caught. You could be expelled. Do you understand?"

Layla's stomach dropped. "I understand completely. Thank you for your wisdom and guidance."

She respectfully dropped her gaze before Dr. Jeannette turned away and left the room.

She stared at the door for several minutes. The rules of the Colony were becoming clearer and clearer every day. Dr. Jeannette didn't want the truth. She wanted a story. One that she insisted was real. Layla took a deep, ragged breath and pulled her blanket up to her chin.

"Yes, I understand completely, Dr. Jeannette."

23

Austin Harris exited Interstate 45 and followed his GPS to the Fairview RV Park, as he'd been instructed. He pulled into lot fifteen, picked up one of his Tracfones, and dialed.

Again, only one ring. "Yes."

He appreciated the efficiency and consistency of the Fixer. "I'm just south of Dallas at the RV park."

"Yes."

"I'll leave tomorrow by eight o'clock."

"Yes."

He waited a couple seconds for any further instructions. None came.

"Okay."

He disconnected the call, hopped out of the RV, and headed toward the office. A bell jingled as he stepped into the trailer labeled Office.

"Good evening. How can I help you?" A heavyset black woman with a deep southern accent greeted him from behind a small desk littered with paper and fast-food wrappers. Her face was perfectly round, and when she smiled, her cheeks dimpled like one of those ugly dolls with the pinched faces. A Garden Patch doll?

"I've pulled into lot fifteen. Reservation for Larry Kohn." He laid a fifty-dollar bill on the counter.

"Yes, Mr. Kohn." She pronounced the name in two syllables: Ko-uhn.

"May I kindly see your driver's license?"

"Actually, if it's all the same to you, I'd like my stay here tonight to be confidential." He laid another two fifty-dollar bills on the counter.

"Yes, Mr. Kohn. Enjoy your stay." She smiled again, her dimples even deeper with the delight of a very nice tip.

He wondered if one extra fifty would have done the trick. Everyone had a price tag, and he bet Little Miss Garden Patch would have been peachy keen with fifty, maybe even twenty. But he wasn't going to risk playing his game during this trip.

Not with the stakes so high.

***

He lay awake staring at the sky through the moonroof of his brand-new 2019 Pleasure-Way Mercedes-Benz widebody recreational vehicle. He couldn't see the stars tonight, thanks to the city lights of Dallas, but he smiled anyway. His enjoyment of this trip was surprising. He felt young and free again, as he had in his mid-twenties backpacking through Germany, though now he enjoyed a much higher quality of travel. But it wasn't the luxury RV that made him smile; it was the simplicity of his singular focus. No tedious task lists or absurd presentations, no pushing the limits of his EQ to appear compassionate to his staff, no coddling the fragile and inflated egos of his pompous physicians. Hell, he didn't even have to listen to his whiny kids and nagging wife, as family vacations usually went. He felt positively liberated.

Despite that, he couldn't let his guard down even for a second. He'd been financing this contingency plan for months, unsure if and when it might be needed, and it hadn't been easy or cheap. But foolproof plans came with a cost.

The financial part had been easy—it was good to be wealthy—but staying out of sight hadn't been so simple. The whole world is captured on camera every second, he was told by the Fixer, and it was nearly impossible to disappear. The Fixer, whose name or face he didn't know, had managed every detail of his extraction, providing complete albeit terse updates on the status of the search for him, including the extensive scope of the FBI's APB. Austin had also been warned about the hungry flock of fugitive recovery agents that were in all likelihood on his trail. Skipping bail wasn't important enough for a TV news story, but the reward for Austin's return would be plenty attractive to a bounty hunter, a lot more than a typical target. And if that wasn't enough, the Fixer had said Austin's very own wife had hired a private detective to spy on him back in New Jersey. Bitch.

Jackie was fiercely independent. It's what had originally attracted him to her in the first place—in addition to her raging-hot body, of course—but now he despised it. In those flawlessly gorgeous eyes boiled a look of both challenge and superiority: *Go ahead and try to do better than me.* The look had always made him want to slap her across the face, but he never had. She was an important part of his plan.

But he did try to do better than her. He tried often, in fact—flight attendants, cocktail waitresses, secretaries, you name it. *Thanks for the suggestion, Jackie.*

He felt a vibration next to him and shuffled through four Tracfones. He glanced at the small piece of tape he'd used to label the phone and answered. "Kiran."

"We have a situation."

Austin waited.

"Allison Stevens."

He didn't need or care about all the details of Allison's little excursion yesterday, but he allowed Kiran to deliver the blow-by-blow. He felt his face tighten into a scowl. He'd underestimated her, and it wasn't like him to mischaracterize those in his inner circle. She'd been strategically groomed for this role, docile and obedient. This wouldn't do.

"I'll take care of it." He disconnected the call and stared at his phone. "You sneaky little girl." He smirked.

He dialed Allison's number.

24

Allison poured a third vodka tonic, this time with more vodka than tonic. She couldn't stop thinking about her ominous call with Kiran earlier that afternoon, and the Spiragene invoices were ringing alarm bells in her head. This wasn't just smoke; these were real fires.

She needed someone to talk to, but her someone had always been Austin. Her vision blurred, and she took a long pull from her glass in an effort to swallow back the tears. The booze made her more emotional, but she didn't care. She was utterly alone. Friendless. Faced with something both intriguing and intimidating, and not a soul to share it with. Her face contorted, and she stifled a sob with a gulp from her glass.

She lay back against the sofa cushions and closed her eyes. It was her own fault. She'd allowed Austin to manipulate her until her meager social life had completely eroded.

It's girls' night tonight, she'd insisted one night as she freshened her mascara.

Cancel it. I'll come over. I'll bring Indian food and beer, and we can work on the DMD program strategy. Austin sounded especially sexy through her iPhone speaker. He knew Indian food was her favorite. But he'd been taking up all her time the past several months, and what few friends she had left were getting annoyed.

I can't cancel. Anyway, maybe you should go home to Jackie. It came out haughtier than she'd intended.

His tone changed from sexy to indignant. *I thought you were serious about our work. Maybe I've misjudged you. There are plenty other professionals out there who'd be far more dedicated to your DMD program.*

At the time, she'd chalked it up to jealousy. He was in love with her, after all, and he had a possessive side she found endearing. Still, it only took a few more conversations like that before she'd stopped making plans with anyone else. God, that must have been three, four years ago.

Her phone vibrated, and she answered with a sleepy "Allison Stevens."

"Hi, baby. Do you miss me?"

She leaped off the sofa, instantly growing light-headed, then lowered herself to the edge of the cushion.

"Austin?"

What a dumb thing to say. She knew it was Austin.

"Yeah, sweetheart. I'm okay. I'm on the road, keeping a low profile. How's my girl?"

His girl had been falling to pieces for days now. "Fine, um, I guess." God, why did she suddenly sound like a stupid child?

"How's Quandary? Are you keeping the programs going? You're not hiding out in your apartment all day, are you?"

She walked over to her window and looked out over the dimly lit parking lot. He couldn't be out there, could he?

"Um, well, um, we lost Jakob. From the study." Her legs trembled. What the fuck was wrong with her?

"Oh, baby. I'm so sorry. God, that must have broken your heart." He sounded genuinely sad.

"Yeah."

"And how's Ryan doing? Are you guys still working with Kiran? I'm sure the board will be meeting soon to decide an ad interim CEO."

"Yeah."

Her chest ached, under the weight of her conflicting emotions. One part of her wanted to ostracize him, to accuse him of keeping Spiragene a secret and shutting her out of his pain program. The other part of her—the larger part—just wanted to tell him she loved him and to please come home and make this all better. His voice was intoxicating. She would give anything to erase all that had happened over the last two weeks and just go back to business as usual. Maybe he'd come out of wherever he was hiding and stay with her tonight.

Instead, she asked in her little-girl voice, "So do you know who they'll name for that?"

"Doubt anyone's going to ask me."

"Oh." She picked up her glass and watched the ice swirl, but she didn't take a sip.

"Listen, Al, I'm sorry I disappointed you. I cared very much for you. I still do. And I know you felt the same. And now you probably think I'm a jackass."

She closed her eyes, and her face tightened again.

"But I want you to know that this … How can I say it? … This sabbatical is a temporary arrangement. It's like a mission. Something I need to do. And when I'm done, I'll be back, and it'll be just like the old days."

His voice was so comforting and he sounded so genuine that she couldn't help relaxing. "A mission? Like helping a third-world country?"

"Something like that. Listen, I understand you visited a company we've been working with. Spiragene."

She went rigid.

"Barbara said you stopped by to get a full portfolio status for an urgent board meeting. Is that right?"

It was so unexpected that she couldn't think of a response.

He chuckled. "It's okay, it's okay. Take your time. Have a sip of your vodka."

He knew her far too well. Or maybe … She glanced over at her window again.

"Austin, I found … an invoice." Her voice cracked. "I just—I didn't know what it was, and you weren't answering my calls, and—"

"Honey, honey, it's okay. It's fine."

"—the auditors were here, and my signature was on the invoice, and I was afraid that I'd done something wrong—" Her voice rose.

"Shh, shh. Hey, listen, baby. It's fine. You didn't know. You were just doing your job. It's okay, really."

She stepped into the kitchen, in dire need of a glass of water.

"It's fine," he continued. "I smoothed it over with Barbara. She really liked you, by the way. She says you have a lot of potential."

Her nervousness turned into confusion. Why was he calling?

"But here's the thing." His tone changed from soothing to sharp. "It's important that you never visit them again, okay? And if you find any other invoices or documents that you don't understand, the best thing would be to just shred them. I don't want you to get into any trouble. Do you hear what I'm saying?"

She braced one hand on the counter. Trouble? "What are you talking about? Am I in some kind of danger? Did you involve me in—" She didn't know what he was involved in. "Is there something going on that you haven't told me?"

He laughed then, a callous slap across her face. She winced.

"I've always loved your innocence. It's really your best quality. Hang onto that as long as you can. Meanwhile, let me be a bit clearer. This … How can I say it? … This venture I'm involved in right now is more important than anything. It will change the course of medical history. I've been building this for years, planning every tiny detail—including you. You play an important role in all this, Al. You're my right-hand man, aren't you, baby? Your role is to go back to work and just behave like everything is normal. Keep the train on the tracks. That's why I hired you."

She squinted. She still didn't understand what he was getting at. "How am I supposed to just—"

"Don't talk. Just listen." His voice deepened, taking on a threatening tone that she'd never heard before. "You will go back to work and do your job each day, protect what we've built. Do you understand? Am I being clear enough for you?"

Allison felt a hot flush crawl up her face. "Who the fuck—"

"Shut up!"

She froze. Seconds ticked by in silence.

Austin's tone changed again, as though he were talking to a child. "I only have one more minute, honey, then I have to run. But this is the important part, so pay attention. You're an important element in my planning—my scapegoat until this plays out. Do as I tell you, and you won't get hurt."

She squeezed her eyes shut. This wasn't Austin. This wasn't the man she loved.

"From this moment on, I need you to forget everything you saw and heard at Spiragene. Forget all about the LXR portfolio. Just pretend it never existed. Don't get all detective-like, and don't talk to the police. This is bigger than both you and me. So go back to your job each day and play your role. Keep the train on the tracks."

A memory flashed through her mind of Austin lounging next to her on the couch giving her a foot rub as she sipped wine. She glanced over at the sofa. That hadn't been even three weeks ago.

"Say it. Keep the train on the tracks."

Her tongue felt like sandpaper. She sipped her water, but it seemed to pour into her mouth like volcanic ash.

"Say it." His voice was a demonic snarl.

She could only whisper. "Keep the tr—"

Someone was banging on a door. Austin's door.

A muffled voice called out, "Dr. Harris, I have a warrant for your arrest. Let's not make this difficult."

"I'm not armed," Austin called back.

Allison tottered backward, banging against the wall. Her water glass crashed to the floor, spraying glass and liquid across her kitchen. Her hand flew to her mouth. They'd found him.

Two explosive gunshots followed. She dropped her phone. Dropping to her knees among the glass shards, she clambered for it.

"Austin?" Her voice was just a squeak.

Silence.

25

F uck, fuck, fuck.

The Tracfone flew from Austin's hand, banged against the driver's seat, and flipped closed as he reflexively dropped to his knees, then fell face down onto his stomach, breathing fast and shallow. He shielded his head with his arms. This was it. After everything he'd built, this was it.

In the next instant, before his short-circuited brain could even process whether the bullets had entered his body, the RV doors unlocked. Both the driver and passenger doors opened, and two men climbed into the vehicle. The man behind the steering wheel soberly started the truck and pulled out of the lot.

Holding his breath, Austin patted his body for blood. Nothing. He hadn't been shot. He exhaled and pulled himself onto his hands and knees, but he couldn't stand as the RV rattled and swayed down the dirt road. Vibrating with the terror, his tongue felt glued to the top of his mouth.

The driver broke the silence. "Dr. Harris, my sincere apologies for the intrusion. This intervention wasn't optimal, but it was necessary to prevent your arrest and return to Connecticut."

Austin blinked in stunned silence.

"My colleague and I are with the operation assigned to your safe transport into Mexico."

The man in the passenger seat swiveled to face him, and Austin gaped. The guy must've been in his twenties. He was just a kid. In fact, both these thugs were kids.

The kid's voice was gentle. "Sir, please collect your important items. We'll be changing vehicles in less than one minute."

Finally, Austin gathered his bearings. "What the hell is going on here? Who the hell are you? What the fuck just happened?" His tone escalated with each question.

"Please, Dr. Harris, kindly gather your important items. We'll be leaving this vehicle behind."

The driver apologized again, his eyes still on the road. "We're sorry about this interruption in your schedule, sir. Once we change cars, we'll explain. Please ensure you have the Tracfones."

The gravity of the situation finally settled in. He was a fugitive, and someone looking for him had just been shot. He did as he was told and collected his duffel bag, which contained all his money, identification, and phones. He slipped on his pants and shoes and perched on the edge of the bed, shakily clutching his bag.

"Here we are. Dr. Harris, please exit the RV as quickly as possible and get into the back seat of the Expedition."

A black Ford Expedition sat at the far end of a liquor store parking lot. The RV driver held the door as Austin scrambled out, still clutching his bag against his chest, and followed the driver to the SUV.

"Thirty seconds," the driver said to his partner.

The partner pulled from the center console a pair of gloves, a respirator, and a spray bottle and moved quickly back to the RV. As Austin slid into the back seat, the driver resumed his position at the wheel, watching the RV through the rearview mirror, glancing at his watch every few seconds. Austin craned to watch through the back window. A few seconds later, his partner emerged from the RV with a bag and held up the key fob, presumably locking the doors, on his way to the passenger side of the Ford.

"Clean," he said as he slammed the door.

Seconds later, they were driving down the highway.

Austin could no longer remain silent. "Would you kindly explain what's happening here?" He recognized with dismay that he sounded like a fussy customer dissatisfied with the temperature of his filet mignon. "This is not what I discussed with your boss. I need to speak with him."

"Of course. Please feel free to call him."

He whipped out the phone, his fury building. Goddammit! He'd been explicit about his requirements for this exit strategy and had been assured that his demands would be met. He'd been unmistakably clear that no one could be hurt or killed, and the Fixer had agreed. He'd paid a lot of goddamn money for this.

"Yes." The Fixer's unflappable demeanor infuriated him further.

"What the hell is going on? Do you realize what you've just done? This isn't acceptable. Now my safety is—"

"Dr. Harris."

"—seriously compromised, not to mention that if I'm caught—"

"Dr. Harris."

"—I'll be tried for murder, even though I didn't pull—"

"Dr. *Harris.*"

The Fixer raised his voice just slightly, but it was such a change from his otherwise emotionless tone that it unsettled Austin. He paused, breathing hard.

The Fixer's voice returned to normal. "I apologize for the change in strategy. Unfortunately, we're unable to continue with the original implementation of the contract."

"But I'm the one who paid for the fucking contract!" His voice cracked.

"Your safe delivery over the border is our highest priority, and we'll accomplish that despite the obstacles. But you must do exactly as we say, exactly when we say it. Do I make myself clear?"

"I don't understand." The roller coaster of the last fifteen minutes had drained his energy, and his hands shook. Who were these people?

"The best thing for you to do right now is relax and listen carefully to the instructions of your escorts. You need to understand that this situation is now beyond your control. If you want to achieve your objective, you need to follow our instructions."

The line disconnected.

Austin lowered the phone to his lap. He listened to his drumming heart and raspy breath. He felt powerless and intimidated like he was unraveling. The operation had gone off the rails, and someone had been killed. Certainly, the police would track the man's death to him.

The situation is now beyond your control. But why? This was his contract. He was supposed to be the boss. For the first time since he was a child, and with all the will he could muster, Austin fought back tears of genuine, primal fear.

26

"**M**r. Richmond, this is the team working on your daughter's case," Wang said as he led Lyle Richmond into Malloy's office.

Richmond could only be described as a burly man, hardly what you'd expect of the father of petite, athletic Karen Richmond. He had a Grizzly Adams look, with a large beer gut and a flannel shirt over a T-shirt that read Ban Idiots, Not Guns. Given the hundred-degree heat, Malloy presumed the flannel overshirt was the man's rendition of a suit jacket.

Malloy shook Richmond's hand, determined to remain professional, even though he was fuming inside. Richmond had lied to his team about the treatments his daughter had been taking.

"I'm Peter Malloy," he said. "This is Danny Garcia, and you met Vincent Wang already."

He gestured to a chair at his office conference table, and Richmond sat, nervously scratching the beard on his neck.

"How about some coffee?" Malloy asked, in an effort to ease the tension.

"Oh, yeah. Thanks. Appreciate that."

Malloy nodded to Garcia, who gave him a "What the fuck?" expression before leaving the room. Richmond had been resistant, even combative, when the team had interviewed him after his daughter's death. They needed to handle this interrogation today with kid gloves. If Richmond had a short fuse, he could get up and walk out as easily as he'd walked in, burying Malloy in paperwork and warrants to get him back again. You could catch more bees with honey than vinegar, as Suzanne used to say.

"How are the kids? Enjoying the summer?"

"Oh, well. Yeah, you know. Doin' the best we can. It ain't been easy."

"I lost my wife, Suzanne, a few years ago—cancer," Malloy said. "I remember those months where it just felt like all I could do was wake up and draw breath. Sometimes even getting up took more than I had. Anything more than that would have required a damn miracle."

Richmond's shoulders slumped. "Yeah."

Garcia walked in with a cup of black coffee and handed it to Richmond, who thanked him politely. Malloy picked up his own coffee cup, which was now cold and he had no intention of drinking, and sat down at the table with Richmond. He'd mastered the tactic of "mirroring" years ago as an easy way to build rapport and, more importantly, trust.

Wang joined him at the table, but Garcia took his usual stance against the wall.

"Thank you for coming in today," he began.

"After your secretary called me, I decided I needed to come forward. I'm a man o' God. It's the right thing to do."

Richmond had a faraway look in his eyes, and Malloy sensed he had something to say. He remained silent, waiting for Richmond to continue. A full thirty seconds passed.

"My daughter, Karen, was an angel in our family." Richmond's lips tightened into a thin line. "A true angel. She gave her heart and soul to God and the community, and so when they approached her with an answer for her pain and a large amount of money to boot, it only seemed like God was answering her prayers. All our prayers."

Malloy chose his words carefully. "Who approached Karen with an answer for her pain?"

"I dunno. I wadn't there when it happened. Karen never spoke of 'em, and I never asked. Just assumed it was some marketing thing. You know, where you try something for a couple months and then you get your picture on a TV commercial or sumpin' like that. But they said her sciatica would be gone." His eyes shot up to Malloy's. "She was crippled. Couldn't even walk to the kitchen for dinner. And they said she'd be running fine, just like before. They wanted to pay her. Lots of money."

"How much money?" Malloy asked, straining to keep his voice even.

Richmond dropped his eyes down to his still untouched coffee on his lap, like he was embarrassed. "Fifty thousand."

"They gave her $50,000 to take their drug? And they promised she'd feel better?"

"That's right. I'm sorry. I know I shoulda tole you folks when you come to the house a couple months back. But thing is, we really needed that money, and I didn't wanna give it back. I been outta work a long time, and I have a family to support."

"We won't take the money from you. It's yours to keep. But is it okay if I ask you some questions about it? It might help us track down the people who killed Karen and the seven others. You know, two of the others were kids—younger than Karen, in fact." Malloy hoped a man of God would see the horrible crime in that. Children were a heritage from the lord, according to Proverbs or Psalms or one of those.

"Don't know too much, but I'll tell you what I can."

"Did you receive the payment by a check?"

Richmond shook his head. "Karen set up a new bank account at MidFirst, separate from our home account. They'd given her clear instructions. If she did anything different, they wouldn't give her the second payment. Money just showed up."

"There was a second payment?" Malloy leaned forward slightly and noticed that Richmond leaned back in response. He leaned back and crossed his legs.

"Supposed to be another fifty. But it never came through."

"Is the money still there? In that new account?"

"Nah, we pulled it out right away. We were afraid it wouldn't be real, you know? After y'all come knockin', I closed up the account."

Now for the million-dollar question. "Do you have any papers from the bank or a statement that might have information about where that deposit came from?"

"'Fraid not, sorry. Bank never sent us a statement, and as I said, the account's all closed up now."

Wang looked at Malloy as if asking permission to speak. Malloy nodded.

"Mr. Richmond, do you know who performed the surgery to implant the spinal port in Karen's back?"

Richmond turned his whole body toward Wang. "No, sir. She never tole me the details. Wadn't supposed to. I don't know anything about the folks who she was involved with. Way she talked, they seemed like the real deal. Medical doctor types."

"And did you do the injections for her?"

"Yes. Yes, I did. Every day. One syringeful for three months. We had us a full box of vials, but I took 'em to the dump after Karen … after she …"

"How did she respond to the treatment?" Wang asked.

"It was like God himself reached down from heaven and touched her. Within the first couple weeks, she was walking. After another week or two, she was back to jogging. By the end of the second month, she was running marathons again. Like she hadn't missed a day."

Mark Vespe's PCP expression flashed through Malloy's mind. "Did she behave differently while she was taking the treatment? Did she seem loopy? Do anything strange?"

"No, sir. She was same old Kare Bear. Happy to be alive and happy to be moving around again."

Malloy noticed Richmond's knee had begun shaking, and he decided the man had had enough interrogation, gentle though it was. It didn't appear he knew much more that could help them. "You've done a very good thing by coming forward today. My colleagues and I are grateful for everything you've told us. If you can think of anything else that might help, no matter how small, please call me. My cell phone is right here." Malloy handed him a card and pointed to his mobile number.

Richmond pushed his chair back and set his full cup of coffee on the table. "I have one more thing." He pulled a cell phone from his shirt pocket. "They gave her this." He handed the phone to Malloy. "It ain't never been used, far as I can tell. No calls in the log comin' in or goin' out. But maybe you can trace it to somebody."

Malloy handed it straight to Garcia, who gave him a nod of understanding, but Malloy wasn't optimistic. It was a Tracfone, and likely the most they'd learn is which Walmart had sold the damn thing.

"Sorry about the coffee. I haven't been eating or drinking much of anything lately. Karen used to …"

"Mr. Richmond, I'll walk you out." Wang saved him from a memory that might have caused him to tear up.

Richmond shook hands with Malloy and Garcia. "Funny." He pointed to Garcia's vintage T-shirt that read Robot Is the Future. "Karen once told me they were pumpin' tiny robots into her. I called her crazy, but maybe that ain't far from the truth."

He croaked a hollow laugh and followed Wang out of Malloy's office.

Malloy closed the door after them. "Start the paperwork for a warrant—"

"—for Karen Richmond's bank account. On it, boss."

"And see what you can get on that Tracfone. I doubt we'll get any good fingerprints, but give it a try."

"Yup." He slammed the door behind him.

Malloy's phone rang, and he glanced down at the caller ID: John Cramer, FBI. He hadn't spoken to Cramer since he'd dumped this case on Malloy weeks ago.

He picked up. "John, what's going on? Don't tell me the FBI has another vic."

"On the contrary, I have some good news for you."

"I could use some."

"The FBI received some intel about that drug you're chasing, the one with the spinal port. The case has been reclassified, and the FBI is reclaiming it. Full stop for your team."

Malloy leaned against the edge of his desk. "Are you joking?"

"Like Christmas in August, huh?"

27

Allison gasped awake as if she'd stopped breathing. It took several moments before she realized where she was, and she groaned, turning her face from the stench of vomit that lay in a semi-dried pool just inches away on the kitchen floor. Her head pounded. As she tried to pull herself to her knees, a wave of dizziness flattened her to the blessedly cool ceramic tile.

Her foot tapped something hard, which rolled across the floor and into the wall. *Plink*. Without moving her head, she tracked its path. An empty bottle. Not vodka, but—oh god. She'd drunk the full bottle of Austin's bourbon, a gift she'd given him last year that he'd not gotten around to trying. Her stomach heaved, and she took a deep breath to avoid another round of vomiting.

She wiped her mouth and nose with the back of her sleeve and rolled onto all fours. Pain shot into her knee, and she jerked her leg up and pulled a shard of glass from her kneecap. Too dizzy to stand, she crawled to the living room in search of her phone. She found it on the floor under the coffee table. No messages, but dozens of outgoing calls to Austin after one five-minute-and-forty-second incoming call from an unknown number.

A muffled warble escaped her lips, a voice that didn't sound like her own. She squeezed her eyes shut. Her head throbbed and she pressed her knuckles against her eyes to relieve the pressure.

No, no, no.

She turned onto her side and opened a browser window on her phone. Her thumbs trembled as she keyed in "Austin Harris" and selected news results.

Nothing.

Had she dreamed the gunshots?

Dr. Harris, I have a warrant for your arrest. Let's not make this difficult.

I'm not armed.

Two unmistakable gunshots. Then silence.

Were they police? Did they kill him? Tremors wracked her body.

Her phone vibrated. The office. Maybe they had news.

She sat up, and the room spun. She cleared her throat. "Hi, Carol."

Her assistant's voice was barely above a whisper. "Oh, hi, Allison. I'm sorry to bother you. I'm sure you're, uh, busy, but there are two FBI agents here. They want to speak with you."

This was it. Austin was ... dead.

Her vision swam.

"I'm coming," she croaked.

***

Carol hurried over as soon as Allison entered the lobby.

"I sent them to the conference room. They seemed"—Carol glanced over her shoulder, as if they might have sneaked up on her—"angry."

Allison swallowed and peered past Carol toward the conference room. "I'm sure it's nothing to be worried about." Her armpits were already damp and her stomach still hadn't settled, despite forcing herself to eat a sleeve of saltines. She was neither physically nor mentally prepared for this.

"Do you think it has something to do with Austin?"

She ignored the question.

She stepped into the conference room and approached the agents with her hand out, ready to offer a firm handshake. But her confidence drained as the agent turned toward her. It was the agent who arrested Austin at that bar in Boston. There was nothing friendly about the sneer on his face.

She dropped her hand. "Can I help you?" She flinched inwardly at her sheepish tone.

"Ms. Stevens. You probably don't remember, but we met briefly once before. Up in Boston." That deep, scratchy voice was unforgettable. "It's nice to see you again. I don't think we formally met, though. I'm Special Agent Gary Gadorski with the FBI. This is Agent Paul Wymer. Could we have a few minutes of your time?"

Allison gestured to the conference table. Gadorski sat at the head of the table, and Wymer sat to the right, in Allison's usual seat as Austin's chief of staff. Such an insignificant detail, the random choice of seating, but it made her feel even more insecure.

"What can I do for you?" She eyed the badges they displayed on the table in front of her, flashing back to the bar in Boston.

"I love your ring," Agent Wymer said. "I've been looking for a ring for my wife. You know, an anniversary gift."

She pulled her hand back, momentarily confused. Did they think small talk would soften the blow? "Well, this one isn't real. Cubic zirconia."

Gadorski took the lead. "We've been reaching out to some of Dr. Harris's friends and family in an effort to find him. We were hoping we could ask you a few questions."

"Uh, of course." She dropped her shaking hands to her lap.

"If I recall correctly, you and Dr. Harris are in a physical relationship. Is that right?"

She drew back slightly.

"Is that right?" Gadorski looked down at his notebook.

She took a bottle of water from the bowl in the center of the table. "That's right." No point in lying about it. "We're obviously not now."

"Is that because you had a falling out?"

"It's because Austin was a fugitive. Is a fugitive." Shit.

Gadorski looked up and appraised her. She shoved her hands under her legs to keep from fidgeting.

"How would you characterize your relationship with Austin before he left?"

"I'm sorry?"

"Your relationship with Austin. Would you say you were extremely close?"

"We worked together and occasionally spent time together outside the office."

"Has he contacted you since he left his home in Connecticut?"

Don't talk to the police. This is bigger than you and me. Didn't Gadorski know what happened last night? Was he testing her?

"Has he contacted you, Ms. Stevens?" Gadorski pressed.

Allison didn't know anything about the law or her rights in this particular situation, but she did know one thing, thanks to hundreds of hours of crime TV shows. Don't talk to the police until you have an attorney beside you.

"Cat got your tongue?" Gadorski leaned forward on his elbows. His unblinking eyes bore into her.

She hated that expression. She shifted back to put some space between them. She was sure Gadorski could sense her nervousness.

"Actually, Agent, uh, Gadorski," she read from his badge, "I don't think I want to proceed in this line of questioning without an attorney." She sat up straight and lifted her chin.

"Is that so?" Gadorski asked, the corners of his mouth turned upward.

Was he mocking her?

His tone remained even. "Have you heard from Dr. Harris since August fourth? The day he left for his fictitious trip to California?"

"I'd really like an attorney present for this questioning." Her stomach churned, threatening to toss the handful of crackers she'd eaten. Her face felt slick with sweat.

"You're not under arrest, Allison." Gadorski rolled his eyes and sounded like he was talking to a child. "We're just trying to track down our fugitive. It seems likely that a woman who's in a physical relationship with him might know his whereabouts. It's perfectly safe to answer the question. Unless you have something to hide."

"I'd like to call Kiran Parsons, our legal advisor here at Quandary. He should be part of this meeting." She stood up, feeling confident once again.

"Sit down." The words came out in a low growl, like a junkyard dog facing off with an intruder. The half-smile he'd been struggling to hide vanished from his face. "You're not going anywhere."

28

Allison sat back down slowly and folded her arms, gripping her elbows.

Agent Gadorski's facial muscles relaxed a little. "Let me reiterate. You haven't been charged with a crime, Allison. Not yet, anyway. You don't need to exercise your fifth amendment rights."

He opened his briefcase and pulled out a large yellow envelope containing a stack of photos, which he began laying out on the table in a straight line in front of her. He moved slowly, lining them up perfectly. She knew this was for dramatic flair, to show his authority and his power over her. Just like addressing her by her first name. Her time wasn't important in his eyes, and he wanted her to know it.

"But I'm sure you're beginning to see why you might be a person of interest in my case."

Adrenaline washed through her, making the images swim before her eyes. Perhaps this was nothing more than one of her anxiety dreams. She'd wake up at home, alone and sweating and scared, but so much safer than trapped in a conference room next to a bully with a badge.

But Gadorski didn't melt away; he was very real and very serious.

The pictures appeared to be candid shots taken from … who? The FBI? A private investigator? Someone had been watching them? The first image was her and Austin on a ski trip in Switzerland. She had her arms around him in a loving embrace. They'd taken an extra weekend after a conference presentation, and it was the happiest two days Allison had ever had with Austin. They'd been completely in love and spent every moment of the weekend kissing, hugging, making love, and having fun. She'd become convinced that weekend that she and Austin would live happily ever after as the king and queen of Quandary Therapeutics.

The remaining photos were more of the same. The two of them hiking in the Redwoods, the two of them kissing on the green at UCLA, Allison on Austin's back on a beach in Cancun, their arms entwined as they shared a glass of champagne in the Signature Room at the 95th in Chicago.

Emptiness from the loss of Austin consumed her. They'd been so perfect together. How had it come to this? When had it all changed?

"You and Austin sure do make a cute couple. That looks to me like love." Gadorski was watching her intently.

She turned away from the pictures and fixed her gaze on the whiteboard, still refusing to speak.

"In fact, it looks to me like you built a pretty good life together. You're practically married." Gadorski set one last picture on the table.

Her eyes widened. What the hell?

She leaned closer to get a better look. She and Austin stood with their arms around each other on the lawn in front of a house. A For Sale sign hung from the post staked into the grass behind them, and she was holding up the small vinyl Sold sign, grinning from ear to ear.

But that had never happened.

She wanted to pick up the picture and take a closer look, but she refused to touch it. That was definitely her face, so real and so perfect that she had to stop to think. Had she bought a house with Austin?

It was ludicrous. She was photoshopped into the image. She didn't know Photoshop, but she knew the capabilities of producing exactly this kind of doctored picture were readily available.

She hoped her face appeared passive and uninterested as she leaned back.

Gadorski pulled one another sheet from his vile little envelope of lies.

"Nice house. It took us a while to find it, but we did." He produced a certificate of title, and indeed her name was on it. "I couldn't afford a nice house like that, mortgage-free, in my twenties. What about you, Paul?"

"Not on my salary."

"In fact, you seem awfully well-heeled for a girl in her twenties." He twirled a finger at her. "Biotech must really pay well. Looks like we picked the wrong line of work." They nodded with mutual understanding.

Allison's hand drifted to her necklace. Fucking cop had no idea what she'd sacrificed. How dare he imply that anything in her life came without a price?

"Where did you get that kind of money, Allison?" Gadorski's voice softened, as if he were trying to switch to the good cop role: *Just tell Uncle Gary the whole story.*

She took the last sip of her water bottle and prayed they'd get tired of her silent treatment and leave.

Instead, Gadorski picked up the picture of the UCLA lawn and showed it to his partner. "Paul, you ever been this in love?"

"Sure haven't. Not many couples get so lucky, I figure. Oops, don't tell my wife I said that." He snickered at his joke.

She didn't.

Gadorski chuckled, of course. It was part of their act. "That's the truth. If I were that in love, I'd probably do anything for her, anything she ever asked me to do. Is that it, Allison? Did you collude with Austin and steal from your investors so that you could build a life together? Are you hiding him somewhere to keep him from going to jail?"

She felt sweat drip down her back. *You're an important element in my planning—my scapegoat.* Gadorski stared at her for a full minute before turning to Wymer. The two of them shared a look that Allison read as she was obviously hiding something.

At long last, he stood and gathered the pictures. "Well, Ms. Stevens, we really appreciate your hospitality. We'll be in touch real soon. If you'd like to talk, here's my number." He set a card on the table. "Oh, one more thing."

He pulled one last document from his briefcase, which he set down gently on the table in front of her. He tapped it with his finger and smirked. "You might want to rethink that cubic zirconia story. We'll show ourselves out."

Allison watched them step out of the main office toward the elevators before she slumped back in her chair. She felt as though she hadn't taken a breath for the last ten minutes. She filled her lungs completely, coughed, and exhaled.

Gadorski had left a diamond certificate on the table, complete with an enlarged image of her very own ring. Somehow, she wasn't surprised to see her own name as the owner with her own signature. She was, however, surprised to see the value of the ring: $32,000. Shit. She didn't know a ring could even cost that much.

She glanced down at the massive sparkling gems studding the eternity ring around her finger. How many times had she caught Austin admiring it? A sarcastic laugh escaped her. She'd thought it was their future together he was admiring.

She was such an idiot.

She stoically left the conference room, walking as naturally as she could past Carol's desk with an "okay" gesture and into her office. Behind closed doors, she slid limply down until her backside was on the ground and hugged her knees to her chest. She drew a deep, shaky breath and exhaled again. It didn't work, and she broke into sobs. They weren't a physical reaction to her terror. They weren't a crash, the kind she sometimes felt after a really stressful presentation. These were plain old tears of betrayal.

Austin hadn't changed. He'd set her up from the day they'd met. He'd never loved her. Now he was gone forever, and she was left to wonder what he could have done that was so important it had turned cops into killers.

She palmed her eyes and caught a glimpse of her reflection in the shiny steel leg of her desk, cowering in a ball in the corner of her office. Her sour stomach threatened to heave, so she lay down in the fetal position, her head closer to her reflection in the steel. Her blotchy face looked distorted, her mouth curved in an unnatural way—a circus freak, bought and exploited.

She whispered to her mutant self.

"Why did you do this to me, Austin? What's so wrong with me?"

29

Malloy rocked gently in the oversized recliner on FBI Special Agent in Charge John Cramer's back porch. Cramer let the screen door slam loudly behind him, handed Malloy a tumbler of scotch, and settled with a grunt into the chair next to him.

"Macallan Rare Cask," he bragged. "Birthday present from Marie."

"She's too good for you."

"Ain't that the truth."

The sun had set and the night temperature had dropped to a very comfortable eighty-two degrees in Fountain Hills. Malloy inhaled slowly. The air quality was so much better at this elevation, and he wondered why he'd chosen to stay down in Phoenix all these years. Not that he was in the mood for admiring Cramer's golf course view or drinking his scotch while they engaged in vacuous small talk. Frankly, he was pissed he'd had to drive all this way to have a conversation he shouldn't have needed to have in the first place. He'd known Cramer since the academy. A reclassification of an ongoing investigation could only mean one thing: bullshit.

He set his scotch down on the glass table between them. "John, we've made progress on the LXR case. We learned there was a large payment made to the victims, one of them at least. We need to question the other victims' families again, and if I can get a warrant, I can track down the bank and account responsible for the transfer. Why would you shut us down now that we finally have a lead?"

The tone of his voice was clearly accusatory, and he felt a twinge of guilt. Cramer was his friend, and he wanted to give him a chance to explain.

Cramer stared out over his expansive lawn, which glowed with landscape lighting and an occasional firefly.

Malloy pressed. "Eight people have died. That can't be swept away."

Cramer squinted down at his drink, which he swirled gently. Malloy turned back to the lawn and waited.

"Pete, remember that year we all went to Club Med back east?" Cramer asked. "The kids were, what, thirteen? Fourteen?"

Malloy couldn't help smiling at the memory.

"Robbie and Ava were in that ridiculous skit where they played a couple who couldn't stop fighting. Remember that? They had the whole audience rolling."

He remembered. They'd been so convincing; they would've made a perfect couple.

"Suzanne and Marie spent the rest of the trip planning their wedding," Malloy added. He'd sat at the bar with Cramer that night as their wives conspired in the corner, literally writing out a guest list.

Cramer laughed. "Yeah, that's right."

Malloy felt the familiar tightening in his chest at the memory of Suzanne during that trip. She'd insisted on savoring the full resort experience, participating in every sport the facility had to offer, up every morning at seven a.m. for tennis lessons, volleyball lessons, golf lessons, yoga, even trapeze school. She dragged Malloy onto a sailboat to join the regatta, and they'd laughed and laughed as they sat motionless in the bay for twenty minutes.

"Robbie's like a son to me," Cramer said, "and I know Ava's like a daughter to you." He shook his head, his lips in a tight line. He swallowed. "If anything were to happen to Robbie, it would destroy me, same as it would destroy you if anything happened to Ava."

Malloy gaped, searching for a crack in his serious expression. The sky had grown dusky already, and Cramer's features were shaded, making him appear ominous. But his eyes shined in the moonlight, and Malloy could read them clear as writing.

"How high up does this go?" he asked.

"Higher than both our pay grades added together."

"Why didn't you tell me?"

"I'm telling you now."

"Never thought we'd be having this conversation again."

It had been years ago. Malloy had been working with the FBI on a case to exploit a drug operation run by a powerful mafia family in Las Vegas. The mob didn't waste police officers or agents. Instead, they used bribes and threats to family members to thwart any investigation into their business dealings. Malloy and Cramer had been ordered to close the case without explanation, but Malloy had continued the investigation, unwilling to be bullied by the mafia and whatever corrupt officials they'd manipulated at the DEA. He'd been young then. He'd still believed the hero always won.

But his naive idealism had been shattered the day that Robbie, then a kindergartner, had been collected from school by a uniformed police officer whose name was never captured. Robbie was gone for three hours, unbeknownst to Suzanne, then dropped off up the street from their home. He'd run into the house, excitedly telling his mother about his amazing field trip, then handed her a sealed envelope. The envelope was filled with Polaroid pictures of Robbie having a wonderful time at the zoo, but in several pictures, a gun was pointed to the back of Robbie's head—police issue, for fuck's sake. Robbie had never realized it. Suzanne sobbed the entire night, and Malloy had closed the case the following day.

Was Robbie really any safer now, out in California working on his PhD? Did they have that kind of reach? Would they send someone all the way to Caltech?

Cramer leaned toward him, his face solemn. "Listen, Pete, I don't know much more than you do about this case, but I was told it was some Olympic training group outside the country, some doping ring testing performance enhancers that sneak past the standard drug tests. Said only eight people in the US took the drug. It's over."

Malloy had never heard such bullshit come out of Cramer's mouth. "That doesn't make any sense. A performance drug given to four homeless—"

The screen door opened, and Marie stepped onto the porch. "Pete, I'm putting a steak on the grill for you. You'll stay, won't you?"

"Ah, no, I can't, really. I just came by to drink John's expensive scotch."

"I'll take it personally."

He wasn't interested in spending another minute listening to lies and cover-ups. He stood up and gave Marie a hug. "Next time, I promise."

Cramer stood too and rested a hand on his shoulder. "Take a few days off, man. You work too hard. We all need a break sometimes for some self-reflection. You gotta make sure your priorities are in the right place. And you have your team to think about, too."

Malloy heard the plea as he shook his friend's hand, and he wondered, with deep disappointment, how Cramer had become part of the problem.

Two blocks later, he pulled off the road and pounded the steering wheel with his palms. Fuck. Whatever this was really about meant no one at the bureau would be looking into the deaths or the operation behind it. How could he live with himself if he walked away now? How could he tell his team the case was closed, after all their hard work?

Fuck it. He dialed Darcy.

"Uh-oh. You're not soused, are you?"

He chuckled despite his foul mood. Darcy had a quick, tomboyish wit he was really starting to love. So different from Suzanne's girlish charm.

"Good evening to you, too. And no."

"Well, if you're looking for a booty call, I've long since jammied up for the night."

"How would you like to spend a few days with me? Drive up the California coast. Head out tomorrow bright and early."

Silence. He knew what she was thinking. He didn't take vacations at all, let alone last-minute ones. Or maybe she was thinking she couldn't possibly leave her clinic with no notice.

It was a dumb idea, and he opened his mouth to say so.

"I'd love to."

He exhaled. When you're in love, you'll drop everything, Suzanne had told him years ago. Maybe if Darcy could drop everything, he could drop one corrupt case.

30

Austin stepped out of the Escalade. His lower back ached and his legs were cramped after almost two straight days of driving with barely a handful of stops to take a piss. He reached out to the side of the truck to brace himself while he stretched.

"Shit." He yanked his hand back from the burning-hot chrome trim.

Mexico City—god, he hated this country. It smelled like rotten fruit. But his mood lifted as he took in the property. At the end of the driveway, a cast-iron gate opened to beautifully manicured grounds. Shrubs lined an expansive mosaic cobblestone walkway leading to a cement colonial house. The grounds were artfully decorated, giving the place a warm, inviting look.

"Dr. Harris, it's been a pleasure serving you."

Austin turned to see his escort, the driver, holding out his hand. He reflexively shook it, then felt stupid. A hostage shaking hands with his captor?

"What do you mean?" he asked. "Where are you going?"

"Our operation has completed. You'll be greeted by your host and his employees momentarily. Very best of luck to you in your future endeavors, sir." The driver handed him a leather zipper bag containing his passport and cash, then stepped back into the Escalade and drove off.

His small duffel bag sat waiting on the walkway—everything he owned in the entire world, right there in a bag on a sidewalk in goddamn Mexico. He closed his eyes and rolled his shoulders, turned back to the house, and took a hesitant step toward it.

In an instant, he was greeted by a very tall, very broad, much older Hispanic man. The man was dressed in a military uniform and wore an earpiece like Austin's escorts; however, this man was in no way trying to be subtle. The thick leather belt around his waist held a pistol, a nightstick, and a walkie-talkie.

Austin took a step back. Was this where the Fixer lived? Why this diversion?

"Dr. Harris, welcome to the Hacienda del Sol. Please follow me."

He led Austin down the long walkway, as an attendant picked up his bag and followed them. Austin glanced over at a gardener, who immediately stopped working and stood straight with his hands clasped behind his back. He offered a respectful nod as Austin passed.

A woman in a servant's uniform took his bag from the attendant and greeted him with a nod as they stepped into the foyer.

"Buenas tardes, Señor Harris," she said politely.

Austin couldn't help feeling a bit like a celebrity.

The lobby was understated compared to the grounds, but once Austin stepped through the large wooden double doors into the living room, he breathed in sharply. It was the most beautiful room he'd ever seen. Two stories tall and at least twice the size of his own great room back in Connecticut, adorned with what had to be authentic Venetian antique furnishings. Impressive. The back wall featured a quarry fireplace large enough that he could have stepped into it upright. Double French doors led to the magnificent garden.

Austin noticed the discreet surveillance cameras in the corners of the ceiling capturing both the interior and the outdoor approaches. For a home straight out of the 1700s, the security was definitely twenty-first century.

"Austin Harris!" boomed an unfamiliar voice from behind him.

The man who entered the room appeared young and fit, an American in his early forties, maybe, with wavy brown hair and perfectly trimmed three-day stubble. He strode over to Austin with such energy and confidence that

Austin felt his own energy sag a bit. Still, Austin wasn't one to be intimidated by alpha males. He stood tall and took a step toward his host.

"Stewart Hammond." The man reached out his hand. "I've been waiting a very long time to meet you. Huge fan of your work."

Austin shook Hammond's hand warily. "And what work is that?"

Hammond's smile oozed patronizing arrogance. "Your reputation precedes you, Dr. Harris. I've been following your career and your work in human genetics very closely."

"Well, I wish you'd spent less time doing that and more time planning my extraction, which has been a fucking train wreck." Austin glared at this new irritant in his life. Damn Fixer had almost screwed up the whole plan. "The experience over the past week was not what we agreed to nor what I paid for."

Hammond's smile faded as he took a step closer, violating Austin's personal space and enraging him further. "I think you may misunderstand. I'm not the one who extracted you from your situation. I own the operation that extracted you as well as many other organizations you should hope never to encounter, including some task forces within the FBI. As you are well aware, your extraction didn't go precisely to plan, which isn't uncommon with a complicated exit strategy such as yours, especially given the mistakes you made. Frankly, you're lucky to have made it this far."

Austin flinched, taken aback the change of tone. He took a small step back despite his anger.

"What you need to appreciate is that I'm here to help you out of your current bind," Hammond continued, "and for the moment at least, I'm your ally. If you prefer, I could turn you over to the FBI, who I'm sure would be delighted to escort you back to Connecticut."

Hammond tilted his head slightly and raised his eyebrows as his implacable smile spread across his face.

Austin's stomach turned as he processed this option. He stepped toward an opulent chair and dropped into it with a long exhalation. "Fine, Mr. ... Hammond, was it? My apologies if I seem a bit irritable. I've had a stressful week, and given what I've been through"—he couldn't help reminding his host—"as a captive led blindly over the border, a complete deviation from my original contract, I obviously may not have all the facts. So let's start over. I appreciate your help, but I'll be more comfortable once I understand what our connection is and what it is you want from me."

"That's much better, Austin." Hammond gave him a friendly slap on the back.

Austin noted the shift to his first name. It was a tactic he frequently used himself to level the playing field when he was dealing with powerful, arrogant types.

"Let's not let confusion spoil our relationship," Hammond said. "We have so much to talk about! But you've had a very long trip, and I'm afraid that I'm to blame for at least part of your digression from the plan. I'd like to try to make it up to you. Would you join me for dinner?" He tapped a button on the wall next to the door. "Bring us two glasses of the Hirsch Reserve 27-Year. Dr. Harris prefers his neat." He turned back to Austin. "I know you're a Knob Creek guy, so I think you'll really like this one."

Was this guy kidding? He'd paid $400 for a glass of Hirsch Reserve 16-Year a few years ago. The things Hammond seemed to know about him were absolutely unnerving— but he had to admit his mouth was watering.

***

The evening sun had set, casting shadows across the ornate dining room. Now showered, shaved, and feeling much more like himself than he had for the first time in days, Austin sat at the dining room table opposite Hammond. He spread a bit of warm walnut-encrusted brie on a slice of Italian bread. It was so nice to be eating something other than diner take-out. He would never eat another turkey club sandwich for the rest of his life. He sipped his Turley Zinfandel 2015—boy, a good year for Turley. Hammond had excellent taste.

Hammond also monopolized the conversation as Austin fixated on his dinner and wine. Fine with him.

"Money always came easy, Austin. I built a name for myself in quantitative financial analysis. I always had a good sense for the fundamentals. But my real money came from sniffing out high-value private equity. I was aggressive and ruthless. I made my first billion before I was thirty-two."

Austin was impressed. He'd always considered himself pretty ambitious, but at forty-two, he wasn't anywhere near his first billion.

Hammond continued. "I think when individuals have that kind of financial success, it changes them, you know?"

Austin nodded, even though he didn't know. Or care. God, this was a particularly bold and fruity Zinfandel. He wondered how much it cost.

"So I started looking for other things to amuse me. I raced sports cars for a while, but that wasn't very fulfilling. I looked into US politics, considered running for the Senate, but then I decided that even with all my energy, my influence would be minimal in that bureaucratic shitshow. Some men don't think ..."

The next course was being served. Crispy sautéed bronzini with vegetable succotash. Excellent choice for a main course. The voluptuous server smiled seductively as she refilled his glass of Zinfandel, and he stole a glimpse at her cleavage. He wondered if she lived on the property. He had to admit, he was very much enjoying the hospitality. Hammond might not be such a bad guy to know. Maybe one day he'd invite him to his property in—

" ... something far more noble: the human race. Agreed?"

Austin was instantly back in the conversation. "Sorry?"

"Gene editing for the betterment of humans. I believe that with the right technologies and the most brilliant minds behind them, we can make a real difference in this world. That's why I wanted to meet you. To talk to you."

Austin finally understood. Hammond wanted his CRISPR/Cas9 gene editing platform. He probably had a soft spot for crippled kids or moms with MS; everything on TV these days was geared to the bleeding-heart liberals. Now it made sense. Quandary was the first to deliver larger genes into the cell, as evidenced by Enigmax and some of their other early drugs, and Austin held several patents on this technology. He certainly wouldn't be giving it away for cheap, especially to a multibillionaire.

Austin sat up a bit taller. Ah, it felt great to have the upper hand again, to have something someone else wanted. He sipped his wine, pretending to be thoughtful about it. "Well, Stewart, I've put a lot of time and money into my technology. My patents are extensive. What did you have in mind?"

Hammond looked at him quizzically. Then he laughed and leaned forward. "Oh god, I'm sorry, I should have been more explicit. I'm not interested in your CRISPR platform. In fact, I have a better one, and I can't wait to show it to you."

Austin was baffled. "Then what is it you want?"

Hammond's eyes literally twinkled in the low light of the chandelier. "What I want, Austin, is your pain colony."

31

Austin took a sip of wine to hide his astonishment. With every bit of vocal control he could exert, he said, "Excuse me?"

"You heard me right. Your colony."

Austin laughed. "I'm sorry, but I really don't know what you're—"

Hammond flopped back dramatically in his chair, arms out to his sides, staring upward. "Austin, please. Can we finally drop the act? We're getting along so well. How can you still not trust me?"

Austin sat silently, unwilling to acknowledge this conversation. He had gravely underestimated Hammond, and now he had once again lost his footing in this peculiar relationship. Who was this guy, and how did he know so much about him? This asshole had turned him into a ridiculous pawn on some huge chessboard he couldn't even see.

And he fucking hated chess.

Austin set down his wine. He shouldn't have drunk so much. If he'd had any idea where this evening would lead, he'd have kept his wits about him.

Hammond looked at him woefully. "Okay, perhaps it was unsporting of me to spring this on you after a long night. You're probably exhausted. Let's retire to the smoking room, and I'll revive you with some incredible Cuban cigars."

Hammond stood up. Austin didn't know what else to do, so he followed him.

They sat quietly, taking short puffs on their cigars. Austin wasn't a fan of smoking of any sort, even expensive cigars, but he was desperate for the nicotine to help him clear his head. He sat back in the overly cushioned lounge chair and watched the smoke fill the room.

Hammond broke the silence. "I got this box of Cubans from a client back when I was working on Wall Street. He was a big name in finance, had all the banks wrapped around his finger. One day he comes in through the front door of our building—how he got past security, I have no idea. Anyway, he waltzes into my office—literally just opens the door and walks in, as if I had nothing else going on—and sets this box down on my desk. Then he leaves. Doesn't say a word. Meanwhile, the entire office had witnessed the scene, so they come running in. 'What did he want? What did he say?' Naturally, I'd already stashed the box, so I have to make something up. You won't believe what I said."

"What?" Austin was feeling better already.

"I tell them, 'He told me to short Goldman Sachs.' I hated those arrogant pricks, and it just popped into my head. And would you believe it? Goldman dropped nine points that day." Hammond laughed at the memory. "Took 'em three weeks to gain it back."

Hammond leaned forward. "You know, I think that might've been the first time in my young life that I realized just how pliable people are." He paused as though he was going to say something else, but then leaned back into his lounge chair and puffed his cigar. "How do you like the stogie?"

"I'm not much of an expert, but it sure feels smooth." He was kind of enjoying it.

"I've been watching you for a long time. I followed your work at Quandary to see what kind of a businessman you are. I watched you in the public eye, presentations, ad-board meetings, that kind of thing, because I wanted to understand your people skills. I saw your bad judgment with the insider trading and fraud, but I understood why you did it. It was calculated, and you had a sweet thing going, but it was also reckless for a man like you. Still, I didn't interpret it as a character flaw."

Austin bristled. He didn't like being appraised, but he was interested in where this was going.

"The truth is, I think we're a lot alike. And that's important to me when I look for a business partner." Hammond took a drag from his cigar and closed his eyes as he let the smoke linger in his mouth. He exhaled slowly and rolled the tip of the cigar across the ashtray. "So let's get back to the colony. I've been following twelve colonies throughout the world."

Austin startled, and Hammond caught it.

"Yeah, I'll bet you thought you were the only one, right? All of 'em do." Hammond laughed. "Actually, the others are much older. Two of them have been running for four generations, long before you and I were even born. But most of them cover at least two generations. They're not purposed for the same objective as yours, obviously. They're not all doing genetic work. But they're all experimental biohacking programs using human subjects, trying to learn something for the betterment of science. And in most cases, the subjects aren't aware of the experiment."

Austin shook his head in disbelief.

"Take the colony in China, for example. Before the Chinese government enacted the new family planning policy to allow couples to have two children, the colony became a home for many second births or first female births. Now, as you can imagine, it's slowed down a bit, but the colony is already functioning and self-sustaining. It's quite successful. Over fifteen thousand subjects. They've done some great work in cosmetic enhancement and started doing genetic research in muscle development a few years back, but they were a bit premature and they've had a lot of failures."

The door to the study opened, and a server entered the room with two taster's glasses and a bottle of Rémy Martin. He couldn't read the label as the server poured double shots, but he had no doubt it was Louis XIII.

"The colony in Bangladesh has done some good work with intelligence genes, but their recruitment efforts haven't been as successful, so I'm afraid it's dying out. Then there're two in Poland, one in Russia, even one in the UK." He waved his hand dismissively. "And a few others."

"Where did ... How did you find these? How do you know they exist?"

He was feeling childishly envious.

"This esoteric world is small but tight, Austin. You'll find out soon enough." Hammond rolled out his cigar in the ashtray and picked up his glass of cognac. "But I don't want to talk about the others. I want to talk about yours."

Austin crossed his arms over his chest protectively. He wasn't interested in a show and tell about his program. And he certainly had no intention of selling it. Or even partnering it.

"I like your pain experimentation work. You've been aggressive with delivery of these megagenes in humans. And I gotta say, I didn't think your origami strategy would work, but so far you have a—what, sixty-, seventy-percent success rate? How many subjects have you lost on the LXR-016 gene?"

Austin gaped. How did he know all this?

"Well, it doesn't matter. But I'll tell you this. Your pain cocktail—oh wait, you call it an elixir, right? clever, by the way—your pain elixir is foolish. All animals need to feel some pain to protect them from environmental threats. You know that's why your field cohort failed, right? I mean, your subjects might be safe while they're shielded behind the walls of your colony, but what about after their reentry into society?"

That was enough. Austin dropped his cigar in the tray and stood up. "Whatever it is you're trying to work me for, I'm not interested."

Hammond stood as well. "You haven't heard my proposal yet."

As soon as Austin took a step toward the door, the goon who'd met him outside stepped into the room and stood soldier like against the back wall. Austin's eyes darted to the corners of the room in search of a camera. It appeared he wouldn't be leaving anytime soon.

Hammond continued. "I'll clean up your mess with the field cohort. It won't be easy or cheap, and I'm not happy about it, but you left those families hanging. You know what people do when they get stiffed? They talk to the police."

Austin clenched his jaw to curb an explosive reply. He was well aware how people behaved when they felt they hadn't been appropriately compensated. He'd been doing this for years. And he hadn't purposely cheated those families. Had Hammond not noticed he'd been a little busy lately getting arrested and running from the law?

"And I don't approve of your Vitality program, either. That'll have to go."

Fatigue washed over him. He sat back down on the edge of the cushy leather chair and tried to hide his unease. "It pays the bills."

Hammond sat back down as well, mimicking Austin's position on the edge of his own chair. He met Austin's eyes and spoke with intense sincerity. "My proposal will not only make you wealthier than you've ever imagined, but this will be the most important work you'll ever do. You'll leave a legacy for a thousand generations to come."

Wealthier than he'd ever imagined. His eyes darted to the fancy black walnut liquor cabinet, and he recognized bottles he himself had never owned. This whole night might have been an elaborate set up to recruit him into—what, he still didn't know, but he had no doubt Hammond had the kind of money he'd been bragging about all night.

Austin leaned forward. "I'm listening."

***

Austin collapsed on to the plush pillow-top bed in the Hacienda's lavish guest house just after two in the morning. He was mentally and physically exhausted, but there was no way he would be falling asleep any time soon. He stared, starry-eyed, at the ceiling. So much to think about. So many ideas and paths forward. He felt awestruck and revitalized.

He felt reborn.

32

ayla's eyes were closed, and despite the cool evening desert breeze, her hair dripped sweat down her face. She sat in heel-sit position in the jagged, sun-heated gravel of the garden.

"Thank you, Father," she said as the ache in her legs began to melt away. She was indeed grateful to the Father for helping her release the pain, but she didn't feel deserving of his kindness today. A new level of suffering during her meditation was necessary. The jagged rocks beneath her added to her experience, but they weren't enough.

She shifted onto her backside with her legs out in front and rolled the marathon stick up and down her knotted shins to inflame her bruises. As the pressure increased, she ground her teeth and groaned. She wished she had other pain mechanisms in her arsenal, but burning and cutting were prohibited. Lashing and caning were allowed when administered by a pure, but inductees were permitted to supplement their experience only using the hard rollers of the marathon stick, as long as it didn't break the skin. They couldn't risk infection.

"With pain comes peace," Layla murmured between gritted teeth. She pulled the stick upward across her shin, relishing the throbbing ache that radiated from the point of contact.

She was deeply conflicted, and she didn't know where to turn for help. It had been barely two weeks since the memory of her father's funeral, and flashes of her past were coming more frequently now, in small clips, sometimes so quickly that she didn't have a chance to commit them to memory. Often she caught just a brief image, sometimes just a voice. While she knew in her heart that these images and voices were real, she also knew that they were harming her progress toward purification. What she saw in her mind's eye was not what the Father wanted her to see. Dr. Jeannette had made that perfectly clear.

So Layla had stayed quiet about her real memories. But her silence had earned her nothing but disdain from her therapist. *You're acting like you don't even care about purification,* Dr. Jeannette had told her this morning. It was a dagger to her spirit. How could Dr. Jeannette think she didn't care, when it was all she thought about, morning to night?

Your progress seems to have completely stalled. Another of Dr. Jeannette's daggers.

Maybe you're just not good enough. Dr. Jeannette had sighed after this one, removing her glasses and tossing them onto her desk, her signature sign of disapproval.

Layla could still picture Dr. Jeannette's scornful look as she sat tall in her chair, literally looking down at her. Layla pressed the marathon stick against her shins harder. She knew it was wrong to be angry with Dr. Jeannette. But did Dr. Jeannette really like her? No. She was sure of it. And she was certain Dr. Jeannette didn't want to hear about her real memories.

She traced her fingers up and down her bumpy shins, reveling in the burn. The physical pain gave her confidence. The Father would see her devotion, even if Dr. Jeannette couldn't. She rolled back into a heel-sit position and exhaled, allowing her shins to sink into the rough, uneven gravel. She clenched her jaw tightly and closed her eyes to focus on her mind's eye.

With pain comes peace. With pain comes peace. With pain comes peace.

A helicopter was approaching in the distance. The green military helicopters, which she'd learned in class were used to monitor the impures on their way to try crossing the border into the United States, usually flew over the Colony in groups of five or six. She liked watching them. The sound of the beating blades growing louder as they neared gave her a feeling of excitement, as though something dramatic and powerful were about to happen.

She rocked back a bit more, applying more pressure on her shins. Her thighs burned from the stretch. The helicopters were coming closer, but she kept her eyes closed to keep her salty sweat from burning them.

"I love helicopters," she whispered in an effort to distract herself from the pain.

***

"I know you do." Mom smiles down at me as I look up at the helicopter. It's hanging just above us, with KTVU written on the side. It's a TV helicopter, and I wonder if I'll be on the news later.

The crowd behind us cheers, and I look down the road.

"He's coming!" I yell, jumping up and down. "Look!"

At the bottom of the long hill, the wheelchairs have just rounded the corner and are beginning the final climb to the finish line. They slow down as the climb becomes more demanding.

Mom's cheering wildly. "Go, Mike! Go, nineteen!"

I look at her shirt, same as mine, which says Robert Joseph Foundation Wheelchair Marathon, plus a one and a nine in extra-big numbers.

"Go, nineteen!" I yell, to be like her. "Go, Daddy, go!"

As Dad's wheelchair gets closer to where we're standing behind the ribbons, I can see his red, sweat-covered face. It's filled with pain and anguish. His mouth is open, trying to breathe as much air as his lungs can hold, and he's panting. His eyes are wide. His arms shake as he pushes the wheels, white-knuckled, to make them turn. He's working harder than I've ever seen him work.

He needs me. He needs me to help him finish the race.

Without asking Mom, I duck underneath the ribbon and run onto the road. I catch up with him, running beside him as fast as my small legs will move.

"I'll finish this race with you, Daddy," I say. "I'll be your guardian angel to the end."

But in only seconds, my lungs begin to burn and my legs slow down. Dad's getting ahead of me, and I can't catch him. I push harder, but I still fall behind. I see the finish line getting closer, but I can't make my legs go any faster, and my chest hurts so much. I'm afraid I'll stop. I won't make it. I won't be his angel to the end.

"Don't you quit on me, Butch!" Dad calls out. "You're almost there!"

I look up and see the finish line, so close.

"I won't, Daddy," I pant between fast breaths. I so badly want to do this for him. I want to cross the finish line with him. I want him to know I'll always be by his side, I'll always take care of him. We can accomplish anything together.

I push one last time to increase my speed, and just as I near the back of his wheel, my feet somehow tangle. I fall down hard on the pavement. Daddy rolls across the line without me.

My skinned knees are burning, and they start to bleed. "I failed, Daddy. I didn't make it."

But I know he can no longer hear me.

***

Layla opened her eyes to see the last helicopter in the group pass overhead. The evening became quiet again.

She rolled off her shins and looked at her bruised, swollen knees. Even though the image was still fresh, she couldn't remember if she got scabs on her knees. She couldn't remember if her mom had run into the road to pick her up. The memories came on their terms, and no matter how much she begged, no matter how hard she squeezed her eyes shut to return to the scene, they never gave her more once they were finished.

Instead, they tormented her emotions. The feeling of failing her dad when he needed her sapped her resolve, and she sat in the sharp-edged gravel and let the sadness trickle away.

"Layla."

Brother James towered over her. He looked freshly showered, his brown hair shiny and combed back. She tried to stand, to be respectful, but her weakened legs crumpled beneath her weight.

Brother James rescued her. To her horror, he scooped her into a cradle hold and carried her to the bench near the rose garden. She felt like a baby in his arms.

She lowered her head, too embarrassed to look at him. "I'm sorry. I … I just … I didn't …"

She wasn't sure what she was apologizing for, maybe for covering him with dirt and sweat, but she knew it was nervous babble. She seemed to apologize a lot when Brother James spoke to her. She stared down at her legs, black and blue, red and inflamed. How ugly they were. She tugged down her pant legs to cover them.

She waited for Brother James to say something, but he sat silently with an odd smirk on his face. She focused on the stunningly large rose blooms across the garden to avoid his eyes, wanting to offer another apology for being so shy. For being so plain. For being so bruised.

"Layla."

She glanced up nervously.

"How is it possible that a woman as beautiful and charming and intelligent as you is so self-conscious?"

She couldn't possibly answer such a ridiculous question.

"Layla."

Her already crimson face grew hotter.

"Okay, okay. I didn't come to torture you. I just saw you in the garden, and I came over to say hi." He sounded defeated.

Instantly, she felt she'd disappointed him again. Why was everything with Brother James so difficult? He was her friend. He was supportive of her.

She sat up taller. "Hi, Brother James."

He chuckled. "Whew, glad we got that over with."

She smiled shyly.

"I wanted to talk to you about how you're feeling these days. Dr. Jeremy says you missed your checkup on Monday."

She knew it was wrong to skip her weekly body check. But she also knew that Dr. Jeremy would scold her. She hadn't been following her nutritional plan and her weight was sinking again. And she hadn't wanted him to see the new self-inflicted bruises and swelling across her shins.

"You know how important the body checks are for inductees during the pain rituals. You can't be pure if you're not physically healthy. Tell me what's wrong."

She desperately wanted to tell him everything from her first vision of her father's funeral until now. She wanted to confess how she'd lied to Dr. Jeannette. She wanted to admit how jealous she was of Nicole and everyone else who could remember their past, everyone who'd been chosen before her. But mostly she wanted him to hug her and tell her that she was okay, that the Father loved her and she could still be pure.

Instead, she forced a smile. "Nothing's wrong. I'm just doing as Dr. Jeannette says, trying to open my unconscious mind so that I can remember my poisoned life. She says it's really the only thing that's preventing me from progressing to purification."

"Give me your leg," he said.

"Huh?"

"Your leg. Right up here." He patted his lap.

She looked down at her legs, still unsure she'd understood him.

"Yep. Here." He patted his lap again.

She did as she was told and lifted her left leg onto his lap.

He rolled her pants leg up and winced at the bruises and swelling. He slid his fingers very gently over the knots. "This is too much, Layla. It's not good for you."

She flinched at the reproach in his voice, and a wave of panic washed through her. "Is the Father unhappy with me?"

"No, beautiful girl, he's not. But he doesn't need you to suffer this much." He pulled her pants leg down and set her foot gently back on the ground. "Layla, you're different than the others here at the Colony. I don't know if you are aware of that. The Father has chosen you for a special purpose. He sees purity in you, deeper and brighter than in any other inductee. I can't tell you more than that because it's not for me to do so, but you'll learn your destiny here at the Colony from the Father, when your time comes. When you're ready for your purification."

She gaped up at him, and he grinned as he nudged her chin to close her mouth.

"He sees your diligence. He sees your impact within the community. He sees your beauty the same as I do, your charm, your grace, your goodness. He's already chosen you, Layla. All you need to do now is carry on with your daily schedule, get strong and healthy, and continue being the model inductee that you are. Let your memories come in their own time. You're doing a wonderful job."

Relief and joy swept over her, stripping away her fear and embarrassment. She threw her arms around Brother James and squeezed him as hard as she could from her awkward position next to him on the bench, pressing her face into his broad chest.

He laughed and hugged her back.

She held on tightly, savoring the scent of his bath soap. God, he smelled so good. She tilted her head slightly, and her lips brushed the skin of his neck. She gasped and pulled away.

He didn't seem to notice. He stood up, offering his hand. "Can you walk yet?"

Her legs were shaking, but she wasn't sure if it was from the meditation or nervousness.

"You seem a bit wobbly. I better walk you back."

He held her hand and walked beside her, along the path directly into the most beautiful sunset she could ever remember. The cool breeze dried her sweat, and she felt a little less filthy. He began humming a tune as they walked, her hand completely enveloped in his grip and their arms swinging together between them.

Layla heard a chirp. More came from all around them. She craned her neck but saw no birds overhead.

He stopped walking and cocked his head. "Uh-oh. We've upset them."

"Who?"

"The other colonists," he said in a low, ominous tone.

"What?" Her eyes shot left and right, as though she were expecting to be ambushed by some unknown enemy.

Brother James laughed. "Prairie dogs. They're barking to warn the others that evil bipeds are nearby. And what a treat. They should be in bed by now."

"Prairie dogs," she repeated slowly, trying to remember what they looked like. No image came.

"Gunnison's prairie dogs, to be exact. Did you know they live in a colony, just like us? With underground tunnels that lead to their little houses. They come up to the surface through small holes, popping their heads up and standing on their hind legs to see what's going on."

He did an impression of a prairie dog, and Layla giggled.

"I wish I could show you how funny they are, but they live on the other side of the wall."

Layla turned and gazed at the towering cement wall that protected the entire Colony. It must have been twice the height of Brother James, and miles in length. For the first time, she wondered why the walls were necessary.

"Why does the Father want walls to keep us in here? Are we … are we prisoners?" She immediately regretted asking. The Father would be disappointed in her distrust of him.

Brother James put a hand on each of her arms and drew her to face him.

"No, beautiful girl, of course not. The walls are there to keep the poisoned world out."

***

The rain on Layla's dorm room window came in pounding bursts, as if someone were throwing buckets of water against the tiny panes. In the moments between the waves, a soft *tink-tink-tink* of drops hit the window frame.

You are superior to me and all other impures, Madeline had told her.

She caressed the opal necklace in the dark, running her thumb around the diamond circle. The symbol of purity. Madeline had given the necklace to her, not Nicole or anyone else.

He's already chosen you. Brother James's words echoed in her head, and her stomach fluttered. She'd been chosen. She was protected from the poisoned world lurking on the other side of the imposing cement walls.

She was special.

33

ollow the money. It was a phrase Allison had learned in her one and only political science class. If you wanted to learn the truth, you had to follow the money. The FBI would certainly be looking for the smoking gun, a bank account large enough to buy that $32,000 diamond ring, which now resided in a small safe at the bottom of her dresser, and a goddamn house. Somewhere, deep in the detail, she'd find a transaction. Or a suspicious account. But Quandary's archaic financial systems, which Austin had refused to upgrade, were not searchable. It was like looking for a needle in a haystack.

She drilled into the data like a madman. Printed spreadsheets highlighted in bold florescent colors covered the desk and walls. At least a dozen half-full coffee cups from the weekend, reeking of sour milk, littered every surface. The trash can overflowed with wadded paper and grease-stained bags from Wendy's.

Carol ignored the handwritten Do Not Disturb sign Allison had taped up and cracked the door just enough to sidle inside.

"Golly," she breathed.

She tiptoed around the stacks of folders lined up on the floor and set a pile of mail on Allison's chair. "Um, Austin liked doing his own mail. I've been storing it for him, but the pile was getting kind of big, and I wasn't sure what to do with everything. I guess it all should go to you for now, right?"

She sounded weepy, but Allison was in no mood to show any empathy. "Okay."

She swiped yellow across another line item: United Airlines EWR to PHX $1,076. She twirled the highlighter. It was the sixth trip he'd taken to Phoenix this year. What had Austin been doing in Phoenix?

"Anyway, I took out all the usual administrative stuff," Carol continued, "but I didn't know what to do with the rest."

"I'll take care of it." Allison highlighted a trip to Las Vegas.

She pulled her eyes from her paper only long enough to watch Carol shuffle glumly back to her desk. She understood why the staff moped around. Austin had been the heart and soul of Quandary. He had a way with people, made every single employee feel special. He remembered everyone's name and joked with them in the coffee room. He was the embodiment of charisma. Men wanted to be him, women wanted to sleep with him, and motherly secretaries wanted to hand-deliver his mail.

And all that time, it had been a lie. A big fucking lie.

She threw her highlighter across her office. They'd been tricked. His employees meant nothing to him. She meant nothing to him. And now he was gone. She'd never get an explanation.

Why? Why, Austin? She pounded her forehead with her fist several times.

She pushed her hair from her eyes. Outside in the main office, Carol stood next to her desk watching Allison closely, her brow furrowed.

Keep the train on the tracks.

Allison forced a smile and began picking through Austin's mail, which seemed to be one invitation after another to some benefit dinner or special interest group meeting. She grabbed the trash bin and set it in front of her. Alzheimer's Association. She tossed it into the trash. Movement Disorder Society. Trash. Benefit for the Children's Hospital of Philadelphia. Trash. The Pain Institute.

She stopped.

The Pain Institute. Dr. Jonathan Chambers. Ryan said he and Austin were planning a meeting at the Pain Institute? She'd completely forgotten.

She tore open the card, a dinner meeting with key opinion leaders, experts in pain management. No details other than the topic, Future Directions in Pain Management. It was uncharacteristically vague for a KOL meeting.

She marched over to Carol's desk. "Do you still have Austin's calendar?"

"Mm-hmm."

"Could you do me a favor and see if Austin had a meeting on his calendar for the twenty-fourth?"

"Well, his calendar still has a ton of meetings, even now that he's—"

Allison cringed. The echo of the two gunshots still rang in her head.

Carol's face was a wrinkled mask of discomfort. "Are you looking for one in particular?"

"The Pain Institute. It should be a dinner."

"Oh, with Jonathan? I believe that's been canceled. Jonathan's traveling abroad this entire month. Doctors Without Borders, I think, or one of those volunteer things." Carol turned back to her computer.

"Wait, you know him? Jonathan Chambers?" Allison asked, surprised.

"Of course. Austin has a one-on-one call with him every week, ever since the outreach program started. They're both so crazy busy, Elaine and I are always trying to find a good time to reschedule." Carol shook her head as if the task of rescheduling a meeting was truly unbearable.

"What's the outreach program?"

Carol took her hands off her keyboard. "Oh yeah, you weren't here yet. It was a disaster from the beginning. All the time and effort poor Austin put into it, but he loved it like a baby. Jonathan was his partner, though I know Elaine did all the work, that poor woman. Even with her regular day job. She works crazy hours for that man."

Carol had a tangential way of communicating that Allison found truly annoying. It was like talking to her grandmother.

"Elaine?"

"Jonathan's assistant. I just can't imagine what she has to go through each day. I mean, the guy's mean as the devil. Elaine says that any time she makes even the tiniest mistake, he screams and makes her cry. One time, he threw a pen at her, jabbed her in the arm. I told her that's a hostile work environment and she really should quit—I mean, no one should have to deal with that kind of treatment. But she never will. She's too scared, I think. You know, like those abused wives? It's like he has her handcuffed. Gosh, I'm so glad Austin wasn't that way."

Carol's shoulders slumped at the thought of Austin.

"So Austin meets with Jonathan Chambers every week for this outreach program?"

"Oh, no. The outreach clinics closed down years ago. They were a ton of work, and I don't think they had much success. Austin was sad when they went under. He disappeared for weeks at a time. If you ask me, he went into a bit of a depression. He'd worked his tail off on those sites, and watching them fail pretty much killed him."

"He disappeared? To where?" Allison leaned forward.

"He was traveling a lot. But Quandary was small back then, and we didn't have much going on, so no one complained." Carol laughed. "I remember one day he came into the office after a long stint away, and he'd grown a thick beard. We thought he must have been on some spiritual journey in Tibet or something. It made him look fifty years old, but everyone was too afraid to tell him to shave it."

Now that was weird. Austin despised facial hair. But she didn't want to encourage a campfire night of storytelling, so she reined Carol back in. "So what are Austin and Jonathan discussing every week now?"

"Beats me. Austin was always very secretive about it, and Elaine says they were doing some research thing together. Jonathan keeps all his notes and files in a special cabinet in his office. Doesn't even ask Elaine to file them, which is strange since she does everything else." Carol's face turned suspicious. "I personally think they've come up with some miracle cure that the world isn't ready for yet. You know how brilliant and leading-edge Austin is. He's always ahead of his time."

The work I'm doing is more important than Quandary. It's bigger than you and me.

Allison's stomach fluttered. "Does anyone else participate in the weekly calls?"

"I think so. I've heard Austin's voice through the walls, and I think there's a large team of people. But I'm only responsible for Austin's and Jonathan's calendars. I guess the others just join if they can. Who knows?"

"Huh." More secrets to digest. More research. "Well, thanks, Carol. You've been really helpful. I appreciate it."

Carol looked surprised at the compliment, and Allison wondered when she'd last uttered the words thank you to Carol or any of the staff, for that matter.

Back at her desk, it took only a moment to find a local NJ.com article: "Venture Capitalist, Local Physician and Biotech CEO Band Together to Confront Rising Opioid Crisis."

Austin Harris of Quandary Therapeutics and Jonathan Chambers of the Pain Institute have received financial backing from venture capitalist Madeline Barnett to set up an outpatient clinic to provide opioid free-pain treatments at little or no cost to patients in economically disadvantaged areas. The clinic will educate teenagers and young adults and provide alternative therapies designed to prevent opioid addiction, which is on the rise, particularly in urban areas.

Newark, New Jersey, will be the site of the first such outreach program. Drs. Chambers and Harris are in process of establishing similar outreach programs across the country with the continued support of Barnett. Early locations will include Chicago, Las Vegas and Austin, Texas.

"We're providing a much-needed service to these communities," Chambers said in a formal statement. "There are many ways to manage pain, such as acupuncture, hypnosis and guided imagery, that most people aren't aware of. These approaches have proven successful over decades but only now seem to be embraced by millennials and younger folks who've grown up in overmedicated families. We're even looking into adding more natural THC-based therapies for pain management in states where marijuana is legal."

Allison enlarged the picture of Austin and Dr. Chambers with Madeline Barnett. She radiated confidence and elegance. The kind of woman who is accustomed to being photographed. The three of them stood casually in front of a small shop on Market Street, right next to a bodega, under a sign that read "Newark Pain Clinic. Most Services Free." They all smiled broadly for the camera, and Austin had an arm around Barnett's shoulder.

Allison felt a fiery pang of jealousy. The article was dated more than five years ago. Austin had never once mentioned the clinics to her—or Dr. Chambers or Madeline Barnett, for that matter.

She typed "Madeline Barnett" into the search bar and scrolled down the page.

"Phoenix's Priciest Home Purchased by Billionaire Venture Capitalist Madeline Barnett for $37.5 Million."

It was a blow to her gut. She doubled over, clutching her torso. Phoenix. Austin went to Phoenix to see her. God, she'd come to believe that Austin had lied and used her, but she hadn't really felt it until that moment. She closed her eyes and bargained with herself: She could cry tonight with her vodka and tonic, but right now she needed to think.

Austin's threat from the night before echoed: *Don't get all detective-like.* He was hiding something, something big. *Forget all about the LXR portfolio,* he'd said. The LXR portfolio of pain genes. *Just pretend it never existed.*

Shut up! Austin had never raised his voice to her before. She'd heard the rage in those words, and something else too. Desperation, maybe?

Two deafening gunshots.

She shrank back into her chair.

In the wake of losing Austin, she had crumbled. She loved him so deeply that she couldn't bear the thought of not realizing their happily ever after. But last week, everything had changed. His betrayal, the threatening call trying to intimidate her, to scare her into the corner like an obedient little girl … It enraged her. And if Austin was dead—

She wouldn't think about that.

She stared at the picture on her screen as her mind raced. They looked so chummy together, and yet she'd never even heard of these relationships. Were Chambers and Barnett in on Austin's secret venture?

You're my scapegoat.

She was in on it, too, apparently. She just didn't know what it was.

And the FBI was watching her. They believed she was helping Austin. They were probably building a case against her right now. If she was going to prove herself innocent, she'd have to find out what Austin had been doing.

She tapped her pencil nervously. Jonathan Chambers. He was a physician working with patients. He kept his files at his office, but they were too private for his assistant to file.

Her resolve strengthened, and finally she smiled as a plan formed in her mind.

34

Dr. Jeannette looked tired. She had dark, baggy circles under her eyes, and Layla didn't remember noticing all the deep wrinkles across her forehead. She wondered how old Dr. Jeannette was. Fifty? Sixty? Dr. Jeannette continued sipping tea and silently appraising her, as if trying to read her mind.

Finally, Dr. Jeannette spoke. "Have some tea, Layla."

"No, thank you. I don't actually like green tea." Layla focused on her posture, fighting the impulse to hunch forward and look down.

Dr. Jeannette set her teacup down, as if Layla's unpleasant attitude had turned it suddenly bitter. "I've seen a change in you lately, my dear." Her tone was flat, not her usual singsong voice.

"Really? How so?" Layla didn't care that she sounded flippant.

"You seem to be more interested in challenging me than in respecting and appreciating the guidance I provide to you. It's as if you no longer value my help in your preparation for purification."

Dr. Jeannette was observant. Layla expected that from a therapist, but she was surprised by her candor. She didn't reply.

"All these months, I've been on your side, trying to help you with your memories. Encouraging you and supporting you in all your activities. I've helped you grow here at the Colony. Frankly, I don't really understand how I've become the enemy."

He's already chosen you, Layla.

Layla lifted her chin. "My confidence has grown a lot here at the Colony. I've been here a long time now, and perhaps I don't need as much support as I did before."

Dr. Jeannette didn't respond.

"Of course, I'm so grateful for all you've done for me." She meant it, although she knew it sounded haughty.

"Interesting, because that's not the vibe I'm getting from you."

She felt too jittery to sit still, and she couldn't hold Dr. Jeannette's penetrating stare any longer. She stood up and strolled around the room, eyeing the various wall hangings and decorative vases. She picked up a statuette of a woman warrior holding a bow and arrow atop a globe that resembled the earth.

"What additional things do you think I need to do in order to be called for purification?" she asked. "What do you believe I'm still missing?"

"I've discussed this at great length with you. You know the answer."

"My poisoned life memories, right?"

"Yes. A poisoned life cannot be—"

"—purified until it is fully understood. As an impure. I must acknowledge, accept, and despise the poison inside of me so that I can be free of it."

"That's right." Dr. Jeannette smiled smugly.

"Okay. But what I don't understand is why do I have to remember everything about my poisoned life? I've already acknowledged, accepted, and despised the poison. You know I have. Don't you think that makes me ready for purification? Not everyone can remember everything about their poisoned lives. Even Nicole admits she can't remember her teachers' names from school, and yet she received the calling."

Dr. Jeannette stood up, and Layla could tell she'd crossed the line. The doctor picked up both teacups and took them to her small coffee bar, setting them down with a clatter. Layla flinched.

"First of all, Layla, you're not Nicole. You're on a different path than Nicole, as is every inductee at the Colony. Second, you may think you're special here at the Colony, but I assure you that you're not. You would do yourself a great service by finding your humility, and you'll be sorry if you make me your adversary."

In Layla's hands, the warrior woman stood tall and strong. Her well-defined muscles and stoic facial expression inspired envy. Did a warrior woman feel humility? She set the statuette back on the table. She was already chosen by the Father, and she didn't need Dr. Jeannette's support.

"I can see that our session today is not going to be productive," Dr. Jeannette said. "I'd like you to leave."

Layla shrugged and walked to the door. "If I can be perfectly honest, I feel like you don't want me to be called for purification. I don't understand how I've become *your* enemy."

And Layla stalked out of the office.

35

The Pain Institute resembled an expensive private school more than a doctor's office. The two-story building's seventeenth-century windows and doors gave it a historical look, all the way down to the pillars on either side of the broad front porch. Although Allison had studied her destination with the help of the miracle of Google Images and one very helpful YouTube video, a local news interview with Dr. Chambers that had taken place in his luxurious office, she'd still been intimidated from the moment she'd climbed the three steps to the imposing double front doors. Cameras in each corner of the porch peered down upon her.

She knew her plan was a long shot. A very long shot. But whatever Austin had been doing, whatever this venture of his had been, must lie somewhere in Dr. Chambers's file cabinet—the one that his assistant, Elaine, wasn't allowed to touch. If Allison could just find out what was going on, she could tell the FBI, and—

But she was lying to herself. This wasn't about proving her innocence. The truth was her curiosity about Austin's pain program and his relationships with Dr. Chambers and that woman had mushroomed into a full-blown obsession. The idea that he had kept this secret from her, had worked with some practically invisible consultant, was driving her mad. What could he possibly have been hiding? And what did he need a scapegoat for?

Besides, she wasn't really doing anything illegal. If there was something going on that involved Quandary, she should know about it, right? She was only looking for documents that she had a right to review. Just a quick look.

She glanced at her watch. 4:50 p.m. Time to go.

She stepped into the waiting room of the Pain Institute, relieved to see that there were no patients waiting to be seen. Dr. Chambers's PA would be finishing up or already gone for the day.

She walked over to the receptionist with as much confidence as she could muster. "Hi, I just need to pick something up from Elaine."

The receptionist looked at her warily. Allison drummed her nervous fingers against her leg.

"One second, let me see if she's still here. Your name?"

"Allison. With Quandary Therapeutics." She stepped away and took a seat in a fancy leather console.

A few minutes later, a heavyset woman in her late fifties stepped into the waiting room.

"Uh, Allison?" She was timid, clearly not used to dealing with the public.

"Hi, Elaine." Allison offered her hand.

Elaine seemed confused by the gesture, then returned a slightly sweaty hand for a limp handshake. Poor woman. She seemed fragile.

"Um, what can I do for you?" Elaine asked.

"Oh, sorry, I thought you were expecting me." Allison laughed uncomfortably in an effort to appear taciturn. "I'm just here to pick up the folder from Jonathan. I'm so sorry that I didn't come sooner, but it's been crazy lately, with Austin being unavailable."

Elaine looked at her with utter bewilderment. "Um, I don't know what folder you're talking about."

Allison drew her eyebrows together. "The folder. You know, from Jonathan? Oh my god, please tell me you have it. The board is going to be furious if you don't."

Elaine's eyes widened with fear, and Allison felt a twinge of regret. As impatient as she was with people, she wasn't accustomed to forcibly upsetting them.

"Um, okay. Can you describe it?"

"It's either a folder or a manila envelope. It should be addressed to Quandary? Maybe? Or to Austin?"

"Dr. Chambers didn't give me an envelope for Quandary," Elaine said, but Allison could see the fear in her eyes. She was questioning herself.

"Maybe it's in his office. Maybe he just forgot to give it to you?"

"Um, okay, I guess I can take a look."

Allison followed her uninvited. "God, it's been so long since I've been here, I forgot how nice it was. I wish our offices were as nice as yours. It must be so great to work here. Plus, you have a Starbucks right next door! You must spend a fortune on coffee." Her small talk was meant to distract Elaine from telling her to wait up front.

"Um, well, I don't really drink coffee ..." Elaine's voice trailed off as she opened her second desk drawer and fished out the key to Dr. Chambers's office from a coffee cup with the Pain Institute logo.

"Should I wait here?" Allison gave her best innocent face.

"Sure, I'll be right back. Hopefully it'll be on his desk."

Allison felt guilty again. This woman would fret about the envelope until her boss returned to work.

She waited less than a minute before she casually followed Elaine into Dr. Chambers's office.

"Let me help."

As she helped Elaine unstack and restack folders on his desk, she spotted a two-drawer lateral file cabinet, the same high-quality cherrywood as the rest of the office furniture, tucked discreetly in a corner of the room.

"I don't see anything." Elaine's voice rang of closure, a *thanks for stopping by*.

Time to raise the stakes.

"Oh, Jesus," Allison moaned, pulling her fists to her mouth. "This can't be happening. This can't be happening."

Elaine frowned. "Is it really important that we find it this afternoon? It can't wait until the morning?"

"This is all my fault. I should have come sooner. The board of directors is going to kill me. The patients—oh my god … And their treatments—oh god …" Allison forced her voice to tighten, a clear indication that tears would be coming soon.

Elaine put a hand on her arm. "Okay, okay. Don't worry, we'll find it."

Allison drifted toward the two-drawer file cabinet, still whimpering. She was preparing to perform a full-on emotional meltdown, which she'd practiced over the weekend, when Elaine's cell phone rang.

Elaine glanced at the screen. "Excuse me one moment. It's my son's school."

And just like that, the gods smiled down on her. Allison was alone in Dr. Chambers's office.

36

Layla peered inside Brother James's office. The light was on, so she took a seat in the chair opposite his desk to wait for him. She was so utterly appalled by her behavior in Dr. Jeannette's office, she'd locked herself inside the sweatbox for two hours of deep meditation with the marathon stick. The hot metal floor of the box against her fresh bruises had improved her focus, but she still felt impure. What had gotten into her? Dr. Jeannette may have been a bit harsh, but Layla needed her on her side. She could not make her an adversary.

The poison inside her was too strong, and she wanted Brother James's guidance.

She gingerly knelt beside her chair. "Please forgive my insolence, Father. Please don't let this stop my progression. Please forgive my insolence, Father. Please don't let this stop my progression."

If she stayed on her wracked knees much longer, she might not be able to pass her body check tomorrow morning. She clambered back into the chair to wait. His office wasn't as tidy as it should be. File folders were stacked on his desk and floor. Boxes of books stood along a wall, probably another donation of books for the library. She got up to peruse the new titles. She fingered through the stack of Nancy Drew books. They were for young girls and completely outdated, but for some reason she loved the mysteries. She dug deeper into the top box. *A Tale of Two Cities. The Princess Bride.*

She picked up *The Princess Bride*. It seemed familiar. Had she read it before, in her poisoned life? She couldn't remember what it was about, but she definitely remembered the cover. She kept it out. She'd ask Brother James if she could borrow it.

She stepped outside his office and looked up and down the gravel path. Still no sign of him. She went back inside and picked up the book. Only then did she notice her name on the file sitting on his desk. Of course, he had files on all the inductees. He would certainly have one for her.

She glanced at the open door. No sound came from down the path.

She set the book aside and opened the folder.

"So that's what I look like," she breathed.

She was much more beautiful than she'd expected. In the picture, her hair was blond, which she knew, but only shoulder length. Her hair now was long, nearly to the base of her spine. She wore eye makeup, which surprised her, and a sleek black knee-length dress and high-heeled shoes, as if she were going to a fancy party.

Did she still look like that? She looked down at her body, now clothed in the Colony's loose-fitting white linen. She lifted her pants leg just a few inches and recoiled at her bruised, bumpy shins. She turned back to the image of her smooth, tanned legs. And for just a second, she felt envious of life before the Colony. She looked simply radiant.

She closed her eyes tightly. "I'm sorry, Father. I despise my poisoned life."

She should have closed the folder right then. But she looked at the next page, which included handwritten notes. At the top of the page was her name, followed by "Cohort 2: Renewed. Treatment: LXR204909, delivered on intake, consented."

It meant nothing to her. She read further. "Layla continues to respond positively to coercion therapy and easily recites back her post-hypnotic suggestions. However, she continues to resist internalization. Hypnotic suggestibility remains undetermined. She displays a heightened sensitivity to nonverbal communication. She shows growing enthusiasm for the purification process. At this time, however—"

She heard voices approaching.

" … don't think you're listening to me." It was Dr. Jeannette. Her voice grew louder as they approached Brother James's office.

Layla looked down at the folder she was holding, unable to move. Her breath caught.

"Her attitude is changing. She's …"

She'd be expelled. She wasn't supposed to be here. She'd be sent back to the impure world.

" … more assertive, more willful, more …"

"Jeannette," Brother James said. "You're too close to her in the moment of transition. Your assessments …"

She could only think of one thing to do. She had to hide. Right now. She slid the folder back onto the pile.

" … biased. You have to give her a little space to get there on her own terms."

Brother James stepped into his office just as Layla's inflamed knees slammed down on the cement floor behind his desk.

37

Allison bolted over to the file cabinet, offering a small prayer—*please, God*—and yanked the top drawer. It opened.

She wasn't sure what she'd expected to find, but she was surprised to see a collection of expandable folders, each labeled *VWC* and dated. She opened the first folder, labeled *2013*. What a disappointment—patient files.

Leonard Felix, age twenty-four, Hispanic. Condition: sciatic nerve pain resulting in debilitating numbness and leg buckling. Cause: unresectable bone spur, S5. Prior treatments: Neurontin, oxycodone. Recommendation: inpatient admission, Vitapura Wellness Center.

She shrugged and read the next profile.

Sayid Al-Amari, age twenty-eight, Arab. Condition: idiopathic neuropathy. Cause: no known cause. Prior treatments: Neurontin, oxycodone, self-medicated with alcohol and marijuana. Recommendation: inpatient admission, Vitapura Wellness Center.

Emelia Antonucci, age twenty-six, African American, again recommended to the Vitapura Wellness Center after treatment for fibromyalgia. Wow, Emelia was striking. She looked like a model.

She shuffled through twenty or so profiles, glancing at the photos. The patients came from a variety of ethnic backgrounds, but they were all in their early twenties. Odd. So many young people with chronic pain. Dr. Chambers sure had found himself a niche market to tap.

Elaine's voice outside the office reminded her that time was of the essence. She retied the expandable folder and closed the drawer. The second drawer looked much more likely, green hanging folders packed with tabbed manila folders. She ran her finger along the labels. There. *B. Elliott Intakes.* That was surely—

"Allison? What are you doing?"

She jerked back her hand.

"Those are private files. You aren't supposed to be in there. What are you doing?" Elaine's voice vacillated somewhere between angry and fearful.

Allison stood up slowly. "Listen, Elaine. Dr. Chambers is involved in something with Quandary that involves me personally, and it may even be illegal, and I'm just trying to find out what it is. I have a right and a responsibility for—"

"I'm calling Dr. Chambers. You're not supposed to be reading those."

Allison surged across the room until she stood six inches from Elaine's face. Elaine cowered as though she expected to be struck, but she couldn't back away because she was already pressed against the wall.

Allison glowered, her face inches from Elaine's. "You'll do no such thing. What would Dr. Chambers do if he learned you'd invited me right into his office, showed me where you keep the key in your desk, and let me follow you inside? I'll tell Austin that you knew about these files and you wanted me to have them. I'll tell him Dr. Chambers treats you like shit and you wanted to get even for all those years of abuse. What will he do to you then? Is that what you want?"

Elaine crouched against the wall, frozen in fear.

"You will *not* speak of this, understand?" Allison's chin quivered. "I need to find out what Austin—"

"Elaine?"

Allison spun around to see a man in a white coat in the doorway—the physician's assistant, presumably.

"What's going on? What are you doing in here?" he asked. "You have no business being in Dr. Chambers's office while he's away. Who are you?"

He uncapped his pen, ready to take notes.

"We were just looking for a folder." Elaine's voice was barely a whisper. "Allison came by to—"

He jabbed a finger at her. "I'm not speaking to you!"

Still reeling with adrenaline, Allison nearly exploded. "Hey, don't you talk to her like that. She's just doing her job."

"Both of you. Get out of here immediately."

She took a deep breath to calm herself and turned back to Elaine with a smile. "Elaine, thank you so much for your help. I'll let Austin know we couldn't find the folder." She glared at the PA. "And that some jackass interrupted our search."

She felt slightly dizzy as she marched out of Dr. Chambers's office. It wasn't until she stepped out the front door onto the porch that she started trembling.

38

An explosion of stars announced the impact of Layla's bruised legs against the hard floor, and her teeth caught hard against her tongue as she stifled a reflexive cry. Her brain registered the nauseating taste of copper before the pain, and her mouth instantly filled with blood. She opened her mouth slightly to keep from vomiting, then let the blood trickle from her mouth into her cupped hands. Through it all, she made no sound.

Brother James stood in the doorway with Dr. Jeannette.

"James, please. Talk to him about one more dose of 909. I believe she's having visions that are not part of the coercion program."

Layla dropped into a tighter ball, making her legs throb even more. Blood continued to drip into her cupped hands, and her abs clenched for another wave of heaving. She opened her mouth wider to get more air. The bleeding slowed, and she focused on counting the drops to ease her stomach.

"It cannot happen. The memory elixir is too toxic for a third dose. Look at what happened to Kelly."

Kelly? Layla heard him take a step closer to his desk. She shook with fear, but instead of moving behind it where she crouched doubled over in pain, he stopped in front of the desk. She heard him sweep the pile of folders into his arms.

"I'm not taking that risk with Layla. Just keep up with the hypnosis—"

"This is what I'm trying to tell you," Dr. Jeannette said. "She's not suggestible. She doesn't respond. Nothing I've given her has stuck, not one image, even in the deepest state."

They were talking about her. But what—

Something banged against the desk and a scorpion emerged from behind the trash can, skittering right into her mess of long hair splayed on the cement.

" … only one in the renewed cohort that hasn't embraced her false narrative. She's high risk …"

She squeezed her eyes and mouth as tightly as she could, fighting the irresistible impulse to jump up and shake her head. She held her breath and somehow remained still.

" … no guarantee that she can be controlled. Doesn't this worry you?"

"Listen, Jeannette. We both know how important Layla is to this program. She'll be the face of the renewed cohort. Think about how hard she's struggled after having her memories erased, and yet she's still fully committed …"

Her hair twitched as the entangled scorpion struggled to break free, but it seemed to be only climbing closer to her scalp. A choked whimper escaped her.

" … lead all the others who follow her in this cohort. When they struggle with trying to rebuild a whole new impure past, she'll be their champion. Peer mentors have a much better success rate than formal therapy. You know this."

"And what if she's not a champion? She doesn't fit our model, and you know it."

Layla shuddered. She shook her head vigorously until she could no longer feel the crawling.

Brother James raised his voice. "This isn't open for discussion."

She'd never heard that tone from him before.

"We're wasting valuable time," he continued. "Get her on the advancement schedule. Do your job and make it happen. No excuses, and no more hesitation. The success of this program is bigger than our egos."

Dr. Jeannette sounded angry. "I don't think I'm the one who's lost objectivity here. It's obvious you favor the girl."

Layla opened one eye in time to see the scorpion scuttle away.

"It's 4:01, James. Don't you have a new recruit meeting? You better go do your job. Remember, the program is bigger than our egos."

Dr. Jeannette's heels clicked out the door and away from the building.

"Damn it," Brother James muttered.

The light went off, and the door clicked shut to silence.

***

Layla silently counted to one hundred, trembling and sweating, blood and saliva still dripping from her mouth, before rolling to her backside and sliding against the wall away from the direction of the scorpion.

Please forgive me, Father.

She tipped the contents of her cupped hands into Brother James's trash container and wiped her hands on some wadded paper and rearranged them in the trash bin to conceal the blood. She stood up unsteadily and surveyed the office, half expecting to see Brother James sitting quietly in the corner, ready to declare her the traitor that she was. But he was gone, and the room was empty.

She steadied herself on the edge of the desk. That had been a very close call, and she silently thanked the Father for offering her a path to redemption. Her nausea from the blood had finally passed, but her tongue was sore and swollen and she was still trembling as she slipped back into the desert heat.

As she hobbled down the path, she replayed Brother James's words in her head. She would lead the others. She would be their champion. Layla slowed her pace and looked around the campus at the other inductees, realizing how rarely she looked up. She stood tall and flexed her leg muscles.

Girl power! her dad's voice said.

She flexed her biceps. There was barely a perceptible bulge. If she was going to lead others in the cohort, whatever that meant, she would have to get stronger.

"Girl power," she agreed and walked back to her dorm.

39

Malloy had turned his work phone off during the extended weekend with Darcy, so he wasn't particularly surprised to find Garcia in his office when he rolled in on Wednesday morning. What did surprise him is that it wasn't even seven a.m.

Garcia didn't look happy. His first instinct was that Garcia was going to resign. Garcia had friends at the bureau, and he'd probably already heard the LXR case was being shut down. Unlike Malloy, who'd spent years building a thick skin for law enforcement corruption, Garcia was young and naive. He was likely to walk off the job on principle, shouting a litany of curses and burning every bridge he'd built.

Malloy felt the pain in his gut. He didn't want to lose Garcia.

He strode straight to his desk, avoiding eye contact. "Awfully early for you to be awake, let alone sitting in my office."

When a reply didn't come, he looked up.

Garcia's face was colorless. "We have another vic."

It caught him off guard. Cramer had assured him that he wouldn't have to see another body or talk to another goddamn family.

"I got a call early this morning from Stacy Cordone, from—"

"Stop." Malloy sat down. "Just let me—"

He rubbed his eyes with his palms and sat back in his chair, staring at the ceiling. It wasn't anger he was feeling; it was exasperation. Cramer's warning had been clear enough to convince him this case wasn't worth his career or personal safety, but he still lay awake at night questioning his integrity. And now another victim.

His mind was already ticking ahead to the next steps. How was he supposed to process the vic? Was he expected to simply ignore it? Cramer had told him the bureau would assign a lead, but Malloy wasn't dumb. This case was destined for the graveyard.

"Let's hear it." He sat up straight, ready for the download.

Garcia spoke mechanically, like he was dictating a forensics report. "Twenty-four-year-old male found in a dumpster behind a drug den in Flagstaff."

Malloy opened his desk drawer and grabbed his Tums. Goddammit, he wasn't going to deal with this alone. He'd call Cramer, make him take some of the responsibility, not to mention some of the damn burden on his conscience.

"Test results show very high levels of heroin, and physical appearance of the body suggests death by overdose. Stacy called me when she found a partially healed wound exactly the location and size of a spinal port."

Malloy perked up. "But no actual port? Maybe it's not one of ours. Give me the file."

He chewed up two Tums. Maybe he'd just hand the file straight over to Cramer and let him shove it in the face of whoever was sweeping things under the rug. Why did he even need to get involved at this point?

"He's one of ours, all right," Garcia said. "You'll know when you see the image of the wound."

"Give me the file," he repeated. Maybe as each new body rolled in, he'd start stacking them up in the corner of his office. Fuck 'em.

Garcia just looked at him, holding the file in his hand.

"Give me the goddamn file!" Malloy demanded, standing up and holding out his hand. This day was off to a shitty start.

Garcia exhaled. "It's Tyler Steele."

The name registered as if Garcia had spoken in slow motion. Malloy felt the blood drain from his face as he stood rigid, mouth agape. He stared at

Garcia, waiting for—praying for—a smirk, a wave of his hand to say *just joking, boss.*

But Garcia didn't speak.

"No," Malloy insisted through clenched teeth. "No way." He refused to imagine it, even as his eyes shifted to the framed picture of Suzanne, Robbie, and Tyler at the beach, the one that had sat on his bookshelf for over fifteen years.

Garcia stood with his head lowered, his jaw set, his eyes downcast.

A wave of nausea ran through Malloy, and the taste of copper filled his mouth.

"Garcia!" he hissed.

His chest tightened as his hands clenched into fists. He wanted to explode in a fit of rage, to tell Garcia he was a fucking idiot and throw him out of his office. Throw him out of the building. He would have done it except that his throat had closed and he couldn't speak. His muscles began quivering as his rage melted away and grief racked his body. In an instant, all the energy drained out of him, and he fell back into his chair. His vicious, accusatory stare at Garcia turned into a plea, but no words formed. Instead, his mouth twisted, and his eyes blurred as involuntary tears welled up.

Garcia waited, respectful but helpless, as Malloy hunched with his head buried in his hands.

***

Malloy tried to ignore the nausea created by motion sickness and the reek of cigarette smoke that filled the cab of Garcia's Ford Ranger. Neither of them bothered to turn on the radio. Garcia stared straight ahead from behind the wheel, his face expressionless, lost in his own thoughts. Malloy gazed out at the long line of cars stopped on the other side of the freeway, and for once in his life wished he were sitting in it, heading back into the office instead of north to Flagstaff to examine the corpse of Tyler Steele.

It's Tyler Steele. Malloy still couldn't grasp that in a world of seven billion people, one of barely a handful of people he loved had ended up in a file on his desk. What else could possibly have those kinds of odds? He had a higher probability of being struck by lightning. He thought his breakfast might come back up, and he lowered his window to get some air. The hot gust that hit him in the face offered no relief.

"You all right, boss?" Garcia asked without looking over.

He rolled up the window but didn't answer, afraid to open his mouth. He breathed through his nose and distracted himself with sad memories. His mind rolled back through the years of Tyler, like old home videos. Suzanne trying to convince Robbie and Tyler that peas were actually LeBron James's all-time favorite food. Robbie and Tyler running through the house with armloads of sticks and rope to complete their wilderness shelter in the backyard. Both boys strutting down the stairs dressed in collared shirts and ties that Suzanne had bought them for their eighth-grade dance.

He'd practically raised Tyler. Tyler's mom was single and she worked during the day, leaving Tyler without a ride home after school. Suzanne would collect Robbie and Tyler from school, supervise them as they did their homework, and then let them play together until evening. Tyler had a string of objectionable male role models, men he referred to in later years as the "fuck of the month." Most nights, he stayed at the Malloys' until bedtime or even overnight.

Tyler and Robbie remained best friends until their sophomore year in high school. As Robbie became involved in sports and clubs, Tyler found a new crowd and drugs. To Malloy's deep disappointment, Tyler disappeared before finishing high school. It wasn't until three years ago that Malloy found him. His very own DEA team raided a small-time meth cooking operation in a suburban home in Tempe. Tyler was one of the group arrested.

Malloy had offered Tyler the deal of a lifetime: He would drop the charges if Tyler agreed to rehab. It was a long shot, given how long Tyler had been using and the abysmal success rate for meth addiction rehabilitation. But saving Tyler was something Malloy desperately needed so soon after the loss of Suzanne, and he knew she would have wanted him to do it.

So with a heavy dose of tough love from Garcia and a heavy dose of genuine love from Malloy, Tyler recovered. He moved to Prescott and got a job as a server at a Claim Jumper restaurant. In six months, he was promoted to store manager. Malloy and Garcia visited whenever they were doing fieldwork in the area. Tyler proudly showed them his office and some of the new ideas that he'd implemented.

The last time they were there, just as they were getting ready to leave, Malloy had patted Tyler on the back and told him he was proud of him. Tyler pulled him in for a hug, the first time he'd ever shown such an overt sign of affection, and said, "I love you, Pete. You're the only dad I ever had. Thank you." That had been six, maybe eight months ago.

Now Malloy sat shell-shocked, with his head pressed against the window. His chest felt hollow, but his head was raging with questions. Why? Why Tyler? He knew that later he'd be ready to really answer that question, using his professional experience, attention to detail, and knack for analytical thinking. But not yet.

For now, he just needed to be angry with a god he didn't even believe in.

40

D r. Will Lozano, the forensic pathologist in Flagstaff, stepped into the dimly lit waiting room and introduced himself to Malloy and Garcia.

"I'm really sorry about your friend," he said as he led them to the exam room. "Stacy mentioned you knew the victim."

"Thank you." Malloy didn't mean to sound terse, but he didn't want it to turn into a conversation.

Lozano seemed to get the message. He held the door for them. "Right this way. It's fortunate he was found not long after his time of death. I'd say about nineteen hours. I'm getting ready to do the internal exam, but I wanted to give you the opportunity to see the victim before I cut."

Malloy had witnessed a handful of autopsies over his career, but he was physically and emotionally unprepared for this one as he stepped into the sterile, over-lit room. The sour, acidic smell of bile and decomposition seemed to pour down his throat. He swayed and caught himself with a rolling gurney, which shifted under his weight. The metal instruments crashed to the floor.

"I got it, boss. I got it." Garcia dropped down to clean up the mess. It was a kind gesture to save him some humiliation, but it didn't work.

Malloy walked to the furthest corner of the room to collect himself. It wasn't Tyler's body emitting the stench. Decomposition gasses took days to build up to a truly foul odor. The stench had to be coming from a different corpse, but it still took him a full minute to convince himself to return to Tyler's table. His lips were press so tightly together, his jaw ached, and when the doctor asked him if he was okay, he could only nod.

Lozano pulled back the sheet, exposing Tyler's body.

Malloy swallowed hard and looked down. God. His heart broke again, and he swallowed a second time to fight back tears.

Garcia cursed through gritted teeth. This was also hard for him.

Malloy lingered on Tyler's peaceful, childlike expression. Even though he'd promised himself he wouldn't allow it, his head filled with memories. *Pete! Spray me!* as he and Robbie ran through the wet grass while Malloy watered the garden, pretending he couldn't hear them until they got close enough for a good dousing. *Pete! How do you like my birdhouse?* which he'd brought home from art class and to this very day sat on a shelf in the Malloy family room. Tyler had always wanted his approval, and he had been generous with it.

He pulled away and forced himself to survey the rest of Tyler's trim body. His eyes stopped at shin level. "What happened there?"

"The bruises appear to have been sustained at different times. See here." Lozano pointed his pen to the lower shin. "These bruises are yellowish, nearly healed. I'd say at least a week old, maybe two." He shifted his pen to the other left leg. "These couldn't be more than a day or two old. Still inflamed."

"What does it mean?" Garcia pulled a rubber band off his wrist and tied his hair back, as though it was in the way of his vision.

"I've seen similar bruises on fighters, particularly in martial arts or kickboxing," Lozano said. "Maybe he was taking some classes."

Malloy and Garcia exchanged a glance. Highly doubtful.

"It could also be the result of self-mutilation, which we've seen in some drug users, though it's not typical for a heroin user."

Garcia visibly bristled. "He wasn't a heroin user. He was a recovered meth addict. Emphasis on the 'recovered.'"

Lozano instinctively took a step backward.

"I'm sorry," Malloy said. "He was close to the victim as well."

He shot Garcia a look of warning. He was in no mood to abide Garcia's temper.

"I understand," Lozano said. "But you raise an interesting point that I wanted to discuss. Take a look at his arms."

Malloy bent forward for a closer inspection, then shrugged. "I don't see anything."

"Exactly. The victim has evidence of drug use in the past. Look—some very old scars here." He pointed to faint track marks inside the elbow of Tyler's left arm. "What's curious is that he shows no sign of recent drug use. I found no trace of methamphetamines in his system. I looked closely at the usual injection sites and then his entire body for the needle hole that resulted in his demise. I couldn't find it. We usually see damaged, even collapsed veins in drug abusers, but his veins look very healthy. This leads me to the possibility that the heroin was injected into the spinal artery."

Malloy nodded. He meant through the wound where the port once was.

"If that were the case," Lozano continued, "it likely would have resulted in anterior spinal artery syndrome, which could have led to paralysis in his limbs."

"Oh god." Malloy stared, frozen, at Tyler's bruised shins.

"I'm not officially connecting the dots on this yet," Lozano said. "But something for you to think about."

Malloy was grateful for a moment of silence. He didn't see any obvious relationship between Tyler and the previous eight victims besides the spinal port. Maybe Tyler's death was something entirely different.

"Physically, the victim is healthy and fit," Lozano continued.

Garcia stepped closer. "Look at his body. I know addicts, especially tweakers and junkies. They're thin and weak. Tyler isn't. Look, he has muscle tone, like he's been working out. How many addicts do you know who exercise?"

Lozano nodded. "His teeth are healthy. In fact, they've been cleaned professionally. His fingernails, clean. But there's more I need to show you."

Lozano matter-of-factly rolled the body face down.

"Jesus fucking god!" Garcia yelled.

Malloy queasily turned away.

"What is that?" Garcia asked. "It looks like he was whipped."

"That's what it looks like to me, as well," Lozano said. "The directionality of the lashes looks more like the markings of a whip. They're not characteristic of burn scars, and given their width and depth, they're not knife wounds. But these wounds are in fact healed completely. If he was whipped, it was weeks, maybe months ago."

"What does that mean? He was tortured?" Garcia's voice cracked.

Lozano didn't answer. "Finally, we have a small wound between L2 and L3 on the lower spine, which appears to be similar to your victims who were found with intrathecal access ports. The wound is only partially healed, as you can see, and there was no bandage or dressing covering the wound when the victim was found, even though the body was found fully clothed."

Malloy peered at the wound, willing it to be something else—a skin infection, maybe, or a cyst. But its location was so precise, and it appeared to be the exact size of a port.

"What the fu—I mean ..." Garcia looked defeated. "What happened here? Why? What's going on?"

Lozano sighed. "The manner of death is accidental drug overdose."

"Doc, come on," Garcia pleaded.

"The only other thing I can tell you is this. I've examined hundreds of OD deaths, and I've never seen a case like this. I'm a pathologist hired to provide a medical assessment, but if I were an investigator, I'd have an awful lot of questions about circumstances that don't match the usual pattern."

Malloy's stomach threatened to heave. There was nothing more to learn today.

"Thank you for your time, Dr. Lozano. We won't hold you up from completing your exam, and we need to get back to Phoenix. We appreciate that you called and let us come. If you find anything else that might help, please call." He handed Lozano a business card.

"You're welcome." Lozano handed him a vial of blood in a sealed biohazard bag—the sample from Tyler. "As you requested. I'll send the brain tissue sample to your lab if you'll kindly leave the information with my assistant up front."

He turned back to the body, then spoke over his shoulder. "Agent Malloy, one other thing that perhaps you already knew. The victim was HIV positive."

***

Malloy and Garcia walked in silence to the parked pickup truck.

Garcia pulled out a pack of cigarettes and tapped one into his palm. "Boss, I don't like what's happening here." He rested the cigarette between his lips, pulled a lighter, and lit it.

Malloy sat down in the cab to avoid the smoke and gazed out the window at the empty parking lot. He didn't like what was happening, either. He felt that something evil had tapped, quite literally, into the blood of these victims, like a bad sci-fi movie where aliens collect humans and attach them to tubes to suck their life energy.

A minute later, Garcia put out the cigarette and sat down behind the wheel, but he didn't start driving. He stared vacantly out the window. "There's something very wrong going on. That kid was tortured. He was tortured and killed. His killers knew he had a drug history, and they shot him up and dumped the body, far from home, far from anyone who would know him. Tyler had nothing on him but clothing, and he never would've been IDed if he hadn't already been fingerprinted from a prior. The killers probably hadn't banked on that. Just a useless, HIV-infected drug addict found in a dumpster."

Malloy was still stunned by the HIV result, even though he was certain Tyler never would have confided such devastating news. Tyler wouldn't have been able to bear the disappointment on Malloy's face.

"Make sure you get that blood sample to Jordan Jennings's lab," he said.

He needed to collect his thoughts. He was deeply inductive in his approach, and he needed time alone to think. He couldn't see the connections, find the pattern, with chatter in his ears.

Garcia understood this and remained silent as he pulled out of the parking lot.

Tyler's case was different. The first eight victims had died by their own hands, doing something risky and deadly, driven by wild-eyed euphoria. And while it appeared that Tyler had ODed, Malloy didn't believe it. Like Garcia, he believed Tyler had been injected with heroin, likely through the port, resulting in paralysis.

What if they'd dumped him before his heart had stopped beating? What if he'd awakened in the dumpster, unable to get out? Jesus Christ. He felt his face tighten and shook his head, willing the image to disappear.

His phone rang, and he quickly palmed the tears from his eyes. He fished around for his phone and finally found it in the side pocket of his bag. Melanie. He hit the speaker.

"Yeah." His voice caught, and he cleared his throat.

"Sir, I've got an agent from the bureau here to collect case files for elixir."

There it was. That word. "Sorry?"

"The files for L-X-R?"

Damn it, he'd forgotten all about the bureau's reclaiming the files. He wasn't ready to part with them yet. He needed to look for connections between the vics and Tyler. He pounded his fist on his forehead. Why hadn't he copied them?

"Fine," he barked.

"They already have the files for the eight victims, but I told them another had come in."

Ack, he'd spoken too quickly. Melanie knew they were in the field investigating. He grappled for an explanation. "False alarm. The vic isn't related to the LXR case. Just a typical heroin overdose. We drove two hours for a wild goose chase."

"Oh, good! They seemed awfully confused when I said that. Okay, I'll set it straight. Thanks."

Malloy dropped the phone into his bag.

"What the fuck is going on?" Garcia asked through gritted teeth.

Malloy pulled out his Tums and shook two into his hand.

"Boss."

He tossed the Tums into his mouth and chewed slowly. Facing forward, because he was too ashamed to look Garcia in the eyes, he answered. "We're on our own."

Garcia pounded his palms on the steering wheel.

"Shit."

41

Austin triumphantly slapped his notebook down on the table after crossing off the last thing from his list. The upcoming summit was now just two weeks away. This would be a night to remember.

Hammond's face glowed with childlike joy. "Austin, wait until you meet this team. I mean, it's so amazing to connect with a group of brilliant people who not only have the same vision as you but are just as deeply focused and driven to make it successful. It's incredible. This summit is going to be life-changing for you."

Austin was indeed excited. He'd begun planning his part of the talk already—nothing on paper just yet, but some key points he wanted to make. If this group was really who Hammond said they were, he planned to put on the best show he'd ever done. These were people with so much wealth they could buy entire governments. They could change the course of history.

Well, that was the plan, wasn't it?

He was overcome with respect for Hammond. Who else had the ability and resources to gather and mobilize this kind of money and influence?

Like he'd read Austin's mind, Hammond added, "And remember, when you're planning your presentation, these folks are wealthy investors. Businessmen and politicians. They aren't medically trained. Keep it light."

There was nothing light about what he and Hammond were planning to propose. In fact, the times had never been darker. But if all went well, maybe there would be light at the end of the tunnel.

"And don't throw in that bit about your grandmother smelling like mold."

Austin laughed. "As dumb as it is, it gets a roar of laughter every time." He took a sip of bourbon. He loved his new life.

"I know, I know …"

The conference table speakerphone jingled. Austin recognized the voice of the Fixer on the other end.

"Sir, we have a situation. Allison Stevens attempted to break into Jonathan Chambers's office. She was alone in his private office less than four minutes, but evidently, she found the files with the confidential documents. My operative is unsure which files she might have viewed before she was discovered and stopped."

Shit. Adrenaline shot through Austin's veins. Goddamn the insolence of that girl. Why couldn't she just do what she was told?

Hammond scowled, and his nostrils flared as he inhaled dramatically. "This is really unfortunate to hear. I made it clear that we have zero room for error." Hammond spoke to the man on the phone, but Austin knew the comment was directed at him.

"I understand, sir. Would you like me to eliminate Ms. Stevens?"

The suggestion made Austin dizzy, and he had to grab the edge of the table to steady himself. Without Allison, he'd lose everything, but he wasn't about to tip his hand to Hammond this early in the negotiation process. Allison was his wildcard, and without her this whole deal would collapse. He had to diffuse this.

Hammond buried his head in his hands, making fists in his hair.

Austin eased back in his chair and crossed one leg over the other. "We can eliminate her if you think it's best, Stewart, but believe me, Allison Stevens is a mouse, not a cat. She might have a curious side, but I can assure you she's not tough enough to take it any further."

He wondered if Hammond could hear the tremor in his voice. He forced himself to take a sip from his bourbon, even though he was so nervous he could barely swallow.

Hammond looked up, seething.

Austin swirled the ice in his glass. "I'd hate to lose my linchpin for Quandary. I really need her to keep up appearances." He kept his gaze on his drink, hoping Hammond couldn't read the desperation on his face. Maybe he was being too aloof. He tried another tack and sat up straight, looking Hammond in the eye. "But it's your call. If you think she's too much of a risk, I'll just have to find another way to manage things back in New Jersey."

Stewart eyed him balefully. "Some mice, when they feel threatened, go on the attack."

"I'm sorry, sir?"

Austin had almost forgot the Fixer was on the phone. He held his composure and waited.

Finally, Stewart averted his stare and spoke to the phone. "Dr. Harris has made it clear that it's in our best interest to keep the girl alive. Because of our partnership, I'll trust his judgment. Put a tail on her."

Austin exhaled with relief, and Hammond caught it. The corners of Hammond's mouth turned up in a smirk. "A close tail. I want to know if she deviates from her instructions again."

"Yes, sir."

Hammond disconnected the call and left, slamming the door shut behind him.

Austin slumped back in his chair with a groan. Bullet dodged. But his relief was fleeting. What in god's name was she doing? The FBI must be watching her closely now. She should be dutifully following her orders.

If it hadn't been for that damn misplaced invoice. The biggest goddamn mistake of his life.

He considered his situation. He wasn't ready to use Allison yet. He just needed another two or three weeks to seal the deal with Hammond. But Allison's unpredictability made her too risky. He couldn't have her poking around like this.

He scrubbed his hands over his face and waited another minute to make sure Hammond wasn't returning. Then he redialed the number of the last incoming call.

"Yes."

Austin kept his eyes on the conference room door. "Stewart and I are in agreement. There's a change of plans."

42

"**A**llison …"

She had just slammed the door of her Toyota Camry when a tap on her shoulder startled her. Her Wendy's bag thunked onto the pavement.

"Damn." She picked up the bag before turning to look at the offender who'd come up on her so suddenly.

It took a moment for her to recognize Dr. Chambers's assistant. "Elaine?"

"I'm sorry, I didn't mean to sneak up on you. I wanted to speak with you, but I didn't want to go into the building."

Allison didn't know how to respond, so she waited.

"I was wondering if we could sit in your car. I have something to show you." Elaine stood tall and spoke with confidence—nothing like the insecure mouse Allison had intimidated barely a week ago.

"Uh, okay." She opened the door and slid back into the driver's seat as Elaine walked to the passenger side and hoisted a large quilted purse onto her lap.

Elaine got right to the point. "I need my job with Dr. Chambers. You're right, he's a verbally abusive man, and yes, he intimidates me. He has a quick temper that usually gets the better of him. But he does care about his patients. One of them is my son, who suffers a genetic disease called erythromelalgia. Have you heard of it?"

Allison shook her head.

"There are only a handful of patients diagnosed with the disease. His symptoms started when he was eleven. He stopped wearing shoes because he said his feet burned. As he got older, the burning sensation spread to his legs, his arms, his hands. I didn't understand why, and had I known his father, which I didn't, I might have learned he had inherited it. It's a genetic mutation of the SCN9A gene."

Now it came to her: Man on Fire Syndrome. She'd read up on it after the Spiragene meeting. Her hand rose involuntarily to her mouth.

Elaine continued. "Jeff spent most of his days indoors to be near chests of ice to put his feet in. He had ice packs for his hands and arms. He couldn't go to school. He couldn't play with his friends." Tears welled, but only for a moment. "No doctors in my HMO plan could help him, and I finally reached out to Dr. Chambers. I begged him to help, but I couldn't afford his fees. I was working as a low-paid nurse at the time, and I agreed to work for him as his administrative assistant if he'd take Jeff as a patient. Dr. Chambers had a reputation for being tough, and he had a difficult time retaining secretaries. Go figure. Anyway, he took over Jeff's treatment, and we tried everything. Nothing except morphine ever worked for Jeff."

"God." Allison shook her head in sympathy.

"Then a couple years ago, Dr. Chambers asked if we wanted to try a new gene therapy. It wasn't an approved drug—it wasn't even an experimental drug—and it hadn't yet been fully tested in animals. I said yes. God, I had no choice. Jeff was wasting away with no quality of life. He slept through his days, had lost nearly half his body weight. He looked like—" She swallowed hard. "He looked like a hospice patient."

"So you gave him the drug?" Jesus. It was unheard of. How could a mother give an untested drug to her own child?

Elaine clasped her hands. "I knew it was illegal and risky. Dr. Chambers said we could never, ever speak of it to anyone. Even in the office, we only referred to it as the elixir. But it works. It was like a miracle. Jeff took the drug for six months through a spinal port, and it cured him completely.

Now he only returns once every six months for another dose. He has a life. For the first time, he has a normal life."

Elaine grew lost in thought, stony-faced as she stared at the concrete wall in front of the car. Allison waited for her to continue.

"You visited me on Tuesday, August the fifteenth," Elaine said. "I wrote it down in my scheduler, where I write down every aspect of my day. That same night, I received a call from Dr. Chambers letting me know that he'd be away an additional two weeks. Just before I hung up, he asked if Dr. Harris had called. I know Austin's in trouble with the law, so I found it odd that Dr. Chambers would be expecting a call from him. That's when I replayed the moment I caught you looking through his files. You said something illegal might be going on."

Allison squirmed as a chill slithered up her spine. She gripped her knees in an effort to keep still.

"I was worried someone might've found out about Jeff's medication, so I decided to look through Dr. Chambers's file cabinet myself to see what he's been hiding. And I found something."

Elaine pulled a file folder from her purse.

"I debated whether to bring this to you. I don't want anything to get in the way of Jeff's injections, and what I've found ... I mean, if this gets out ... well." She sighed heavily. "I know I took a huge risk allowing Dr. Chambers to give this drug to my son, and I was prepared to suffer the consequences if the drug didn't—"

"I understand," Allison whispered.

"But I wouldn't be able to live with myself if I didn't show you what I found."

Allison looked down at the folder. It was labeled B. Elliott. She could barely resist yanking it right from Elaine's hands.

Elaine's lips tightened into a thin line. "Dr. Chambers thinks I'm a dummy. He assumes just because I'm fat and shy that I'm dumb. A lot of people have that perception, really."

"That's not true." But Allison knew the obesity stigma was real. Hadn't she herself found Elaine an easy target for manipulation and bullying?

"Yes, it is. But it gives me an advantage. He underestimates me. He thinks I don't understand when I listen to his conversations or when I read his documents. But I do." She smiled ominously and opened the folder. "So let me tell you what I think is going on. I found a folder labeled Field Cohort that had profiles of eight patients. Have a look."

Allison scanned the names: Elvis Doe, age 31. Eric Sparks, age 21. Faye, age unknown (20–30 yrs.). Karen Richmond, age 23.

"Have you ever heard of any of these people?" Elaine asked.

Allison shrugged.

"They were given a drug, see?" She pointed to a section labeled TREATMENT. "The drug they were given is called LXR102016. It's similar to the drug that was given to Jeff, which was LXR10—"

Allison's mouth fell open. Spiragene. Austin's secret research. "Oh my god, I know this drug! I know the LXR drugs. There's a whole family of them in research."

Elaine looked at her with skepticism. "But you don't know the patients? Have another look."

Allison read the remaining names: Jake Graventoll, Mark Vespe, A. J. Reese, Reuben Smith. She frowned. "Uh-uh, I've never heard of any of them."

"Because apparently you paid them to participate in the study."

The next document Elaine handed her was an Excel printout that looked exactly like one of her own, with the same color scheme and column headers. She looked at the line items. Payment to Eric Sparks, $50,000, Account DBB 889805532, Account Holder Allison Stevens. Another payment to Karen Richmond, $50,000. Jake Graventoll and Mark Vespe were also paid $50,000 from the account in Allison's name. The remaining four patients were paid $1,000 in cash.

"I didn't pay anyone." Her voice was a whimper as her gaze locked on the account holder name: Allison Stevens.

"I think they were part of a biohacking group, just like my son." Elaine spoke in a whisper, as if they weren't alone in the car.

This was it. This was Austin's secret project. His venture. Austin was biohacking gene therapies. The LXR drugs. She swayed slightly and braced herself with a hand on the steering wheel.

"There is no LXR gene therapy in a legitimate clinical study," Elaine said. "I looked through the FDA's website. That means you paid patients to participate in an illegal clinical trial."

"But I didn't!" Allison insisted. "This isn't my account."

"I believe you."

"I didn't even know about it." Suddenly being accused of buying a house and a diamond ring seemed like trivial nonsense. Her chest tightened with panic.

"I know you didn't."

"I'm not responsible for this!" She was practically yelling, her voice an octave higher.

"Allison, I know you didn't do it." Elaine lowered her voice to almost a whisper. "I know you didn't because I'm the one who opened the bank account. In your name."

43

I *drop my backpack on the kitchen table and listen. The house is quiet except for the small TV in Mom's room. I walk over to Daddy's wheelchair, which Mom let me keep after the funeral, and adjust Teddy Morey, who'd slipped down in the chair with one chubby leg hanging off. I give him a kiss and walk upstairs and down the dark hall, hoping Mom's awake. I know she won't be.*

"Mom?" I ask quietly just outside her door. There's no answer. "Mom?" I repeat, a little louder. "Are you awake?" She still doesn't answer. I wait a minute, wondering if I should open the door or not. I decide to open it just a crack and peek in. The shades are drawn, and the room is almost completely dark. I see the shape of Mom lying on her side under her heavy comforter.

I walk back downstairs to the kitchen. I'm starving. I open the fridge and find that moldy cheese still in there. I'm afraid to touch it, so I quickly close the door. The pantry hasn't improved this week, either. I take the last sleeve of Ritz crackers and the jar of peanut butter into the living room. I'm not allowed to eat in the living room, but I know Teddy Morey won't tattle. I roll Teddy Morey's chair next to the living room sofa so he can watch TV with me. Then I turn on the TV and flop onto the sofa.

Mom doesn't wake up till late, while I'm watching Friends. She wanders into the living room and squints from the light.

"Hi, honey. How was school?"

"Fine," I answer, looking back at the TV.

"Did you do your homework?"

"Yep." I know she won't check like she used to.

"Okay. Did you have something for dinner?"

"Yep."

"Okay, good."

I wonder if she's going to ask me more questions. Monica and Chandler are getting married, and I've been waiting all week to see it.

"Okay, well, I'm really tired, so I'm going to bed. Can you tuck yourself in?"

"Sure." Chandler's speech is so sweet. He really does want to marry Monica, even though Joey almost messed it all up.

The mention of dinner makes me realize I'm hungry. During the commercials, I dash into the kitchen to see what's left in the pantry. I find a can of fruit cocktail hidden behind the stewed tomatoes, and I grab a spoon and run back to the sofa before the show starts up again.

*** *

Layla opened her eyes to an empty room. It wasn't the first time she was last in the community building after devotions. She sighed and rolled off her knees onto her hip. Her legs were completely numb. She lifted each calf with her hands and straightened her legs, exhaling from the dull throb as the blood refilled her muscles.

Brother James had warned her to take it easy, but with greater physical suffering her memories seemed to be more detailed, more intense, and more emotional. Her craving for new memories grew with each passing day.

They weren't all great memories, obviously, and some of them held no meaning at all. But one thing she knew for certain: Her poisoned life was filled with far more suffering, pain, and loneliness than she'd ever experienced at the Colony. She had no interest in going back to that life, but she continued to be curious about it. She wanted to understand how she'd become the woman she was today, how she'd ultimately come to be at the Colony. All those memories resided deep inside her unconscious mind, just as Dr. Jeannette had been telling her all this time. They would continue to emerge, one puzzle piece at a time, until one day she'd be able to put the whole thing together.

She lay back, feeling tiny and insignificant beneath the soaring cathedral ceiling of the community building. The stones in the ceiling formed an enormous, intricate circle. It comforted her to see that the spot she lay was directly in the center of the stones. She felt protected.

Circles could be found everywhere in the Colony. Even the garden had been planted in an elaborate circle of tangled branches and stems, with a small break in the ring where Colony residents could enter to meditate. Circles symbolized purity and wholeness.

But Brother James had told her that the circle had an even deeper significance that most members of the Colony weren't aware of: a ring representing eternity, the immortality of a pure society, the only sustainable future of the world. And the colonists would lead the purification of the earth. It sounded beautiful when he explained it.

Her chest swelled with pride at being among the leaders of the purification of the earth. She would be a warrior for the Father. She would be a champion.

If only the Father allowed it.

She rolled onto her stomach and pushed herself up into a plank position. Sweat dripped from her forehead and splatted onto the cement floor as she counted her breaths. Her arms trembled, threatening to give out, but she held on for ten more breaths. *You always have ten percent more than you think,* her yogi had told her one day after the rest of the class had packed up and left the studio. *You'll find your warrior self in that remaining ten percent, not the ninety percent before that.*

With slow, controlled movements, as she'd been instructed, she lowered herself to the floor. She wasn't a warrior woman yet, but she was on her way. Every day, her counts went longer. She would show Brother James and Dr. Jeannette that she was capable.

She flipped over and pushed herself into an upward plank pose, ignoring the pain in her awkwardly twisted wrists. Oh, yes. She'd find her inner warrior.

She squinted as she stepped outside, the sun already blinding as it pushed higher on the horizon. She spotted Brother James walking toward the courtyard. Excited, she skipped over to him. She hadn't seen him in nearly a week.

"Well hello, Brother James," she said, her voice a bit too flirty. "Where have you been lately? Not out partying, I hope."

She'd prepared the line days ago, waiting for an opportunity to use it.

He didn't respond to her teasing. Instead, he stiffly said, "Ah, Layla. I'd like to meet with you after your work and activities today. Could you kindly come to the Intake Room? Four o'clock?"

Layla rocked back on her heels, startled by the formality. "Um, yes. Of course." She dropped her gaze. "I'm sorry, I shouldn't have—"

"Nothing to be sorry about. I'll see you then." He raised his voice and called over Layla's shoulder, making her flinch. "Brother Leo! Can I have a word?"

He strode away.

Layla stared after him, her heart crushed.

***

Layla arrived seven minutes early. The Intake Room was empty. She tapped her heels nervously. She assumed she'd been here before, but she didn't remember it. It was like so much of her impure life; she only knew what she'd been told. She fidgeted, picking at her hangnails, waiting for Brother James.

She'd spent zero time with Brother James since he'd captivated her in the garden, and she missed him. She'd gone back to the garden for meditation every night, hoping he'd be there, but he hadn't shown. He hadn't even appeared to lead morning devotions. Now, after this morning's curiously formal interaction outside the community building, she was left wondering if he still believed in her. Had she done something wrong? Had he learned of her hiding in his office? Had the Father told him?

She took a deep breath, but it felt shallow. She reached under the table and pounded her bruised shins with her fists in an effort to relax. Perhaps Dr. Jeannette had finally convinced Brother James that she was unworthy of purification. She was certain Dr. Jeannette hadn't yet gotten over their last interaction, and Dr. Jeannette didn't strike her as the forgiving type. The Father was surely angry. She'd meditated endlessly for forgiveness for her insolent behavior, but it didn't feel like it was working. The Father wasn't listening to her.

She sauntered over to the fruit bowl and picked through the fruits squeezing each to check for ripeness. Fresh fruit and flowers were abundant in most of the common areas. It was a way to appear inviting to recruits after they'd completed their early program. Not every recruit was invited to induction, but those who were called to this next level were courted. *Roll out the red carpet*, she'd heard Brother James say. This room was one of the first places they would see. They would get an immediate warm feeling about the Colony, and rightly so. They'd quickly learn how blessed they were to live in such a sacred world, doing the important work of the Father.

She pivoted restlessly. At least it was cool in here. A soothing painting of a lily pond counteracted the blazing energy of the world outside, the gallery light above it giving it a magical sort of illumination. The picture felt familiar to her, but all she could place was sadness. Maybe her unconscious was giving her a lingering taste of her own intake. Still, it was a beautiful painting. She read the signature: Claude Monet. The name was familiar. Brother Claude? Maybe he was a resident of the Colony. If so, she planned to find him and tell him she liked his painting.

The door opened and Layla jolted, then quickly sat down in her chair. It was Dr. Jeannette. Layla's heart knocked hard against her chest.

"Hello, Layla." Dr. Jeannette's voice was cool.

"Um, hi." Why was Dr. Jeannette here?

Dr. Jeannette sat down across the table and began writing on her notepad without another word. Layla clasped her hands and looked down at the table.

The door opened again.

"What I'm saying is that he has a pattern of delinquency." Brother James entered the room, deep in conversation with Sister Mia.

She tensed. She'd thought she would only be meeting with Brother

James.

"Hi, Layla," Brother James's tone matched his earlier invitation: stiff, as if he were talking to an employee. He glanced at her only briefly before continuing his conversation with Sister Mia. "What we've tried isn't working. Let's discuss a new approach for him later."

Layla shoved her hands under her legs and stared at a knot in the glossy cherrywood table.

Two more people entered the room. Sister Pauline, the inductee residence hall manager, and Brother Sayid, her supervisor in the dining hall. Layla's apprehension turned to dread. What was going on? Brother James opened his bag and pulled out Layla's folder and a book. Layla strained to see it: *The Princess Bride.*

Panic struck. They'd caught her in Brother James's office. She was being expelled.

The air thickened, and she began breathing shallowly. Her mind raced to figure out what she could do to save herself. She could beg forgiveness. She'd tell them anything they wanted to hear and then beg to stay. She would do anything. She would happily suffer some kind of harsh punishment, like isolation or hard physical labor. She could offer to go back to the recruit program. Anything to stay.

Please, Father. Please help me. Please. I'll do anything.

Sweat beaded on her forehead, but frozen with fear, she couldn't wipe it away.

"Okay, let's get started," Brother James announced.

Everyone stopped chatting.

Brother James opened the folder in front of him and looked at her soberly. "Layla, we've called you here today to discuss your future with the Colony."

44

Allison stared at Elaine, aghast. "You? You did this to me?"

"No! Well, I didn't mean to do anything to you. Dr. Chambers asked me to set up an account. He had documents, power of attorney, and everything looked correct. I didn't have any idea I was doing anything illegal. I swear it was just a logistical thing, setting up the account. Carol was away that week taking her daughter to college. He just asked me to do it because Carol was away. I didn't know. I'm sorry. I didn't know."

She regarded Elaine with distrust, as Elaine rambled her apology.

"But there's something else," Elaine continued, "and this is the important part. This is why I decided to come and talk to you."

She handed Allison a small envelope. On the outside was written "B. Elliott."

"Bradley." It was all she could think of to say. She opened the envelope to find a short note and a flash drive inside.

Brad,

I've been trying to contact you for several days regarding the protocol for LXR102016. We've had some setbacks, as you'll see from the video included. Please contact me as soon as possible so we can discuss next steps for this model. We'd also like to discuss the other models, especially the germline animals, as we fear we may observe the same dose-limiting toxicity.

Regards, Jenna

Allison twisted to reach her laptop and powered it on.

"This is really something," Elaine said. "I just want you to be prepared."

She inserted the flash drive and loaded the video. The Camry filled with the sound of screeching monkeys. She fumbled for the volume button. The video appeared to have been taken inside a large warehouse, where several huge chain-link cages—maybe three stories tall and elaborately equipped with ropes and jungle gyms—stood lined up in a row. Each cage contained six to eight chimpanzees.

Quandary had never conducted studies with chimps. It wasn't easy to find primate labs that used chimpanzee models anymore. The chimps were climbing and jumping, hollering at each other. Normal chimp behavior as far as Allison could tell. She wrung her hands as she waited for something to happen.

A woman's voice spoke from behind the camera. "This is the day 120 video observation of Cohorts 3 and 4. The date is July 9, 2019. I'm Jenna Wolfe, lead researcher in the primate bay."

The camera bobbed toward one of the cages, then stabilized. Wolfe stepped in front and spoke to the camera.

"This unit is Cohort 3. All animals were injected seven days ago with their fourth dose of LXR102016, 1.4 milligrams per kilogram of body weight. As predicted, the subjects appear to have no pain. They not only walk across the hot plate to get food, but they stand and sit comfortably on the hot plate. The plate is currently set to 120 degrees Fahrenheit, which causes first-degree burns. We've increased the temperature to 140 degrees and see no reaction from the subjects, even after they sustain second-degree burns. The additional pain sensitivity tests, which include pricking and piercing the skin, ice compression, capsaicin subcu injections, and pressure algometry, all show negative pain sensitivity. As you can see, the animals appear happy and comfortable."

Wolfe moved out of the camera's view to show the full cage. Eight chimpanzees moved easily about. Several walked across or sat on the hot plate. Wolfe lured them off the plate with some banana slices.

The camera shook again as it was repositioned to focus on the next cage, and Wolfe again moved in front of the camera.

"This unit is Cohort 4. These animals have been injected with their fifth dose of 016, which was escalated from 1.4 milligrams per kilogram to 1.6 milligrams per kilogram. The subjects have the same pain reaction as Cohort 3. They seem to have no pain sensitivity, as per all the same tests we used in Cohort 3. However, the Cohort 4 animals are exhibiting a new behavior pattern we haven't observed in the earlier cohorts, and as a result, we've had to tranquilize and restrain the animals. For the sake of this video observation, I'll remove the restraints of two of the subjects."

Wolfe stepped out of the way, and Allison gasped. Two chimps had been restrained by cuffs attached to the cage and accessible from the outside. They were awake but sat despondently.

"Oh my god," Allison whispered. She'd never seen such horrifying animal cruelty. How long had they been in those restraints? She wanted to choke Jenna Wolfe.

Wolfe walked around the cage and unlocked the cuffs of one chimp. He snapped out of his depressive state and scampered to the top of the cage, relieved be unshackled. She freed the second chimp, who did the same.

The first chimp let out a shriek and hurled himself off the platform at the top of the cage. He grabbed for a rope swing, but it was too far away, and he plummeted the full three stories and hit the ground with a thud.

Allison's breath caught in her throat. The chimp didn't move at all for a long moment; an attempt to roll over was unsuccessful. His spine appeared to be broken. She stared at the screen, unblinking, not breathing.

The second chimp observed all this, shrieking excitedly from atop the platform. He flailed his arms as he darted back and forth across the plank a couple of times, and then—

"No!" Allison yelled at the screen.

The chimp jumped with all his might toward the rope swing. But he didn't come close, and he too fell to the ground.

Allison clamped her hands over her mouth.

Wolfe shot two tranquilizer darts at each animal, and they lay still. She came back onto the screen, visibly upset. Her voice was scratchy, and her chin trembled as she spoke.

"Three of the eight subjects jumped from the platform before I was able to tranquilize the whole unit. We caged the animals individually so they couldn't hurt themselves or each other. One of the animals experienced a brain hemorrhage after beating his head against the cage bars in an attempt to break out. Another animal bit off his tongue. We euthanized both as quickly as possible to eliminate their suffering."

Wolfe turned from the camera to wipe her nose with a tissue. "After some discussion with the other researchers, I've surmised this behavior is caused by drug-related shrinkage of the amygdala, which is increasing high-risk behavior and impulsivity and decreasing the fear response. With the exception of these two animals, which we retained only for the purpose of this video, the cohort has been euthanized. We will complete the task tonight and document the results."

Wolfe's voice broke. "The behavior we've witnessed appears to be observed only at this escalated dose level. However, due to the severity of this self-destructive behavior, we have stopped dosing all animals at all levels and closed the study. We will also discontinue dosing of the germline models."

The video ended.

Allison stared at the screen, devastated and unable to move.

"The drug those chimps took is the same drug that was given to the eight subjects," Elaine said. "102016."

Allison turned her stare on Elaine.

"Do you understand?" Elaine asked. "Those patients are in serious danger."

Allison blinked. She understood, all right. She just didn't know where to start.

"I know you're overwhelmed right now, but did you hear the last part when Jenna referred to the germline models?"

Allison had worked on clinical trials her entire career. Nothing was more important than the safety of the patients on study. She clutched the file folder against her laptop and opened the car door.

"Allison?" Elaine tried to stop her as she stepped out of the car. "Wait, there's more."

"I have to call them."

"No, wait!"

"I have to call the patients!" she shouted over her shoulder.

She picked up her pace toward the building, swerving with annoyance around a car parked illegally in front of the building. The man leaning casually against the car nodded and smiled as she brushed past. She did a double take. The FBI guy from the other day. Gadorski, was it?

Goddamn it. They were watching her.

45

Layla was melting into her chair under the weight of all the eyes on her. Disappointment hardened each face. *Layla had such great potential,* they were probably thinking. *It's too bad she had to throw it away. Some impures just can't be helped.*

She lowered her gaze. *Please Father, please Father, please Father.*

She envisioned being escorted to the heavy iron gate that kept the Colony free of impures. Brother James would hand her a small bag with some food and clothes and motion for her to step through. Then he'd latch the gate closed with Layla on the other side. *Good luck in the poisoned world, Layla,* he would say with a bitter smile. Layla would look at the dusty and desolate road ahead of her, and—

"You've been with us for"—Brother James lifted the first page of her file—"wow, Layla, you've been with us for almost a year and a half."

God. Had it really been that long? Where had the time gone?

"We'd like to know what your experience has been here in the induction program." He leaned forward on his elbows, his fingers threaded.

Layla sat unmoving, uncertain what he wanted her to say. Was this a trick? Was he offering her a chance to confess her transgressions?

"Um, well, it's been wonderful, actually," she finally answered. She braced herself for an accusation and prepared to fall to her knees and beg.

"How so?"

She glanced at Brother Claude's painting for moral support.

"Well, every day I wake up happy to go to devotions. The feeling I get when I release the pain is so comforting, and I know I've pleased the Father. I love my tasks at the dining hall"—her eyes flashed to her boss, whose face remained impassive—"and I've made a lot of friends here. I love all the activities and helping others …"

"And tell us about your commitment to purification." Brother James's eyes drilled into her. They did not radiate warmth. They demanded an answer. The truth.

In an instant, Layla pushed out her chair and dropped onto her knees. Although she heard Sister Mia audibly gasp, she didn't cry out or whimper with the pain. She exhaled as quietly as she could and dropped her gaze.

"Layla," Brother James began.

But she didn't let him finish. The moment was on her, she was certain. This was her one and only chance to make her case.

She spoke without looking up. "Brother James, and everyone, I know that I'm not perfect. I know I have a lot of learning and growing to do within the Colony. But for more than a year now, I've dedicated every ounce of my being to preparing for the process of purification. There's nothing more important to me than being pure, and if you'll let me stay—if you'll *please* let me stay—I'll do anything to continue my path. If it requires less sleep, more pain, and more chores, I promise you I'll give one hundred percent. I'll dig deeper into my unconscious mind for my memories. Whatever you require. But please let me stay. I belong here. It's my destiny."

"Layla." Brother James's voice was gentle now, nearly a whisper. He came around the table until he was standing next to her.

Layla dared not look up. She locked her tear-filled eyes on the cement floor seam beneath her and clamped her teeth shut to keep them from chattering from dread.

In her peripheral vision, she saw Brother James hold out his hand. She looked up slowly. His warm smile had returned. She took his hand and allowed him to help her back into her chair, where she clasped her hands on her lap and kept her eyes on the table, terrified to meet the gaze of her superiors.

"Thank you, Layla. Let's continue." Brother James turned to Brother Sayid. "How has Layla been performing in the kitchen prep?"

"Layla's a model worker," Brother Sayid replied. "She's never late, and she does a terrific job. In all my years at the Colony, I've never had a better salad preparer. But everyone knows that."

Layla finally looked up, confused by the change in the tone of the meeting. Was Brother Sayid trying to protect her from getting expelled?

Brother James directed the next question to Sister Pauline. "And how would you characterize Layla's behavior in residence?"

"Not very good, I'm afraid." Sister Pauline shook her head and frowned. Layla sucked in her breath.

"Layla is so involved in the community that she's practically never in her room. I have no way to evaluate her." Sister Pauline winked at her.

She couldn't appreciate the teasing or the compliment. *Please let me stay, Father. Please let me stay.*

Finally, Brother James turned to Dr. Jeannette, and Layla froze. This was it. "Dr. Jeannette, how has Layla been doing in therapy? How has she been dealing with her memories?"

Layla avoided Dr. Jeannette's gaze and looked down at her hands. They were trembling.

Dr. Jeannette didn't speak. Not a word, for five seconds. Ten seconds.

The wait was agonizing, and Layla finally looked up right into Dr. Jeannette's piercing eyes. She desperately wanted to look away, but she held Dr. Jeannette's stare. Dr. Jeannette's jaw was clenched and slightly quivering. Fear engulfed Layla again and she wanted to sit tall and be brave, but she cowered in her chair as if she were going to be struck.

At long last, Dr. Jeannette smiled at everyone at the table.

"Layla's been doing wonderfully," she said in her singsong voice. "Our therapy sessions have been very productive. Her memories from her poisoned life are slow to return, but I don't see that as a hindrance in her progression toward purification."

"Excellent. Thank you, everyone. I will discuss it with the Father this evening, and I know he will be thrilled to get Layla started." He turned back to Layla. "Sister Layla, it's with great pride that I inform you that you have been called for purification. You will begin your conditioning as soon as you meet with Dr. Jeremy."

Layla's eyes filled with tears—tears of joy, tears of relief, tears of exhaustion. But she smiled as she cried and looked around the table as all her mentors applauded her. All but Dr. Jeannette, who busied herself writing notes in her pad.

"And as a congratulation, I brought you a gift. This book was donated for our library, but I recall you'd mentioned it was one of your favorites. It happens to be one of my favorites, as well. I'd like you to have it."

Layla took the book from Brother James and hugged it to her chest. Had she told him she loved this book? She didn't remember.

"Thank you so much, Brother James. Thank you." She held the book out to look at the cover, then hugged it again.

***

Today was the best day of Layla's entire life.

She lay in her bed, unable to sleep. It was early, not even ten p.m., but she no longer attended evening devotions. She was a trainee now and would soon attend her first day of conditioning. The next phase of her life would begin in just two days, and she couldn't imagine how she would survive until then.

She picked up the book Brother James had given to her. *The Princess Bride* by William Goldman. Hmm. She ran her fingers over the cover. A man wearing a black mask held a sword, while a woman with long, flowing hair— Layla could only assume she was the actual princess bride—stood by his side. The book was slightly worn, but it didn't matter to Layla. It was a gift from Brother James to her.

Layla opened the cover, breathing in the musty smell of the old book. It reminded her of something. A smell from her past that she couldn't quite put her finger on.

She fanned the book pages and inhaled again, savoring the moment. Finally, when she could hold out no longer, she turned to the first page and was surprised to see a handwritten inscription inside.

To my beautiful girl,

As you wish.

Brother James

She didn't understand the note, but her stomach filled with butterflies. What could it mean?

She skipped past several pages of introduction and stopped to look at the map. The Cliffs of Insanity. The Fire Swamp. It all sounded so familiar. She smiled. Then she turned to page one and began reading: "This is my favorite book in all the world, though I have never read it."

What a wonderful first line.

46

Allison's office window vibrated as she slammed the door shut and she flinched, thinking it might shatter. She glanced through the window to see Carol jump up from her desk and look worriedly over. Allison mouthed "Sorry!" and opened her laptop to appear to be addressing an urgent matter. Which she was.

She leafed through the patient documents that Elaine had shown her. Four of them listed no known address or phone number, so she started with Jake Graventoll. She picked up her receiver, then set it down. What if the FBI were monitoring her calls? Couldn't they do that from the office of a known fugitive?

She rifled through her purse and retrieved her cell phone. She dialed the number on Graventoll's profile, but it was out of service.

"Dammit," she whispered as she moved to the next profile.

Mark Vespe. She dialed and let the phone ring eight times before hanging up.

The third number was picked up after a single ring.

"Hello?" A male voice.

"Uh, hi, is this Eric Sparks?"

"Hang on."

She heard a loud whisper on the other end of the phone. "Carla. *Carla!* It's them."

A woman took the phone. "Hello? Who am I speaking with?" She sounded frantic—or maybe angry?

"My name is Allison Stevens, and I'm with a biotech company, Quandary Therapeutics. I'm looking for—"

"Listen to me, you fucking bitch. You owe us $50,000. Do you hear me? We want our money right fucking now. We followed all your fucking rules. We didn't talk to the cops. Now give us our money!"

Allison sat stunned, unable to breathe, let alone speak.

"You killed my brother with your stupid drug. I lost my brother because of you fucking bastards!" The woman screamed into the phone. "Now give us our fucking money!"

Finally, Allison spoke, barely a whisper. "I don't know what you mean."

That seemed only to infuriate the woman further. "I have your number now, you fucking bitch. I have your number! I'm gonna track you down. I have friends who will fuck you up. I'm gonna kill you."

Allison disconnected the call. Jesus Christ. Her breathing was shallow and fast. She glanced down at the one remaining profile with a phone number, Karen Richmond. With quivering fingers, she started dialing.

But before she could finish, a text message popped onto her screen. It was a video. She tapped the small triangle in the middle of the screen.

A man dressed in a football uniform pulled off his helmet and tossed it aside. He looked into the camera. "Okay, ready?"

"Yeah." The cameraman panned out to get the full view of the street.

"Okay. Hi, I'm Eric Sparks. Welcome to Jackass Live Edition!"

Eric started running at a full-out sprint. The shaky camera turned to follow him. Eric headed straight for an oncoming pickup truck, which seemed to be accelerating as it approached him. It looked like he was playing a stunt man version of the game chicken.

It took less than five seconds for the truck to meet Eric at what had to have been twenty or thirty miles an hour. Eric sprung off his feet to hurdle the oncoming vehicle. His leading foot landed with a sickening twist on the hood of the truck before his body cartwheeled. His head slammed into the windshield and then again on the tailgate as the truck sped past. The impact should have knocked him unconscious, if not killed him.

Instead, he sat up, shook his head as if clearing the cobwebs, and looked directly into the camera with a bloody smile.

"Did you get it? *DID YOU FUCKING GET THAT SHIT?!*" he screamed, his words noticeably slurred.

The video ended, and Allison read the message that followed: "This is what you turned him into. Rot in hell, bitch."

A picture of Eric Sparks lying unconscious in a hospital bed appeared next, as though the video wasn't convincing enough. Sparks was dead. The LXR drug had killed him. It had made him crazy, just like the chimpanzees.

Oh god.

The tingle in Allison's fingers spread up her arms and through her body, until every muscle trembled.

Another text message: "You killed my brother, bitch. Now I'm coming for you."

She dropped her phone onto the desk as if it had burned her hands. She stood up. Her legs buckled underneath her, and she collapsed back into her chair. She lay her head on her arms and closed her eyes.

So this was it. Austin had used her to pay for an illegal drug study that killed a subject. He'd framed her for this heinous crime. She might not rot in hell, but if she didn't figure out how to get herself out of this, she'd certainly rot in prison.

47

Malloy looked up at a gentle rap on his office door. Wang stepped into the office and closed the door behind him.

"I'm sorry to hear about your friend," Wang said.

"Thanks. I appreciate that."

"I received a call last night from my supervisor in Newark. My assignment here with the Phoenix office has ended. I'll be returning to New Jersey this afternoon."

"I assumed that would be the case. Thanks for all you've done for us." Despite Wang's unwavering formality, Malloy had grown fond of him.

"Sir, since I'll be back at my desk job, what if I called around to a few biotechs on the East Coast? Just see if we can get any leads? I know a lot of people there. Maybe if we hit the streets ..."

Malloy was touched by the gesture. It was evident that Wang wasn't just a bureaucratic desk jockey, and Malloy could see he was bothered by what could only be a bribe by some big-money pharma lobby. But like Garcia, Wang didn't understand the stakes, and Malloy wasn't willing to allow the man, who had a lovely wife and daughter back in New Jersey, to put himself or his family in harm's way.

He scowled and stood up from his chair, leaning over his desk. "Agent Wang, which part of 'the case is closed' did you not understand?"

Wang rocked back a step, startled. "None of it, sir."

"I don't know how you do things out there on the East Coast, but here we follow orders. Our criminal justice system was built on integrity, and part of that integrity requires compliance, even if we don't have full understanding of the reasons behind decisions that are made above our pay grade."

Malloy hated himself. He sat back down and turned toward his computer.

"I understand, sir." Wang left without another word.

"Shit." Malloy shook his head, disgusted, and picked up his phone receiver. "Garcia, get in here."

Garcia sauntered in and stood against the wall. He stretched a hairband off his wrist, pulled his hair back into a ponytail, and waited.

Malloy slumped over his desk with both hands wrapped around his coffee cup. The heat from the sunlight, which poured into the room through the west-facing windows, had long since overpowered the building's ancient AC system, but his hands were cold and clammy. He walked to the window, hoping the sun rays might form a fireball to blast right through the window and stop him from what he was about to do.

None came.

"I've been thinking," he began.

He didn't have to do this. There had to be other ways.

"Maybe we need to take a more aggressive approach."

Fuck. There it was. Out there, goddammit.

Garcia remained silent, and Malloy wondered if his message was too subtle. He could still back out.

But Garcia answered. "Yup."

It's Tyler Steele. Garcia's voice still rang in his head. He kept his gaze focused in the parking lot. "I sure would like to know what bank account deposited $50,000 into Karen Richmond's secret account."

He instantly regretted it and turned quickly, trying to find a way to take it back.

Garcia nodded. "Week or so." He left.

Malloy slowly returned to his desk and sat down, staring vacantly at his computer screen. His lips tightened over his teeth in an effort to hold in the barrage of curse words he needed to spew. He banged his fists on his desk, sloshing coffee onto his lap.

"Shit." He rolled his chair backward and brushed off the droplets.

He'd been thinking about that account ever since Lyle Richmond confessed. It was like a bad earworm, constantly nagging him to get off his ass and do something. He'd contacted the three other victims' families and gotten nothing. Either they hadn't gotten paid, or they didn't know anything about the source of the payment. It was possible they were lying, but it didn't matter. If they weren't going to give it up, he certainly wasn't going to pressure them. It was risky enough contacting them at all, given the circumstances of the case's closure.

But it had taken great courage for Lyle Richmond to come around. Sure, he did it because he was a man of God and probably thought his seat in heaven was at risk, but the man was clearly suffering. Malloy owed it to him to do his best to find the bad guys.

He got up and walked back to the window, where he stood with his hands on his hips, arching his back to relieve his aching lower back. He felt old. Old and tired and achy.

Lyle was just an excuse, he knew. Quite simply, this was all about Tyler Steele. He wouldn't let Tyler's death go unpunished any more than his own son's. But it was difficult to ignore orders, especially when the consequences of ignoring them had been made perfectly clear. And he had a lead, goddammit, something to follow other than scientific babble beyond his comprehension. A bank account was something he understood.

Follow the money. Every law enforcement agent knew it. Find the source of the money, and you find the source of the crime. But it wasn't easy to follow the money when you couldn't get a warrant, and right now, asking for help from a judge would likely get him fired. Or worse.

So now he'd done what any emotional cop who'd lost his objectivity would have done. He'd thrown his morality under the bus and gone for the nuclear option: Garcia's special gift.

Garcia's gift came in the form of a vast concealed network of ethically challenged associates who helped each other from time to time with just this kind of thing. Garcia didn't hide the fact that he had connections. The bureau had tried to recruit him precisely because of his channel into various hacking groups, and Garcia had refused their offer precisely because he wasn't ready to give it up. It was a valuable helpline when he needed to access it, but Garcia also didn't want to, as he had put it, wake up buried alive in a box six feet under somewhere in the middle of the Sonoran Desert.

Malloy had told Garcia from the beginning he didn't want to know anything about the network, and he'd never asked him to use it. Ever. Until today. It seemed like a small, inconsequential request, and Garcia's reaction—or more accurately, his nonreaction—probably meant that it was. But Malloy still felt ashamed, like a recovered addict who'd finally broken down and taken the hit. He wondered if this was the start of the downward spiral of his career. It happened to cops, he knew. Once they started working outside the law, it became too easy to continue. The golden seal had been broken.

Sweat beaded on his forehead as he stood in front of the unforgiving Arizona sun. He'd done enough unscrupulous work for the week. He packed his things and went home.

48

Layla was ten minutes early as she approached a small group of inductees standing together in the garden. Apparently, she wasn't the only one who was excited to be getting started with conditioning for purification.

"Layla! Oh my god!" Nicole ran over and threw her arms around her. "How come you didn't tell me?" She punched Layla in the arm a bit too hard.

Layla only smiled and enthusiastically greeted the others. "Sofia! Jonah! You guys were both selected?"

"This is so exciting!" Sofia exclaimed as she hugged Layla. "We'll be in the same class."

Jonah hugged Layla, too, picking her up off her feet. "Well, the Princess of Pain finally gets her calling."

"Don't call me that." She grimaced. The nickname had been around for as long as she'd been here, but she hated it. It was disrespectful to the process of purification, and she was certain that the father didn't approve of that kind of arrogance.

"Uh, could someone direct me to the trainee party?" A voice came from behind them.

"Isaac!" Nicole squealed, causing Layla to flinch.

Isaac dismissed Nicole and high-fived Jonah. Layla caught a brief glimpse of Nicole's crestfallen look and couldn't resist putting an arm around her friend's shoulder to cheer her up. As melodramatic as Nicole could be, she had a good heart.

"Who else is starting?" Sofia asked.

Sister Mia came over. "This is it, the five of you. Congratulations again, everyone." She hugged each of them. Then her face became somber, her voice reverent. "Let's sit in the garden together."

She led them to a quiet, secluded spot and lowered herself into the heel-sit position. Her hands lay gently across her legs, her head lowered slightly. Layla and the others followed her lead and lowered themselves into the same position, whispering "Thank you, Father," as they exhaled to release the pain of the pressure against their bruised shins. They sat silently, breathing in and out.

Finally, Sister Mia began. "Today I'm going to introduce you to the next phase of your journey, conditioning for purification. Let's express our gratitude to the Father and thank your own body and mind for what you've been able to accomplish."

Thank you, Father, for this opportunity and for giving me strength. Thank you, Layla, for accepting the gift of the Father, the gift of strength in mind and body, for enduring what was necessary to progress to this stage of purification.

"During the induction phase of your journey, you learned how to devote yourself—your entire being, mind, body, and spirit—to suffering," Sister Mia said. "You've endured extraordinary physical pain and sleep deprivation to help you overcome significant, even profound, mental and emotional obstacles. Reflect on your own development and give thanks."

Thank you, Father.

"As a result of your exceptional effort and endurance, your complete dedication to the Colony, and your devotion to the Father and his work here, you are among the very few chosen to become pure."

Layla could barely contain her excitement. She was chosen. Finally.

"As you all have been told many times over the course of your induction, the pure have a special place in our society. They have a duty and a moral obligation to lead the impure. They have a social responsibility to uphold and encourage the values of the Colony. And above all, they must comply with the requests of the Father and his leadership team. You are here today because you have proven ready to take this step. I am so proud of each one of you. Come."

Sister Mia stood and opened her arms.

Layla moved into Sister Mia's embrace, as did the others. She didn't know why, but she was crying. She turned her head and saw that Jonah was crying too. Sister Mia held them as they held each other, for several minutes. Layla didn't know if she'd ever felt such love, such a sense of family, of unity.

Of purpose.

***

"As trainees, the next several months will be quite taxing for you," Sister Mia said.

Layla hadn't known what happened during purification, but she hadn't thought it would require months. She glanced at Sofia, who shrugged back.

"I'm sure you have all expected that becoming pure is just a magic injection," Sister Mia continued. "Most incoming trainees have that impression. But I can assure you, there's so much more to it than that. It's what we call the conditioning process."

They followed Sister Mia, down past the river and into the grasslands toward the mountain.

"Your days will be filled from the moment you awaken to the moment you sleep. Your schedule will be tight. Strict. Every day, you'll train your body, mind, and spirit. You might think you've already experienced the most difficult part of the purification process, but no, this next step will shape who you will become here at the Colony or outside the Colony. How you progress over this next stage will determine your calling from the Father."

Layla replayed Sister Mia's words as they silently continued along the path. She was ready to do whatever would be asked of her.

Several minutes went by before Sister Mia spoke again. "We're coming to the trainee center, which is a special campus reserved only for conditioning and readiness for purification. For the next several days, I will introduce you to the many individuals who will be supporting you through your conditioning. Our trainees, which now include all of you, are our highest priority. We have world-class physical trainers and educators here who've given up their careers and lives in the impure world to develop our pure society. I want you to reflect on that. I want you to understand just what a privilege it is to be in this elite group."

Layla was too giddy to clear her thoughts long enough to thank the Father.

Sister Mia stopped at the door of a small building, which she opened with a key card. They entered into a small, unimpressive lobby with three elevator doors along one wall. Sister Mia pressed the call button. An elevator. Layla couldn't remember if she'd been on an elevator.

The door opened and they all shuffled into the small space. Layla felt a familiar stomach-dropping sensation as soon as the elevator began moving.

Okay, ready, Butch? One, two, three ... jump!

Her father's voice in her head startled her so much that she stumbled backward. Jonah caught her just as her tailbone touched the floor.

"Are you okay, Layla?" Sister Mia asked. "What happened?"

Layla chuckled and rubbed her tailbone, trying to appear nonchalant.

"She probably doesn't remember how to ride an elevator." Nicole was trying to be helpful in her garish way. "Right, Layla?"

But Layla could only grin ear to ear, flooded with joy at the memory of riding up and down the hospital elevators a dozen times with her dad. She wanted to close her eyes and relive it a while longer, but the door opened.

They stepped out of the elevator into an enormous room.

"Holy cow!" Jonah said.

"This is fantastic!" Isaac turned in a full circle.

Sophia was significantly less impressed. "A gym? We have to exercise?"

"Every day," Sister Mia said with a nod, "and you're all going to love it. Sofia, I once said the same thing. I was skinny my whole life and never felt like I needed to exercise, but this actually became my favorite part of the conditioning. It will make you feel amazing, with endless energy and strength."

A deep voice with a strong accent thundered from behind them. "Look at you, Mia, my girl, so strong. This, best part of conditioning. First and best."

Layla wheeled around as a six-foot bodybuilder strode toward them. He was dressed in form-fitting white shorts and a tank, definitely not Colony attire, and he had the largest biceps Layla had ever seen. His spikey neon-yellow hair stood two inches straight up, and Layla wondered if that could be his real hair color.

Sofia's smile told her that Sofia was about to have a miraculous change of heart about the gym.

"Welcome to my training center," he said, articulating each word carefully. His accent was thick. "My name is Dimitri. I am lead trainer. Congratulations to you. Your lives will change much in next months, starting here with me, yes?"

Layla glanced at Sofia, who was practically drooling, and smirked.

"You wonder my accent, yes? I come from Russia. I was professional bodybuilder and boxer, and I train others for top competition. One year ago, I come here to Colony to develop new trainees to be pure." He glanced down at his flip chart and gestured at them. "Who starting today? Nicole, Sofia, Layla. My new girls." He sized up Sophia and Layla. "You are too skinny, like small girls. Children. I will fix." He looked at Nicole. "You, good. Built solid. But not so much dessert, yes?" He winked at her, and opened his arms to the men.

Isaac and Jonah introduced themselves as Dimitri squeezed their biceps. "Good muscle tone, but I will make better. Tomorrow you begin physical conditioning first thing. Today I show you my gym, yes? This way."

He led them to a large area with treadmills, bikes, and other equipment that Layla had never seen. He moved into the center of the section, stepped onto a treadmill platform, and faced them.

"This is cardio center. Each day, you come here. You do one hour cardio training exercise of your choice: bike, treadmill, elliptical, AMT, rower. Each machine with fitness monitor. We record data each day to see progress for you." Dimitri flattened his palm across his chest, and his face changed from excited to somber. "The heart is most important muscle in body. Your heart become stronger each day. You push yourself harder each day."

He stated this as though it were law, nonnegotiable. Layla wondered if she could handle Dimitri's gym. She'd never really done much exercise except yoga, and he didn't seem like the type to appreciate a good backbend.

He led them to a well-equipped free weight area. "And you do weight training every day, one and half hour. Why, you ask? Because pure have special responsibility. Pure must be stronger, more physical than impure in poisoned world. Powerful. Superior."

He flexed his bicep, and Sofia sighed audibly.

"Yes? Understand? You must be extra, extra strong with top health to be ready for pure." He seemed to want to make this point very clear.

"Your training begin tomorrow morning. I will be here to guide you."

And with no goodbye, he turned and walked away.

***

Layla filled her lunch tray with turkey and mashed potatoes, even treated herself to a slice of pumpkin pie, and walked over to the picnic table where her group sat. Sofia had everyone's attention as she animatedly acted out a story.

She liked Sofia a lot and was thrilled that they would be roommates. They'd laughed and joked while trying to scoot the heavy bureaus to reorganize their new room. Sofia told stories about her job organizing the Colony's enormous brand-new shipping and receiving building, and Layla explained the secrets to making delicious salads. She admired Sofia's even temperament and relaxed, confident style, so different from her own shy, nervous demeanor. Maybe Sofia's personality would rub off over time.

She sat down and took a large drink of cucumber-infused water.

"I'm looking forward to the fitness program," Jonah said. "I was a wrestler in high school, and I was pretty good. Well, until I got mixed up in drugs."

"You were an addict?" Nicole asked through a mouthful of Italian bread.

He nodded. "Not something I'm proud of. It was always so hard for me to make weight, so I started taking drugs to control my appetite. You know what they say about gateway drugs. Long story short, I ended up in a drug den, high on heroin."

"Is that where you met the Colony recruiters?" Sofia asked.

"Sure is. I see it as perfect serendipity. If I hadn't been there, the recruiters never would have come across me. I'm not embarrassed by my poisoned life. It was just a step in becoming something better. I told Dr. Jeannette that when I'm pure, I want to join the recruiting team. Help others who were just like me."

"Wow, I never would've believed it," Sofia said. "You always seem so well put together—and no, I'm not flirting. You're not my type."

Nicole rolled her eyes. "Yeah, I think we all know what your type is. Yellow-haired Russian, maybe?"

"What? I don't know what you're talking about." Sophia gave a wave and changed the subject. "Isaac, did you do sports in high school?"

Isaac shook his head and swallowed a bite of chicken. "I don't think so. Maybe I did stuff when I was young, but I don't have any memories of my past."

"Are you a renewed?" Jonah was incredulous.

He nodded.

Layla put down her fork, her interest piqued at the word *memories*.

"What's that?" Sofia asked.

"People who don't have any memories of their poisoned life. We came here for a fresh start."

"Like Layla!" Nicole pointed a finger at her.

Layla shot her a look. She wished she'd never told Nicole about her lost memories.

But Sophia's attention was on Isaac. "What? You're kidding. Why would you do that?" She stared at him, a forkful of watermelon in the air, seemingly having forgotten she was eating.

"I had post-traumatic stress disorder."

She shoved her unfinished lunch to the side and leaned forward until her elbows were on the table. "Okay, stop right there. I want to hear this story from the beginning."

Isaac tossed his napkin on his half-eaten food, his appetite now ruined. "It's not a very nice story, and I only learned it from Dr. Jeannette. Apparently, our family lived in this bad neighborhood in Austin, Texas. I'd gotten caught up in a gang. One day, they killed a five-year-old girl who'd just moved into the neighborhood. It was a hate crime." He shook his head. "I guess they were sending a message that whites weren't welcome in our black neighborhood."

"Oh my god." Sophia looked riveted.

"So what the cops think happened is that I must have left the gang, or maybe I was going to turn them in, I don't know. Dr. Jeannette says I wouldn't even talk about it during hypnosis. But anyway, I guess they wanted to get even with me and deliver a message to others. They came to my house and killed my family."

Layla couldn't believe how impassively he spoke.

"When they found me, I was tied to a chair, badly beaten but alive. My little sister had been raped. My parents were beaten beyond recognition. The word 'traitor' was spray-painted across our living room wall."

"Jesus." Jonah straddled the bench so he could face his friend.

Isaac remained shockingly unemotional. "I ended up getting into the mess of social services, moved to a couple foster homes, bounced around for a few months. I hadn't spoken a word all that time. I guess I was too traumatized or something. Finally, some caseworker called Brother James, thinking it might be the only way I could be helped."

"Then what happened?"

"Dr. Jeannette showed me a video of my intake." His face clouded over. "God, I was so thin. My face was gaunt and ashy. I looked like I was just ...

just wasting away, like I was on the verge of disintegrating into a pile of dust."

He had a faraway look on his face, lost in the memory.

"Anyway, so in the video, Brother James asked for my consent to remove the memory of my poisoned life. I watched myself just stare at him with a completely blank look on my face, like I wasn't even in there. Finally, he said, 'Isaac, we need you to verbally give us permission to give you this treatment. You have to say yes. If you don't consent, we can't help you. But if you do consent, you'll have the opportunity for a whole new life. You can have a fresh start.' I croaked out the word yes. And that's the story." Now Isaac smiled. "The memory elixir saved me."

"The memory elixir," Layla repeated, unaware that she'd spoken aloud until everyone turned to her. "I've heard of that."

She'd heard of it, but where?

"Yeah, lots of people here are in the renewed cluster. It's a miracle, a savior for anyone who's had something horrible happen to them."

"But you don't have any memory of it? You don't remember your family at all, not even before that night?" Didn't he have visions?

He shook his head.

"Then how do you know it's true? How do you know all that horrible stuff happened?"

Isaac looked at her as if she was crazy. "Because that's what Dr. Jeannette told me. Why would she make it up?"

Sofia ran around the table to wrap her arms around Isaac, cooing how sorry she was for him. Nicole crawled over Layla to get in on the embrace.

Layla got up and stepped out of the way. She eyed Isaac, who politely hugged the girls in return but didn't seem in the least tormented by his own story. He didn't feel the pain or the loss of that night. He didn't have real memories. Layla didn't join the group hug. She didn't feel sorry for Isaac or his family.

Dr. Jeannette had told him that tale, and she didn't believe a word of it.

49

"**O**kay, you guys, this is some crazy, weird shit. Are you ready for this?"

Malloy cowered next to Garcia in a quiet booth in an unopen section of the Green Lizard Grill, apprehensively awaiting the results of Tyler Steele's blood and tissue analysis. Garcia had a Skype window open on his laptop, and Jordan Jennings' bushy head bobbed on and off of the video screen. Malloy hadn't told Jordan the victim was a friend—it hadn't seemed relevant—but now he feared that Jordan might be crass in reporting his findings, and he couldn't risk reacting emotionally instead of analytically.

Too late to worry about that now.

"Go on."

"Okay, here we go. Most important: This victim is different than the others. He doesn't have the mutated SCN9A gene the other patients had, so we did whole blood sequencing to look for anything unnatural. And you'll never guess where we found some highly unlikely mutations."

He turned from the camera and typed something onto his computer.

"Here it is. First, we noticed a mutation of the rs7294919 gene, which is on chromosome 12q24. This is common in older people and manifests as early Alzheimer's disease, but because he was so young, we thought this was weird enough to dig deeper. We expanded our analysis to other genes associated with Alzheimer's and found mutations in three more genes related to episodic memory and the largest Frankengene I've seen yet, a very strange rebuild of the KIBRA gene. Bizarre, right?"

"So what are you saying?" Garcia asked. "Someone wanted to give Tyler Alzheimer's disease?"

Jordan shook his head. "It's just my opinion, but I think this kid was a pincushion. I think he was being used for human experimentation with different genetic mutations related to episodic memory. Whoever did this sure did a number on this poor kid's brain. Probably completely scrambled it. Who knows what was left of him."

There it was. Malloy recoiled.

"See, here's the thing. Neurons and brain cells, which were the target of these modified genes, don't replicate like other cells. That means in order for the modified gene to work, you'd have to keep dosing again and again to eventually hit every cell."

Garcia turned to Malloy. "Like Lyle Richmond. He said he had to keep dosing Karen over a couple months, right?"

"So in our analysis, we used PCR to measure copy numbers of each of these genes, and the copy numbers varied significantly. If we assume they were using the same CRISPR platform to deliver the modified genes, it looks to me like they dosed him with different drugs over the course of some time. Months maybe. They might have been adding on new genes to the original ones or mixing cocktails of multiple Frankengenes to see what would happen."

An image of Nazi human experiments flashed through Malloy's mind.

"Fucking why?" Garcia moved to the edge of his chair, his face flushed.

"My guess is they were trying to figure out how to erase his memory, or aspects of his memory, without turning him into a vegetable."

"Did they? Did they turn him into a vegetable?" Malloy asked with a croak. He cleared his throat.

Jordan shrugged off the question. "There's more. The modified genes weren't restricted to the brain. We found them in the blood, and that wasn't the case for the other victims. The mad scientist seems to have refined his technology to transfect every cell type, and they delivered the drug systemically—intravenously, instead of through the port."

"What does that mean?" Garcia asked.

"I'm not sure why they would do that. These memory genes are only expressed in neurons, in the brain, and the Frankengenes these guys created are far too big to cross the blood–brain barrier. It doesn't make sense to inject them into the blood. All I can think of is that they were trying to prove that these megagenes can be delivered systemically with high uptake. Maybe they were just using this kid to see if there would be any toxic effects."

Malloy couldn't get the pincushion metaphor out of his head. "What did this do to him before they killed him? Was he a vegetable? Did he suffer?"

"I don't know." Jordan must have seen the grief on his face, because he visibly softened. "I just don't know. They hit him with so much over such a short period. No one's done this kind of thing before. I can't imagine what kind of adverse reactions he might have had." He dropped his head into his hands and ran his fingers through his hair, then looked intently into his camera. "But I can tell you this. If he was what I think he was, a human subject for what should have been an animal toxicology study, he'd have to have been dosed at a clinic of some kind, or there'd be an obvious needle pattern that the medical examiner would have found. Whoever did this to him knew what they were doing. Probably injected him at points all over his body."

"They didn't even need the spinal port." Malloy shook his head. Maybe that's why it had been removed.

"Why did they kill him?" Garcia asked.

Jordan's lips tightened and he shook his head. "When researchers run animal tox studies like this ... Well, if I ever tried this type of experimentation on an animal, even a mouse, I'd humanely euthanize it right after obtaining the results."

For the first time, Malloy hoped that what Jordan was suggesting was true. A heroin overdose was an awfully peaceful way to leave this life, especially for someone who'd been tortured like a lab rat.

"There's one additional finding I think might be important. We found an allele variation of stathmin, which is related to amygdala function."

Malloy rubbed his temples. It was already too much science to process in his heightened emotional state. "Jordan, please try to dumb this down to a level we can understand. Think fourth grade." He really wanted the call to be over.

"I skipped fourth grade," Jordan replied with a grin.

"The amygdala—it's the fight-or-flight organ," Garcia said.

Malloy gaped at him.

"Word." Jordan's enormous head bounced up and down in agreement. "I've heard it described as the alarm circuit of the body. A poorly functioning amygdala would turn that alarm off or at least quiet it, if that makes sense. This mutation was found in this victim, and guess what? We also found it in all the other victims."

Malloy leaped up, now excited. "The original eight victims. They couldn't feel pain—"

"—and they had no alarm system," Garcia finished. "They had no survival instinct."

The PCP behavior. That was it.

"Jesus. Garcia, we gotta find that clinic."

50

Layla wrapped the hospital gown around her tightly as she waited for Dr. Jeremy. Her feet dangled off the exam table, and she wished she had some booties. She passed the time by picking at her hangnails. It was a terrible habit, she knew. When she was pure, she was certain the impulse would be gone.

Dr. Jeremy entered the room, his eyes buried in a medical chart. "Layla, how are you today?"

He was always enthusiastic. He seemed to love his job. "Fine, Doctor."

"Any incidents like the one you had a couple of weeks ago?"

"No."

"And how have you been eating? And drinking?"

"Fine, I think."

"You know, down here, we have to drink a lot more. You may not be used to drinking as much as you need to in this part of the world, and now that your conditioning has begun, you'll need even more."

"I know. Eight glasses a day."

"Let's see how you're doing." He pulled his stethoscope into his ears and began his exam.

Twenty minutes later, Layla was dressed and sitting opposite him across his luxurious office desk. He appeared pleased with her exam.

"Aside from that bite in your tongue, which should heal in a couple of weeks, you're healthy as an ox." He shook his head. "I can remember when you first started induction. You were so weak, so frail, I thought you might break during your cleanse. But now you're a good, healthy weight. Your menstrual cycles are regular again, and assuming your Pap results are normal, you're the perfect trainee."

She beamed with pride as he turned to type his report. Now it was time for the question she'd been waiting to ask since the moment she'd walked into Dr. Jeremy's office. She hoped it wouldn't mar his positive opinion of her.

She gathered her courage. "Dr. Jeremy, am I part of the renewed cluster?"

He seemed surprised by the question. "Yes, you are."

"What does that mean?"

"Well, we have a number of members here at the Colony who've either lost their memories or chosen to have them erased."

Dr. Jeannette had told her she lost her memories in a traumatic event, but she was sure she'd overheard her talking about the memory elixir. "Were my memories erased? Was I given the memory elixir like Isaac?"

His eyes were on his computer screen, and he seemed to not hear her question. "Those in the renewed cohort are particularly fortunate. You should feel very privileged and grateful."

"But why? What does the memory elixir—"

He pivoted to face her with an admonishing look. "Layla, there are many aspects of our Colony that are beyond our understanding, and showing your readiness for purification means showing your unconditional devotion to the Father. You need to trust his plan for you. When you question your circumstances here at the Colony, that's a sure sign that you're not ready for purification."

Although he spoke in a soft, measured tone, Layla heard the warning. She pressed her lips tightly together. He resumed typing his report, and she sat back in her chair and pouted. So many questions. If they'd purposely wiped out her memories, why was Dr. Jeannette trying to make her remember a past that wasn't real? Why had Dr. Jeannette lied to her about her poisoned life? Why did Layla feel compelled to keep her memories a secret?

Dr. Jeremy must have sensed her frustration. He stood up and moved around to her side of the desk and half sat on it, facing her.

"Listen, Dr. Jeannette may disagree with me on this, but if you want my opinion, I think you should spend less time thinking about your past and more time planning for your future. The next weeks and months are crucial. You need to give one hundred percent to your conditioning. Don't worry so much about what you can't remember."

She took the opportunity to press further. "But what if I can remember some things? What if my memory isn't a hundred percent gone?"

"Well, no one's memory is ever a hundred percent gone. That's why you can walk and talk. And some memories are deeply ingrained. Emotions, for example. You might remember something that made you extremely sad or angry or happy."

She seemed to have plenty of memories that made her sad.

"Music, art, creative moments … These are also difficult to lose." He pointed to a painting hanging on the wall opposite his desk. "Take a look at that. Any idea who painted it?"

Brilliant colors splattered and dripped across the canvas. The piece filled her with both wild exuberance and deep loss.

The name sprang to her lips. "Jackson Pollock." She gasped, awestruck by her own memory.

"There you have it." He smiled briefly. "But keep in mind, the brain is a complex organ. It's capable of repressing memories deep into your unconscious, but it's also capable of creating false memories of events that never actually occurred."

He regarded her carefully while she processed his words. Was he suggesting the memories she'd had of her real dad might not be real?

He returned to his chair. "Okay, we need to schedule your next appointment. Please track the exact days of your menstruation for next time. And I'll be taking blood then so we can check your labs. That means I expect to see the positive impact of your new diet. And keep up the good work with Dimitri. You got me?"

"Yes, sir." She saluted him. It was a peculiar thing for her to do. Where had she learned that?

"I'll put you in for next Wednesday. How's that sound?"

"Okay. Is that when I'll get my purification port?" Layla knew she sounded too anxious, but she couldn't help it.

Dr. Jeremy tilted his head. "Purification port? Where'd you hear about that?"

"Nicole. She told me about a friend who had gotten a port in his back. You know, for the injections."

"Ah, well, the ports are a thing of the past. The injections now are intravenous."

"Oh." She was disappointed. She'd been looking forward to the port. It was like a trophy.

"If you have any questions, give me a call or stop by. And good luck with your conditioning."

He closed the door as soon as Layla stepped through.

***

Layla climbed into her new bed. Sofia was jabbering away about something related to her physical exam, but she wasn't listening. She felt around under her bed and pulled out the book she'd hidden there. Even at ten o'clock, the sky hadn't completely darkened, and she could still make out Westley's and Buttercup's features. She closed her eyes and tried to envision herself as Buttercup, with her flowing dress and long, silky hair.

"Are you even listening?" Sofia demanded.

"Yes, well ... Sorry, what was the last part?"

"I don't understand why he thinks I'm too skinny. Thin people are healthy people. He's making me drink an extra protein shake every day. They're so gross."

"He's just trying to make you healthy as an ox. Purification is tough on the body." Layla smiled with satisfaction. For once, she wasn't the underweight one of the group.

"I don't know why I have to be an ox. Why can't I be a beautiful and slender cheetah? Or maybe a sly, fast-as-lightning fox?" Sofia yawned.

Layla opened the front cover, feeling the overwhelming whoosh of butterflies fill her insides. Then holding back as long as she could, she read Brother James's words: "As you wish." Her stomach fluttered again. She turned to the earmarked page and read to herself, mouthing the words of the hero, Westley: *You thought I was answering 'As you wish' but that's because you were hearing wrong. 'I love you' was what it was, but you never heard, and you never heard.*

She smiled, as she did every night when she read the passage. Brother James had sent her a secret message in his inscription. He loved her. He loved her! Despite the fluttering in her stomach, she could barely keep her eyes open, so she tucked the book under her covers and closed her eyes.

***

"Hey, Butch!" Daddy calls from the bottom of the stairs.

"Busy!" I call back.

Vanessa and I are having a contest for who can make the best spin-art to give as a gift to Mr. Marokesh. I personally think mine is better, but she insists that purple and yellow are better colors for man teachers than red and pink. I decide to try a green and purple. I pour in the colors.

"Why does he call you that?" Vanessa asks.

I roll my eyes dramatically and sigh. "There's some dumb cowboy called Butch who has my middle name." I hate having a cowboy's name. And I really hate being called Butch.

I hit the spin button and wait.

"Butch Cassidy!" I hear again from downstairs.

"Hang on, be right back." I jump off the bed.

"I got you something," he taunts in a singsong voice.

"What is it, Daddy?"

I bounce down half the stairs, then hop with one butt-cheek onto the banister, slide to the bottom, and land on his lap. He catches me before I crush him with my sixty-four pounds. It's our amazing daddy-daughter stunt, which we've perfected over two years. He says I only have six more pounds, max, before I'll squash him through the floor.

"Check it out." He rolls me over to the table and opens a bag. He pulls out a slightly battered VHS tape. "This is only the greatest movie of all time. It's the film that made your mother fall in love with me. I highly resemble the hero in the movie."

"Funny," Mom calls from the kitchen.

"I thought it's about time you watch it. That way, you'll have an idea of what true love is supposed to look like."

"Ew." I make a face. I'm not at all interested in a boring love movie, and I need to get back to my spin-art before Vanessa uses the rest of the blue. "Okay, thanks!"

I grab the movie and hop off his lap.

But Vanessa wants to watch it because it has the word princess *in the title. So we put away the spinner, but only after we decide that my green and purple design is the best. I eject* A Bug's Life *and push the new tape into the VCR. We hop up onto the bed, lie on our bellies with our chins cradled in our palms, and watch the movie.*

It's the best movie of all time. I dream of being Buttercup, living happily ever after with my Westley.

***

Layla's eyes popped open, and she felt immediately disoriented. She turned toward the only light in the room and saw it was 4:47. From the other side of the room, she could hear Sofia softly breathing.

She closed her eyes, trying to fall back into the dream. She wanted one more slide down the banister into her dad's lap. She could feel the slick wood under her right cheek. It was so familiar. She must have done it a million times.

"I have to kick off with my foot before I hit the knob at the bottom," she whispers, "or I'll get one doozy of a bruise on my hip."

Whoa, Butch, that's one doozy of a bruise.

Doozy. She liked the word.

She drifted back to sleep.

51

*Y*ou killed my brother with your stupid drug.

Allison woke up to the sound of her phone vibrating. She pulled the covers over her head and rolled over.

I have friends who will fuck you up.

The vibrating stopped for a minute and then started again. Annoyed, she felt around for her phone and, opening only one eye a crack, read the display. Ryan Garner. The call disconnected and her display read, "Ryan Garner, 14 Missed Calls."

Grunting, she dropped her phone and staggered to the bathroom. What day was it? How many days of work had she missed? Three? Four?

She shuffled to the window and shifted the blackout blinds an inch to scan the parking lot. Agent Gadorski's car was still parked next to hers, though she couldn't tell if he was sitting inside. She dropped the blinds and looked around the room. Maybe he'd bugged her apartment. Maybe he'd installed hidden cameras. He could be watching her right now.

Her legs started to wobble, and she moved back to the edge of the bed, bracing herself through a wave of dizziness. Once it passed, she reached for the emergency bottle of oxycodone that sat open on her bedside table. She shook the remaining pills into her hand. Two. A rush of panic swept through her, and her head throbbed. She fisted them tightly, afraid they'd disappear, then picked up the closest vodka bottle and filled a glass three fingers high to wash the pills down.

The smell of the vodka sent another wave of dizziness through her, and she lay back until it passed. Her fist clenched tighter around the pills. She took a deep breath and exhaled with a groan. The vibration from the groan eased her stomach for a second, but she still couldn't sit back up. She closed her eyes and felt the room spin. It kept spinning, and spinning, until she finally slid back into blessed sleep.

***

Someone was trying to drive a nail through her skull. Or at least that's what it sounded like, but as she stirred awake, she realized the hammering was coming from her apartment door. She groaned and squeezed her eyes shut and waited for it to stop, but the pounding continued. Thirty seconds, one minute. God, they were relentless.

Furious, she stood up and wrapped herself in her blanket, wiping stringy, dried saliva from her mouth as she shuffled to the door and opened it a crack. The sunlight was so blinding she stepped back, tripped on the blanket, and landed on her backside with a *whump*.

"Cruella, where the fuck have you—"

Ryan caught his breath as he stepped in the door and looked down at her.

"Allison?"

She didn't answer.

"Jesus." He closed the door behind him and looked around the apartment. "Jesus."

In her head, she answered him with *It's nothing, I'm fine.* What came out was "Nossin. Fahn."

"Jesus, god." He pulled her off the ground. He held her steady with a firm grip around each arm, but her neck felt like rubber and her head wobbled. He looked deep into her eyes. "Allison. The board meeting. I've been trying to call you for days. Today's the board meeting. It starts in an hour."

She thought she might collapse.

"Do you hear me, Allison? Are you in there? You need to go take a shower now and get dressed. Jesus." In a whisper, he asked, "What did you take?"

She looked away. The fog was starting to clear, and she felt ashamed. "I'm fine."

"Oh my god."

He spun her around and half dragged her through the bedroom to the bathroom. He dropped her onto the toilet and turned on the shower.

"No, stop."

But she was no match for him, and he forcibly shoved her into the shower, fully clothed.

"You need to sober up right now, Allison Stevens. You're about to flush your entire career down the toilet."

The water was frigid and she gasped and sputtered, clawing at him and struggling to get out. He held her there, his dress shirt and tie completely soaked. Her stomach contracted, and she turned and vomited. She fell to her knees and vomited again. And again. Ryan pulled her wet hair away from her face and waited. But the heaving continued for what felt like forever.

***

Allison closed the office door behind her. She really needed some time alone, but Carol hadn't seemed to get the message and knocked twice before opening the door and poking her head inside.

"What happened?" Carol asked. "Is the board meeting over?"

She shook her head. "I was asked to leave."

"Really? Well, you probably aren't missing much. Austin was always complaining about how boring the discussions were."

She sighed. She still felt ill, and she didn't have the energy to engage in a long, drawn-out story with her gossipy assistant.

"No, I was asked to leave Quandary. Forever. I was fucking the boss, you see, and the board frowns upon on that. Since I have no scientific skill, or really any skill whatsoever other than"—she pointed two thumbs at her pelvis—"the obvious, they suggested I look for employment elsewhere."

Carol gaped.

Allison moved toward the door, forcing Carol to step backward out of her office. "Now, if you'll excuse me, I'd like to get packed up."

She closed the door and stood with her back against it.

She looked around the office and realized she had nothing worth packing up. Not a single picture on her desk or framed achievement propped up on a bookshelf. The desk held nothing but office supplies. Her computer belonged to Quandary. Her DMD program files would go to whoever replaced her.

She listlessly picked up her gym bag. She hadn't used it in weeks.

As she turned to leave, her eye caught the yellow file folder with the title B. Elliott, the file that Elaine had given to her. God, that felt like ages ago.

She picked it up, dropped it into her gym bag, and trundled out the door.

52

M alloy stepped out of the car into the late morning sun. The parking lot of the Claim Jumper Restaurant in Prescott was nearly empty, and Malloy figured the timing was perfect. He wanted to have a conversation with the on-duty manager, which would be impossible during the lunch rush.

Their interview list was short, which probably was for the best, given this was technically unofficial business. Malloy's jaw clenched at the memory of Tyler's half-smirk, a characteristic expression for as long as Malloy could remember. *All I do is work and binge Netflix*, Tyler had told Malloy months ago, content with his new, quiet life.

Garcia moved next to him, and they walked inside. The sweet smell of warm apple pie filled the lobby, and he knew they wouldn't be leaving until Garcia had a slice in his bottomless pit of a stomach.

"Hey there, two for lunch?" A smiling hostess greeted them.

"Please."

As they sat down, Malloy said, "We'd like to have a word with the manager. Is he or she available?"

"Um, I'm not sure. I can check. I know he was wrapped up in some paperwork."

Garcia wasn't wasting any time. He pulled out his badge. "We're with the DEA, working on a high-priority case. Let him know it's urgent."

The hostess's eyes grew wide. "Uh, okay. I'll tell him." She scurried into the kitchen.

Malloy shot Garcia a silent look. Teaching moments were a thing of the past. Garcia would always be emotional and impatient, with a strong preference for colorful language, but he was such a good agent that Malloy was willing to overlook these minor flaws.

After a few minutes, a man dressed too casually to be a store manager strode over to Malloy's table. "Carl Hutton. What can I do for you?"

Malloy sensed he was irritated and decided he'd talk to Garcia about his professionalism after all on the drive back to Phoenix.

"Mr. Hutton, I'm Special Agent Peter Malloy and this is Agent Garcia. We were wondering if we could have a few minutes of your time regarding an employee of this restaurant."

"Who is it?" Hutton pulled a chair from another table and sat at the end of the booth.

"Tyler Steele."

"Tyler hasn't worked here for months," Hutton said, still irritated. "Just quit, didn't give notice, not even a call. He just didn't show up for work and never came back. Unprofessional as hell. They called me over here from North Phoenix temporarily, and they're still looking for a permanent store manager."

"Do you have any idea why he left?"

"Nope. Never even met the guy."

"Did he make contact after he left?"

"Not with me. What's this about? Is he busted for drugs or something?"

Malloy ignored the question. "Did he leave any of his belongings behind? In a locker or something?"

"Nope." Hutton sat back and crossed his arms over his chest. "Listen, I don't know what he's done, but I can tell you, if he comes crawling back and thinks he'll be able to get his old job back, he's gonna be awfully disappointed. This ship has left the station."

Malloy stifled a smirk at the botched idiom, but Garcia was beginning to fume. Hutton wasn't going to be much help. "Well, Mr. Hutton, thanks for your time. We don't have any other questions."

Hutton walked away without another word.

"What an asshole," Garcia grumbled.

The hostess brought over two glasses of water and set them down, then glanced over her shoulder to see if Hutton was still in the front. "I'm sorry for eavesdropping, but I heard you asking about Tyler."

"Do you know him?" Garcia asked eagerly. "Do you know why he left?"

"We were friends." She looked over her shoulder toward the kitchen again. "I'm pretty sure he joined a cult."

"A cult?" Malloy wasn't sure he heard correctly. He caught a glance at the waitress's name tag. Tori.

"Yeah, well, some people came into the restaurant one day," she said. "It was slow, sort of like how it is now. They sat at a booth and started talking to some of the staff about some place. You know, like a better place. I thought they were like those Mormons who go around trying to get people to join?"

"Missionaries," Garcia offered.

"Right. Yeah, so at first, we were all sort of giggling, but then they started talking about something else. It wasn't like religious. They were talking about like a way to cleanse your body and soul from poison. They said we could start our lives all over, like remove all the bad from ourselves and have a new beginning. They talked about how they cured someone who had brain cancer. It was a little creepy to me, so I didn't hang around. I went and told Tyler, and he came out of the office to throw them out. You know, like, no soliciting. But he started listening to them."

Tori glanced back at the door to make sure no one was waiting to be seated.

Malloy's pulse picked up.

"Yeah. He sat down in the booth with the three of them, and they talked to him for like hours. The whole dinner shift came and went, and we were all working. And he was still there, listening and nodding."

"Do you know who they were?" Garcia asked. "Was it a specific religion?"

"I don't think it was a religion. It seemed more like just a cult. You know, like where you'd go to drink peyote and grow your own vegetables."

"Did they have any material? A pamphlet?" Malloy racked his brain trying to think of any cult-like operations or compounds in the area. Nothing came to mind.

She shook her head.

"So then what happened?" Garcia asked.

"They finally just left. Tyler went back into the office. I followed him and asked him what he thought of them. He just shrugged and said he didn't know. But then a couple days later, he was asking all the staff if anyone wanted to buy his Kia. I would've loved to, but he wanted four thousand and I didn't have that kind of money."

She shook her head at the absurdity.

"He was trying to sell the car because he was planning to leave?" Malloy asked.

"He never said. That's just what I put together. Then a couple weeks later, he sent me a text and said he wouldn't be coming back to work. He was going to go live in the middle of the desert and become pure. Here." She pulled out her phone from her apron. "I kept his text, just because, you know, if he, like, shows up someday with superpowers ..."

Malloy and Garcia leaned over in unison to read the text message, including her reply, "Whatever they give you, bring some back for me." He was sure they were thinking the same thing: Tyler must have thought they could cure his HIV.

"Anyways," she continued, "when you find him, tell him I miss him. Carl's kind of a hard ass, if you know what I mean."

***

It wasn't until Garcia merged onto I-17 that Malloy finally spoke.

"When we get back to Phoenix, see if you can find anything about any new age centers, compounds, spiritual groups, healing groups ..." He fished around his bag for his Tums.

"Sure thing, boss."

"Not the usual suspects." They'd already investigated several pop-up camps in the area, particularly near the spiritual center of Sedona. Most were small and low-tech, often no more than groups of twenty-somethings set up in tents around campfires to explore the ego-altering effects of hallucinogens in an attempt to elevate themselves to a god-like status. Those groups rarely lasted through the winter. Evidently, God finally got cold too. "We'll be looking for a legitimate operation. Brick and mortar. A place that would have the resources to engage a dedicated recruiting team."

"Yep."

Malloy didn't want to ask, but he felt emboldened by this new turn of events. "Anything on the bank account?"

"Not yet. But I've been chasing another lead. I found this pain clinic in Las Vegas. They offer free pain services to anyone who doesn't have insurance, and it's not far from the largest shelter in Vegas. Supposed to be working in alternative medicines and THC. Anyway, the clinic seems to be closed, but I found out who opened it. Guy by the name of Jonathan Chambers."

"Why do I know that name?" Malloy shook two Tums from his bottle.

"He's all over the news. Vocal about the opioid crisis, and I guess he's involved in some drug legislation in New Jersey. Anyway, I have a call in to his office, wanna see if I can get hold of someone from that clinic. Maybe they've seen the Does with the port."

Malloy cracked the Tums with a sharp tap of his teeth. Things were looking up.

53

"Hi there, sweetie. What can I getcha?" The Morristown Diner waitress was far too perky for Allison's mood.

"Turkey club and a Diet Coke, please," she responded with far less friendliness. Austin's favorite diner meal was the turkey club, and she used to tease him about how he lacked a refined palate. *You always go with the safe bet in these kinds of places,* he'd told her. She wasn't sure why she'd just ordered Austin's goddamn sandwich—for breakfast, no less. Guess she needed one safe bet in her life.

Because all other bets were off. No job, no family, no friends. Instability was her Achilles heel, and she felt like she was drifting away. Like she'd lost every anchor that kept her feet solidly on the ground. Even the threat of being arrested no longer alarmed her. Being locked in a cell might just keep her from floating off into oblivion.

But one thing was certain. When she walked into the office of the FBI, she'd be prepared. She'd have the complete story with documented proof of Austin's reprehensible study and how he'd set her up to take the fall. And just like all good stories, it would start with the illegal bank account. Follow the money. The bank statements would tell the story. They always did.

She glanced at her watch. Forty-five minutes until the Delbarton Bank opened for business.

She pulled the B. Elliott folder from her bag and began what now felt like a ritualistic review of the patients who'd taken LXR102016. She'd scoured the names a dozen times already, spent most of the night dissecting the patient profiles. Four of them couldn't be found on the internet. They'd been paid $1,000 in cash, and based on their sparse personal information and disheveled profile photos, she assumed they'd been homeless. Were they still alive? She had no way of knowing.

But she was fully aware of the death of Jake Graventoll, the BASE jumper who died during a particularly dangerous jump, and Mark Vespe, the college student who died at a frat party. She was certain the LXR drug had somehow been responsible for their deaths. *This is what you turned him into*, the woman on Eric Sparks's phone had said.

She closed her eyes and silently recited a prayer. *In your hands, O Lord, we humbly entrust our brothers and sisters. In this life you embraced them with your tender love; deliver them now from every evil and bid them eternal rest.* She crossed herself. She hadn't done that for years, but it still felt natural.

The last patient, Karen Richmond, was a mystery. There were a lot of Karen Richmonds out there, and Allison had found none related to a recent death. She traced Karen's image with her finger. Short, straight light brown hair. A very pretty face but no smile. She looked unhappy. If she were still alive, she could—

"Hello, Allison. It's nice to see you." Agent Gadorski stood at the end of her table.

She slammed the folder shut.

"Are you okay? You look upset." He smiled as warmly as his boorish detective face could.

"Are you here to arrest me?" She knew he wasn't, or he'd have walked her out of the restaurant. She remembered how impersonal and efficient he'd been when he arrested Austin. He certainly hadn't bothered with niceties then.

He lost his smile. "Mind if I join you?" He sat down opposite her in the booth before she could answer.

"Actually, I was just—"

"About to eat a turkey club, right? I won't stay long. I just wanted to let you know I had a nice chat with Jackie Harris yesterday. She seems to know you quite well. You know, she hired a private detective to follow you. She knows all about your long relationship with her husband."

He leaned down on his elbows, closing the distance between them with his face only inches from hers. Allison understood the importance of body language in a power situation, and she didn't move, even though he was radically invading her space.

"Do you know what I think, Allison?" His breath was hot on her face, and his voice became even huskier than usual. "I think you're in on this with Austin. Before, I thought you were probably just an accessory, but now I think you're an accomplice. Do you know the difference? As an accomplice, you can be arrested and tried for these criminal activities all by yourself, even if Austin's never found."

Is this what Austin had been hoping for? That she would serve his sentence?

"And do you know why I think this? Two reasons. One, you're ideally positioned as his lover and his, what do you call it, chief of staff? Yeah. Until you regretfully got fired, you were perfectly primed to have an influence on the board of directors. To buy time with the SEC auditors, create a diversion whenever we got close. This is something the two of you have been building for years, isn't it?"

He paused as though he expected an answer.

"Two, Austin Harris is a brilliant, calculating criminal with enough charm and money to convince a small army to work with him. But far as I can tell, the only person he picked to stand by his side was you. If he wasn't sure you could be trusted as his partner, he would have set up an insurance plan. I don't see an insurance plan. I just see you. And I don't think you're capable of saying no to the man you're in love with."

Gadorski sat back and gestured to the whole of the diner. "What else do you have in this life, Allison? Nothing. You know who summed it up nicely? Jackie Harris. 'Gary,' she said to me, 'that little bitch has been trying to steal my life with Austin from the day she met him.'"

He was taunting her into a confession, and she almost gave in.

Almost.

"Are you absolutely sure you don't have something you want to tell me? Something that will make me think you're on the right side of the law?"

"Not today, Gary. Maybe tomorrow." Her appetite, poor as it was these days, was gone. She stood up, gathered her things, and strode away from the table, not bothering to alert her waitress.

"Good to hear," he called after her. "I'll check in with you again, Allison."

Her time was running out.

54

Vincent Wang hoisted himself out of his SUV into the oppressive ninety-percent humidity. The sun hid behind clouds, but the air temperature was already in the high eighties, and he simply wasn't built for heat. Sweat dripped down his chest and trickled into the folds of skin around his midsection. He withdrew his handkerchief from his pants pocket and mopped his face. He would lose the weight this year. It was a promise he made every year when the New Jersey heat became unbearable. He already missed the dry heat of Arizona. Maybe he'd request a transfer to the Phoenix office. He really liked Special Agent Malloy, even if he was a bit on the rough side.

He leaned back against his truck, gathering his courage. The LXR case had truly been an adventure compared to the drivel he dealt with on a daily basis—FDA audits, site inspections, trips to Newark International to ensure the proper shipping documents accompanied boxes of drug substance. But when Garcia had called asking for a favor, he'd hesitated. Calling biotechs or engaging his professional network was one thing, but schmoozing was not his strength, especially when the schmoozing required getting bank account information for which he had no warrant.

"Malloy won't call you for help," Garcia had said. "He's just not that kinda guy. But listen, we're so close to finding these bad guys. My buddies found the bank and the account number that paid Karen Richmond, but the personal details are kept on a different server. It'll be days before I can get a name."

"Danny, it's illegal. They're not going to give me anything."

"Come on, man, give it a try. Just feel 'em out. Wear your badge where they can see it. Worst they can do is ask you to come back with a warrant. If that happens, just smile and leave."

He'd still hesitated.

"Please, man. Please. Tyler. He was a friend. He was a son to Malloy. You know it."

Garcia had won, and here he stood.

He glanced at the door of the Delbarton Bank, wishing desperately that Garcia were here to do this instead. Skills aside, Garcia's handsome, eccentric Mexican-American Indian look opened a lot more doors than the pleading face of a sweaty, obese, middle-aged Asian.

A woman with a child came out just as a young woman stepped inside. It would probably be easiest to do this when the bank had customers. They'd be more likely to move him along. It was now or never.

He mopped his face one last time and walked toward the bank.

55

Allison stood in the teller line of Delbarton Bank, nervously chewing the skin on her thumb. As she neared the front, she reached into her folder for the page with the account information. Where was it? She knelt and opened the folder on the floor, riffling through the documents.

"Excuse me, ma'am."

A heavyset man loomed over her. He wore a badge that read DEA on a lanyard around his neck. His face was shiny with sweat, and his eyes turned into small crescent moons with his smile, which might have made Allison smile back under different circumstances.

"I just need to get by you, sorry." He pointed to the cubicle on the other side of the line. On the outside of the cubby hung a placard that read Julia Esposito, Assistant Branch Manager.

"Oh, uh, sorry. Of course." She snatched up her papers and rose, stepping back to let him pass. Her eyes followed him as he ambled over to the cubicle and said something to the woman behind the desk that she couldn't hear.

"Next, please." The teller was motioning her to step forward.

"Uh, sorry—I just need to, uh …" She moved over to the island counter, her attention glued to the man at the desk of the assistant manager.

"This is quite urgent, as I'm sure you can imagine," she heard him say.

"We believe the owner of this account might be responsible for a drug that has killed several people."

Oh god. He was looking for her.

She jerked away from the counter and her purse tangled in the chain of a counter pen, spilling its contents all over the marble floor. Every head turned in her direction.

The DEA agent was the only one who got up to help.

"Are you okay there?" He awkwardly bent down on one knee to help her pick up her things.

"Yeah. I—I just ... my purse just hooked ..." She jammed the papers back into the folder, then picked up her sunglasses. One of the lenses had popped out, and she scanned the floor for it.

"Here you go, Allison."

Her head spun around.

"Your name—right here on your phone." He held out her phone, one finger pointing to the business card she'd taped to the case. He smiled, and the crescent moons appeared again.

"Thank you." She could only whisper, waiting for him to say *I'm afraid I'm going to have to place you under arrest.*

He put one hand on his large knee and stood back up with a grunt. "Happens to the best of us." He winked at her with one crescent moon.

She forced a smile and walked to the door as calmly as she could. Once in the parking lot, she ran to her car.

56

Allison pulled into a shady picnic area near Lake Parsippany and turned off the engine. Except for a handful of crows pecking at scattered trash, she was alone. Not surprising with the heat and humidity at its highest. The place would be packed by five o'clock. She watched the entrance to the parking lot for several minutes, expecting a police car to pull in next to her. Today would be her last day of freedom. As soon as that DEA agent in the bank realized that those patients had been paid from her account, there would be a warrant for her arrest. Her time was up.

She needed a lawyer. She pulled out her phone.

You killed my brother with your stupid drug.

Her mouth felt as dry as straw, and the thought of hiring an attorney seemed somehow so overwhelming that she simply stared at the Google search page, her brain paralyzed.

Without thinking, she texted Ryan. "Wanna grab a beer?"

Shit. What was she doing? It wasn't even noon yet.

A quick reply. "Sorry—AC. Ad board for the Alz Dis portfolio."

Her heart sank. She was supposed to have been in Atlantic City at that advisory board meeting with Austin. He'd been excited about moving into Alzheimer's disease.

A second text appeared. "Oops. I probably shouldn't have told you that. Pls delete."

Jerk. Did he really think she was going to immediately pick up her phone and dial some biotech stock analyst—

Her phone whistled again with a third text. "We probably shouldn't hang out anymore."

That stung, and she collapsed over the steering wheel, wanting to sob, but no tears would come. She couldn't blame Ryan for walking away. They weren't friends, really. She'd been aloof, probably downright hostile, toward him since he'd joined Quandary. He'd responded by dubbing her Cruella de Vil and shutting her out of his deals. And of course, there was the unpleasant scene at her apartment yesterday.

Her face crumpled and she shook her head. How had she ended up here? In this place in life?

She opened the glove compartment and pulled out a flask Austin had given her when she graduated with her master's. She read the inscription: To Ease the "Pain."

Just one swig to loosen her up. She took a long drink of the vodka and put it back. She dialed a number by memory and took a deep breath, exhaling slowly while the phone rang on the other end.

"Hello?"

"Hi, Mom." Her voice cracked and tears welled up in her eyes.

"Allison?"

"Yeah."

After a long pause, "Why are you calling? Are you in trouble?"

Still unable to speak without sobbing, she grabbed a handful of hair and pulled, hoping the physical pain would override her emotional anguish.

"Jesus, Allison, what is it? Money? Is that why you're calling me? Of course, it is."

"No, I—"

"Charles," her mom called out. "It's Allison. She's calling for money."

Allison disconnected the call. She hurled the phone onto the seat next to her and threw open the car door. She surged out of the car and bellowed, "Fuck you! Fuck everyone!"

You killed my brother with your stupid drug.

All the energy drained out of her, and she felt heavy. Her head was pounding, and her body ached. She looked at the parking lot entrance again, wishing the police would pull in. Just get it over with.

But none did.

Ten minutes later, she sat back down in the car. She had only one more card to play. She pulled out the B. Elliott folder. Karen Richmond's profile was on top. She looked over the details again, even though she already felt like she knew Karen. So young, and such a pretty face.

She dialed *67 to block her number—she couldn't stomach another disturbing text image—and dialed Karen Richmond's phone. Time to finish this. If Karen was dead, she'd go to the police. Tell them everything she knew.

A man picked up the phone on the third ring. "Hello?"

She gathered her courage. "Hi. My name is Allison, and I'm looking for Karen Richmond. Is she available?"

57

Malloy's office door swung open with such force that he heard the crunch of drywall cracking as the door handle lodged in the wall. Garcia stomped through the doorway.

"What the fuck?" Malloy stood and braced himself, ready for a fight.

Wide-eyed, Garcia held a cell phone to his ear and pointed madly at it.

Malloy shrugged his shoulders and mouthed *What?*

"My name is Dan," Garcia said into the phone. "I do know Karen Richmond, but unfortunately, she isn't available. She died in an accident about two months ago. Were you a friend?"

Garcia feverishly turned left and right, in search of something. He snatched a Sharpie from the pen cup and using his whole forearm, swept all the folders and papers off Malloy's desk and onto the floor. He wrote directly on the desk: *Allison?*

Malloy ran to the other side of his desk, unsure how to react to such a gesture.

Garcia continued to pace from one side of the office to the other, nervously twirling the Sharpie. Garcia was typically anything but overdramatic. His state of agitation was so out of character that Malloy stayed silent.

"Wait, please don't hang up. My brother, Tyler Steele, took the LXR drug, just like Karen. He's dead now too, and I've been trying to find out who gave him the drug. Do you know him? If you can help me, if you have any information, I'd really be grateful. All I want is to find out how this all happened."

Malloy finally caught on. Someone had called Karen Richmond's phone. *They gave this to her*, Lyle Richmond had said. The phone had never been used. Until now.

At long last, they had their man. Or woman.

"Give it to me," Malloy ordered in a hoarse whisper. He held out his hand.

Garcia stared, his eyes as wide as silver dollars. He rapidly shook his head side to side and continued speaking. "Do you know about the other victims? I've learned that there were others. Did you know?"

Despite his deer-in-the-headlights look, Garcia's voice was soft. Calm.

Give it to me, Malloy mouthed, now through gritted teeth.

Garcia wrote on Malloy's desk again. "No cops."

"Listen, please, Allison." Garcia was pleading. Malloy had never heard this voice. "I just want to know what happened to my brother. I know some things about it—like, I know it was a gene-altering drug they gave him. And I know it made him unable to feel pain. I've learned some other things too. Listen, maybe we can help each other. I mean, if you're looking for information about Karen? Please, he was my brother. I miss him so much. You're my only hope."

With the Sharpie, Garcia tapped the question mark he'd written after *Allison?* several times.

Malloy sat down, stunned. The woman on the other end had called the Tracfone, and she hadn't provided a last name. If she was calling from an unlisted number, they wouldn't have a prayer of finding her if she hung up right now. Goddammit, Garcia had good instincts.

"Please help me. Tyler was only nineteen. He was my baby brother. He was going to be a teacher, an elementary school teacher. He was the best thing in my life. Please." Garcia's voice was so soft, Malloy wondered if she could hear him from the other end.

There was a long pause, and he was just about to demand the phone when Garcia started speaking again. "Oh, hey, hey," Garcia cooed, "it's okay, it's okay. What is it? What's wrong?"

Malloy could hear sobs on the other end of the phone. Garcia picked up the marker and frantically scribbled on the desk. Malloy could only make out a few of the words: *Quandary. LXR. Chimps. 8 vics. Jake. Eric. DBB. Harris. Chambers. FBI.* The writing continued for several minutes as Garcia soothed the crying woman, encouraging her to let it out, just let it out.

Finally, Garcia wrote *She paid them!* and underlined it twice.

Jesus. He'd done it.

"Can you send it to me? I'll give you my email address." Garcia walked out of the office.

Malloy plopped down in his chair. His entire body seemed to melt into the chair as relief washed over him. The feeling was so overwhelming, he just couldn't help it. His eyes filled with tears.

They'd found Tyler's bad guys.

58

Tuesday nights weren't typically busy at Frank's Tavern, but tonight the bar was overloaded with some kind of reunion party. Frank, the proprietor, had been running around since Allison had arrived. She sat at the bar nursing a tasteless beer as she forwarded the video of the chimps from her phone. Her eyes still felt puffy, but the call to that guy Dan had somehow been cathartic. Poor guy had lost his brother, and he deserved to see what the drug had done to those chimpanzees. First thing in the morning, she would turn over the video and the patient profiles to the police.

But not before one last drink, even if it tasted like water.

A twenty-something girl shrieked as two handsome twenty-something boys strolled in. "Oh my god! I haven't seen you in so long!" She jumped off the stool and kissed them exuberantly, once on each cheek.

Allison glanced at Frank.

He rolled his eyes and mimicked putting his finger down his throat, the universal sign for *I'm going to puke.*

She smiled weakly. She'd been frequenting his bar, which was perfectly situated three blocks from her apartment, since she'd moved into this sleepy suburban town. She'd sit at the end of the bar, just as she did now, and watch him subtly insult the customers. She usually enjoyed being in on his fun, but tonight there was no joy anywhere in her to be found.

The new gang of three didn't stay. The cutesy girl dropped a bill on the bar and hollered "Bye, Frankie!" as she left with the boys.

Frank ambled over and grabbed the empty glasses off the bar. "I have to admit my acceptable range of human voice frequency has narrowed as I've gotten older. That girl could've been a squirrel for all I could tell."

She forced a courtesy chuckle and considered leaving. Agent Gadorski was likely stationed in his favorite parking spot in front of her apartment, waiting to arrest her.

On second thought, perhaps she'd stay a little longer.

She was about to ask Frank to make her a vodka tonic when someone sat at the other end of the bar.

Frank approached the newcomer. "Hi there. What can I getcha?"

"What do you have up for an IPA?"

"Let's see, I have a Kane Overhead Imperial IPA, delicious. I have Smuttynose Finestkind, solid 4.1 from BeerAdvocate and a masterful representation of the style, and I have a Goose IPA for those beer drinkers who lack a palate."

She laughed despite herself, and the newcomer smiled in her direction with gleaming teeth and sparkling eyes. His hair was dark blond and thick, slightly too long, and he sported a week's worth of stubble. She might have found him handsome if he hadn't been a bit on the short side for her taste. Not that she was in the mood for socializing.

"Well, I guess it's the Kane. Thanks."

Frank pulled his beer, gave her a sly smile, and raised his eyebrows at her.

"Cheers." The newcomer lifted his beer in Allison's direction.

She lifted her glass. He turned to look at his vibrating phone. She took a sip and returned to watching the bubbles.

The bar emptied in a rush. She guessed that meant the bill had been paid. Austin had loved to host Quandary happy hours. After an hour he'd announce *Last call before Dad picks up the check. Drinks after that come out of your own wallets!* Once the check was paid, everyone scattered to the wind. She smiled at the memory, then hated herself for feeling sentimental.

"What's going on here?"

She glanced up at Frank, who stood against the bar, looking between her and the newcomer. They glanced at each other questioningly.

"That's the problem with you young folks. You have your faces buried in your phones, and you don't talk. Look around! You're the only two people here. This is a bar, for Christ's sake! A place for social gathering."

She smiled apologetically at the newcomer.

"This is my friend, Allison," Frank said with dramatic flair. "She's twenty-nine, single, and loves IPA most nights." He stalked to the other side of the bar.

She felt the heat rise from her chest to her face. "Sorry about that."

The newcomer laughed and moved over two seats to sit next to her, politely leaving one stool between them. "I'm Luke. I'm thirty-two, single, and I love IPA. Should we get right to the wedding planning, then?"

He had an earnest look about his deep-set blue eyes, and she found herself wanting to like him. But today was not the day. She pulled her purse onto her lap and dropped her phone into it.

"Sorry," he said, looking back down at his beer. "Too soon for wedding jokes?"

She smiled politely. "I've had a rough day—and believe me, I'm not the right girl for wedding jokes or even dating jokes."

"That sounds like a challenge."

She gave Frank a subtle glare. If this guy was trying to flirt with her, he would be sorely disappointed. But she didn't want to be rude.

"Okay, let's hear your best dating joke." She didn't smile, but Luke didn't appear to notice.

"Oh, the pressure." He took a couple of rapid breaths. "Okay, ready? A guy walks into the bar with his date. The bartender says, 'I'm sorry, we don't serve food here.'"

She repressed a grin. It was a really dumb joke.

"Get it? Date? The fruit? Brilliant, right?"

She exhaled. "I'm really sorry, but this has been the worst week of my life."

"Maybe it wouldn't be so bad if you got it off your chest. They say telling a stranger your problems is therapeutic."

God, he wouldn't go away. "You must not be from New Jersey."

"Nope." He sat back on his stool and relaxed his shoulders. Maybe he thought he'd successfully broken the ice. "I live in the boondocks of South Carolina."

"Well, Luke, here in New Jersey, we don't talk about our shitty lives. We just internalize it until it eats us from the inside like a cancer, and we shrivel up and die."

"Whale hail, hon, now that ain't no way da live."

The sudden shift into a southern accent caught her off guard. She looked at him and smirked.

"How bad can it be, sweet thang?" he said.

He just couldn't take a hint. "Okay, for starters, I got fired from my job today. I used to be in the business of curing young children of debilitating diseases. Now I'm nothing."

"Okay, okay. There's always another job."

"Second, I've been framed for fraud and embezzlement. I'll probably be arrested any minute now, and I'll spend the next year trying to prove I didn't do it."

"Shit." His smile faded, and his grave expression was somehow satisfying to her.

How do you like them apples?

"Oh, but there's more. My boss, who I was sleeping with, seems to have created a genetic drug that's killed a whole bunch of people. And he's involved me in that, too." She clapped her hands excitedly.

He gaped at her.

"So tomorrow, I'll look for an attorney that I can't afford, and then I'll drive to the office of the FBI to give them a statement. They'll likely arrest me. I won't have any money to post bail, so I'll begin my stay in the county jail while the attorney I can't afford decides it's too much trouble to get to the bottom of this conspiracy and I end up getting lost in the system and spending the rest of my life in an orange jumpsuit."

She opened her purse, pulled out a ten-dollar bill, and dropped it on the counter. "Now if you'll excuse me, I'm going home so I can get one last good night of sleep."

She was already across the street when he caught up to her. She kept moving.

"At least let me walk you home," he said. "My momma'd tan my dad-gum hide if she learned I let a honey walk home all by herself from the saloon, boy howdy."

It wasn't even dark yet. She clutched her bag against her side and picked up her pace.

"Listen, I don't know anything about this stuff, but my brother's an attorney," he said quietly. "A litigator back at home. I can call him and you can talk to him. Maybe he'd have some advice. One thing I know for sure is that you shouldn't talk to the police without an attorney present, and it's going to be hard to find one this late at night."

She sighed. He actually seemed like he cared. She so badly needed a friend.

"Let's just call him," he continued. "Maybe he knows a good attorney here. He's really connected in the legal community."

She knew she needed good legal advice. She wasn't usually superstitious, but maybe meeting this guy at just this time was more than a coincidence. Maybe it was serendipity.

She stopped walking and finally looked him in the eyes. "Okay. That would be really kind. Thank you."

59

The sky was just beginning to darken when Wang pulled onto a side street and parked in a No Parking zone. From this spot, Allison Stevens's apartment and the parking lot in front of her house were in his direct line of sight, and he had some shade from an overhanging oak tree. He ignored the sign. He didn't plan to get out of his truck just yet anyway.

He pulled out his binoculars and scanned the parking lot until he found the license plate number he'd written down. Yep, that was it, the white Camry. He aimed the glasses at her apartment window. The curtains were open, but the apartment was dark. Maybe she was already asleep.

With a sigh, he laid the binoculars on the seat beside him and reviewed his current dilemma. He'd successfully dodged Garcia's calls all day. Once he'd convinced the branch manager at Delbarton Bank to release the name on the account, his memory had brought up not one but two coincidental interactions. *Here you go, Allison,* he'd said just minutes before. The woman's look of fear at the mention of her name had compelled him to point out her business card on her phone. Still, the way she scurried out of the bank and ran to her car was peculiar, and now he knew why. She'd known he was looking for her. And what was she doing at the bank, anyway? Closing that account, perhaps? Trying to destroy the evidence that she had paid Karen Richmond to take an illegal drug?

The other interaction had occurred weeks ago. He'd spoken with her as the acting CEO of Quandary Therapeutics during his initial cold-calling of biotech companies. She hadn't finished answering his questions before she'd ended the call abruptly—hung up on him, in fact. He'd found it nothing more than insulting at the time, but now he saw it a bit differently. Now he knew all about her fugitive boss, Austin Harris.

All the pieces of the puzzle were falling into place.

He would call Agent Malloy first thing tomorrow, but he wanted to question the girl himself before he turned her over to the Phoenix office. If they spooked her, she might try to make a run for it, probably join up with Harris and they'd be too far away to stop her. Plus, Wang had a knack for reading people's faces. He'd know right away if she was lying.

Movement caught his eye, and he turned to see two figures climbing the stairs to the upper floors. He held up his binoculars just in time to see one of the figures turn and run back down the stairs.

60

"Uh, there's a guy in the parking lot staring at us," Luke said as they took the stairs to Allison's apartment on the third floor. "He looks like a cop."

She looked in the same direction, then smiled ironically at Luke. "Yep, that's Special Agent Gary Gadorski, FBI. He's been following me for days. I think he's trying to scare me into a confession or waiting for me to screw up. He's probably bugged my apartment."

"Are you fucking kidding?" He stopped midstride. "You know he can't profile you at your home like this, right? He can follow you in public, but he can't harass you at home."

"Well, it's too late to care about that now. I'm going to give him a statement tomorrow, anyway. In fact, let me just go—"

To her horror, Luke was pounding back down the stairs, two at time. He reached the bottom and strode purposefully toward the parking lot. She began descending.

Luke shouted. "Hey! Hey, asshole! What are you doing here? Are you stalking my friend?"

He barreled straight over to Gadorski, who was leaning against his car. Gadorski straightened and took several steps toward Luke, not ceding any ground.

"Back the fuck up!" Gadorski yelled, as he reached around his back for his firearm.

"Luke!" she called. Jesus, this guy was going to get shot.

Luke stopped ten feet in front of Gadorski. "This is police harassment. My brother is a prominent attorney, and he'd be happy to help Allison out with this abuse of authority." He pulled out his phone, and Allison thought he was going to call his brother, but instead he snapped several pictures of Gadorski standing by his car. "Unless you're planning to arrest her, you can't have her under constant surveillance like this and invade her privacy. We're calling my brother. What is your full name and badge number?"

Gadorski sneered in his usual way. "Are you done with your speech, little fella?"

Luke stood firm as Allison caught up to him.

"I'm sure Ms. Stevens told you that the FBI has reason to believe she's been involved in a crime," Gadorski said. "So while you're talking to your brother, perhaps you should have him explain to you the difference between police work and police harassment. And while you're at it, ask him what the penalties are for conspiracy. If you plan to spend time with Ms. Stevens, you might want to get familiar with the process."

Luke leaned in with his cell phone as though he was capturing every word.

"Ms. Stevens, I'm happy to see that you're moving on from Austin Harris," Gadorski said, "but rest assured, you're still under investigation. You'll be on my radar until this case is closed to our satisfaction."

He opened his car door. "You two have a nice night now."

He got into the car and drove away.

61

W ang looked down at his phone, his hands shaking, hoping he'd captured at least one good image. He'd observed the entire scene in the parking lot from his binoculars while simultaneously trying to aim his phone for an image of Gadorski in conversation with Stevens and her friend.

It was entirely unexpected. He'd only been hoping to speak to Allison Stevens, but now he'd hit the jackpot. Allison Stevens and Agent Gary Gadorski. This could be the linchpin he'd been waiting for, the evidence that proved what he knew to be true, that the corrupt FBI had shut down the LXR case to protect Austin Harris and that Allison Stevens was colluding with the FBI.

If it had been anyone else at the bureau, Wang might have second-guessed the purpose of this meeting. But Gadorski was practically a celebrity with his long record of abuses of authority, complaints from suspects he'd harassed, and complaints of racial slurs and verbal abuse even within the department. Gadorski had been investigated by Internal Affairs and suspended several times. Yet somehow, he'd managed not only to keep his job but to get promoted. Gadorski was as dirty as a Porta-John at a carnival.

It was time to contact Malloy. The call went straight to voicemail. He hung up. This complicated string of events couldn't be left in a message.

He looked back over at the now quiet parking lot. How had he missed Gadorski's arrival? If he'd noticed, he would have moved in closer, maybe overheard some of the conversation. Damn it. He chewed his lip and flipped through the blurry photos on his phone. Not great, but a couple were clear enough to identify Allison Stevens and Gary Gadorski together.

A loud knock on his window caused him to drop his phone on the seat. God, all this excitement had made him skittish. A tall, well-dressed young man was smiling down at him apologetically, pointing at his cell phone screen and turning it toward Wang to reveal a mapping application and a blinking GPS location symbol.

Wang rolled down his window.

"Can I help you?" He knew he sounded irritated, but he didn't even live in this area. He wasn't going to be any help.

He leaned out just a bit to squint at the man's phone in his left hand, but from his peripheral vision, he caught swift, sweeping movement from the man's right hand. He didn't even have time to draw a breath before a six-inch blade buried into his throat.

He felt no pain, just a detached feeling that something was very wrong with his neck. His chest, which was covered in sweat just seconds ago was already cooling, numbing, and he felt a growing sense of disconnection from his body.

If only he were in better shape, maybe he could've responded faster, defended himself better.

He was vaguely aware of the man reaching over him into the car for something. For what?

He didn't pray for God to save him. Instead, he promised himself that when he recovered from this, he was going to lose the weight. This year, for sure. He'd tell Lin no more desserts, and he'd go to the gym every day. His mind drifted to his daughter's wedding next year. How thin he would be—how proud he would make her—as he walked her down the aisle.

Then his vision darkened, and he knew he would never see her wedding day, fat or thin.

62

Allison returned from the bathroom as Luke brought two glasses from the kitchen. Her nerves were shot after the confrontation out in the parking lot, but it had been gratifying to see someone stand up to that bully. She hated Gadorski. Yes, she was going to talk to the FBI, but she refused to give her statement to him.

Luke handed her a glass. "Matty's just leaving the office. He said he'll call me back in five from his car."

"Okay." She wanted to say no to the vodka but instead found herself taking a long drink from the glass. Her whole body relaxed. Maybe she had more of an alcohol problem than she wanted to admit.

Luke looked ashamed. "I'm really sorry for the scene out there. It's just that I hate to see cops abusing their power, you know? Civilians have rights in this country, and I don't think people really know that. Has that asshole tried to interview you?"

"Couple times." She said, feeling more indignant than before. "He came into my workplace and everything."

"Did you tell him anything?"

"Nothing. Nothing at all. I told him I wanted a lawyer."

"That's good." He nodded.

She pulled her legs underneath herself and leaned back on the cushion. She felt comfortable with Luke. It felt good to have a friend, someone on her side. They sat in silence for a few minutes.

"What does one do in the boondocks of South Carolina?"

He answered with that adorable accent. "Keep to m'self most o' the time. Spend my days down at my daddy's catfish pond settin' trot lines with my brothers."

She put her glass down and lay on her arm for a pillow with a smile. "Tell me more." She felt drained and slightly light-headed from all the excitement. She didn't feel like talking.

"Well, I kin tell you how to get from Sassafras Mountain to Hell Hole Bay without never seeing no police officer. And one time, when I's about, I dunno, six or seven, I swiped ten bucks from my momma's purse, and me and my brothers hitched all the way to Greenville."

She felt him get up from the sofa, and she took the opportunity to wriggle down flat.

Then Luke switched off the accent and said, "Come now. She's ready."

63

Layla glanced down at her stats as the treadmill belt zoomed by underneath her feet. Her legs felt like they were on fire, as did her lungs, and she relished it—the comfort of pain she hadn't enjoyed since her last devotion.

"Thank you, Father," she said, gasping for air between each word.

Heart rate 183. Miles per hour 8.2.

Don't you quit on me, Butch.

"I won't, Daddy."

She stretched her neck to each side. Running felt natural. Her long stride, the way her feet struck the belt mid-sole—she knew she had the correct form. Her arms were slightly bent as they swung at her sides, her hands were loose. Her breathing was fast but in cadence with each footfall.

It felt too good. She wasn't pushing hard enough. She turned up the speed to 9.0 miles per hour, and a wave of nausea swept over her as her heart rate accelerated to 197 beats per minute.

Dimitri was by her side in seconds, pressing the speed back to 8.0.

"No, Layla. That is no good for you, yes? You know it. The heart." He put his hand on his chest and furrowed his brow, shaking his head reproachfully.

She scowled back and returned to her pace, trying to get back into her zone. She tuned out the rest of the room, now filled with trainees. She ticked her pace to 8.5 miles per hour. Another wave of nausea came and went as her pulse crept upward.

Her heart rate stabilized at 185, and Dimitri walked by and gave her a warning look. As soon as he rounded the corner, she ticked it up again to 8.7 miles per hour. Her head cleared as she stared, with laser focus, at a single rivet in the steel wall in front of her.

***

I stand at a lectern, looking out over a huge crowd. All their eyes are on me, waiting expectantly—impatiently, really—for me to say something. I search the audience, scanning rows of faces, but I don't see him. He's not here. He didn't come.

My eyes blur with tears of disappointment as I look down at my notecard. He promised to be here.

"Go on, honey," Principal Whelan urges.

But I can't remember what I was going to say, and the words on my card are blurry.

I look up again at the waiting audience. Moms, dads, and kids fan themselves with the folded single-sheet program of the evening's awards. Two babies are crying. Everyone's bored, and I know my delay is just keeping them from the cookies and juice outside the auditorium.

A voice booms from the side of the stage. "What's wrong, little girl? Are you too timid to speak?"

I whip my head around. Dad's rolling in from the emergency exit door, a large bouquet of flowers on his lap and mom behind him, smiling broadly. Relief washes over me.

"Girls aren't good enough to be on a stage," he yells. "They belong in the kitchen!"

The audience gasps. What kind of a parent would say such a thing? But I know what he's doing. That's just the kind of thing my dad does. Aha! Triggered ya! he'd say.

I glance down at my note card one last time, but I don't need it. I've read it so many times I'll have it memorized forever. I clear my throat and stand up as tall as I can.

"I'd like to thank Principal Whelan for the President's Top Fitness Award for District 129. And I want all girls out there to know that we are not inferior to boys, physically or mentally. We are not weaklings! We can do anything that they can do, and sometimes we can do it better. My dad taught me that with determination, anything is possible, even with a physical limitation."

I raise my skinny arms and make fists to flex my tiny biceps, then turn to my dad. One, two, three, *I mouth.*

On cue, he yells out in unison with me, "How do you like them apples?"

The audience erupts with laughter and applause, but I really only hear the whooping of my dad as I self-consciously run off the stage toward him.

"Girl power!" he yells.

"Wait! Your trophy!" Principal Whelan calls after me.

***

Something whacked her hard on the back of the head, and her eyes snapped open. Stabbing pain shot through her skull. She squeezed her eyes shut.

"Layla, are you okay? Oh my god, Layla!"

Voices sounded far away, echoing like they were coming from the other end of a long tunnel.

A male voice thundered above her. "Back up, back up. Give me some room."

She started to doze and then felt herself being lifted onto a stretcher. She tried to cover her ears to stop the piercing ringing, but her arms didn't move. The ringing began to fade as she was wheeled away, and then she lost consciousness.

64

Allison stirred from the dead. Or at least that's what it felt like as she opened her eyes after what seemed like a long, dreamless nap. The hammering between her temples was unbearable, and she moaned and closed her eyes again, willing herself back to sleep. She turned, then realized she wasn't in her own bed. She wasn't in a bed at all. She was in the back seat of a truck.

"Hello?" she croaked.

"Ms. Stevens, there's some water and Advil in the cooler on the floor. Take that, and your head will start to feel much better."

Was it the guy from the bar? Luke? His toneless instructions were alarming, and she rose on one elbow, barely able to hold herself in that position. She could only see his profile. His hair was short now, almost military style, and he'd shaved the stubble.

"What's going on?" Her throat was dry and her voice sounded croaky, as if she'd been asleep for days.

She squinted into the sunlit front seat and saw two figures. Luke was driving and didn't answer.

It was the second man in the passenger's seat who spoke. "Go ahead and take the Advil. Drink some water. You're probably quite dehydrated." Neither he nor Luke looked back at her.

She was in fact very thirsty. She drained a full bottle of water and washed down two Advil, then slid back down on the seat. The rocking motion of the truck and the gentle hum of the engine were so soothing. She closed her eyes and fell back to sleep.

She woke some time later with a start. Her head was clear, and she sat up, concerned. "Where am I? Luke, what's happening?"

Out the window, familiar rows of cornstalks whizzed past. She had to be somewhere in the Midwest. Was she going home? Was he taking her to South Carolina?

Luke responded without looking back. "I apologize for the awkward situation. You'll be in our custody for the next several days. We've been instructed to transport you to a new location."

"What are you talking about? What happened?"

Neither Luke nor his partner answered.

"What the hell is going on?" She scooted forward on the seat.

Luke nodded to his colleague, who removed his seatbelt and turned to face her.

"Ms. Stevens, your presence has been requested by our employer, and we'll be your escorts for the next several days. It's our goal to make this a comfortable trip for you; however, if you say or do anything that impedes our ability to complete our assignment, we're prepared to make your time with us considerably less comfortable."

The coldness of his voice made the hair stand up on the nape of her neck. She leaned away, sensing danger. Her eyes darted to the door handle.

"I wouldn't try that if I were you." Luke met her eyes in the rearview mirror. His voice was calm and emotionless. "We're driving fifty-five miles an hour, and it's awfully quiet out here. Even if you survived the jump, there's nowhere to go."

"I don't understand." She felt breathless.

The colleague pulled out a phone and made a call. "Sir, Ms. Stevens is awake."

He turned and handed the phone to her, but she didn't get a good grip on it and it bounced off her knee to the floor and jittered away under the seat.

She felt the car slow slightly as she leaned down to reach under the seat for the phone. Luke turned to look at her, as his colleague moved to his knees, facing backward.

She didn't have time to think. Instead of picking up the phone, she pulled the door handle. Then, grabbing the headrest in front of her, she tucked her legs underneath herself and kicked the door open. Still hanging onto the headrest, she scooted to the edge of the seat and prepared to lunge for the opening.

But Luke was a step ahead of her. He cranked the wheel, causing the car to swerve dangerously and the car door to swing back into her. Her reflexes weren't quick enough, and she heard the chilling sound of bones crunching as the door slammed against her left foot. She fell back onto the seat, breathless and mesmerized by how quickly her foot turned grotesquely purple, swelling right over the top of her Rothy's flat. She could only whimper.

Luke pulled to the side of the road. "Get the towel!"

Her whimpers had become cries by the time a towel smothered her, and she breathed in the sweet, coppery taste of what she knew was chloroform. She thrashed but was immobilized by Luke's knees on either side of her head, breathing hard and fast, clawing at his back and bucking her hips and twisting her torso without success.

Luke's partner apparently found the phone. "I'm sorry, sir. Ms. Stevens will need to be anesthetized. I'll provide a status this evening."

She fought for a full six minutes until finally her strength left her and her body went limp.

65

Layla woke to voices outside her room. She wasn't in her bed; she was in the infirmary. The dull thrumming between her ears reminded her that she'd had an accident. Did she fall?

"Then there's no sense in her staying in the program," Brother James's voice was sharp. "We're wasting time. And you know he's getting anxious to implant the proband embryo."

"What you should be concerned about is her readiness," Dr. Jeremy said. "She's right on the cusp of the weight requirement for a carrier, but she fluctuates quite a bit. I can't in good faith recommend progressing at this point."

"That's not your decision," Brother James snapped.

"It damn well better be. You're no longer thinking objectively, James. She is a trainee, and she has a long way to go."

"I am the only one in this facility who knows her. I brought her here. I fostered her growth from the start. I'll decide when she's ready."

The door opened, and Dr. Jeremy stomped into the room, his face flushed with anger. He seemed surprised to see her looking back at him. "Ah, you're awake. How are you feeling?"

"Fine," she murmured, looking past him for Brother James. To her disappointment, he seemed to be gone.

Dr. Jeremy picked up her chart. "Your vitals look fine. You took quite a blow to your head, but we saw no sign of bleeding or swelling from your

CT and MRI scan. You're extremely lucky." He closed his chart and looked at her reproachfully. "I won't insult your intelligence by recapping how you landed in my infirmary. But I will tell you—"

"Dr. Jeremy, I'm so—"

"Don't talk, and don't apologize. Listen."

She startled at his tone. He'd never spoken one angry word to her before.

"The Colony has made an enormous investment in you, Layla. You may not realize this, but your progression to purification requires hundreds of thousands of dollars, not to mention the time and effort of dozens of people and the hundreds who support the entire infrastructure of the Colony. When you put yourself in danger, you not only waste our time and money, but you impede our ability to accomplish our objectives. You need to remember this isn't about you, it's about the vision and work of the Colony. If you ignore Dimitri again, I'll stop your training and you'll go back to induction. Do you understand me?"

She nodded, too ashamed to speak.

He didn't bother to soften the closing of the door, and it echoed in the small, sterile exam room.

"Father, please forgive me," she whispered in the silence. But the plea felt empty. Could the Father even hear her? Was he like a god or a just a normal person? Brother James seemed to talk to him all the time. In fact, Brother James talked with everyone and seemed to know everything about the Colony.

And everything about her.

Her face felt hot. Without another thought, she quickly dressed in the standard-issue linens and slides she found in the closet and snuck out of the infirmary, as quickly as her weak legs would move.

Brother James was all the way across the courtyard when she called out to him.

He spun around at her voice and retraced his path. "What are you doing out here? You should be resting."

She stood defiantly. "I'd like to speak with you."

He waited.

"What did you mean when you said you brought me here?"

He looked startled.

"I heard you tell Dr. Jeremy, 'I brought her here. I fostered her growth.' What did you mean? Did you find me that night in the city, when I was all beat up? Were you in the van?"

"Listen, you've had a really rough day. I'm going to walk you—"

"Brother James, please. I just want to know the truth. I have to know what I was like when you found me. What did I say? Did I tell you what happened? Did I mention my family or anything?" She desperately searched his face. "Please. If you know something about my poisoned life, something that might help me remember who I was—"

Brother James pressed a finger to her lips. She froze.

"I have an idea."

He turned toward the path and gestured for her to follow. They walked slowly and wordlessly, but her thoughts were racing. Why had he never told her he was the one who found her? Why was everything such a secret here?

They arrived at the garden, her favorite place in the whole Colony, and she felt some tension release. The garden had a way of washing away her anxiety.

But instead of sitting on the bench, he took her hand and pulled her close to the flower bushes. "Have you ever wondered how we created such a beautiful garden here at the Colony? With colors so incredibly vibrant, the flowers so big and lush?"

"Well, no, I guess not." She shrugged. "I just assumed that's what the earth produced."

"No way, not flowers like those. Look at them. Each of those rose blooms must be, what, six or eight inches in diameter? Bigger than the earth can produce on its own. And look at the colors. Blue isn't a natural rose color. It looks like it's been painted, doesn't it? And think about how long they last. Have you ever seen one of our roses wilt and die?"

She hadn't even considered it until now. She shook her head.

"The roses are special here at the Colony. Just like our people. The roses are pure."

She stepped closer to the rose bush and looked carefully at a plump blue blossom. "Really?"

"Really. Come on. There's more."

He held her hand and led her through the rose bushes down a path Layla had never noticed before. His large hand over hers felt so good. So protective.

"Where are we going?"

"There." He pointed to an enormous glass building still quite a way ahead of them.

After several minutes of walking, which was enough to remind her how uncomfortable slides were, they reached the door. To her dismay, Brother James let go of her hand to open the door and usher her inside.

An onslaught of humidity made her suck in her breath.

"Sorry, I should have warned you. We keep the greenhouse quite warm and humid. It helps the plants."

He flipped on a light, and she stood paralyzed by what she saw. The greenhouse was bigger than any building she'd seen on campus, probably four times the size of the cafeteria. The walls and dome ceiling were all glass, glistening with condensation now that the sun had gone down and the air outside had cooled. Along the walls stood rows and rows of planters. There must have been a hundred of them, filled with all different types of flowers, plants, and even fruit trees. Planters hung from irrigation pipes between the rows. The colors were amazing, more colors than she even knew existed.

"Wow," She breathed, as if speaking louder would break the spell. Without asking permission, she moved down the center aisle, taking in each planter as she walked. "Are all these plants and flowers pure like the roses?"

He hung back, leaning against the door. "Mm-hmm. We're always learning new things and making changes to their genetic structure to see how they adapt. Sometimes we get something totally unexpected and wonderful, like that one on your left."

Huge blue and magenta chrysanthemum blooms tumbled from the large planter on her left. She'd never seen anything like them.

"They're beautiful," she cooed.

"But wait."

He turned off the light. The greenhouse went dark, but the chrysanthemums remained brightly lit, luminous.

"They glow in the dark! Oh my god!"

Brother James drew closer. "The earth produces magnificent things, Layla. The world is full of beauty, even outside our walls at the Colony. But the earth has also produced poisonous things. Poisonous people, poisonous plants, even poisonous air and water in some places. They make the world uglier, less desirable to live in, even unsafe." He leaned down and cupped a chrysanthemum in his hands. "Imagine if we could take all the beautiful flowers in this greenhouse and spread them through the Colony. After they began to grow and spread on their own, we could plant them outside our Colony, across the whole earth. What if we could keep spreading such beauty until there wasn't any more room for poisonous, ugly plants to grow? Wouldn't that be wonderful? Wouldn't you want to be part of that?"

"I would very much want to be part of that." Her eyes locked on his, and she couldn't turn away. God, he was so beautiful and so pure. He was perfect. All she wanted was to be with him forever and spend the rest of her life planting beautiful, magical flowers all over the world.

He smiled. "The Father doesn't create beauty. He looks for it, and when he finds it, he takes the beauty that the earth has created—even in the poisoned world, and he makes it better. The flowers are pure. They're better, but they were beautiful already. They just needed to be taken from the poisoned world and cultivated. Just like you."

He swept a lock of hair from her face and kissed her forehead. Whether he meant it to be sensual, she didn't know, but it sent a tingle through her whole body that lingered in her groin. For the first time, she felt something more than devotion and admiration for him.

"As usual, you've distracted me from my schedule," he said. "I have to go. But I have one more thing to tell you before I do."

He took her hand and led her out of the greenhouse, latching the door behind him. She followed compliantly, still reeling from the kiss.

"I spoke with the Father earlier today about you."

She skipped a step to catch up.

"He's so proud of who you've become here at the Colony. He believes you have so much to offer as a pure—so much so that he's ordered your purification procedure."

She stared at him with wide eyes. "I'm going to be pure?"

"You'll be the fastest trainee to become pure in the history of the Colony."

"Oh my god." She swiveled to one side, then the other, wanting to tell someone. Since Brother James was the only one around, she told him.

"Oh my god, Brother James, I'm going to be pure."

66

"**A**llison Stevens?" Garcia whispered. "The girl I talked to on Karen Richmond's phone?"

Malloy had spent half the night trying to connect the dots between Wang and Allison Stevens. He sat back in his chair and exhaled, waiting for Garcia to catch up with his conclusions.

"Impossible," Garcia said, his voice filled with conviction. "Not fucking possible."

Garcia believed he was a flawless judge of character, and his record was impressive. Put Garcia in a room of a hundred scum-sucking thugs, and he could sniff out the perp. Didn't even matter what the crime was. But just like him, Garcia was too close to this case. His judgment was clouded.

"Bureau's been on her tail for weeks. They found a knife covered in blood under her bed mattress. Got confirmation this morning. Wang's DNA, her prints."

Garcia just stood against the wall, shaking his head. Malloy could see him trying to reconcile his first impression of Allison Stevens with the news that she was wanted for questioning in the death of Wang but was now missing in action. As they now understood the situation, her relationship to the fugitive CEO of Quandary Therapeutics, Austin Harris, who was charged with fraud, was more than professional. She'd been his mistress. The situation certainly bore all the signs of complicity, if not conspiracy. And now murder.

"Then why did she call Karen's phone? Why did she confess all that shit to me?"

"I don't know. It isn't our problem anymore."

"It doesn't make sense. We're missing something."

"I'm going to New Jersey to attend Wang's funeral." It flew out of Malloy's mouth like someone else had said it. He hadn't been planning to go, hadn't even considered it. But for some reason it felt like the right thing to do now.

"We have things to do," Garcia said to the floor. "Listen, boss, she sent me something. A video. They gave the LXR drug to chimpanzees—"

Malloy gripped the edge of his desk. "We're done here." Garcia clenched his jaw, and he softened his voice. "With Wang's death, this is no longer a drug case. The bureau will be more than dedicated to finding Allison Stevens and her boss. They'll get to the bottom of it. And ..." He paused to rub his dry, tired eyes. "Nothing we do is going to bring Tyler back. I let this case get too personal. There's a real drug problem out there we've been ignoring."

"What about the eight—"

Malloy wouldn't let him finish. "Goddammit, it cost the life of a good agent. I'm going to New Jersey to pay my respects and to apologize in person to Wang's family. I owe that to them."

"Boss, you got nothing to apologize for. We all know the risks and what we signed up for. Wang did, too."

Malloy was done talking. He opened a search window and typed *PHX to EWR*. He didn't know if Wang's funeral was his true motivation. Maybe he was really just in need of an escape. Someplace far enough away that he could think. Remind himself of his values, and dig deep to forgive himself for failing Tyler.

For the first time in weeks, the heaviness in his chest finally lifted.

67

Allison's arms were numb again, but she didn't bother to roll over and she certainly wouldn't sit up. They'd driven for two days, Luke and the other man alternating the driving as she'd drifted in and out of sleep. They'd stopped on only a couple of occasions for fuel and food and parked once on a quiet back road for a few hours of sleep.

The pain in her foot, which she assumed was broken by the look of it, wasn't much more than a dull throb, but her head pounded, and she ran her tongue over her dry, cracked lips. The cooler on the backseat floor next to her offered snacks, water, and Advil, but she made no effort to open a bottle of water. She had no appetite for food or drink, and she wasn't about to suffer another assisted bathroom break in the woods.

She closed her eyes and prayed to God again. She hadn't been to church in a while, but God wouldn't abandon her. The lord wouldn't cast off his people. She believed it. She could feel his presence. She silently recited a Bible passage from memory. *The Lord is my shepherd; I shall not want. He makes me lie down in green pastures. He leads me beside still waters. He restores my soul. He leads me in paths of righteousness for his name's sake. Even though I walk through the valley of the shadow of death—*

"We have company." It came from the driver, maybe Luke, but she wasn't sure. She'd already forgotten which voice was his.

She opened her eyes but didn't move.

"Private or G-man?"

"Nah. Bloodhound. Probably a freelancer."

She didn't understand their jargon, but she gathered that they were being followed. Maybe someone would rescue her. Or maybe not. She didn't much care.

"Pit stop?"

"Yeah."

The passenger-side escort picked up his phone. "Vehicle maintenance required." He disconnected and turned to speak to her, something they only did when delivering instructions. "Ms. Stevens, we'll be changing vehicles in a few minutes. Until we assist you, please remain in your seat."

She had no intention of doing otherwise, but she shifted slightly and rubbed her arms and hands until the blood flow returned. Another fifteen or twenty minutes passed before the SUV slowed, presumably exiting the highway. The truck came to a stop, and both men stepped out of the vehicle. From her horizontal position, she saw the driver, Luke, lean back against the door and light a cigarette.

Another minute passed before he called out, "Huh? What's that?"

Silence. Then: "Nah, brah, never heard of her."

She couldn't hear who he was addressing.

"Sure, man, knock yourself out."

A stocky middle-aged man with a full beard stepped up to the car and peered down at her through the backseat window. He didn't wear a police uniform, but an ID tag hung from his neck. She couldn't read it.

"Ma'am?" His eyes widened as he scrutinized her.

She must have looked half-dead, her skin dry and her hair tangled and matted. She moved ever so slightly to lift herself up. Her arms felt heavy and weak.

The bearded man didn't open the door or say another word. His face froze as if he were looking at a ghost.

She made it to one elbow. "Help." No sound came out, just a raspy exhale.

He moved closer to the window, as though trying to get a better look at her. Then, to her horror, he lurched forward, spewing blood across the windshield before his face smashed into it. She gasped and recoiled. His eyes remained locked on her as his nose and forehead slid down the window and out of sight. She whimpered, but again it came out as barely a whisper.

The opposite rear door opened, and she pulled herself into a ball, her arms wrapped around her knees. She closed her eyes tightly.

"Time to go."

In one fluid motion, she was lifted out of the car as if she were no bigger than a child. They carried her to another vehicle and set her down in the back seat. She kept her eyes closed through it all, still balled up in fetal position, as three doors closed and the engine started.

Even though I walk through the valley of the shadow of death, I will fear no evil, for you are with me; your rod and your staff, they comfort me. You prepare—

"Our apologies for the unpleasant scene."

—a table before me in the presence of my enemies—

"We'll divert to back roads for the rest of the trip, to reduce the risk of being discovered."

She covered her ears with her hands. Now she'd lost her place in the scripture.

The Lord is my shepherd; I shall not want ...

68

The day had finally arrived, and Austin felt like a kid in a candy store. He looked around the large conference room, trying to add in his head the total net worth of the twenty-five people standing within twenty feet of him, but the excitement of the day, this whole event, was dizzying and he couldn't figure out how many zeros and commas that would be. Not to mention the political power. He was starstruck to see the legendary General Harding, one of just a handful of five-star generals retired from the US Army, in conversation with Hammond barely ten feet away.

Jonathan Chambers must've read his mind as he came up behind Austin. "Sure is a lot of money in this room, Harry." It was a pet name he'd given Austin their first year at UCLA when they'd met as lab partners in microbial science.

"I used to think I was in the elite group." Austin grinned and excused himself to get a glass of champagne. A little social lubrication was definitely necessary.

He glanced up from his glass to see a tall, elegant older woman approaching. The way she held herself brought a single word to mind: well-bred. She looked the way he'd always pictured Jackie would look ten or twenty years from now, someone who'd never had to work for anything her whole life. He wondered whose silver spoon she'd grown up eating from. The Koch family? The Rockefellers?

As she neared him, his eyes practically bugged out of his head. "Maddy?"

"Hello, Austin." She gave him a warm hug.

He reciprocated, but then held her at arm's length so that he could look at her.

"Wow." It was all he could think of to say. He might as well have been looking at a ghost.

She waved her hand dismissively. "Where does the time go, right? We haven't seen each other in, what, a couple of years?"

"Jesus. You look amazing."

"It must be this gorgeous desert air."

He glanced over at Hammond, who excused himself from General Harding and strode toward them.

Austin raised a hand. "Stewart, I'd like you to meet—"

"Madeline Barnett. Hello, sweetheart. You look great! Not a day older than fifty."

Austin shuffled back a step as Hammond moved in. "You've met."

Hammond laughed and leaned conspiratorially toward her. "He thinks he's the only one with connections to influential people."

There it was, that haughtiness Austin had come to despise in their short time together. He felt his expression harden.

Hammond stood back and admired her face and body. "Austin, this was the anti-aging elixir, right?"

"That's right. Maddy was the first. The gene modifications could theoretically add twenty years to her life."

"Amazing. Why aren't we all on this?"

Madeline chimed in. "Well, in my humble nonmedical experience, it's the Vitality Spa that makes the real difference. Most women will pay almost anything for youthfulness over longevity. I mean, who wants to live forever with wrinkles and arthritis?"

Austin grimaced. He wished she hadn't mentioned the Vitality Spa. It was a point of contention between Hammond and himself, a conversation they'd never finished due to Hammond's childishly short fuse. He'd been surprised by Hammond's revulsion when he'd first shown him the Vitality program. What was the point of developing a purpose-bred, pain-desensitized unit of juveniles if not for this type of experimentation?

Hammond's smile returned, but he could tell it was forced. "Well, it certainly does produce remarkable results. You're the youngest seventy-year-old I've ever met."

Madeline chuckled. "Heli-skiing Davos is totally worth every penny. And it's seventy-six, next month. But don't tell anyone." She winked a wrinkle-free eye.

She draped her arm through Hammond's and they moved off into the room. Austin watched them curiously. The two of them together could charm anyone, and he felt out of his league. He walked over to the refreshment table and poured himself a second glass of champagne. It wasn't his custom to drink before giving a talk, but he needed something to calm his nerves. This was not a typical presentation.

"Ladies and gentlemen," Hammond said, his voice raised, "shall we get started?"

The room hushed as everyone found the seat with their name card. Austin took a long swallow of bubbly and left the glass on the refreshment table. He took his seat at the end of the long cherrywood table, opposite Hammond.

"Good morning and welcome to the Vitapura Wellness Center. If you would kindly power off your phones, I'd be grateful. We have a lot of important stuff to discuss, and we don't need anyone butt-dialing his kid's teacher or the pizza delivery guy while we're planning the next phase of humanity."

Everyone laughed.

"Okay, okay. I know you're all just as excited as I am that this day has finally arrived. Our project has been years in the works, and I'd like to thank you all for your support. Not just the financial backing, but your encouragement and ideas, your help discovering and facilitating advancements at various sites around the world, and mostly your dedication to what we're trying to build."

Austin looked at the nods around the table. He wondered if they all knew about his Colony. Had they spied on him? How accessible was his Colony to the outside world? Maybe he wasn't as thorough with security as he thought. No doubt Hammond would have something to say about it.

"With that, let's get on with it. I'd like to start off today with my highest vision. Many of you have suffered my bloviating about this, probably over cigars and scotch, but it may be new to others of you. Then I'll hand it over to Austin to discuss his impressive work here in Arizona."

Hammond picked up his controller and pushed back from the table. As he stood up, the lighting dimmed and a holographic projector hanging from the ceiling above the table whirred softly.

"Our story is one of evolution. It begins here."

Gasps and cries filled the room as a full-size ancient human dropped from above and landed with a crash on the table in front of them. He stood up from his crouched landing position and looked from one person to the next, like he was studying them. His physique was stocky and muscular, though he must've been only about five feet tall. He wore an animal skin draped over his hairy torso but no shoes, revealing callused, hobbit-like feet. His face was covered with a thick black beard that matched his matted hair and extended down his neck and across his chest and back. His beady eyes were wrinkled from sun exposure, and his mouth turned downward in a frown.

He evidently decided he didn't like what saw and raised his spear like he was warning everyone to back off. Several people responded by pushing their chairs back a few inches. The ancient man strutted to the end of the table, leaped over Hammond with a cry, and disappeared into thin air.

Everyone applauded. Austin read the childish delight on Hammond's face, even though he himself found 3-D holographic technology to be cheesy—computer graphics straight from *Jurassic Park* running through a $100,000 projector with surround sound audio. Their vision was far too important to be summarized by a Disney cartoon, yet Hammond had insisted. Austin was embarrassed and annoyed. This was a waste of time.

"That was Winston," Hammond said above the excited chatter. "He's a Cro-Magnon from about thirty thousand years ago, the first Homo sapiens sapiens, evolving from Africa and soon spreading to every continent across the planet."

He splayed his arms dramatically. Austin rolled his eyes.

"When you consider the harsh world Winston and his family had to survive and adapt to over the course of thousands of years, you start to understand our early genetic makeup a little better. It makes sense that we're genetically programmed toward these ancient phenotypes. I mean, if we weren't predisposed to not just survive but proliferate, we wouldn't be here to pat our early ancestors on the back, would we?"

Amid oohs and ahs, Winston returned to the table, walked to the edge, sat down, and crawled off the table, where he appeared to sit right on Hammond's lap.

Hammond mimed patting the hologram on the back. "Great job, Winston."

The group laughed as Winston disappeared. The hologram projector turned off, and the room brightened again.

"But look around the room now," Hammond said. "Not one of us has ever fought a tiger. We've learned how to avoid tornadoes and floods. And while there are still starving people in the world, most countries have an abundance of food. Thanks to genetic science, food becomes more plentiful every day.

"But our genetic predispositions haven't evolved much in those thirty thousand years. We're still driven by our brainstems, looking for tigers to fight. We still have a tribal mentality—us versus them, however you personally define the other guys. We still rely on aggression when we feel threatened. Our fight-or-flight instinct is as strong as it's always been, yet our innate intelligence hasn't evolved one bit. We exist as cavemen in a world so high-tech that artificial intelligence will soon easily surpass us. It's just a matter of time."

Austin marveled at the glistening, starry eyes of every tribal human around the table. They would all stand in Hammond's camp to wage war against anyone who tried to stop them. Religious zealots who preferred to put the future of the human race in the hands of an invisible asshole in the sky. Liberal snowflakes who couldn't accept the suffering of one person even if it stopped the suffering of millions. And pompous bureaucrats who slowed innovation and progress because they were too lazy and too stupid to keep up with it. Yes, they would be at war—because tribalism was still very real.

"The speed at which we'll reach our inevitable demise is moving at the speed of technological advances. Here we are, with our Cro-Magnon DNA, now operating in a world where destruction is lightning fast. Imagine Winston with a fully automatic assault rifle. Imagine Winston with his finger on the nuclear button."

"Some might say we already have a Winston with his finger on the nuclear button," called out a participant Austin thought of as the Marlboro Man. Jack Downs was a billionaire oil tycoon with significant political influence—probably the reason the president had been elected in the first place.

"Exactly my point, Jack." Hammond shook his head. "We don't have to imagine anything at all. Just turn on the TV news. Look at the destruction and the hate, countries fighting for power over each other instead of working together to make the world better."

More nods from the meeting participants.

Hammond turned to Steve Bridges, CEO of Ageant Technologies. "But don't worry, Steve, I'm not saying technology is the problem. Technology has significantly improved the lives and longevity of humans."

"Whew." Bridges pretended to wipe sweat from his brow, which elicited some chuckles. "Thought I was going to need a career change there for a moment."

Hammond stood up and pushed his chair under the table.

"And this brings us to the reason we've gathered today, to initiate our vision of directed human evolution by means of genetic engineering."

Austin loved the sound of it. It was such a simple, practical solution to the most important challenge humans faced: the survival of the species.

Hammond paced the room, seemingly too excited to stand still. "Think about it. Over seven billion people occupy this planet. The earth is shrinking under the weight of overpopulation. As its resources are depleted, our survival instincts force us to react, not think. We all lived through the recent financial crisis, right? People fleeing from a threat to their financial security—a reaction that wasn't in the best interest of individuals or society."

Hammond shook his head like he really was thinking about it. Austin had to hand it to him. He was a great performer.

"Are we getting smarter? Relative to our advancements, no. Bump stocks have allowed gunfire to become faster than our brains can register what we're shooting at. Have we become more thoughtful, more action-oriented when it comes to competing for resources? Nope. Look at the oil wars, right, Jack? And the destructive effects of superstition. Holy wars and radical jihadists. Tribalism. Hate crimes and segregation."

The group murmured in agreement.

"We are fundamentally flawed, and humanity will not achieve evolutionary success if we continue on this path. I'd like to change that."

"Is this about eugenics?" Jonathan asked with a smirk. "I believe it's been tried before, with a less than optimal outcome."

Hammond laughed. "Are you asking if I'm the new Adolf Hitler? Not at all. In fact, I believe all historical efforts at creating a master race have been clumsy and profoundly misdirected. Skin color, facial features, religious beliefs? These are just tribal identities that have absolutely nothing to do with genetic perfection."

Jonathan actually looked nervous. His eyes darted around the room, trying to gauge everyone's reaction to what Hammond was saying. Austin wished he'd briefed his friend ahead of the meeting.

"Hitler was an egomaniac. His barbaric plan was ridiculously dumb, and even worse, his approach was shortsighted. Mass extermination of people with his idea of undesirable traits? How would that benefit the human race? How would it improve our chances of surviving as a species?" Hammond spoke without emotion, and Austin wondered if his concerns lay with the ethics of the Holocaust or merely the stupidity of it.

"Negative eugenics is not the answer. I have no interest in mass extermination or forced sterilization. What I'm talking about is a way to fix the genetic flaws that have formed our species into what it is today, and which—if left alone—will be the cause of our demise."

"So what," Jonathan asked, "you're interested in eliminating genes related to tribalism and violence from the gene pool?"

"Ah, no again." Hammond smiled. "Change the concept of eugenics from negative action to positive action. What do you get?"

"You're introducing positive genes into the gene pool?"

"Exactly!" Hammond appeared as delighted as if he'd just broken through to Helen Keller.

General Harding threw his hands in the air, completely exasperated, and looked around the room for help.

"Since I'm just a dumb trust fund baby, let me say it in layman's terms," Madeline said, provoking laughter from the group. "It's quite simple, actually." She surveyed the refined faces around the conference table as proudly as if the idea were her own.

"Stewart's vision is to reprogram the DNA of the human race."

69

"**W**ell someone's going to have to explain this to me. I like Star Trek as much as the next guy, but I wasn't thinking cyborgs were the future of mankind." Jack Downs laced his fingers behind his head like he was expecting a business unit report from one of his senior VPs.

"I'll do you one better, Jack," Hammond said. "I'm going to turn it over to Austin Harris, the geneticist in our group, who'll tell you about the science behind our idea. Austin?"

Austin sat up proudly as all eyes fell on him. Jack Downs kept his hands behind his head, waiting to be impressed. General Harding frowned with distrust. Others wore looks ranging from curiosity to skepticism. It was the best audience he'd ever had. Nothing bolstered his confidence like a room full of cynics.

Austin smiled and stood up from his chair. "Only a few weeks ago, I listened to this crazy visionary's radical ideas and wondered if he was a genius or a lunatic. Admittedly, I at least had the benefit of Stewart's high-quality bourbon to soften the blow."

He paused for the snickers from the group, moving toward the whiteboard as they resettled.

"Friends, we have the biotechnology now to create just about anything. I'm not going to bore you with a big science lecture, but I'll drop a couple of important concepts you'll want to impress your friends with. The first is called CRISPR."

He wrote the word on the whiteboard like he was lecturing a roomful of students.

"You've heard about it. It's all the rage in the media. I'll sum it up in one sentence: This technology has given us the ability to edit genes. That's right. It's just like editing a movie film back in the old days. You could cut the film tape at any point and splice in some new tape, making the scene different. CRISPR does the same thing, only instead of a reel of tape, we're editing the strand of DNA, or the genetic code, of a human."

It sounded like science fiction to many people, so Austin waited for a comment or question, but none came. But their rigid postures and narrow eyes told him he should pick up the pace.

"Let's take a disease like cancer. Humans often lose the battle against cancer because their immune systems aren't strong enough to fight it. With CRISPR, we can modify immune system T-cells, making them stronger so they can kill the cancer cells. Every day, we're finding more ways to cure diseases using CRISPR."

He turned back to the whiteboard and wrote "DNA nanobots."

"The second key concept that makes all this possible is DNA nanotechnology, or what we often refer to as nanobots. I was among the first to begin working with a company that not only spliced DNA using CRISPR but actually created entirely new genes that could be delivered into cells. These tiny assembly robots carry sections of the genes into the nucleus of the cell and then splice the sections into the existing DNA strand, building the new gene. Since these new genes aren't natural to humans, they give us something more. Something different."

"Like what, special powers?" The question came from a man whose table tent read Richard McNeill, but it didn't include a title. Austin hadn't met the man before and couldn't tell if he was being serious or a smartass. Still, he was grateful for that perfectly worded question.

He nodded. "Exactly. Like special powers."

The room became so quiet he could almost hear their repressed childhood superheroes crying to be set free. Austin relished the moment and the hungry stares from the group. The inferiority complex of just minutes ago had melted away, and he stood tall and powerful, knowing he could ask any one of them for a billion dollars and they'd write him a check in a heartbeat. He wished he could stop talking entirely just to hear them all beg him to continue. But that wasn't the plan.

He hid his smugness behind a wide smile and poured on the charm, walking the room, making eye contact with each person as he spoke.

"Of course, humans will never be able to fly like Superman or breathe underwater like Aquaman. But what if we could build a gene, or a cocktail of genes, that would help humans develop the characteristics necessary for survival of the species in the twenty-first century and beyond? If we assume what we know to be true, that our genes dictate much of our behavior, what might we want to edit for the betterment of the human species?"

He paused, allowing the group to consider the question. "Intelligence? Aggressiveness? Longevity? What about a gene that prevents humans from becoming ill or suffering pain? Or a gene that increases physical strength?"

"Wait a minute," Jack Downs protested. "Are you telling me you can do all these things?"

Austin opened his mouth to answer, but Hammond stepped in. He had to turn to hide his irritation.

"We're very close," Hammond said. "Close enough to start phase one right here at Austin's colony and consider getting started at other select colonies. But let's not spoil the surprise just yet." He clasped his hands. "Austin, let's bring in Brad. This guy is a freaking genius."

Austin gaped at Hammond. He'd prepared an entire presentation drawn from years of genetic development, from his pain cocktail through his latest achievements in episodic memory and wakefulness. Why was Hammond shutting him down now? Spoil what surprise?

"Let's do this." Hammond walked to the door and called out. "Brad! Ready?"

Austin's shoulders slumped. He wouldn't get their attention back now even if he insisted on continuing. The show must go on. His face burned as he pushed onward, already anticipating the diatribe he would launch into at his first private moment with Hammond.

He glanced at Hammond, who stood by the door. "I'm thrilled to show you our experiment right here in Black Canyon City. You've all been staying in our luxurious Vitapura Wellness Center, but the real magic happens just beyond the center walls in our Colony."

Hammond gave him a cheerful thumbs-up.

"However, our science isn't the primary reason Stewart selected my colony as the pilot site. The choice hinged on the success of our recruiting and retainment. I'd like to introduce you to the lead administrator of the Colony, Dr. Bradley Elliott. Dr. Elliott has a PhD in sociocultural anthropology, as well as an honorary doctorate in clinical psychology from Stanford for his rehabilitative work of the fifty-eight college students who were mentally and sexually abused in the Wake of God religious cult in California. He's also widely published, under the pen name B.J. Elliott, in cult societies and behavior."

"This is the guy running the show?" General Harding asked with a snicker.

Austin bristled at the general's arrogance. "That's right. He's been instrumental in establishing the culture of the Colony, but his real gift is the recruitment of new subjects and an impressive ninety-five percent retention rate. Every member of the Colony is here because they want to be. No one has ever been forced to come to the Colony or stay once they've arrived, and this is one aspect that differentiates my colony from other experimental societies. In short, Dr. Elliott is a genius. So without further ado ..."

Austin nodded to Hammond, who opened the door and gestured for Brad to enter.

To Austin's surprise, Brad wasn't dressed in business attire as he'd instructed. Instead, he'd shown up in a white linen tunic and pants—his Colony uniform. He carried a long bamboo cane in one hand and a riding whip in the other. He glided toward Austin's seat, laid the cane and whip on the table in front of him so that everyone could get a good look, and settled into Austin's chair.

He closed his eyes, took a deep breath, and spoke. "With pain comes peace. With gratitude comes the Father's love." He opened his eyes and smiled warmly at everyone in the room.

"Welcome to the Colony. My name is Brother James."

70

Malloy stepped out of the Uber, grabbed the shoulder strap of his duffel bag, and took a deep breath of dry desert air. He was happy to be home, but even after the five-hour flight from New Jersey, he couldn't seem to shake the melancholy of Wang's loss.

The Uber pulled away, leaving him staring up at his house but for some reason unwilling to move. He'd wake up tomorrow and drive into the office just like he'd done over the last thirty years and pick up where he'd left off before the LXR case turned his life upside down. Wang's funeral had given him a sense of closure on the LXR case, which he was grateful for, but somehow he didn't feel like the same cop he used to be. It was like the fire in his belly had gone out. No, that wasn't it. It was as though he still couldn't recover from failing this case. Not only had he not solved it and he'd never be able to look Lyle Richmond or any of the families in the eye again, but he'd never see Tyler's killer pay for what he did.

The storm door slammed as Darcy came out to see what he was doing. "Pete? What's wrong?"

She was a sight for sore eyes. "Hey Darce, good to be home. I was just taking in the fresh Phoenix air. I'll take our pollution over that damn humidity any day." She took his bag, standing on tip-toe to give him a peck on the cheek.

"We have a guest," she announced, raising her eyebrows toward the house.

He looked at her questioningly.

"Jessica Heffner. That friend of yours who called the other day."

He shrugged and headed for the living room.

The woman sat on the sofa and took a swig of Heineken just as he entered the room. She was older, probably in her fifties, with long hair dyed platinum blond, a look he thought made middle-aged women look even older. She was quite thin—emaciated, really—with a face leathery from years of sun exposure. He didn't even have to reach her before he smelled the cigarette smoke from her clothes and hair.

He put out his hand. "Have we met?"

"Pete. It's me, Jessie."

He stared, and she spoke before he made the connection. "Jessie Steele."

Tyler's mom. His hand connected with hers, but instead of shaking it, he pulled her in for a hug. "Jessie. God. It's been such a long time. I'm so sorry I didn't recognize you."

"Well, you know, life has a way ..." She pulled away, clearly uncomfortable with the hug, and sat back down.

He took a seat in the chair across from her. "How are you ..." He wanted to ask how she was doing after Tyler's death, but instead, he finished, "How have you been?"

"I remarried," she said almost apologetically. "Changed my last name."

Tyler had told him his mom was dead. Cancer.

"I'm so sorry about Tyler, Jessie. You know I loved him like a son." He felt the words catch in his throat.

"Yeah. Anyhoo, just thought I'd come by and say thanks for all you did for him. Never would've gone off the needle if y'all hadn't helped him like you did."

Malloy found her demeanor odd, but obviously their relationship had been strained. She'd been dead to Tyler. He'd probably been dead to her, as well.

"You knew about the rehab?"

"He called me. Tried to get me to buy his car off him before he left."

He took a breath to steady his voice and asked as calmly as possible, "Jessie, I understand a few months ago Tyler joined a cult. Do you happen to know ..."

She let out a boisterous laugh, showing a mouthful of very yellow teeth. The laugh turned into a coughing fit, and Darcy handed her a box of tissues, but she waved it off.

"A cult?" she asked, like it was the dumbest thing she'd ever heard. "Like a religious cult? Don't you know anything about that kid?" She laughed again, more softly this time to avoid another coughing fit, which got the best of her anyway and continued longer than the last one.

God, he despised smoking.

"Do you know where he went?" Malloy fought to keep his voice calm, but inside he was practically dancing like a kid in line for Space Mountain.

"Sure as hell wasn't no cult. No sirree Bob, it wasn't no cult." Her smile faded into an angry frown. "He went to the goddamn spa."

"What are you talking about? A spa?" He wasn't even sure he'd heard her correctly.

"Ya know, Pete, I spend my whole life working like a dog, on my feet every single day, carrying heavy trays of meatloaf and barbecue ribs. I'm fifty-six years old, and I can barely walk when I get out of bed in the morning. If anyone should get a free ride at a pain spa, it should be me! What the hell has that kid done in this life, other than become a junkie and catch the AIDS? Why was he so goddamn deserving of living the good life at a spa?"

She looked conspiratorially at Darcy, as if a man wouldn't be able to understand the injustice of it all.

Darcy nodded politely but didn't offer an opinion. "Can I get you another beer? Or maybe some ice water?"

Malloy was grateful for the distraction because he'd visibly recoiled at her rant. Her son had been murdered, and she was resentful?

"Yes, beer please, uh ..."

"Darcy." She smiled.

"Right." Jessie looked back at Malloy, still frowning. "So he has the nerve to call me and try to pawn off that damn car, and then when I don't buy it"—she opened her arms, inviting Malloy to have a good look at her—"I mean, do I look like I'm rolling in money? So when I don't buy it, he says to me, 'Fine, then. I guess you won't be able to come and visit me.' I says, 'Visit you where?' And he says, 'It's a secret.' So I told him I don't care what he does, and he hung up."

Malloy's heart sank.

Darcy appeared with three beers and handed one to Malloy and one to Jessie.

"Thank you, uh …" She looked down at her lap.

Malloy rolled his eyes.

"You're quite welcome," Darcy said.

"So how do you know he went to a spa?"

Jessie swigged her beer and stared at Malloy, like she'd forgotten what the conversation was about. "Oh, yeah. So guess what the little asshole does? He sends me a text message. It says, 'Go to hell, because I'm in heaven' and has this picture attached."

She scrolled through her phone for what seemed like eternity. Malloy tapped his foot nervously and squeezed his thigh with his free hand.

"Yeah, here it is. He sends me this picture. Here."

She handed him the phone. The picture was taken from the back seat of a car or maybe a van, through the front windshield. Based on the angle of the shot, it appeared the photographer might have snapped the shot from his lap. The sun was setting behind the building, silhouetting it and obscuring the details or markings around the front. Malloy couldn't make out a sign. The desert grounds did indeed appear resort quality, with magnificent fountains and palm trees. Arizona alone was home to probably a couple of hundred spas, and he couldn't even be sure he was looking at Arizona desert.

Maybe Garcia could figure it out.

"Can you just believe that little bastard?" She shook her head. "I was so pissed off that I spent the whole night on the internet looking for the place. Finally found it."

"And?" Malloy's eyes widened.

"The goddamn Vitapura, right outside of Black Canyon City." She took a long swallow from her beer and smiled, looking pleased with her detective skills.

"Jesus. That's less than an hour from here."

"Damn straight it is." She set down her empty beer bottle and stood up to leave. "Anyhoo, he's never gonna call me again, so I was hoping you'd give him a message the next time you talk to him. A letter came to the house from the car dealer, said the car's all paid off. I just had to figure out where it was impounded. Cost me two hundred and fifty bucks, but now that sucker's mine. So next time you see him, tell him the goddamn joke's on him!"

71

Austin studied Hammond as Brad presented to the group. Hammond appeared transfixed by Brad's story, and Austin couldn't help feeling resentful. From the moment Hammond met Brad, he'd seemed less interested in the genetics and more interested in Brad's operations at the Colony. Sure, the program was provocative, but it was just the means to the end. The genetic experimentation was the true vision.

"So here's our first group of recruits from Austin and Jonathan's pain clinics," Brad said. "We selected them carefully based on certain criteria. We needed the pioneers to be true believers, and there are distinct qualities that correlate with this personality trait. It took us months to get our first group of twelve."

Brad clicked to a slide Austin had seen many times before: twelve young people in white linen uniforms, smiling happily for a photoshoot. The next slide was a close-up of one of the twelve.

"This is Emelia Antonucci, or as she's known at the Colony, Sister Mia. She was just like all the others. She had debilitating chronic pain that was untreatable by anything other than morphine. She's intelligent and educated and had an established career, but she agreed to walk away from her life for the opportunity of purification, which would remove the poison from her and free her from her pain."

Brad moved to the next slide, and Austin cringed as he always did at this image. In the photo, Brad brandished a whip over an inductee who was strapped over a bench. The cleanse.

"But true believers must be cultivated. I won't bore you with the psychology behind developing a true believer, but in our case one thing was critically important. We had to convince the subjects that pain is a mental phenomenon they could view as negative or positive. Once they embraced their pain as a pleasurable stimulus—a reward, so to speak—we removed it by genetic modification of their pain genes."

Stewart jumped in, overexcited as usual. God, he had the maturity of a six-year-old. "But they didn't know they were getting gene therapy. They believed poison was being removed from their bodies with the help of a mythical figure known as the Father."

Brad offered his award-winning smile, riling Austin even further. "That's right. Mia here was the first to receive the gene therapy. The psychological effect was so dramatic that she fasted for three days as an offering of gratitude to the Father. All our pioneers responded beautifully to the injections, which they had been fostered to believe was a spiritual purification. After they lost their sensitivity to pain, they became our most important assets as champions of the Colony and the purification process, believers from the depths of their souls. They brought in new recruits, but more importantly, they became instrumental in keeping our early inductees from giving up and wanting to leave."

He clicked again to an image that had always made Austin particularly proud. An aerial view taken from a drone. Over seven hundred colonists had gathered and waved up at the sky from below. "Our recruiting has evolved. We now bring in healthy subjects through our pain experimentation program, roughly fifty to a hundred new recruits each season. We no longer have to beat the streets. They come straight to us through a clever social media campaign that Mia developed. We're visible to potential recruits and under the radar of the authorities. It's like hiding in plain sight. And we're growing so fast, we're nearly out of space."

Hammond walked over and stood next to Brad, putting an arm around his shoulder, as though they were a team. Austin took a step forward to join them but halted with Hammond's next assertion.

"Of course, the Colony will no longer be using the pain elixir. Austin's field cohort proved it's simply not safe. Brad and I have been discussing how we can repurpose the Colony with different genetic experiments, but Brad has now convinced me that the pain rituals must continue. They're the foundation of inductee indoctrination. How did you describe it, Brad? A domino effect? The new recruits are cultivated by the previous classes, so even though the new recruits don't have chronic pain, Brad has had great success with his methodology."

Austin felt sucker-punched. He stood stiffly at the back of the room, trying to unscramble his thoughts beneath blind fury. Brad and Hammond had been working together behind his back. They'd purposely excluded him from what was happening in his own damn Colony. He might have expected this of Hammond, but Brad had been his partner for years. How could Brad stab him right between the shoulder blades?

He yearned to speak up, to reestablish his role in this meeting as Hammond's partner, but he was completely in the dark. All he could do was nod and smile. All he wanted to do was to slam Hammond to the ground and choke him to death.

"Tomorrow, Brad will go into more details about the recruiting program and the various phases of progression to purification, and we'll start setting up think-tank groups for implementing Brad's practices at the other sites." Hammond's expression sobered. "But this summit today is more than a big love fest. We're gathered here to discuss something much more critical."

Austin's arms hung stiffly at his sides. His hands had balled into fists.

"Relocation. The Colony needs to be moved out of Black Canyon City, out of the country. We're going to need the assistance and influence of each and every one of you to accomplish this move. And we don't have a lot of time."

Jesus Fucking Christ. Hammond had never even hinted about a move. Austin glowered at Brad. Brad offered an apologetic shrug, but Austin saw the smirk on the edges of his pretty-boy face. The bastard.

"… recent risks have now made this location untenable. First was the poorly designed field cohort, which unfortunately involved the DEA …"

Austin's phone vibrated, and he fished it out of his pocket.

" … increased encounters with the motorsports groups at the security gates …"

That number was the Fixer. It had to be trouble. Jesus, maybe they'd lost Allison en route. Or killed her. He was loathe to miss what Hammond was proposing by stepping out to take the call, but whatever it was, he was positive he didn't want it escalated to Hammond.

Hammond was pointing to a map of Mexico. "We've procured twenty acres in the Chihuahuan Desert across the border, and we've built …"

Austin sidestepped through the door and pulled it shut behind him, then accepted the call.

"Dr. Harris. Ms. Stevens has arrived. She's at the center main gate."

Goddammit, a day sooner than expected. His luck couldn't be worse. He gazed longingly at the conference room door.

"Shit." He desperately wanted to go back into the meeting.

"Sir, my operatives are requesting you take custody of Ms. Stevens."

He let out an exasperated breath. "I'm on my way." He'd have to debrief with Hammond and Brad later.

72

Allison awoke at the sound of gravel under the tires of the SUV. They'd turned onto a dirt road, which meant they must be very close to the destination. She was right.

"We'll be arriving soon. Please drink some more water."

She pulled herself up, waited for the dizziness to pass, and sucked down the last of her nearly empty bottle. Her first attempt at disobeying Luke's instructions had resulted in an experience she preferred not to repeat. Her throat was still scratchy from being force-fed water through a plastic tube. *Our operation is to deliver you in good health, and your behavior is compromising that.*

She rested her head against the window. There was nothing to see except sagebrush and tall cacti, the kind that looked like they were giving you the finger. *Get the hell out of our perfect, unadulterated desert.* She shielded her eyes from the setting sun, which for some reason seemed brighter than she remembered. Through squinted eyes, she saw nothing but empty dirt road ahead. She turned to look behind the truck for any sign of life, but she couldn't make out anything through the dust from their tires. Perhaps she'd be killed and buried out here. The thought didn't alarm her. In fact, she might welcome the closure. *Blessed are the dead which die in the Lord from henceforth.*

They jostled along the long dirt road for another half an hour or so, and the sun had completely fallen behind the hills when they finally approached a stately wrought-iron fence. The driver pulled up to the gate, which opened with a screeching buzz that could be heard even through the sealed windows.

Allison sat up straighter as they crunched down a red rock gravel road toward a desert oasis. It was such a contrast to the dusty brown terrain they'd just driven through that she almost wondered if it was a mirage. This had to be one of those desert spas she'd seen in travel magazines—sunrise yoga and vegan meals.

The truck stopped, and her escorts got out simultaneously. She waited, as she always did, until Luke opened her door and held out his hand. She took it, refusing to make eye contact, and allowed herself to be assisted out of the car, careful to not put weight on her broken foot. Luke put an arm under hers to hold her up. A woman stepped onto the entry porch with a wheelchair. The rustic pine wood sign next to the door read VITAPURA WELLNESS CENTER. It sounded familiar, but she couldn't place it.

Luke released his support on her, and she steadied herself. "Ms. Stevens, it's been a pleasure serving you," he said with complete sincerity. He reached out for a handshake.

"Fuck you," she whispered half-heartedly.

Without another word, he retreated to the truck.

A voice came from just behind her. "Al."

She twisted abruptly, and her injured foot twisted beneath her. She stumbled, but strong arms grabbed her before she could fall. She didn't get a look at his face, but she knew whose arms were around her. She knew his smell and the feel of his chest against her.

In that instant, the emotional storm that had been brewing inside her for weeks released in a tsunami of tears. Her weak body shuddered with her sobs, and her breath caught with each inhalation.

"I, I th-thought …"

"Shh," Austin soothed. "It's okay now, baby. I've got you. You're all good. You're going to be fine. Shh. It's okay."

He held her for a long five minutes, stroking her hair, telling her it was all going to be okay, before gently guiding her into the wheelchair. She buried her head in her hands as he began to push the chair, over the small footbridge and into the building.

73

Malloy looked out over the saguaro-speckled hills as Garcia drove north on Interstate 17. Garcia didn't enjoy small talk, which he was grateful for, so they usually drove in silence unless they had something relevant to the case to discuss. There really wasn't much to talk about.

Well, maybe one thing.

"Jessie didn't know Tyler was dead." His gaze remained out the window, but he could see Garcia turn in the reflection.

"Get outta here."

"She changed her name and moved. No one tried to find her." He knew what Garcia would ask next, so he offered the answer. "I couldn't tell her." He was too embarrassed and ashamed of his behavior to tell Garcia he'd been so enraged by her words—*Tell him the goddamn joke's on him!*—that he'd wanted to slap her. He'd choked up and walked out of the room, leaving Darcy to show her out. It was immature.

Garcia didn't reply, and that meant he didn't approve. Well, Malloy had no intention of getting into the details of the conversation. He wouldn't relive that whole heinous scene.

Garcia exited onto a side road in the booming metropolis of Black Canyon City, population 5,575. If there were over five thousand people here, Malloy had no idea where they might be hiding. It was practically a ghost town. Garcia pulled into the parking lot of the Canyon Café, which appeared to be the only coffee shop in town, and turned off the engine. The parking lot was full, but they were the only street-legal vehicle in the lot. Every other vehicle was an off-road type: side-by-side UTVs, ATVs, and dirt bikes. Evidently, Black Canyon City was a hot spot for motorsports.

The cowbell on the door clanked as they stepped inside the restaurant, and all eyes fell on them. The room quieted. Malloy glanced around at the thirty or so young faces staring back. There wasn't a single adult in the whole restaurant.

"Who ordered the pork?" someone called out, eliciting laughter from the rest of them.

Garcia smirked. He loved this kind of thing.

Malloy shrugged: *Go ahead, then.*

Garcia's voice boomed, immediately silencing the room. "Listen up, you spoiled little cocksuckers. Unless you want to spend the rest of the day here with me while I tear up your fake drivers' licenses and call your mommies, I suggest you get back to your chicken nuggets and applesauce and mind your own fucking business."

They all turned away and went back to their breakfasts. It would do.

"Can I help you?" The waitress was grinning at Garcia's gentlemanly words of advice.

"Two cups of coffee," Malloy said, sliding onto the barstool.

She pulled two cups from under the counter while simultaneously grabbing the coffee pot and filling both cups in one fluid motion, like she'd been doing it her whole life. "Something to eat?"

"No, thanks."

The kids must have decided their breakfast was now ruined, and they all left at once like a herd of cattle squeezing through the doorway. He looked at the waitress, concerned.

"Don't worry, I make them all prepay, a flat ten bucks each before they get so much as a glass of water." She winked. "My daddy didn't raise a fool."

He chuckled and sipped his coffee. It tasted like dirt, but he didn't complain.

"What brings you officers out here?" She clearly wasn't used to serving customers outside of locals and off-road enthusiasts.

He was grateful for the lead-in. "We're investigating the death of a young man, who we learned was a guest at the Vitapura Wellness Center shortly before his death. Do you know much about the center?"

"It's an awfully nice place, that's for sure. Not somewhere I could ever afford to stay."

"What about the people who run the place? What are they like?"

"Wouldn't know. Never met any of them." She excused herself and picked up a bus tub. "They pretty much keep to themselves out there. All their employees live onsite. Great big privacy walls." She talked as she cleaned tables. "Trucks and vans constantly moving supplies in and out, but no one's ever stopped in."

"This is the only road to the center, isn't it?" Garcia asked.

"That's right." She hoisted the tub onto her hip, grabbed five water glasses with the fingers of her free hand, and hustled everything into the back room. She returned a moment later, wiping her hands on the dish towel draped from her belt. "Another cup?"

Malloy accepted, stalling for a few more minutes of conversation. "Do you know why they're so private?"

She shook her head. "Beats me. Funny thing is when they first came to the town with their proposal, what, eight or ten years ago, we were thrilled. Figured they'd bring jobs for folks around here and patrons for the businesses. But they're completely self-sufficient. They don't use a dime of town resources. They pay their property taxes, sure, but otherwise, they're powered by their own solar, served by their own wells and septic. They've never hired a single local, not even to wash dishes. It's like they're not even there."

Malloy and Garcia exchanged a look.

"Well, we appreciate the insight. Thank you very much." Malloy pulled out a ten and laid it on the counter.

"Sure thing. Best o' luck." She picked up their cups as they walked to the door. "Fingers crossed that the town develops a bit after they downsize."

Malloy turned back. "Downsize?"

"Yeah, heard they made an offer to sell half their property back to BLM. Guess not too many people can afford top-shelf R & R after all."

74

Layla couldn't stop grinning as Sister Mia escorted her into the gardens. The sun was barely rising over the desert hills, and despite the chilled air, she couldn't imagine a more perfect start to her day of purification. As she stepped into the circle, she counted fifteen others, all pures, seated in heel-sit position atop white rose petals that had been scattered on the ground. They smiled warmly at her, but her gaze fixed on Brother James, who spoke first.

"Beautiful girl, today is your day. Today, you join us and become pure."

They were the most beautiful words she had ever heard.

"Come sit with us in the circle of purity." He gestured for her to take a seat at the top of the circle. Sister Mia took her place next to her. "This is a big day for you, an important step in your development. You know how important it is, don't you?"

She nodded, still unable to wipe the smile from her face.

"Everyone around this circle has been given a calling within the Colony after their purification. Your calling, similarly, will be your very own. It won't be the same calling as Brother Sayid's or Sister Mia's. Your calling is yours alone, and it will be decided and bestowed upon you by the Father, shared only between the two of you. Do you understand?"

"Yes," Layla croaked. She cleared her voice. She would have something special between just herself and the Father. Her eyes teared up, and she swallowed trying to dry up. She didn't want to appear overly emotional.

"You'll also receive a gift from the Father. Your gift of purification will help you fulfill your calling—and I have no doubt you'll be successful, Layla." His eyes glimmered in the morning sun, and she saw something more than his usual warmth as he held her gaze. A sparkle, like a secret look that belonged only to the two of them.

But he turned from her and addressed the group. "Colleagues, thank you for joining us today for the purification of Layla. Let's hold hands to complete the circle of purity, and I'll ask you to focus your meditation today on Layla's successful transition. Please keep her in your mind's eye as we chant."

He looked back at her with that radiant smile that she dreamed about every night. "Layla, please join us in the chant when you're ready."

He took a deep breath and closed his eyes. "With pain comes perfection. With perfection comes purification. This is the Father's will for me. As a pure, I am responsible for the purification of the Colony and the propagation of purity into the world. This is the Father's will for me."

He inhaled and exhaled to the count of four, then began the chant again. The group joined him. Layla joined the third time. Sister Mia gripped her left hand, and Brother Leo gripped her right hand. She could feel the energy of the fifteen pures pulsing through her like an electrical current. Her body relaxed, and the world around her completely disappeared.

And even as she fought it and tried to stay in the moment, to hold onto her chant and relish the attention and energy of the circle, her mind's eye opened to her.

***

"D-Daddy?" He's reclining in his hospital bed again. I can feel my facial muscles begin to tighten and my eyes tear up. I want to be brave. I do. I want to be brave.

"You listen to me, Butch," Daddy says firmly. "Stop that. Stop that right now."

I sniff hard and wipe my eyes on my sleeve.

"You listen to me." He's talking with such seriousness in his voice that it scares me. "You're the strongest person I've ever met, and the smartest, and the kindest. But mostly the strongest. Do you know what I mean by that?"

I don't really, so I guess by flexing my tiny bicep.

"I mean in here." He taps his head and then taps his chest with his finger. "On the inside. And that's important. You have to be strong on the inside when you lose someone you love."

"No, Daddy!" Tears well up again.

"Stop it. Show me how strong you are and push those tears away. Push them away with your mind. Do it right now."

I try really hard. I swallow a couple of times and wipe my whole face with my sleeve. But I can't stop my chin from quivering.

"I want you to do that every day for me. Do you understand? Every day, you push those tears away with your mind."

"But I don't want to," I gurgle.

"You have to. Because I'll be watching you. Whenever you think about me, I want you to be laughing. I want you to remember all the fun we had, okay? And I want you to laugh at the memories. I'll be watching you from heaven, and I'll be very disappointed if you're crying and not laughing."

My body shudders as I stifle a sob. I don't know what to say. His eyes look sad, but his voice sounds harsh. It's confusing.

His face softens. "Let's practice, okay?"

"Okay."

"Remember that time I put a rubber frog in your lunch box and you opened it at school and screamed?"

I smile. Yes, I remember that very well.

"And remember how I got a call from Principal Frowny-Face, and she scolded me for playing such a mean trick?"

I laugh, but still, a tear drips from my eye. I wipe it away quickly before Daddy gets angry again. Daddy doesn't say anything about the tear, and I take a deep breath.

"Now you try one," he says. "Go ahead."

"Um ..." I try to think of something. "Um ..." But my body erupts into sobs and I tremble, unable to control the shaking. I don't want him to go.

"Come on, Butch. Don't let me down. You're so strong. You can do it."

I turn from him and look at the wall. I concentrate on making the sobs stop. I think of a funny thing. I exhale and turn back to him. I inhale a shuddering breath. "Remember that time we were at the movies and you dumped the whole bucket of popcorn down Mom's shirt?" I smile, but my breaths are still quivering.

"Yes! And then she just said, 'Thanks, Mike! More for me!'" Daddy laughs at the memory.

"And you reached into her shirt and told the lady next to us that it was your popcorn, you paid for it." I'm laughing a little bit now, snorting and wiping my nose on my sleeve.

"And she and her boring husband got up and moved somewhere else." Daddy waves his hand. "Bye-bye, boring people."

"And all three of us laughed while everyone was glaring at us."

I smile at Dad, and he smiles back. But the emptiness inside doesn't go away.

"Go out there in the world, Butch, and be special. Do something good and make me proud of you, okay?"

"I will, Daddy."

***

Layla opened her eyes to see fifteen pairs of eyes looking back at her. Realizing her cheeks were wet and her nose was running, she dropped hands with Brother Leo and Sister Mia and covered her face, embarrassed.

"Sister Layla, I think you're ready." Brother James drew her to her feet and embraced her. He whispered in her ear. "Sister Layla, you will be pure. You will be special."

Then she was in Sister Mia's arms. "Sister Layla, you will be pure. You will be special."

Tears started again and dripped down her cheeks.

Brother Sayid stepped forward with the warm embrace. "Sister Layla, you will be pure. You will be special."

And so it went with long, heartfelt hugs and support from every member around her purification circle. Her tears kept falling.

I am Sister Layla. I will be pure. I will be special.

75

Allison woke to the sound of a shave-and-a-haircut knuckle rap on her door. She was still in the hospital room where she'd been taken the night before so that a doctor could attend to her broken foot and dehydration.

She'd been expecting Austin. It had felt so good to feel his arms around her last night. As he'd wheeled her into the hospital, he'd assured her he would explain everything. He'd show her his work, and she'd understand why he'd done what he did. He said he'd wait as long as it took for her to forgive him.

But when the door opened, a stranger stood in the doorway, tall and muscular enough to fill it completely.

"Allison Stevens," he declared. "Boy, am I a huge fan of yours. I've been dying to meet you."

She didn't respond. He seemed familiar, but she couldn't place him.

"I'm guessing, by your confused look, that Austin didn't tell you I'd be your escort for the day."

She flinched at the word *escort* and waited for instructions.

He stepped inside the door carrying a white linen bag, which he handed to her. "I brought you some clothes. The center is like a great big pajama party"—he gestured to his own white linens—"so if you'd like to freshen up in the tiny bathroom over there, I'll just wait for you outside the door."

With a dramatic bow that would have made her laugh in her old life, he backed out through the door, pulling it shut.

She studied the door for a couple of minutes, unsure of how to proceed. Austin had said he'd see her in the morning. He didn't tell her about this strange man. And what about her doctor? Could she just leave the hospital?

She inspected her arms and hands. Her IV had been removed and covered with a bandage. She threw the blanket off and inspected her newly bandaged foot. It was tightly encased in a white medical walking boot.

She desperately had to urinate. She scooped up the linen bag and shuffled to the bathroom.

Twenty minutes later, she hobbled out of the hospital room with damp hair and a well-scoured body. The linen pants and tunic were spa quality and more comfortable than she expected. She felt refreshed.

She eyed the stranger warily as he lounged in a wheelchair, scrolling on his phone. He hopped out of the wheelchair, dropped his phone into his shirt pocket, and gestured for her to have a seat.

"Your chariot awaits, m'lady."

She was loathe to sit down. Nothing made a person feel more vulnerable than being pushed around in a wheelchair. But she did as she was told, lifting her broken foot onto the footrest.

"Ah, I see you met Dr. Jeremy." He nodded at her newly wrapped and booted foot. "He's the best."

She barely remembered the doctor or Austin's abrupt departure after he dropped her off. She'd been so drained that she'd fallen asleep minutes after being helped into the hospital bed.

"Are you taking me to Austin?" She had a million questions, and she didn't want them answered by this guy.

"Austin is unfortunately stuck this morning giving a tour to the investors, so he's asked me to step in for him. I know, I'm not nearly as charming, but I hope you'll be okay with me as your tour guide." He smiled. "I'm Brad Elliott."

She swung around. "You?! You're Brad?"

He stopped pushing and took a step back. "Oh, uh, well. Maybe not. I mean, who wants to know?"

She rose from the chair with an explosive rage that made her feel more alive than she had in days. "You!"

He didn't move.

"You're the reason I'm here." He was a full foot taller than her, but it didn't stop her from shoving a finger into his chest. "You framed me. Because of you, I was threatened by the FBI and drugged and kidnapped." She punctuated each accusation with a stab of her finger. "And you're the reason I have a broken foot."

She shoved her leg forward and waited for a sensible explanation for all her suffering—or at the very least, a heartfelt apology for what she'd been through over the last month.

She got neither. He looked at her impassively before the corners of his mouth turned upward into a smile. "Aha. There you are, Allison. I was sure hoping you'd be back."

She recoiled. What was he talking about? She drew him back to her point. "And the patients. You're responsible for their deaths."

His smile disappeared. "That wasn't my project. There are many aspects of our work that Austin and I don't agree on."

The sudden change in his demeanor had a sobering effect. "What work have you been doing with Austin all this time? And why the hell did you have to drag me into it?"

He held his hand out to her. "Please, sit down. I know you've been through a lot, and I'm sorry. The trip across country … well, it was the only way to get you here safely under the circumstances. The FBI was moving in to arrest you, and we didn't have much time. But just let me show you what we've built. Once you see it, you'll forgive me. You'll forgive Austin. I swear."

But she wasn't ready to trust him. She wasn't even ready to trust Austin. She surveyed the hospital lobby. Three patients, all elderly, eyed her suspiciously. She was out of place here, and she despised hospitals.

Reluctantly, she slumped back into the chair.

"Thank you."

He pushed her through the hospital lobby door and into the morning sun. The air was already hot even at this early hour, but without the humidity she was accustomed to, it felt comfortingly therapeutic.

"Is it okay if we take a quick detour for some coffee?" he asked. "I had a very early start today, and I need a caffeine hit. And Luca makes the best cappuccino you ever tasted."

He leaned over her to look her directly in the face, pleading as if he were a little boy asking for a candy bar in the check-out line.

Thank God. Coffee. "Fine."

The coffee turned out to be a perfectly brewed café latte, better than her usual Starbucks, but she refused to give him the satisfaction of being right about it.

After a long silence, he finally spoke. "I'm so excited you're here. For years, I've wanted you to see your ideas in action."

She sat back, looking at him reproachfully. "What do you mean? I've had nothing to do with any of this, and you know it." She was in enough trouble already thanks to Austin, and she had no intention of allowing Bradley Elliott to pull her in too, especially if this place was built on stolen money, which she was certain was the case.

"Oh, on the contrary. You were the inspiration." He smiled.

He was clearly trying to rouse her curiosity, but she wasn't going to take the bait. She turned her head, disinterested.

"Your thesis! Your pain research. It's all working here. All your conclusions and implications. I studied everything you did and put it all into practice. And you were right! It's the best social experiment I've ever done, and it wasn't even my theory. It was yours."

He wrapped one arm around her shoulder and she yanked away, trying to understand what he was saying.

"My thesis?"

"Yes! That's what I'm about to show you. Our primary work out here was built on your groundbreaking research on the psychological impact of pain."

Fragments of her thesis and research flew through her mind as she grasped for some aspect of her study that could be applied in a real-world setting.

"Here, hang on." He pulled out his phone and began scrolling through pictures. He stopped and handed the phone to her.

Nostalgia washed over her. It was her, seated at a large table at Friday Night Fireside in the University of Wisconsin student center. It was an open-mic event where students working on their theses could come discuss the significance of their work. The organizers liked the edgier stuff, and Allison had such a huge turnout that they had to bring in extra chairs from the conference center.

She looked up at Brad. "You were there?"

"I've seen nearly every presentation you've ever given." He seemed embarrassed by the admission.

The small arrow in the middle of the screen told her it was a video, and she tapped it to make it play. There she was, young and aspirational, animated as she spoke to the crowd: "Imagine the implications of turning pain from a negative experience to a positive one. For example, think about the millions of people who love to sunbathe at the beach, slathered in sunscreen. Is it because they enjoy being overheated with burning-hot skin and sand in their swimsuits? No. It's because they've created a psychologically positive association with this activity: relaxing on the beach."

Her younger self strode about the room, something she did only when she was feeling extremely confident. She remembered this talk well. It was a greatest hit.

"Or what about those famous polar bear swims? Jumping into ice-cold water in the middle of winter—pain as a positive experience. Eating peppers so hot they make you cry. Body-slamming at a concert. You guys sitting here listening to my talk when you could be out partying."

The room erupted in laughter, and somebody yelled, "Truth!"

"There are examples everywhere. Of course, there are negative examples of pain as a psychological reinforcer. Nonsuicidal self-injury, for example. People who cut or burn themselves to cope with emotional stress or trauma. But whatever the reason for creating pain, one thing is common in all these examples. It works."

Brad sat back with that goofy smile on his face. She still had no idea why he was showing her this video. But as soon as she heard her next words, her pulse quickened.

"Now, don't lynch me. Just open your minds and think about this concept as an alternative to opioid addiction and overdose." Video Allison offered a coy smile. "What if we established a pain management center in the middle of nowhere and collected a large group of people who experience chronic pain on a daily basis? And then through psychological training, peer pressure, and—dare I say it?—groupthink, we converted their perception of pain to pleasure? We could turn their unhappy existence living as outcasts surrounded by normal, pain-free people into a happy existence with a new definition of normal. A place where they could embrace their pain and share it with others, where it could drive them to some higher achievement. If I may quote a fictitious character from my favorite movie, 'Life is pain, Highness. Anyone who says differently is selling something.' If what he says is true, if life is pain, then why try to cure it with addictive chemicals that only make money for the pharmaceutical giants? How is mental or physical numbness a better way to live?"

Video Allison finished with the Fireside Forum's slogan: "It's just something to think about."

The audience howled and applauded, most of them drunk on discreetly flasked rum and cokes.

Allison handed the phone back to Brad. "So that's it? This is what you've built? A giant pain management center in the middle of nowhere? It's not an original concept." Her eyes darted to Luca's fancy chalkboard menu of flavored lattes. She wasn't impressed. The Vitapura Wellness Center was just another overpriced spa.

He stood up. "Huh-uh. This is the wellness center. What I'm going to show you is so much better."

He waggled his eyebrows but said nothing more as he backed her out from the table and pushed her out of the building.

76

"**A**gent Malloy, Agent Garcia, I'm Madeline Barnett, general manager here at the wellness center." Malloy was surprised by her firm handshake. "Welcome."

She smiled, revealing a mouthful of perfectly straight white teeth and dimpled cheeks. At her faint nod, a young woman approached them with two glasses of ice water.

Barnett motioned for them to take a glass. "All our water at the center is drawn from the ground and specially processed to a TDS of thirty parts per million. In other words, it's about the purest water you'll ever drink."

Malloy thanked her and took a glass to be courteous. Garcia took one look at the cucumber slices in the water and shook his head.

Barnett's office was like no office Malloy had ever seen. It reminded him of what might be God's office in some ridiculous Morgan Freeman comedy. Two white leather sofas and recliners surrounded a white coffee table in the center of the room. A large white desk and white desk chair sat catty-corner against the full-length windows. The white walls were bare, and the floor was covered in very plush white shag carpeting.

Garcia hesitated at the door, looking down at his dusty sneakers.

"Please don't worry about your shoes at all," she said. "Come right in. I know what you're thinking: 'How about a little color,' right?" She chuckled. "You'll find white to be thematic here at Vitapura. The color of purity and perfection, light and goodness—it sets a mood we believe is conducive to successful treatment."

She invited them to have a seat, then perched on the edge of one of the recliners. She moved gracefully and sat upright with her knees touching and her ankles gently crossed, like a charm school graduate. "Now then, what can I do for you?"

"We're investigating the death of a young man we believe might have been a guest here with you."

Golden bangles clanked as her manicured fingers flew to cover her mouth. "Oh my god."

"His body was found in Flagstaff two weeks ago, and the last time he was heard from was when he was checking in to your facility. We were wondering if you could help us with any information that might lead to a better understanding of what happened between then and when he was found."

"This is very distressing news—and of course, I'm happy to help any way I can. Can you share his name?"

"Tyler Steele."

She looked thoughtful. "One moment, please."

She stepped out of her office and returned a few minutes later with a folder that looked eerily like Malloy's victim folder.

"Tyler Tobin Steele." She covered her mouth again. "God, just a boy."

"So he was here," Garcia said.

"He checked in with us on May 9, but it appears he only stayed three weeks."

"Why did he leave?"

She read from the chart. "Patient was dissatisfied with the services provided."

"What does that mean?"

"I don't have any more details, but if you'd like to take a short walk with me, I can introduce you to our staff physician. I'm sure he can explain the specifics of Mr. Steele's departure."

They followed Barnett out of the office and through the impeccable grounds.

"Hi, Maddy!" called an elderly woman dressed all in white, from across a pond.

"Hi, Sarah!" Barnett called back. "Don't you sit out in this sun for much longer."

The woman waved in response.

"Sarah is a six-month split," Barnett explained. "She's been coming for years."

"What's a six-month split?" Garcia asked.

"She's here from April to September every year. She's a strong believer in our holistic approach to pain management. In six months, she's able to manage her crippling arthritic pain for the rest of the year. She spends an hour a day in our sensory deprivation tank and another hour a day on an inversion table."

Garcia winced, and Barnett laughed. "You just wait, young man. You'll be thinking differently one day."

Malloy glanced at a handful of people walking together, listening to a guide walking slowly backward as he spoke.

"Investor meeting," she said. "They come out once or twice a year to see our latest technologies. Between you and me, I think they come for the free massage."

They arrived at what looked like a full-service medical center. Malloy raised an eyebrow at Garcia. This place was more than a spa. It could certainly handle spinal port implants.

"We call this the infirmary, creatively enough," Barnett said with a chuckle. "It's similar to an outpatient surgical center. The infirmary was recently renovated with all-new, state-of-the-art surgical technology, but to be honest, it's a pretty quiet place. We mostly do standard physicals and treat an occasional virus."

Malloy kept his expression carefully neutral.

Barnett spoke to the nurse in the reception area, who hopped from her chair and trotted off down the hall.

A few moments later, a doctor emerged. "Hi there. Jeremy Fitzgerald. I'm the attending here at the center." His wavy, shoulder-length hair and deep tan made him look more like a surfer than a medical professional.

Malloy introduced himself, and Garcia and explained why they were there.

Dr. Fitzgerald winced regretfully. "Tyler Steele. Nice kid. I'm so sorry to hear that he's passed."

Malloy hated it when people used the expression "passed," like Tyler had passed into some new dimension where he was alive and well. It particularly irritated him when members of the medical community said it. A doctor of all people should know that Tyler hadn't passed anywhere. He was dead.

"Tyler was a nice young man, but he had the wrong idea about what we do here. He arrived hoping he'd be given easy access to opioids for his pain. However, we're an opioid-free wellness center. We believe there are multiple ways to manage pain, but he wasn't interested in learning. He left not long after arriving, if I recall—what, a couple of weeks?"

He looked to Barnett, who nodded.

"It's a frequent problem with addicts or recovered addicts. They've been rewarded for so long by the immediate and powerful effects of the drugs they've taken that they have a difficult time accepting a drug-free pain strategy that takes days or even weeks to provide significant improvements. It's a shame when we miss an opportunity to educate a young person. It could change the rest of their lives."

Malloy couldn't help noticing the well-equipped surgical room they passed as they walked to his office. "Do any of your therapies involve the use of a spinal port?"

"A pain pump? Absolutely not."

"What about something other than an opioid administered by a spinal port?"

He shook his head. "Why do you ask?"

"The victim was found with a small surgical hole at the base of his spine. We believe he was given a gene editing drug to manage his pain." Malloy pulled out his folder and showed the doctor the picture that had been taken by the medical examiner.

Dr. Fitzgerald studied it carefully. "I'm not calling that a pain pump. I'm not sure what it is. But I can tell you with certainty that there are no approved gene therapies for chronic pain, and certainly none that deliver the drug through the cerebral spinal fluid. I'd be awfully interested if there were." He handed the picture back and looked at his watch. "I do need to get back to work. Is there anything else I can tell you?"

Malloy thanked him, and Barnett pocketed her phone.

"If you'll give me a couple of minutes to rearrange a meeting," she said, "I'll be happy to show you around the facility and introduce you to some of our staff who might be able to offer additional insight. Perhaps we can talk you into a stay with us."

She flicked back a strand of hair with one alabaster hand, and Malloy wondered how old she was. Fifty? Sixty? Heck if he could tell.

"We'd really appreciate that. Thank you."

As soon as Barnett disappeared back into the administrative building, Garcia reached for his cigarettes. Malloy turned away as the breeze sent the smoke into his face and strolled toward a lily pad pond. He couldn't understand how someone could inhale cigarette smoke in this heat. It was hard enough to breathe.

He took a seat on a bench in front of the pond. This really was a beautiful place. Several people, mostly older, were out and about, and a small group had gathered on a raised wooden platform to practice tai chi. Every guest wore the same outfit of white linen, which he found vaguely disturbing. It reminded him of a mental hospital in a horror movie.

His phone vibrated. He didn't recognize the number and sent it to voicemail. Garcia's cigarette smoke seemed to be chasing him, so he stood and walked a few steps out of its path. His phone rang again with the same number. Barnett was nowhere in sight, so he answered the call.

"Malloy."

A roar of white noise made him wince and yank the phone away from his ear. "Peter? Peter, are you there? Is that you?"

He recognized the voice immediately. Was Jordan Jennings standing next to a goddamn jet engine?

"Jordan, I'm kind of in the middle—"

"They're ... germline cells!" Half the words were unintelligible. "The chimpanzees from Danny's video. That's what ... with the Frankengene."

"Wait. Slow down, I can't hear you. Why don't you call me back when you get—"

"It makes perfect sense," Jordan bellowed over the noise. "That's why they delivered the drug intravenously. They're transfecting germ cells. They're creating an F1 generation."

"I don't understand." He glanced up for Barnett, but still no sign of her. "Can you call me back this afternoon?"

"Listen to me! Germline. Gene. Transfer."

He heard every word, but he still didn't know what it meant. "What does that mean? Speak English."

A tall, well-built man pushing a young woman in a wheelchair was waving toward them.

"Excuse me, sir?" the man called to Garcia.

It was the smoking, dammit. This place couldn't possibly allow smoking. Malloy took a preliminary step toward Garcia.

"I'm in the middle of something," he said into the phone. "I'll have to discuss this—"

"Peter! They're making genetically engineered babies! A new generation. You have to find—"

"I'll call you later. I have to go now." Malloy disconnected the line.

77

Allison jounced around in the chair as Brad veered off the path in the direction of two men. One was an older man with a worn, leathery face and thinning blond hair, wearing slacks and a blazer. The other was a Hispanic man with long, straight hair and a T-shirt that read DEA. Cops. Were they looking for Austin? Or ... her?

Thankfully, Brad didn't stop moving. He called out to the younger cop. "I'm sorry, sir, but this is a no-smoking facility. Would you kindly extinguish your cigarette?"

"My bad," the man called back. He put out his cigarette on the sole of his shoe and pocketed the butt. That was nice.

"I despise smoking," Brad said. "And a guy as young as him? Shouldn't he be vaping?"

"Gosh, I can't believe someone in your generation knows the word 'vaping.'" She grinned at her own wit before she remembered she hated Brad.

"Good one." Although she couldn't see his face, she knew he was smiling.

He pushed her down a long, winding path for what seemed like half a mile until they reached a wrought-iron gate with a camera overhead.

"Where are we going?"

"We're leaving the Vitapura and entering the Colony," he said. "You're going to love this place." He pulled out his key card to unlock the gate and pushed her wheelchair through. The gate closed behind them with a slam and latched with a loud click that reminded her of a prison door.

Her skin prickled as they entered what seemed like an entirely different world. "They're kids!"

Several buildings surrounded a large green courtyard. Young people, hundreds of them dressed in the same white linen clothing as she was, chatted animatedly in the courtyard, walked with purpose down the winding stone paths, or sat on the grass reading or writing. A small group sat on their knees in what looked like a meditative state. It looked like a college campus—well, like a college campus in heaven.

Brad pushed her chair to a shady area under a tree that didn't belong in the desert, looking over a courtyard of grass that also didn't belong in the desert. Her spider senses were tingling. Something felt wrong about this.

She turned her face up to Brad. "What is this place?"

"This is the Colony."

She blinked, waiting for the other shoe to drop.

"It's one of the largest studies of genetic engineering in humans in the entire world."

"What do you mean?" It looked like a world from a *Twilight Zone* episode. "They're not human?"

Brad laughed as if she were a cute girl he was trying to pick up in a bar instead of a ditzy blonde who'd just asked the dumbest question of all time. "Yeah, they're human. They've come here from all walks of life, looking for a community of other young folks who can give them a sense of family. Some of them have been recruited from Jonathan's outreach pain clinics across the country, but a lot of them—"

She whipped around to face him. "Wait. You know about the pain clinics? They still exist?"

"Of course, they do. They offer a great service to local communities, especially in lower-income neighborhoods. The clinics are terrific. We move them every year or two to new areas, targeting different ethnic backgrounds. It's important to test our gene therapies in diverse populations."

Indeed, this was the most ethnically diverse group of people she'd ever seen. They didn't cluster together by racial background as she'd so often seen on college campuses, either. She was looking at a completely integrated group of seemingly content people.

"So these people are all taking a genetic drug? Like a clinical trial? Is it … legitimate?"

"Do you mean is it under the oversight of the FDA? No, it isn't. I guess you could call it a very large biohacking experiment."

She was losing focus. A biohacking experiment. Biohacking, for god's sake, like those crazies on YouTube who injected themselves with genetic drugs to try to build muscles or live longer. She'd seen a special on Netflix about it. But that was just some weird scientists who'd gone off the rails. She was now looking at hundreds of people being dosed with an unproven, potentially deadly genetic drug.

God help us.

"Are they all taking that pain drug? The one that killed those people?"

"No, no, these kids here aren't on any gene therapies yet, except for a handful who are testing our new memory elixir. These guys and gals are inductees. They have to prove their worth by showing sacrifice and commitment over time to ensure they're appropriate for testing. And that's where your brilliance comes in."

"How?" She was unable to turn away from a group of people lying on the grass talking. Everyone looked so content. Perhaps they were brainwashed.

"We introduce them to extreme pain, similar to your pain experiments. The pain challenges, right? They learn to embrace pain as a positive experience. It's used here as a tool, just like you used it with your subjects. They are literally living your thesis as inductees."

She stared at him, stunned. Her graduate school thesis. Her pain challenges. Jesus.

Each of her thesis subjects had been challenged to withstand severe pain including electrical stimulation, extreme temperatures and pressure, and cardiovascular pain from endurance running. Using a variety of psychological profiling assessments, she was able to determine the effect of the pain challenges on their emotions, moods, personality traits, and self-image. The results had been undeniable. The subjects who had experienced and endured the most intense levels of pain had significantly higher positive self-images than those in the less challenged group or those who didn't succeed. The challenged subjects described themselves as heroic, more courageous and virtuous than others—even superior to others. Some subjects reported visions and out-of-body experiences. Her experiment had been so innovative it had been published in the highly respected *Journal of Neuroscience.*

But this ... this was a gross misrepresentation of her research. She'd wanted to help people find ways to live with pain, not create a brainwashed, tortured cult.

The air seemed to thicken, and she pressed a palm to her chest. She wanted to leave. She wanted to go back to the wellness center and pretend she'd never seen this place. But the pull of curiosity seemed to be stronger than her instinct to get out of there, because instead of insisting to leave, she asked, "How do you do that?"

Brad beamed at the question. "Let me show you the purge room."

78

"Okay, I'm all yours," Barnett announced as she stepped out of the administration building. "Let me take you through our amazing facilities."

Malloy had no desire to spend even an hour in such a pretentious resort, but just like drinking a second cup of dirt, it gave them an opportunity to ask questions in a way that the witness wouldn't feel interrogated.

"How much does a place like this cost?" Garcia asked, looking around at the perfectly manicured grounds. Grass wasn't easy to keep up in the desert, and there seemed to be plenty of it. Not to mention the ornate stone fountains and koi ponds. And so many trees.

"We have a three-month minimum stay at $18,000 a month. Packages go up from there. Most of our guests come either for the summer or the coldest winter months, which are quite mild here. We have some like Sarah, who you met earlier, who spend six months here."

Garcia exhaled a long whistle. "So $54,000 minimum? Shit."

"Tyler Steele was a restaurant manager," Malloy said. "There's no way he had that kind of money."

"Oh no, of course not." She waved dismissively. "Mr. Steele came in through our nonprofit research corporation, for which we have a significant trust fund from various grants. His costs were covered."

"How does that work?" Malloy asked.

"We have physicians across the US, and even some outside the US, who recommend patients without the ability to pay. For example, you might notice we have a lot of seniors here. But our mission is to find ways to manage pain starting at a young age, so we can develop pain management strategies that can be carried out over a lifetime. But most young folks can't afford our fees."

"Most any-age folks," Garcia added.

"Touché! But that's what the trust is for, to enable younger people suffering from chronic pain to start treatment at an early age. This provides us with data on how younger people respond to some of our therapies. Like this one."

They'd arrived at a small building, and she gestured for them to step inside. The lobby was unimpressive, with two more of the ubiquitous white sofas and a water cooler.

"This way." She led the way to a door and opened it, gesturing for them to enter.

Malloy was instantly spooked. Illuminated only by a black light, the room was bare except for three glowing, egg-shaped contraptions large enough to hold a human. He felt like he'd stepped onto a science fiction movie set. The word that came to mind was *pods*.

Garcia spoke first. "Sensory deprivation tanks."

"Yes, very good!" She clapped. "It's an excellent but costly pain management strategy. The results are undeniable, though scientists can't say definitively that the desensitizing effect is physical. Isolation tanks have quite a psychological effect. It's possible that as our guests experience sensory deprivation, they also convince themselves that they feel no pain."

Malloy looked at her face to see if she really believed that.

"All three are currently occupied," she said, smiling to make her point. "And the effects last long after they leave the tank."

Garcia moved in for a better look at one of the tanks, but Malloy went outside to wait. Just being in the same room with those alien pods made him feel claustrophobic.

Barnett followed him out. "I see you're not a fan."

Slightly embarrassed, he shook his head.

"Let's move on. You probably want to inquire more about Mr. Steele. Let me take you over to our staff psychologist, Jeannette Meyers. Dr. Meyers is an accomplished PhD in both cognitive and behavioral psychology and has trained with some of the world leaders in hypnosis. She's quite talented."

Garcia emerged from the tank room, and they followed her in silence. Malloy turned to Garcia, gesturing a cuckoo sign: *This place is Looney Tunes.* Garcia waggled his eyebrows, a look that said *I wouldn't mind a few weeks here.* Malloy sighed. He frequently felt a generation older than Garcia, but this new age crap made him feel even older. His stomach burned, and he wished he had his Tums. Mostly, he just wanted to get the hell out of there.

79

"With pain comes perfection. With perfection comes purification. This is the Father's will for me. As a pure, I am responsible for the purification of the Colony and the propagation of purity into the world. This is the Father's will for me."

Now alone after her morning of group meditation, Layla lay in the bathtub with her eyes closed, sweat rolling off her forehead and down her face. She chanted continuously, taking a break between each cycle for long breaths in and out to the count of four. The water was hotter than usual, and she looked down to make sure her skin wasn't blistering. The Father would be displeased if he found that she'd been careless on the most important day of her life.

She lifted her knees out of the water and inspected her thighs. They were deep red from the hot water, but they seemed okay. She lifted one leg completely out of the water and admired her muscular thigh, impressed by its new definition. She felt strong. She bent her knee to run her palm up her shin. The bumps were gone and they felt smooth, even though she could still see the bruises. Perhaps after her purification, they'd be gone completely.

She lowered her leg back into the water and flexed her biceps, checking each one to make sure they were symmetrical. Her left bicep was definitely not as defined as the right. *With pain comes perfection.* An imperfect physique was unacceptable. She would do one-armed pushups every day once she was released from the infirmary. Once her purification elixirs had been delivered.

She ran her finger over the long scar across her left wrist, puffy and glaringly white against the red skin on the inside of her left forearm. She didn't remember how she'd gotten the scar, but it was an imperfection she despised. Would purification make it disappear?

She sank deeper into the water, which had cooled significantly, and resumed her chant. But it had lost its meditative effect, and she was just repeating memorized words. Her mind wandered to the procedure. What would it do to her? What would she feel like?

Too impatient to soak any longer, she unplugged the drain with her foot and turned on the shower. She stood up slowly and stood under the shower spray as she removed the paper from a new bar of antibacterial soap. She meticulously soaped her entire body, careful to cover every inch. She scrubbed her fingernails and toenails. Then, just as she'd been instructed, she rinsed completely, opened a second bar of soap, and repeated the procedure.

She stepped out of the shower and removed the plastic wrap from a new terry cloth towel and bathrobe. She dried her body and hair and pulled on the robe, then moved into the empty bedroom to dress. Sofia was at class and a full day of trainee activities, along with the others.

Layla regarded her reflection in the long wall mirror with stoic admiration. *You're the fastest trainee to become a pure in the history of the Colony, Layla.* She was a warrior.

She removed the plastic from her new linen pants and tunic and dressed, then pulled on her new cotton socks and flat-soled slip-ons and checked the clock. Way too early. With a sigh, she scooped Sofia's scattered clothes from the floor and tossed them onto her bed. She loved Sofia, but the girl was far too messy. She settled on the floor in the heel-sit position and closed her eyes, feeling the hot sun on her face.

"With pain comes perfection. With perfection comes purification."

80

D r. Jeannette Meyers, the center's psychiatrist, stood up as Malloy and Garcia entered her office. She was slender and elegant, much like Barnett but without what Suzanne would have called the finishing touches.

She offered a kind smile and welcoming handshake as Barnett introduced them. "I'll bet you're finding the center a bit overwhelming. Most visitors do. We've had several news pieces done over the years that always seem to present us as a bit on the mystical side. Witches and magic potions." She shrugged and shook her head. "Please have a seat."

Malloy settled into the plush leather cushions, struggling to remain upright, while Garcia sprawled out like he was in his own living room having a beer.

"My apologies. Comfort is a big factor in successful hypnosis, and that sofa practically begs for sleepiness, right?" She sat down in her office chair, then glided across the floor until she was in front of them. "Hypnosis is one of the most effective treatments we offer here at the center. The power of suggestion can be as curative as a narcotic."

She sounded like she was reading from a memorized script. Malloy wasn't indulging this nonsense; he wanted to get straight to questions about Tyler. "With all due respect, I've seen stage hypnosis. It's a fun show, but it's entertainment. If your patients are feeling better, it's a placebo effect."

She smiled. "Not a believer?"

"No. Again, with all due respect."

She rolled in closer and held out her open hand. "May I have your palm, Agent Malloy?"

"No."

"Come on, boss," Garcia said. "Prove it doesn't work."

He rolled his eyes and held out his hand. "Okay, fine."

She looked closely at his hand, tracing her finger in a circle on his palm. "You have something here, something that I can take away from you. You don't see it yet but it's here, all right. Once I decide it's mine, I'll take it from you and you'll lose it. You won't have it anymore." Her voice had a mesmerizing tone, just like in the movies. She stared at his palm. "Ah, there it is. Have a look and tell me if you see it."

Curiosity got the best of him, and he looked nervously at his palm.

"Your name. It's mine now. What's your name?"

Malloy stared at her. His mind was blank.

"Your name?" she asked again.

"Shit ..." Garcia breathed, his eyes wide as he gaped at Malloy.

Malloy felt like his brain had just glitched out. He opened his mouth to speak, but no words came to him.

Dr. Meyers dropped his hand, and barely a second later he yelled, "Peter Malloy!"

Garcia and Barnett burst into laughter.

Malloy stood up, completely unnerved.

"I'm sorry," she said. "That was more of a trick. It's quite simple, really. You see, as soon as the patient accepts that his own reality could be false, he opens himself up to an alternative reality. In other words, as soon as you looked at your palm, thinking there was a slight possibility that something was there, even though you were certain your hand was empty, you allowed me to suggest to you that you'd forgotten your name. Just the suggestion convinced you that you had."

Her smile wasn't smug, but he scowled at her anyway.

"That's un-fucking-believable!" Garcia said, clearly smitten with Dr.

Meyers and her hokey bullshit.

Malloy shot him a scalding look.

"So if you can imagine it," she finished, "all we need to do is convince our patients that the pain they're feeling is a false reality, and then suggest a better one. The mind is a powerful tool."

He cleared his throat, trying to regain his composure and steer the conversation back to police work. "Dr. Meyers, did you work with a patient named Tyler Steele?"

Dr. Meyers looked to Barnett for help.

"Young boy with peripheral neuropathy, I believe, related to HIV," Barnett said.

Malloy cringed, still troubled by Tyler's disease.

"Yes, I remember him," Dr. Meyers said. "A very nice boy, but I believe he didn't stay at the center long. It wasn't the right solution for him, I'm afraid."

"What do you mean?" Garcia asked.

"I recall he was more interested in traditional pain management. Medications. I referred him to a neurologist in Phoenix." Dr. Meyers looked between the agents and Barnett. "May I ask what this is about?"

"We're investigating his death. His last known location was this facility."

"Oh dear, I'm so sorry. So young."

"We'd be grateful for any information you'd be willing to provide." He wanted to get a look at her notes from their sessions, but he knew he couldn't get a warrant. He held his breath, hoping she'd comply.

The doctor rolled her chair back to her desk to make a note. "Of course, I'm happy to help in any way I can. I'll have copies of his chart sent over to the reception desk."

Relief washed across his shoulders. "And could you include the neurologist's contact information?"

Dr. Meyers smiled. "Of course."

As they left the office, Malloy gratefully inhaled the hot, dusty desert air. There was something about the wellness center that spooked him. His stomach burned, and his chest felt tight. He looked longingly in the direction of the administration building, but Barnett was leading them down the path in the opposite direction.

81

Allison gaped at the leather straps bolted to the floor at each end of the narrow stone bench. She knew exactly what this was for. She'd drawn an image of this bench for a paper she'd written after reading how it was used in an ancient Eastern European ritual for eliciting visions through whippings.

"You recognize it," Brad said, his voice low, as though they were in a church.

She felt sick to her stomach. Again, her curiosity betrayed her. "Does it work?"

"It's one of our most successful and coveted rituals. We call it the cleanse. The cleanse is a privilege that must be earned. Since it's so desired, inductees arrive at a cleanse in a heightened state of anticipation that contributes to the outcome. Some inductees even request multiple cleanses."

She stared at the spotless marble floors and imagined them smeared with blood. She pictured a naked young woman straddling the bench, wrists and ankles bound while some faceless sadist wearing a long black robe worked a bullwhip across her body. She grimaced, wishing the image had never entered her mind, torn between a perverse sense of pride at seeing her ideas in practice and moral outrage. What kind of deviant would whip someone strapped to that bench?

Brad seemed to understand her struggle. He wheeled her backward out the door.

"Allison." He came around in front of her chair so he could look at her directly. "No one in the Colony is forced to do anything. It's exactly as you predicted all those years ago. The pain is viewed as a reward, and the reward comes in a variety of ways, including a sense of superiority, stronger community connections, and in a lot of cases, visions. People who come here to the Colony, who choose to leave the poisoned world because they can't find the happiness they want out there, find extreme satisfaction here. You saw them yourself."

She sagged in her chair. Her mind seemed paralyzed as she tried to digest what he was telling her. His language unsettled her. The poisoned world. The purge room. It was chilling.

Brad rolled her along the sidewalk until they arrived at a fruit stand, which like everything in the Colony seemed out of place.

A young woman selecting a pear caught her glance and smiled. "I hope you feel better soon."

Had these people been drugged with some sort of antidepressant? Happy pills, her mother used to call them. Brad handed her an apple, and they stopped under another shade tree.

"Are they all on ... some psychoactive drug?"

"Nope. No medications at all, not even Advil." He beamed.

He was attractive in a way she couldn't quite define. Sure, he had that handsome all-American high school quarterback look, but this was something else. Something that emanated from inside him. Confidence and a comfort with his beliefs and this world he'd created.

But she remained skeptical. "Then why is everyone so happy? Why do they stay and live this life?"

"They have a goal. They all have the same single objective."

"The gene editing drug?"

The answer came from a soft female voice behind her.

"Purification."

Allison spun around.

The woman who'd joined them was breathtakingly striking. She might have been Allison's age, with creamy brown skin, long dreadlocks, and a smile straight from a magazine cover. She took a seat next to Brad and crossed one long, thin, white-linen-shrouded leg over the other.

Allison instantly felt insecure and wrapped her arms around her boyish torso.

"Hello, Brother James," the woman said with a nod. "This must be Allison."

Brother James? Oh, this chick was definitely brainwashed.

Brad introduced her. "Allison, this is Mia. Mia's been at the Colony for several years now and is one of our pures. I asked her to join us this morning so you could get another view of life here at the Colony."

Mia held out her hand, but Allison's eyes were locked onto her face. That face. She recognized it now. *Recommendation: Inpatient admission to the Vitapura Wellness Center.*

Vitapura Wellness Center.

"I know you—well, I saw your picture, your profile in Dr. Chambers's office." The unexpected revelation pulled her up from the wheelchair. "Emelia, right? Oh my god, you—and all those people. You ..."

She looked out over the lawn. An entire drawer of folders labeled VWC. How many people were here on Dr. Chambers's recommendation?

"I saw them," she whispered. "I just didn't know."

Mia chuckled. "It's a lot to take in. Don't worry, I totally get it. I'm sure you must be overwhelmed."

Brad guided Allison back into the chair as he explained. "Mia and many others have been referred to the Colony by Dr. Chambers. Mia has chosen her better life here with us. She's chosen to be pure."

Allison stared at Mia's beautiful, happy face, wanting to scream *It's a trap! You've been brainwashed, and you're being used for illegal drug testing. Run! Get out of here!*

But Mia spoke up first. "Purification is really just part of the nomenclature here at the Colony. What we're really doing here is genetic testing."

She drew back. "You—you know about the drug testing?"

"You work in biotech, right?" Mia asked. "Developing gene editing drugs with Austin Harris?"

Her surprise must have been obvious.

"I looked you up on LinkedIn." Mia rolled her eyes. "We do have technology out here in the desert."

"Well, sure …" But were they allowed to use it?

"I know it might appear that we're all brainwashed simpletons, and in your defense, it's an image we've cultivated. But most of us are bright, ambitious people. In my poisoned life, I owned a media design company."

Allison's voice rose to an incredulous shrill. "Then why are you here? Why would you give up that life to live in this—"

"—crazy spiritual cult? Initially, because Dr. Chambers offered a way to cure my disease after every other treatment had failed me. And I was a true believer in all aspects of the Colony. I'm enlightened now, obviously, but I'm still a true believer. We're doing the most important biological work in the world. What we've accomplished here at the Colony in the last five years would have taken twenty years, maybe more, in the biotech industry. Tell me, how long did it take you to get your DMD drug—Enigmax, was it?—into patients who desperately needed it?"

When Allison had come onto Enigmax, Quandary had already invested eight years of research. But because gene therapy was so new, the US and western European health authorities were slow to approve a human clinical study. Drug development moved at a glacial pace. It always had.

"Maybe ten years," she admitted.

"And another three or four years before you could sell the drug to patients all over the world, right?"

She nodded.

"Before the Colony, I was in so much pain I wanted to die. I was very close to taking my own life to stop the suffering. Dr. Chambers offered me an alternative. It turns out I was the first patient to receive the very first gene editing pain drug three years ago, after barely two years of research and minimal animal testing. I wasn't aware of all that at the time, but it saved my life. If it weren't for this Colony, I would be dead now. I'm sure of it." She held out her arms as if to embrace the endless Arizona sky. As if to embrace life. "But look at me. I've never felt better. The modified genes have erased my ability to feel pain."

This woman had been like Elaine's son, sleeping his life away on morphine. Elaine had taken the risk too, and she'd gotten her son back. All because of this unapproved drug, a miracle that otherwise would have been years away.

"Do all these people have a chronic pain disorder?" That girl at the fruit stand hadn't seemed to be suffering.

"Oh, no. Early on, we only accepted pain subjects, but now we recruit a wide variety. Austin has many new cohorts that don't require a disease model for chronic pain."

She winced at Mia's choice of words to describe the people living at the Colony. *Disease models* were animals—rodents, dogs, or even monkeys—that were bred with a pathology or induced with a human disease in order to test new drug therapies. Humans weren't disease models.

Brad interjected. "What Mia means is that we now have many offerings for the colonists. This afternoon, I'll take you to the infirmary, where the infusions are delivered. I'll show you the new elixirs being tested here."

"So what do you think?" Mia asked.

"About what?"

Brad shot Mia a look, but she waved him off. "This is a recruiting pitch, Allison. We'd like you to join us as a member of the administrative team. You'd be such a great addition to the Colony, given your brilliant work in pain psychology. I really hope you'll consider it."

"What?" Allison tensed and sat back. Illegal drug testing? It was ludicrous. She wanted no part of it. In fact, she wanted to leave. Now.

Brad offered a weak smile. "I'd wanted to entice you with more cappuccino and a complete tour of the grounds, but Mia's right. We brought you here to see if you'd join us. The Colony is growing so fast, and we've had such tremendous success that Austin has procured a significant additional investment. Our genetic research is leading edge in the United States, further along than any other country, even China. We need your expertise in pain, and we can benefit from the leadership skills you built during your time at Quandary."

Her leadership skills at Quandary? What a joke.

"Austin's been grooming you for this from the day he met you at that graduate school meet and greet."

She gaped. How did Brad know about that party?

"And just think," Mia said, "you can be with Austin now, living here in this beautiful oasis. Just like you've always wanted, right?"

Brad's face darkened, but he nodded. "That's right."

Allison desperately needed some time to collect her thoughts. Austin had planned this from the start. Had he really loved her? Had his angry call and the gunshots been just part of the plan? God, how badly she wanted to believe it. Could it be true?

"But you'll have plenty of time to discuss this with Austin and make up your mind. For now, let's continue our tour. Mia has to get back to work, and I have so much more to show you." Brad moved behind her and wheeled her back onto the path.

"Bye, Allison. I can't wait for you to join us. We'll be like sisters!"

She chuckled. It was way over the top. But she already liked Mia.

Brad continued the tour, pointing out various buildings, describing the day-to-day activities of new recruits and how the inductees sacrificed and progressed toward purification. But she was only half-listening. Her mind danced over what she now understood: Austin had planned that she be here with him all along. He'd selected her from the start. She was an integral part of this venture. *I've been building this for years, planning every tiny detail, including you.* She had completely misinterpreted his message.

Brad stopped pushing and stepped in front of her. He knelt down on one knee. "I know this is probably overwhelming, but I hope you realize that everything we've built—everything we're doing here—is noble. Our colonists are happier and healthier than they've ever been. Our science is sound and will change the course of history one day. And our culture, which I know seems unconventional, is the foundation that makes us extraordinary. Just look around at the beauty and love and happiness here, and tell me you still don't get it."

His bright blue eyes pleaded with her. He was waiting for an answer.

She couldn't argue that the Colony was idyllic. And Austin had built this. They could be together here. They could be a family.

Her eyes met Brad's, and she almost felt lost in them. He pressed his palms together at his chest, a pleading gesture.

"I get it." The corners of her mouth turned up. "Can we go find Austin now?"

"Yes. Yes, indeed." He took a victory lap around her chair.

82

Barnett, who must have realized that Malloy was losing interest, linked arms with Garcia and continued the tour, pointing out various buildings and guest suites. Malloy was relieved to have a few minutes to collect his thoughts.

She'd said physicians referred patients to the center, but Tyler hadn't been referred that way. He'd been recruited by a few people in a van. It could have been some sort of outreach program, but it seemed peculiar that a fantastic place like this would need to take to the streets to find patients. And how come she hadn't mentioned a field team out recruiting?

The hostess at the restaurant where Tyler had worked in Prescott said that several people had talked to the recruiters but dismissed the sales pitch and walked away. Malloy surveyed the pool as they sauntered past. A gray-haired man huddled under a waterfall, relaxing as the water beat down on his upper back. At the other end, three Jacuzzis remained empty, as did the cushy oversized chairs beneath the umbrellas. Why would anyone walk away from a free stay here? Because the recruiters weren't telling them about the resort. Even Jessie had implied that Tyler didn't know where he was. Why the secrecy?

The opioid story didn't line up, either. The waitress said Tyler had been promised a cure of some kind to remove the poison from him. He would be able to start his life over. *They said they cured someone with brain cancer.* It was an awfully strange sales pitch for a drug-free pain management research program.

Tyler must have expected to be cured of HIV, so when he arrived and learned that he wouldn't be given even a single drug, he'd decided to leave. He knew no amount of hypnosis or sensory deprivation would reduce his viral counts. He'd expected to be cured of his poison. Dr. Fitzgerald and that wack job Dr. Meyers had both said Tyler wanted opioids, but Malloy was certain he'd really wanted HIV treatment. Were they lying? And if so, why?

Malloy hated unanswered questions, but he knew he couldn't dig in without setting off alarms. And without the support of the bureau, his hands were tied.

"Well, this is the end of the line," Barnett said.

No shit. Malloy had to struggle to keep the relief off his face.

"What do you think, Danny Boy? Would you like to come and spend a few months with us?"

Garcia smirked. "Will the research grant cover my costs?"

Malloy scowled. Danny Boy was Barnett's new best friend. He had to admire her sales skills. He turned away from their mutual admiration and let his gaze travel along the excessively tall walls enclosing the wellness center. There was a small unmarked gate at the western end, opposite the main gate. It appeared to have a key card scanner, and two cameras on either side of the gate kept watch over the entry.

"Where does that lead?" He gestured casually toward the gate as they turned back toward the administration building.

"Back there is the engine that runs this gorgeous place. Because we're one hundred percent self-sustaining, that's our staff housing and facilities. We also have vegetable and fruit gardens and a large solar array."

He was reminded of the comment from the waitress at the coffee shop earlier that morning. "We understand you'll be downsizing."

She frowned. "I'm afraid so. We're getting quite a bit of rudeness and negative press from the off-road motorsports organizations. You know, those ATVs? They've been harassing our guests and staff. We've been negotiating with BLM for some time now, and we've reached an agreement to sell some of our land back if they'll enforce our privacy. I don't like those things. It's all just noise pollution, if you ask me." She stuck out her tongue in disgust.

Those little punks in the coffee shop. Yeah, he could understand the problem.

They arrived at the administration building.

"I'm afraid I really have to get back to my schedule today, but I hope your visit has been helpful for your investigation. I am truly sorry to hear about Tyler's death. Let's collect your things up front, and I'll show you out."

He and Garcia waited in the reception area for Barnett to retrieve the copy of Tyler's chart. Following protocol, they didn't speak about their observations. There would be plenty of time to debrief on the hour-long drive back to Phoenix.

Malloy pulled his vibrating phone from his pocket. Cramer. It was the third time he'd called in the last hour. He dropped it back into his shirt pocket. He'd call him back from the car.

Garcia pulled out his pack of cigarettes, clearly yearning to light one. God, it had barely been a couple hours since his last cigarette.

"Reception, Brittany speaking." The perky young girl behind the desk spoke into her handset. "Of course, Dr. Chambers. Just one moment."

Malloy glanced at Garcia to see if he'd caught the name. Garcia gave a barely perceptible nod. Dr. Chambers, renowned pain physician—and one of the names blurted out by Allison Stevens as collaborating with Austin Harris. Malloy had too many years on the job to believe this was just coincidence.

Barnett stepped out.

"Ms. Barnett," Brittany said, "Dr. Chambers is on the line."

Barnett glanced at Malloy and Garcia, then turned back to Brittany. "Please tell him I'll be with him in just a moment."

Was that a nervous smile?

She strode over. "Okay, here you are. It looks like Jeannette has provided you with his full chart as well as, let's see here, oh, the neurologist back in Phoenix. Right. Here you are."

She was babbling. It was such a change in her smooth speech pattern that Malloy was instantly alert. "I'm sorry for eavesdropping, but is that Dr. Jonathan Chambers on the phone? Do you know him?"

"Jonathan? Of course. He's been a referring physician to the center for years. Do you know him? He's really a genius in the field of pain management. Many of our practices here were originally his ideas. But he's based on the East Coast, so we don't see much of him."

He tilted his head slightly. "Do you happen to know a man by the name of Austin Harris?"

She drew back. "Austin Harris? Of Quandary, the genetics biotech? I've seen him on the news. He's a fugitive, right? Insider trading or something?"

Malloy nodded.

"I've never met him personally. Why do you ask?"

He ignored her question. "How about Allison Stevens?"

"I don't think so." She shifted her eyes to Garcia.

There it was. She was hiding something. He'd been watching her body language and communication style carefully since they'd arrived. She carried herself with supreme confidence. Eye contact was her power play, the tool she used to dominate a verbal interchange. Until just now, she hadn't broken eye contact at a single question he'd asked her.

Until Allison Stevens. She knew Stevens. He was sure of it.

"It was truly a pleasure to meet you both." She threw a flirty smile to Garcia. "And if you're ever interested in a brief stay with us, please call me. We'll give you the friends and family discount."

Malloy pulled out his business card. "Thank you very much for your time and for the tour. If you happen to think of anything else that might help us, please call me."

Garcia had a cigarette lit before they were off the front porch. Malloy refrained from looking around. Barnett would be watching them, and he wanted her to believe their interest in the Vitapura Wellness Center was over.

He moved upwind of Garcia as they walked to the truck.

"Well, that was fun," Garcia said. "Do you want to stop by that pie place on the way out? Sign said 'Best Pies on Earth.'"

"We're missing something here."

"Nah, you're just creeped out by the place. You hate this pseudo-science shit."

He was right about that. Malloy couldn't shake the sense of foreboding he'd had since the moment he'd seen those sensory deprivation tanks. But this wasn't about how much he hated the wellness center.

"She was lying about Allison Stevens. I think she knows her. And I'll bet she also knows Austin Harris."

Garcia dropped his cigarette on the ground and stamped it out. "You ready?"

Malloy walked around the truck and sat in the passenger seat. "I want to look around. Didn't we see a service road a little way back?"

Garcia looked over to see how serious he was. He sighed. "I think you're wasting good pie-eating time, but you're the boss."

83

"We call this building the gateway," Brad said as he rolled Allison into the lobby. She looked around the small, single-room building and realized it was little more than a bank of elevators: three elevators along one wall and a long bench against the opposite wall, next to a single unisex bathroom. The room was artfully decorated with native desert plants and cacti. The tiny building was only one story tall.

"Did you run out of budget before you could finish the skyscraper?" she teased.

"Who knew elevators would be so expensive?"

She laughed. God, it felt so good to laugh.

"We have several underground buildings," he said. "This whole area was dug out for copper mines a hundred years ago, and we rebuilt the shafts to provide access between the buildings. We can't have satellite pictures revealing the true size of the Colony."

He parked her near the bench. "Let me just go see where Austin is and make sure he's available to take you through the trainee school. I'll be right back."

He held a keycard against the call button and took the elevator down.

She may have been in love with Austin, but Brad sure was handsome. She felt comfortable around him. Maybe they could be a good team.

She stood up from her wheelchair. Her legs were stiff, and she needed to stretch. She stepped down onto her broken foot. Just a dull ache. She wondered how long it would be before she could jog on it. She limped back and forth between the elevators as though pacing, testing her foot to see how much weight she could bear. It felt good to move around.

Why hadn't Brad taken her down the elevator with him? What was down there? Was there more than one floor?

The outer gateway door opened and, to her surprise, an older couple entered. She hadn't seen anyone over the age of twenty-five since they'd left the wellness center.

"No, it's not a will," the woman was explaining as she pulled out her keycard. "It's a trust. And I told him I don't want to discuss it."

"Why is he getting involved in the first place?" the man asked with irritation in his voice.

The woman held the elevator door open and called over to Allison. "Are you going down?"

Allison smiled. "Yes, please." She hobbled into the elevator.

The inside of the elevator had no buttons. The elevator descended on its own and then opened into a hallway. She stepped out and moved to the side to allow the older couple to pass by. Without a word, they strolled down the hall and turned down another corridor, continuing their conversation. She followed, looking into windows as she passed. Some rooms appeared to be offices. She stopped in front of a large lab, empty except for many cages of mice. This must be where they did animal testing. Perhaps the synthesis of Spiragene's constructs was conducted somewhere down here as well. She'd have to remember to ask Brad.

She lumbered down the corridor, awkwardly swinging the plastic boot, until she reached another window. She peered inside and was surprised to find she was looking down into a huge two-story space the size of a high school auditorium. Dozens of aging adults like the couple on the elevator were engaged in various activities. Three older women chatted while pushing strollers around a track circling the perimeter of the room. Two gray-haired men and a woman sat at a table playing a board game, each with a stroller parked next to their chairs. Several more seniors held babies in oversized recliners as they watched a big-screen TV or used their phones or tablets. It must've been grandchild visiting day at the senior center.

"Magnificent, isn't it?"

She spun around, startled. An elderly woman stood next to her, her hands tightly wrapped around the handles of her walker. She was visibly trembling. Parkinson's disease, maybe.

"Austin Harris is a genius. Truly."

"What is it?" Allison asked.

"You don't know about the Vitality Spa?"

She shook her head.

"It's a parabiosis center. I've been on the wait list for over two years ..."

Allison tried to break down the word to understand its meaning. *Para-*, meaning *next to*—

"... and now, my host is finally available. It'll be born in just two weeks."

—*biosis*, meaning *life*. She didn't get it. "But what are they doing?"

"Bonding. Look closely. See the IV tubing?"

Allison moved closer to the window. Only one of the three women with strollers remained on the track. As she drew nearer, Allison saw thick red tubing hanging from beneath her shirt, as well as a yellow tube dangling beneath the back of her shirt, snaking around her body into the stroller. She was moving at a good pace, bouncing to whatever song was in her headphones, full of energy.

"The matures share a circulatory system with the juveniles. They're pumping each other's blood. Isn't that beautiful?"

"What?" Her eyes were fixed on the woman walking with the stroller. Those were IV tubes. What this woman was saying—

"See that man over there with the checkered shirt?" The woman pointed to the three board game players. "That's Edward. He had end-stage liver disease with irreversible decompensation. After three months of bonding with his host, his liver is completely healthy."

"Three months?" Allison frowned, still confused. Three months of bonding?

"Uh-huh. And Dorothy there, on the track, she's eighty-four. She came here in a wheelchair with spinal cord damage and could barely walk. Her spinal cord has been repaired, and her muscles have completely regenerated. She's been bonded to her host for only nine months."

Oh god. They *were* IV tubes. Allison's mouth went dry. "Bonded?"

"Yeah, look here." The woman grabbed her walker and inched toward a window opposite the one they were looking through. It looked straight into a dorm of some type. A woman lay on her side with a toddler folded in her arms, both of them fast asleep. Their blanket was pulled only waist-high, revealing three tubes, two from the front of the woman's torso and one from the back, similarly attached to the toddler.

"That's Marge. She's been bonded to her host since it was born. Maybe two years now?"

A chill ran through her body. *They're pumping each other's blood.* She stared at the sleeping couple.

"Look," her guide continued. "They share a blood supply and cerebral spinal fluid, so the juvenile's blood is coursing through the veins of the adult, restoring function to all her tissues—the brain, the heart, the liver, even the skin. This doesn't just slow the aging process; it reverses it. Austin Harris is a genius, isn't he? He's the first in the world to implement this concept, you know."

The toddler wasn't moving, and Allison couldn't tell if it was breathing. "Are they dead? The babies?"

"Dead? Of course not." The woman looked at her like she was crazy. "They sleep most of the day. Twenty-two hours, I think Austin said."

"They're taking the blood from the babies?" It wasn't a question, more an expression of her astonishment. This couldn't be real. It had to be a crazy, freakish dream. This was the most disturbing sight she'd ever seen.

"No, silly, they're not taking the blood. They're circulating it through the mature adult. It's all very humane. The juveniles feel nothing. They've been purpose-bred for this by our young ladies right here at the Colony. They're

genetically engineered to have no pain and sleep most of the day. They're—
"

"Babies," Allison whispered.

"What?" The woman seemed confused.

"They're babies. Babies!" She had to restrain herself from grabbing the woman's frail shoulders and shaking her.

"Not really." The old woman chuckled and slapped her arm good-naturedly, as if they were arguing over whether vampires were real. "They're hosts."

Allison gaped at her. "They're babies! They're not juveniles or hosts. They're—oh my god—they're human babies." This was what Austin was doing. This is why he created the Colony. All those young kids out there had been brought here to breed babies to rejuvenate old people. This whole day had been a lie. Her stomach heaved, and she hunched over until it passed. "I need to get out of here."

"I don't understand why you're upset," the woman said. "They're not real babies. They're laboratory humans, no different than laboratory dogs or primates. They don't know a different life—"

Allison hobbled as fast as she could down the hall back to the elevator.

84

Malloy declined another call from Cramer. Jesus, what could be so important?

"Tell me again what Allison Stevens said." Malloy kept his eyes forward, scanning the desert along the service road.

"She was upset by a phone call to a vic, I can't remember which one. Said they blamed her and threatened her. She said Austin Harris was trying to frame her for his fraud with that bank account. She got the victims' information from Chambers's office—his secretary, I think—and she had a bank statement proving that payment to the vics came from an account under her name at Delbarton. But she said she had no awareness of the account. She never mentioned Tyler, though. She didn't know about him."

Malloy chewed the inside of his cheek. He felt the familiar tingle of being on the cusp of a breakthrough. His intuition told him he had all the pieces of the puzzle, and now he needed to get them into the right positions.

"Okay, fast forward. Wang calls my cell phone just before he's killed in front of Allison Stevens's apartment. She disappears. Where does she go?"

Garcia shrugged.

"Put the relationships together. Let's assume Austin Harris set up the Delbarton account in Allison's name, hoping that would give him some separation if he came under investigation. He must have known it was only a matter of time, right? That account paid the vics, and the vics were patients of Dr. Chambers."

"Yeah?" Garcia didn't seem to be making the connection.

"We know that Chambers is associated with the Vitapura. They have a lot of space here. What if Chambers offered Harris a hideout in this place, maybe in the employee housing? And Allison Stevens by now would have been on the FBI's radar. She might have disappeared before she could be arrested. Maybe she made her way here—hiding out with her lover, Harris."

"Listen, boss, that's a lot of what-ifs. Aren't you the one always telling us not to speculate on—"

"Stop here," Malloy ordered.

Garcia hit the brakes. There was nowhere to pull off the road, so he simply put the truck in park and turned off the engine.

"Look up ahead." Malloy nodded to an entrance about a hundred yards up the road. "Some delivery gate?"

Garcia shrugged.

It was difficult to see, but it appeared to be a wrought-iron gate in the same decorative style as Vitapura's front gate, complete with intimidating spikes at the top of the iron bars. He wasn't surprised that he could spot two cameras aimed at the road in front of the gate, and he wondered if there were more. He eyed the long cement brick wall. He didn't spot any cameras, but he did notice something else.

"How tall do you think these walls are?"

Garcia squinted. "Ten feet, maybe? Twelve?"

"The walls at the entry gate were barely taller than me. Certainly not ten or twelve feet. Same with the gate."

Garcia eyed the wall in front of them, and then followed it as it ran parallel to the service road as far as they could see. "Maybe they built them taller out here because of the ATVs. Noise pollution."

"To protect the fragile ears of the help? Doubt it."

They surveyed the gate a minute longer.

"Wanna go poke around?" Garcia asked.

Malloy heard the impatience in Garcia's voice, but he didn't care. He was the boss. "We're at a bad angle here. Let's get a little closer but stay out of sight."

He opened his door and stepped out. A snake slithered between his legs and he yelped, jumping back against the door. Jesus Christ. This place really gave him the creeps.

Garcia reached under the seat and pulled out a shoulder holster.

"Jesus, Garcia. We're just looking around."

"This wasn't my idea."

Malloy picked his way through cacti and sagebrush until he reached the wall. It was easily double his height, and from where he was standing, he couldn't see the end of it. This was one expensive wall. But for what? Were they hiding something in there?

A burst of walkie-talkie static startled him, and he flattened himself against the wall. Probably a security guard stationed inside the gate.

They inched along the wall away from the gate and back toward the truck. Garcia jogged ahead of him, but Malloy continued at a walk. It was nearly noon, and the heat was wearing him down. His raspy breathing burned his dry throat. Garcia was right. They shouldn't be doing this right now. A much better approach would be to go back to the office and see about getting the case reopened. Maybe once he told Cramer his theory, he'd help them get a search warrant.

He stopped to catch his breath, bending over at the waist, when Garcia called out.

"Over here."

Garcia was peering through a two-inch separation in the cement wall. Of course. A cement wall this size couldn't be erected in a single slab. And although they appeared to have filled the spaces between slabs with mortar, the crack had dried and crumbled under the blazing Arizona sun, leaving an opening.

Garcia tramped over some sagebrush to get out of the way, and Malloy leaned in. He couldn't see anything through the narrow slit. "Shit. This is no good." Disappointed, he stepped back and inspected the wall, looking for a larger crack.

Garcia reached down and picked up a pile of dust left by crumbled mortar and spread it across his hands.

"What the hell are you doing?"

Garcia reached up as high as he could and pushed his hands as far into the crack as they would fit. He angled the toe of one sneaker, shoved it into the crack, and lifted himself off the ground. Hand over hand, toe over toe, he climbed the crack until he was high enough to reach the top. He flung one hand over the top to brace himself, keeping the other hand firmly jammed into the crack, and straightened his legs to push himself up a couple more inches. He panted hard as he peered over the top of the wall.

"Jesus." Garcia was a complete mystery to him. "What do you see?"

He didn't answer.

"Garcia!"

Garcia watched for several seconds before lowering himself halfway back down the wall. He jumped the rest of the way.

He dusted off the thighs of his pants. "Boss, that ain't no staff housing."

85

Allison locked the restroom door and clutched the pedestal sink with both hands. Her legs trembled and she heaved again.

It almost worked, Brad, you son of a bitch. You almost had me. You and Mia and your perfectly planned recruitment day. He'd promised that their work was noble, creating a better world, and she'd fallen for it. God, how could she have been so stupid? She should have trusted her instincts; she'd known there was something dark and wrong about this place. She'd felt it from the start. Her emotions had fucked her over again, just like they always did.

She growled and shook the sink as though she would rip it from the wall.

"So what do I do now?" she whispered to her reflection. "What am I supposed to do now?"

The muscles in her face tightened as the realization hit her with full force. *No one in the Colony is forced to do anything,* he'd said. She wouldn't be leaving the Colony, not after what she'd witnessed. No one left the Colony. Ever. The room seemed to darken around her, and the air thickened.

One … two … three … four. Exhale.

She wiped her eyes and face and took one last, deep breath. She opened the restroom door and surveyed the hall. The elevator bank was deserted. She glanced over at her wheelchair, still parked near the bench.

Screw it.

She hobbled quickly across the lobby. Once outside, she looked left, then right. She braced herself for the pain and sprinted toward the outer wall.

There had to be a way out.

86

ith perfection comes purification. Layla delivered her chant one last time, then opened the door and stepped into the room.

"Oh," she breathed. She'd never seen such a beautiful bedroom in her life, at least not the life she could remember. The floors were wood, real wood, unlike the marble and cement she was used to. The bed was centered on a wood-paneled wall, lit by overhead lighting. It was at least double the size of any bed she'd ever slept on, and it was covered by a thick fluffy blanket and four pillows.

Next to the bed on either side were two brown leather armchairs with matching ottomans in front. Would someone be here with her during her procedure? The medical monitors and IV tubing were built into the wall behind the bed, giving the room a very tidy look.

Out the window, fluffy white clouds shrouded the tops of the majestic mountains in the distance, and the long grass on either side of the river below waved softly in the breeze. She loved their new home here so much better than the last one. She hoped they would stay here forever.

She removed her shoes and set them in a corner, then lowered herself into heel-sit position. Her shins no longer hurt, and the pose no longer felt befitting for meditation. She repositioned herself into a perfect plank, which she held for a full minute before starting her chant. By the time Dr. Jeremy entered the room, the burning in her wrists had turned to numbness.

"You, young lady, are supposed to be relaxing, not exercising."

She lowered herself with slow, measured control until she was flat on the ground. She curled into child's pose and then stood up.

"That's how I relax." She gave him a good-natured smile.

"Up on the bed, under the blanket." He opened a door in the wall next to her bed and began typing on a computer keyboard.

She climbed up onto the bed and closed her eyes, sinking into the pillowy mattress. She didn't ever want to leave. The head of the bed inclined with a low buzz until she was seated comfortably upright. She felt like a queen.

Dr. Jeremy rolled over to her on a stool. He attached a blood pressure cuff to her arm. "How's that?"

"Pretty amazing."

"Good, good." He put his stethoscope in his ears and listened to her pulse. "Okay, everything looks fine from my end. I'll be back shortly."

This was it. She was finally here. Thank you, Father. Thank you.

A minute later, the door opened again. She was expecting Dr. Jeremy, but it was someone else.

He closed the door and strode over to her with confidence. With purpose. Although he wore the same white linen pants and tunic as everyone else in the Colony, she knew the instant his eyes met hers who he was. Her voice seemed to have disappeared, and she could only whisper.

"Father."

He walked to the side of Layla's bed and sat on the edge. Putting both hands on her shoulders, he leaned in close to her face, so close he might have kissed her. Instead, he closed his eyes and pressed his forehead against hers.

She exhaled as she felt his purity pouring into her like an electric current. She closed her eyes. *I want to be like you, Father.*

"Thank you," he whispered. "Thank you, Layla, for your sacrifices."

He stayed in that position, with his forehead pressed to hers, eyes closed, for several minutes. He didn't speak, and Layla wondered if he was reading her mind. In case he was, she began chanting. *With pain comes perfection. With perfection comes purification.*

At last, he pulled away, but his hands remained on her shoulders. His intense gray eyes were hypnotic, and although she wanted to show respect by looking down, she found she couldn't break his gaze. She couldn't even blink.

The Father took a deep breath and lowered his hands from her shoulders. "Thank you for coming to us, Layla. Thank you for bringing all the beauty of your impure life to our Colony and for allowing us to make you pure. You have so much to give."

She was so captivated, she didn't know how to respond.

"Today, I bestow upon you your callings, and I bring you your gifts." He smiled, radiating a warmth that seemed to pulse through her entire body. "I've been waiting a long time for this, dear girl."

"Me, too." His smile was infectious, and she smiled back. She didn't feel intimidated or afraid, as she'd expected she would. She felt … well, she felt like family.

He collected both her hands in his own. "Let's begin. I have two callings for you. The first is something I'd been hoping for. I've been watching you to see if you would develop as I'd expected, and indeed, you have not disappointed me. In fact, you've even surprised me."

Layla's stomach fluttered with anticipation.

"Your first calling is one of leadership. I will ask you, alongside Brother James and Sister Mia, to lead our colony. For some time now, I've been intricately involved in the operations of this colony, but now I must spend my time developing the other colonies throughout the world."

She wasn't sure she understood. "There are others?"

He smiled. "Of course. Spreading purification through the world is a big job."

"Oh, sure." She felt dumb.

He looked at her sternly. "Leadership is not granted, however. It's earned through service, trust, and kindness. It comes from within you. I've seen your potential, and I want to see you grow and mature every day. I want you to apply those qualities to build on our core values here at the Colony."

"Yes, Father."

"This is a significant calling. So as a tool to help you be successful, I'm giving you the wakefulness treatment. I am trusting you with this tool because I know you will use it wisely. This elixir will allow you to live comfortably on three or four hours of sleep every night, which will afford you additional hours during the day to accomplish all you need to do, including your physical, emotional, and educational development."

He closed his eyes. Layla was unsure if she should speak or thank him, but he opened his eyes and continued. "In addition, I'm giving you the intelligence treatment panel. I reserve this elixir only for the most dedicated of our colonists. It's a powerful tool. It will allow you to learn at a rate significantly faster than other people. I'll expect you to apply what you learn about effective leadership and the psychology of people. You'll need to understand how to foster confidence in others, how to engage our young people in our community. You'll get to know each and every member of the Colony, and you'll be a mentor and teacher to them. Do you understand?"

"Yes, Father."

"Brother James will discuss this with you in more detail, and he'll work with you as the elixir takes root in your genes. It's not an overnight miracle, and you'll need to continue to exercise your mind, just like your body and spirit."

She nodded. Her mind was racing. Leader of the Colony. Leader. Of. The. Colony.

"My second calling for you makes me the happiest, and I hope it makes you happy as well."

She leaned forward.

"We have perfected the genetic formula to create the first pure generation, the saviors of the human race, a necessary evolution of our species from its current impure state. As you know, impures are weak and fragile, susceptible to disease and infection, and intellectually inadequate. The pure generation will have higher intelligence, stronger bodies, longer lives, and greater empathy toward others. Imagine a world filled with pures, Layla, people like you and me and Brother James and Sister Mia."

Just like the flowers. She imagined the earth covered in beautiful roses and beautiful people.

"It's a vision I've dedicated my life to achieving. We still have a long way to go to propagate purity throughout the world, but now we must take this necessary first step. We must begin with a single child. I would like you to bear this child."

"Oh." She felt the blood drain from her face, and a tingling sensation washed through her. She would bear a child. She was going to have a baby, a pure—the *first*—pure baby.

"You'll be our Eve, and your offspring will begin pure life here in our own Garden of Eden. The first of the F1 generation. What do you think, my dear?"

"I'm … I'm honored."

She couldn't help reaching out and wrapping her arms around him, and when he hugged her back, all she could think was that there was no place in the world more wonderful than the Colony.

"Excellent." He held her at arm's length and looked into her eyes. "I'm so proud of you, Layla. You've become an incredible woman. Truly exemplary."

As the Father walked toward the door, her head stopped swimming and settled on three words: *As you wish.*

"Father, will there be an Adam in our Garden of Eden?"

He looked confused. "My dear, in this age, a conjugal arrangement isn't necessary for conception or childbearing."

Her heart sank. Of course, the work of the Colony was far too important to tolerate foolish brainstem emotions. Fairy tales weren't practical—

His mouth turned upward in a sly smile. "However, should there be someone out there with whom you'd like to share your life, you certainly have my blessing."

87

Austin wanted to throw his phone against the stucco wall of the juvenile center, which he was just getting ready to tour with the investors when he received the call from security.

He rubbed the back of his neck and addressed the group, who'd stopped to admire the outdoor playground. "Folks, I need to step away for a few moments, but Madeline has just rejoined us, and she'll escort you back to the center for brunch. I'll be with you in just a few minutes."

"Coast is clear," Madeline murmured as she passed him.

Her unwavering composure made him want to slap her. He turned abruptly and stalked back toward the gateway.

"Bradley James Fucking Elliott," he muttered under his breath.

This whole thing was Brad's fault. Austin hadn't wanted Allison here in the first place. He'd have been more than happy to let her fall into the cumbersome claws of the justice system, tying her up in legal defense for a year. And goddammit, that strategy was an important piece of the puzzle. The FBI needed to identify a conspirator in order to lose interest in him.

But Brad wanted Allison, and he needed Brad. At least a while longer.

Frankly, he couldn't understand Brad's infatuation with Allison Stevens. With his boyish good looks and high position at the Colony, he could have had any woman he wanted. What could he possibly see in that mousy little bitch? She was a bore, a tiresome homebody always on the verge of an emotional breakdown. And if she'd just minded her own fucking business, this all could've happened later, after the FBI had roughed her up some more and she'd had one of her famous meltdowns. If only they could've swooped in just before sentencing; she'd have been much more malleable.

He quickened his pace across the courtyard. No flurry of activity. It was a typical, dull day at the Colony, which for once he was happy about. He glanced at his phone. No messages. They hadn't found her yet. Goddammit.

Admittedly, he hadn't expected this much fight from her. He knew she wouldn't be an easy sell, but he'd been certain she'd fall in line, given her options. This defiance, however, was unacceptable. Even Brad would have to admit that her behavior couldn't be tolerated. Now she'd have to be eliminated. What a waste of all that investment.

His phone vibrated. "What?"

"Sir, we haven't located Allison Stevens yet, but one of the perimeter guards thought he might have seen someone running near the service gate."

"Pull video from that whole area and increase security over there. If anyone catches sight of her, take her out."

"Sir?"

"Shoot her."

He ended the call.

88

"**W**hat did you say?" Malloy shook his head, disbelieving.

"Hundreds of people." Garcia repeated. "It looks like a cult. And they look young. Like kids, almost. Like Tyler's age. I'm telling you, this is where he was. He wasn't in that wellness center. This is where they kept him. Behind these walls, like a fucking prisoner."

Malloy had to see for himself. Garcia wasn't really known to exaggerate—but hundreds? Certainly, that was way too many to be employed at the Vitapura.

He plodded through the sagebrush, making his way back toward the gate.

"Boss, we need to call for backup."

"Not yet. Just let me see." He needed to know if Garcia was right. He needed to see if this was where Tyler had been held, if this is where they took young kids and did experiments on them, destroying their brains, killing them, and leaving them to die in a dumpster. He tried to pick up his pace, but his legs just wouldn't go faster. He felt light-headed partly because of the heat but mostly because he felt on the verge of the answer to the question he'd been asking himself every single day since the day he'd learned of Tyler's death.

"The gate is guarded. If this is something illegal, they'll be packin'."

Malloy didn't care.

"Fuck." Garcia moved in next to him.

89

Allison stood breathless with her back against the shed door. She was trapped. She knew it had been a dumb move, running into a building barely bigger than a closet, but she knew the guards had seen her, half skipping and half hobbling in the bulky medical boot. She just needed a minute to catch her breath and come up with a plan.

Sweat fell from her hair and stung her eyes. She wiped it away and peered through the narrow air vent. There it was, the gate she'd been unable to find while she was running, maybe a hundred yards away. She wondered if she could squeeze between the iron bars.

She looked around the shed for a place to hide, but the shelving offered not even the smallest concealed corner. Boxes and plastic containers lined the shelves, and she tore through them, looking for anything she might be able to brandish as a weapon. Anything that might at least buy her a couple of seconds. All she found were bundles of laundered clothing, towels, dishcloths, and bedsheets. So much white. What was their obsession with white? She yanked boxes and bundles off the shelves, uttering satisfied grunts as their impact with the gravel floor sent dust flying, coating the fancy-schmancy spa bedding.

She'd hurled the last bundle before she noticed a box, colorfully illustrated, that didn't belong there. Some poor delivery driver must have stashed it here for fear of getting fired for bringing poisoned world contraband inside the walls. She picked it up by the metal handle. It was lighter than she expected. She ran her finger around the metal lid. The hinge squeaked as she opened the latch. Empty.

Voices came from outside the shed. Shit. She dropped to her knees and lay the open box on the ground beside her. She had an idea. It wasn't a very good plan, but it was all she had.

90

Austin's eyes darted across the security monitors.

"Go back five minutes."

The staffer's fingers flew over the keys of the single keyboard that controlled all twenty-four monitors in the security room. Austin scanned the screens looking for atypical activity. Where was the little bitch? The whole damn security detail dressed in the same cozy whites as everyone else—Brad's mind-fuckingly idiotic idea. Now they could only recognize their own staff by the way they moved expeditiously around the grounds.

"There!" he yelled. "Did you see that? Back up again."

The staffer started the video replay again. "The linen supply," he confirmed.

"Alert me if you see her leave the shed." Austin grabbed a walkie-talkie and bolted from the room.

And of all the goddamn days for cops to show up and want to poke around. He couldn't believe his bad luck. But now the situation would be contained and additional collateral damage avoided. He tried to calm himself with a deep breath.

Not that it meant he wouldn't be getting another lecture from Hammond. He'd put his own ass on the line with Hammond, all for Brad's obsession with the whore, and now he'd surely pay for it. But he'd sure as hell make Brad pay right along with him. Wait until Hammond learned this whole thing was Brad's doing.

He plastered a hard smile on his face and waved to the inductees as he walked with purpose along the path. They didn't know him, thankfully, and he was able to move along without the obligatory hugs. Fucking Brad—or rather Brother James, another infuriating Colony custom—and all the goddamn hugging. Brad was a genius, that part was true, but catering to these lowlife assholes was nonsensical. For god's sake, these losers were lab rats. They didn't need the life Brad was giving them. A hundred thousand here, a quarter million there. Organic food, pillow-top mattresses. A new goddamn gym. What the hell was wrong with the old gym?

His pulse picked up as he neared the shed. He'd drag her out of there by her hair and hold her down so the guard could put a perfect bullet hole between those dopey eyes. He couldn't wait to deliver the news of Allison Stevens's unfortunate demise. He could practically hear Brad's heart breaking right in half.

91

alloy kept his eyes on the cameras above the gate and pressed his body against the wall to stay out of their range. He leaned around just barely enough to see through the bars of the gate. At that angle, he could see a dozen or so people dressed in the eerie white pajamas. They were walking, some alone, some in groups. He leaned a bit further and saw a large building with people going in and out.

Garcia was right about one thing: They all seemed to be young people. But he didn't see hundreds of them, maybe a dozen or so. He noticed an empty chair on the other side of the gate, with several empty bottles of water beside it. The guard had to be taking a piss.

A band of tightness snugged around his chest. Now would not be a good time for a heart attack. *Come for a jog, Pete,* Darcy was always nagging him. *You're gonna be dead before you're sixty.*

He moved out of his hidden position and stood fully in front of the gate. He couldn't see a goddamn thing behind the two large buildings on either side of the road.

Garcia moved to the other side of the gate and gestured frantically. "Boss. Here."

Malloy moved next to him, and his view opened to what looked like a grassy field with trees off in the distance. It looked like paradise in the desert, even more beautiful than the grounds at the wellness center.

And people everywhere. Hundreds of people.

His phone vibrated for the hundredth time. Goddammit.

"John, this is not a good time. I'm in the middle—"

"Pete. Listen to me. You need to leave right now. Get in your car, and drive away. Right. Fucking. Now."

Malloy's eyes shot up to the security cameras. Did Cramer know where he was?

"Pete. Just turn and walk away."

"Excuse me, this area is for service vehicles only," a man said, approaching the gate from the inside. He wore the white pajamas too, and Malloy didn't see any sign of a weapon. "Are you looking for the wellness center main entrance? I'll be happy to direct you."

"Pete. Can you hear me? You don't know—"

Malloy disconnected the phone and reached for his badge.

92

The voices didn't seem to be getting closer, but Allison's time was running out. She untied the dust-covered medical boot. It was slowing her significantly with its rigid support, and she needed ankle mobility to dodge anyone who tried to grab her. She unwound the elastic wrap from her foot and ankle and quickly rewrapped it, tighter around her foot, looser around her ankle. Her breath came fast and hard as sweat dripped off her hair and pooled in the gravel beneath her.

She wasn't worried about the pain. She'd once finished third in a 5K with a pulled hamstring; she could certainly run a hundred yards on a broken foot. But she knew she'd make it worse.

She stood up and surveyed the gate again. Two men stood just outside the gate, talking with a guard. She wiped the sweat from her eyes with the backs of her dirt-caked hands and squinted for a better look. The cops! She was sure of it. She couldn't see their faces, but that long, straight black hair... It had to be that DEA guy. Excited, she groped for the door handle just as a walkie-talkie blatted right outside the shed door.

Shit. She retreated two steps. If the guard came in, he'd close the door and silence her until the cops were gone. If she wanted to make a run for it, she had to get past him first. It was back to Plan A.

She knelt down on the ground and waited, panting, her right hand gripping the handle of the box.

93

Austin rounded the corner and stopped dead in his tracks.

"Fuck."

Those cops hadn't left the grounds after all. Why hadn't security informed him? Goddammit, this day was turning into complete shit.

He turned the dial on the walkie-talkie and spoke in low voice. "Call off the search for Allison. I need all guards away from the service gate. Keep a visual on the shed."

He moved cautiously along the outer wall of the cafeteria until he had no further cover. Then he moved slowly along the path, with his head bowed slightly toward the gate. He could hear voices but couldn't make out the conversation. Presumably, the guard at the gate was explaining that all inquiries about the wellness center must be handled at the front gate.

Remain calm and smile—and under no circumstances, even if a warrant is presented, is the gate to be opened.

Sticking to the stone path, Austin turned left and headed toward the linen shed. He'd step inside like he was on a routine errand, pull Allison to the floor, and cover her mouth until the coast was clear. With any luck, he'd suffocate her during the wait.

A scant few yards from the shed, his walkie-talkie hissed. He winced and turned the dial to silence it. He shot a furtive glance at the cops. They seemed to be in a heated conversation with the guard, but the gate was staying closed, per protocol.

He stepped to the shed door and turned the handle.

94

Three.

Two.

One.

Allison held her breath.

The door opened, and one shoe stepped through the door. As soon as she saw the second, she stood up and with a mighty grunt, swung the heavy box as hard as she could at the side of her assailant's head.

She'd underestimated her momentum and the weight of the box. It struck his right temple with such force that the box burst open, spraying gravel, dirt, and rocks across the shed like bullets. He crumpled face down onto the ground. She glanced to make sure he wasn't moving, then carefully stepped over him and was reaching for the door when she saw the blood.

Thick, dark blood was pooling beneath his head, seeping into the gravel beneath him.

Her body shook violently.

Oh my god. She'd killed him. Killed him.

She looked over at the dented lunch box, splayed open in the gravel. Scooby-Doo and his smiling gang were now savagely doused in scarlet. She froze, unable to help the man who lay bleeding yet unable to make a break toward the police at the gate.

Something warm and wet touched her toes. Her white elastic bandage was wicking blood from the ground. Blood splattered her white clothes like the first swing of Pollock's paintbrush across a fresh canvas. The crimson pool beneath the man continued to expand, now soaking into the white bed linens that lay strewn on the ground. She stood mesmerized, watching the blood soak into his crisp white dress shirt and spread down the sleeves toward his wrists and—

No. No, no, no.

The gold cufflinks. Her gift to him on their one-year anniversary of dating.

Engraved with AH.

Bile filled her throat, and she heaved. She stumbled out the door to vomit, but nothing came up. She turned back, desperately wanting to believe it wasn't real. It couldn't be real.

Oh god. Austin. Oh god.

She staggered out of the shed. Sweat and tears burned her eyes, and she couldn't see the gate.

"Help me, please! Help me! My name is Allison Stevens." She wiped her eyes with her dirty hands, which only intensified the burning. She moved toward the gate as fast as she could.

"I'm being held here! My name is Allison Stevens!"

She heard yelling. She blinked several times, and new tears cleared her vision somewhat. She'd closed half the distance.

The young cop took a step back and pulled a firearm, holding it out in front of him.

Something tripped her and she fell hard, sprawling with her hands in front of her, her face in the dirt. She sputtered and started to get up, but the weight of another body pancaked her to the ground. A hand ground her head into the dirt as her wrists were cuffed behind her back. She listened for a gunshot but heard nothing.

And then everything went black.

95

Malloy swung around at the cries of a woman, who was running toward them. What had she shouted? Allison Stevens?

Garcia had heard it, too. He took a step back and pulled his gun.

"Open the gate!" Garcia shouted, his Glock 21 trained on the guard.

Oh, Jesus.

The guard held his hands up, palms forward. "Don't shoot!"

"Open the motherfucking gate!"

"Put the gun down, Garcia." Malloy tried to keep his voice steady as he observed the takedown of the woman. The calculated movements of the two men who tackled her told him they were no mall cops. These men had military training.

"I'm gonna open the gate. Don't shoot." The guard moved cautiously toward them, his palms still facing forward.

"Garcia, lower your weapon," Malloy growled. "Do it right now."

Malloy wasn't interested in the gate guard. He was, however, very concerned about the group of men flanking them. Six, maybe? Seven? They stayed in a tight group as they edged toward the gate, and they didn't have the look of curious bystanders.

"Okay, okay, I'm opening the gate," the guard repeated loudly as he advanced.

Instead of reaching for the keypad, the guard took two quick, deliberate steps backward. Malloy's mouth went dry, and he lunged toward Garcia just as he heard the single, sharp report. Garcia crumpled to the ground in a single motion, like his body had no bones.

Garcia. Jesus! No. God, no.

He didn't need to look closer to know what had happened. The high-caliber bullet had exited the back of his head in a spray of blood and bone. Garcia was dead before he hit the ground.

"I'm sorry, Agent Malloy, but you left us no choice," the gate guard called, his voice calm and almost sympathetic.

Malloy could barely hear him over the ringing in his ears and the sound of his own pounding heartbeat. His chest tightened, and he felt a pain shoot up his arm. He pressed one hand to his chest, and his vision narrowed to the scene in front of him.

Fucking Garcia and that Clint Eastwood attitude. How many times had he told him—

"Your partner put our operation at risk."

The ringing in his ears seemed to be quieting, and his heart rate slowed as he became hyperaware of his surroundings. He turned from Garcia and looked through the gate.

Where had the shot come from?

The group of six. Yes, he could now see six hard-eyed men, who looked very calm and focused, given the circumstances, in a fan formation fifty feet out. No one moved toward him. They were waiting. For what?

The stabbing pain in his chest made it difficult to inhale.

"We do not choose violence here, Agent Malloy. It is important to us that you understand that. We value human life. It is you who trespassed here, bringing aggression from your impure world."

He watched two men pick up the woman who claimed to be Allison Stevens. He couldn't tell if she was dead or unconscious.

Malloy stood frozen. In all his years as an agent, he'd never encountered a scene like the one unraveling in front of him, and he didn't know how to respond. This sort of violence simply didn't happen to DEA officers in broad daylight. Garcia's long hair splayed around him, blacker than ever as it soaked up the blood that pooled beneath him. Fucking Garcia and that hair. His gut clenched.

"But our work here is too important."

The earnestness of the guard's words is what convinced Malloy that his own life was over. *Robbie. I love you. I'll tell mom how proud I am of you.* He didn't believe in an afterlife, and he wasn't sure why he'd thought that. *No regrets, Pete,* Suzanne had said on her death bed. But Malloy was filled with regrets. He'd failed Tyler. And Garcia. And Suzanne. And now Robbie, Darcy— he'd failed everyone he'd ever loved. A sense of anguish washed over him. He had unfinished business. He wasn't ready to die.

"Your sacrifice is for the greater good of humanity. May you rest in peace, sir."

As Malloy dropped to his knees under the crushing pain in his chest, he caught a glint of sunlight in his peripheral vision that his police instinct briefly registered as the scope of a rooftop sniper. The brilliant light of the southwestern sun made the scene impossibly bright. He barely caught the brief muzzle flash before the whole world turned white and he knew no more.

96

ayla picked at the hangnail on her thumb. Then, fearful that it would start to bleed, she laid her hands gently at her sides. She didn't want to yank the IVs in each arm. The needle in her spine was the most unsettling, and although the nurse told her it was perfectly fine to lie back, she was afraid she'd dislodge it. She wanted to ensure nothing would compromise her treatments.

She closed her eyes. "With pain comes perfection. With perfection comes purification. This is the Father's will for me. As a pure, I am responsible for the purification of the Colony and the propagation of purity into the world. This is the Father's will for me."

Propagation. Spreading purity. She would spread purity into the world.

She put her hand on her stomach. Her child would be pure. He or she would be the first, the F1 generation. She would be a mother, just like the Christian fairy tale of Adam and Eve.

She so badly wanted Brother James to be her Adam.

And then he stepped into the room. She felt herself blush, as if he'd read her thoughts.

He walked to her bedside and sat on the edge of the bed, just as the Father had. He lifted her chin to meet his eyes. "You look absolutely radiant."

"So do you. Are you getting a treatment today too?"

He laughed, and she did too. She couldn't believe she'd said something so witty.

He turned his head slightly and looked at her oddly. Suspiciously. Then he stood up and pulled the chair around so that it faced her. He sat down but didn't speak.

"Cat got your tongue?" she asked. She didn't know where she'd heard that expression. It was kind of terrifying, if she thought about it. A cat taking your tongue? She wished she hadn't said that.

He didn't smile. Instead he looked down, as if he were disappointed in her. Maybe not. Maybe he was … nervous?

Still with his gaze in his lap, he said, "I have to tell you something I should have told you before."

"Um, okay." She was nervous too. He wasn't himself.

He met her eyes. "I knew you, Layla. I knew you in your poisoned life."

"What?"

"You didn't know me, but I knew you. I was"—he searched for the right word—"I was enchanted by you."

Layla's heart thumped.

"I just wanted you to know that before the next phase of your life begins. I needed to be honest with you."

"You knew me? How?"

"You were in college when I saw you the first time. You were so smart and so funny, and you were beautiful. Just like now." He sat up again. "And I always wanted to meet you, I did. But our circumstances … well, I guess it just wasn't the right time. But then when you came to us at the Colony in Arizona that first day, I realized how special you are. Even during your intake, I knew. But I had to let you decide if you were meant to stay with us. Then when we migrated the Colony to Mexico, that's when you really blossomed into this wonderful—"

Dr. Jeremy burst through the door, his eyes on his chart. "Okay, I think we're all set."

Brother James stopped talking.

"Ready to get started?" the doctor asked with a grin.

She searched Brother James's face. She needed to hear what he was going to say. She had to know if he really loved her. But he had turned his attention to the doctor.

Reluctantly, she answered, "Ready as I'll ever be."

As Dr. Jeremy gathered several vials and syringes, Brother James pushed his chair back. "Well, I guess I better leave you to it."

God, she didn't want him to go. He started toward the door, and panic seized her. She might never see him again. But then her smiling dad flashed across her mind's eye. She had his memory now, and he had believed she was special. It was enough to give her strength. Confidence.

She called out just as Brother James stepped through the door. "Will you stay with me?"

He stopped midstep as if he were thinking about it. Then he pivoted back.

"As you wish, beautiful girl." He gently lifted her hand and wrapped both of his around it. "I'll stay with you forever."

97

"**W**hat happened to the cops?"

Allison sat across the conference table while Brad set up a camera. She'd slept most of the last day, or maybe two, refusing food and water, but evidently showers were not negotiable. Her hair was still damp after being forcefully held by a guard under the hot, streaming water, and she wore a fresh pair of white pajamas. She despised white.

He didn't acknowledge the question.

"Did you kill them?" She knew they were dead. If they weren't, the FBI would have been here by now, possibly with the National Guard. "They'll come looking for those agents, you know. Cops can't just disappear."

He reached into his bag and pulled out a newspaper, folded. He pushed it toward her.

DEA officers killed in meth lab raid in Tempe.

She shoved the paper away.

"It was an unintended and unfortunate consequence of their interference. We don't like to take lives, but our work here must continue."

Disgusted, she turned away toward the painting over a table that held a fruit bowl. Wholesomeness was the message they wanted to impart to new recruits, wholesome goodness. The painting was a goddamn water lily pond. It had to be Claude Fucking Monet. She hated Monet. They should have hung some Pablo Picasso in this house of horrors—or better yet, Salvador

Dali.

"We're ready to begin. You've signed a consent form to participate in this program, and we're going to video this intake interview in the event that your consent is challenged by yourself or anyone on your behalf. Do you understand?"

"Does it matter?" Of course, she'd signed the consent form. What choice did she have?

"Will you please state your full name and your date of birth?"

She looked at the red blinking light on the small recorder that stood on a tripod next to Brad, then turned and answered to the wall. "Allison Cassidy Stevens, December 7, 1990."

"Thank you. And what are the names of your parents?"

"Michael Thomas Stevens and Rachel Leigh Cassidy."

"Thank you." He made some notes on her chart. She tried to read it, but she couldn't make it out.

"How is your relationship with your father?"

"My father is deceased. He died when I was twelve." She fingered the pendant hanging from her neck, running her index finger around the circle of diamonds. *It symbolizes eternity,* he'd told her on his deathbed. *It means I'll always be in your heart. And you'll always be in mine, even though I'll be in heaven.*

"How did he die?"

"Assisted suicide. He had bone and spinal cancer. He was in considerable pain and was allergic to opioids. Is all this questioning really necessary?"

"He gave you that opal necklace?"

She dropped her hand back to the table. None of his fucking business.

"And your mother?"

She began scratching at a hangnail on her thumb. This interview was gratuitous. "My mother and I don't speak."

"And why is that?"

"I thought you just wanted my verbal consent."

"I'm sorry. I know it's not always easy to discuss your poisoned life, but we'd like to have a record of why you've chosen to leave it."

"It's not a poisoned life. I don't know why you use that creepy terminology. It's just, you know, my life." Her very shitty life.

"Of course." He smiled, and she scowled at the condescension in it. "Your mother?"

"She remarried and started a new life. A new family." A new family that wouldn't remind her that she'd lost everything. A new daughter who didn't tell her to her face that she wished she'd died instead of her dad. Perfect little Beth who didn't get into trouble or attempt to kill herself all the time.

"And can you describe any other close relationships you've had since your parents?"

"No."

Brad sighed. "We really need your cooperation here."

"Okay, Brad, let me tell you—"

"It's James. Brother James."

"Okay, *Brad*, first, you aren't my brother. You're just some nutjob who seems to get off on controlling people. Second, I'm not being uncooperative. I don't have any other close relationships. That's why I can't describe them to you."

She grabbed two fistfuls of her hair, and a guttural cry escaped her. Except Austin. Just Austin.

Enraged, she stood up and leaned over the table. "Have you not been following the plot here? Do you think I'd be sitting at this table right now if I had anywhere else to go?" She slammed her hands on the table. "Do you think I'd be giving up my last remaining grip on reality to be brainwashed by a bunch of crazy cult scientists and poked and prodded like a goddamn lab rat?"

He remained silent.

She felt her strength draining. "You want to know who I am? I'm a basket case. When my dad died, my mom died with him. She gave up on life and left me to raise myself. I was twelve. Fucking twelve!" She looked right into the camera. "I had to steal groceries for a month because my mom wouldn't get out of bed, even to hit the goddamn ATM machine. I quit going to school. My friends abandoned me, and I had nothing." She looked back at Brad. "You're a shrink, Brad. You tell me what happens to a kid who loses both her parents."

"She becomes detached and has difficulty bonding with others." His soft, kind voice was absolutely maddening. "And please call me Brother James."

"You're not my fucking brother!" she screamed. "You're not my friend. You're nothing but a demented, baby-torturing monster."

He flinched at the insult, and she felt momentarily satisfied until that look of false compassion returned to his face. "How did you do it? How did you recover from that trauma? The loss of your dad and then the rejection of your mother?"

She was done answering Brad's bullshit questions.

Brad leaned forward on the table so that he was just a foot in front of her. "You have a choice. You. Have. A. Choice. We don't force anyone to stay."

A sarcastic laugh escaped her. "Right." She leaned back in her chair and returned her gaze to the wall.

He pulled out his iPhone. "Tell you what. Here." He unlocked it and set it down on the table. "Call someone. Tell them where you are. They can come and get you."

She picked up the phone, carefully eyeing him to see if he'd make a move to grab it back. It had to be a trick.

"Go ahead. I'm not going to stop you." He stood up and backed away from the table to make the point. "But I should tell you that there's currently a manhunt for you, initiated by the FBI. You're wanted for questioning regarding a DEA agent who was killed not far from your apartment, as well as a potential charge of conspiracy with Austin Harris." He softened his voice, again trying to appear genuinely concerned about her.

He was good, too, the slimy bastard.

"So whoever you call should be someone you wholeheartedly trust to not turn you over to the police." He nodded at her to go ahead.

She stared down at the phone in her hands. Friends? She had none. The closest friend she had was Ryan. *We probably shouldn't hang out anymore.* Family? All she had was her mom. *It's Allison. She's calling for money.*

With a cry of rage, she threw the phone at him. He ducked just in time to avoid it hitting him in the face. The phone shattered against the wall behind him, spraying glass and plastic across the suffocating room.

She collapsed onto the table, burying her face in her arms.

"Austin was your best friend, wasn't he?" he asked softly. "He would have come for you. He loved you and you loved him, right?"

Wrenching sobs tore from her throat, making it hard to breathe, to speak. Hard to absolve herself.

"He's dead," she wailed. "Austin is dead. I killed him! I killed him with my own two hands."

She covered her head with her arms and sobbed, finally embracing the grief of losing Austin once and for all. The only person she'd ever loved since her father, and he was gone from her world forever. The scene in the shed now haunted her: The vibration up her arm as the rock-filled lunch box slammed into his temple. The spray of gravel across the shed. The blood. All that blood.

Brad rested his hand gently on her shoulder.

She jerked away and sat up, wiping her eyes and nose with her hands. "Don't you ever touch me again."

"Do you want to start your life over again? We can give you that. Here, we can give you another chance for happiness. We can make you forget every bad thing in your life."

He handed her a tissue from the box on the table. His compassion enraged her. What she wanted was her life back. She wanted to wake up from this nightmare and go back to her perfect world. She wanted Austin. She wanted little Jakob to walk again. She wanted to sit at Frank's bar and drink an IPA with nothing to worry about except whether she needed to call an Uber.

But it was all over. There was nothing for her outside these goddamn walls except prison and probably insanity. This sick, unethical, biohacking hellhole for addicts and hookers was all she had left.

She slumped in her chair, defeated.

Brad waited.

She palmed her wet eyes. "Can you make me forget about what happened?"

The question came out like a challenge.

"Can you? Can you make me forget Austin?"

"Yes."

Her chin quivered. "I can't live like this. I don't want to be so alone." She drew in a long, stuttering breath.

"You'll never be alone again, here. I promise."

She felt nothing but emptiness.

"Would you like to stay here with us?"

The fight was over. She gave a slight nod and looked down.

"I need a verbal agreement from you. I need a yes." His face was filled with pity. Or maybe it was sadness, but it didn't matter.

"Yes." It came out as a whisper.

Don't you quit on me, Butch.

I failed, Daddy. I didn't make it.

She wiped fresh tears from her eyes, cleared her throat, and looked directly at the camera. "Yes."

Thirty seconds of blissful silence passed.

Then Brad switched off the video, his eyes shining with what might have been tears. "Well then, beautiful girl, welcome to the Colony."

98

"**C**an you hear me?"

I try to open my eyes, but they won't open. Through my eyelids, the room looks bright. It's morning.

"What's wrong with her? I thought you said she was conscious." A man's voice.

"She's fine. She's just coming to." A woman.

Finally, my eyes open, but I close them again. The room's far too bright.

"Oh, hey there."

I feel a gentle hand on the side of my face, and I squint to see who it is. A man I've never met. He's big, with dark brown hair and black-rimmed glasses. Or maybe he just seems big next to the very small nurse standing next to him.

"How are you feeling?"

"Fine," I say, but it comes out as a whisper. My voice seems to be gone.

"Water, please," he says to the very small nurse.

She whisks out of the room.

"Where am I?" I whisper.

"You're in a hospital bed in a hospital room in a wonderful place called the Colony. Do you remember arriving at the Colony?"

I think hard. Really hard. "No."

The small nurse bustles back into the room and thrusts a cup of water with a bendy straw in front of me. I take a drink. God, it's the best-tasting water I've ever had.

"You've been through quite an ordeal, but we're going to take care of you, okay?"

"Okay." I try to remember what happened. Was I in an accident or something?

"Can you tell me your name?"

My name? My name. I feel like it's right on the tip of my tongue, like a dream after I wake up in the morning. But it's just not there. I close my eyes again, concentrating hard. I try to envision it written on a piece of paper. I start to panic, and I open my eyes.

The man seems to read the fear on my face, and he soothes me. "It's okay, it's okay. Give it some time. It'll come back. Just rest."

But the idea that I can't remember my name is too upsetting. Do I have amnesia? Dammit. I concentrate hard, squinting my eyes as if that will help wake up my groggy brain. I focus on an imaginary pencil and paper. I hold the pencil in my hand: straight line down, straight line over. Straight line down, straight line over.

"It's an L," I announce, as if that solves the mystery.

"Okay, that's a start," the man says.

I'm annoyed that he's talking to me as though I were a child. Straight line down, straight line over, and straight line down, straight line over.

"Two Ls." This small effort has exhausted me and I want to go back to sleep, but just as I start to fade, I hear loud footsteps enter the room.

"Well, who do we have here?" a voice booms over me.

I can barely open my eyes and they won't focus, but I see a blurry doctor looking down at me. He shines a penlight into my eyes, and they close reflexively. He lifts my wrist to feel for my pulse.

"Do you have a name, miss?" he asks.

I feel stupid and embarrassed. "Yes, it's … it's …"

I blink several times to clear my vision and turn to the man in the glasses, imploring him for help. His impossibly bright blue eyes meet mine, but there is sadness in them.

He breaks from my pleading gaze to address the doctor. "Dr. Jeremy, this is Layla."

From the Author

Thanks for reading *The Pain Colony*. I sincerely hope you enjoyed it. The second book in *The Colony* series, *The Rage Colony*, is now available for pre-order on Amazon.

Meanwhile, if you'd like a glimpse into Layla's recruitment into the Colony, be sure to get the free companion short story *With Pain Comes Peace*, a diary written by Layla. Enjoy the first chapter at the end of this book, and download the full book here: **https://dl.bookfunnel.com/zlg4dr1w5c**

Also, I'd be ever grateful if you would consider putting up some stars on the Amazon store page for *The Pain Colony*. Reviews are the life blood of new independent authors, and your review would have a huge impact on my book's visibility to other readers.

Just a quick acknowledgement...

Thank you with all my heart to my husband, Steve Ritland, for the countless hours of scientific advice and endless encouragement. Thanks to my scientist friends and alpha readers, Anne Clewell, Adrienne Farid, Laomi Harewood, and Nancy Lewis for suffering through the terrible, lengthy first draft and still assuring me that I wasn't a hack.

And an enormous thank you to Lisa Poisso, who not only provided a masterful editorial review and line edit, but taught me the art and science of story-telling.

Finally, feel free to visit my website (shanonhuntbooks.com), where you can sign up to be notified of my next book, friend me on Facebook (Shanon Hunt Books), follow me on Instagram (shanonhuntbooks), or write to me at shanon.hunt@gmail.com. I answer every email.

The Colony series continues...

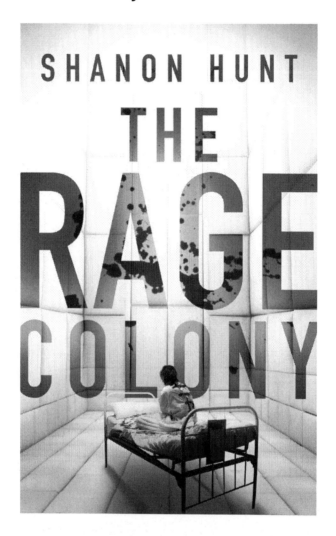

SHANON HUNT

THE RAGE COLONY

In a secret society where human experimentation is
performed at any cost...

There are bound to be mistakes.

With Pain Comes Peace

A Companion Short Story to The Pain Colony

My name is Layla. Or so they tell me.

In no world could I be a Layla. Layla's a feminine name. It's for someone tall and graceful with flawless skin and thick silky hair. I'm five foot six with stringy hair and a round baby face. Slender but a little beefy in the thighs. Graceful? No. I walked right into a sliding glass door just this morning. I feel I'm more of a somewhat klutzy tomboy, more of a Charlie or an Alex.

I've been rescued and rehabilitated by a curious place called the Colony. Rescued from what, I don't know. Possibly a life not worth living, since I was found unconscious and bloody with a broken foot. Hiding from someone (or something) in a dirty dumpster alley in a bad part of Phoenix.

Or so the story goes.

The hospital they brought me to is awfully impressive. Behind impossibly clean glass doors, the rooms are ultramodern, with high-tech machines and all sorts of robotics, like something you'd see in a science fiction movie. The doctors and staff are courteous and caring. No one from the billing department has stopped by to ask how I'm going to pay for this. I've even had a few sessions with the resident shrink. Everyone seems to want to help.

But I have a weird feeling about this place. Not that I can really trust my instincts at the moment. As it turns out, amnesia really hinders your sense of self-awareness. Dr. Jeannette, the shrink, has been gracious enough to explain my situation and provide some motherly reassurance.

"You just need a little time, my dear," she told me last week. "Retrograde amnesia after traumatic brain injury is very common and almost always very temporary. Just like your broken foot, your brain will heal and you'll be able to tell us who you are and where you came from. Simple as that. Try not to get frustrated. When you let your mind rest, your brain will start to repair."

I appreciate what she's saying, but it's impossible not to get frustrated. You know how something gets on the tip of your tongue, and it drives you crazy? That's everything for me. My name, my job, my friends and family. I have a general idea of the world I've lived in for twenty-something years, but nothing personal seems to connect. Like I know I drink coffee, but I can't remember ever buying one. I know how to read, but I don't remember ever reading anything.

Anyway, as I was saying, I have a weird feeling about this place. I think it might be a religious cult. Here's why.

A couple of days ago, I was visited by one of the hospital staff. He's tall with broad shoulders and intense blue eyes that make me slightly uncomfortable, even behind his thick-rimmed glasses. He came in wearing the standard white hospital scrubs.

"How are you feeling today?" he asked me. His perfect white teeth seemed as perfect as the rest of him. Under normal circumstances, I might have found him … well, perfect.

"Okay, Doctor," I answered, all raspy. My vocal cords still haven't fully recovered.

"Well, that's good to hear, but I'm not a doctor."

"Oh, sorry. It's the, uh, outfit." I twirled a finger at him.

"I suppose we haven't been properly introduced. I'm Brother James."

"And I'm 'Layla.'" I added air quotes. The gesture was flippant, and I instantly regretted it. My situation wasn't their fault, and they had to call me something.

I cleared my scratchy throat and changed the subject. "Are you a priest?"

He didn't answer me at first, just loomed over me, grinning. I pulled my blanket up to my chest.

"No, no, not a priest." He fell into the chair next to my bed. "We're a community of open-minded people who are working to make the world a better place. Those who've demonstrated commitment to our cause earn the distinguished title of Brother or Sister. It creates a culture of unity, like a big, happy family."

I couldn't tell if his tone was serious or sarcastic, but it was definitely unnerving.

He glanced back toward the door and said in a low voice, "Between you and me, I always found it to be a little corny. But I've been here a long time, and I suppose it's grown on me. We do extremely meaningful work here, and that's what's most important to me."

"What meaningful work do you do?"

"Experiments."

"Experimenting with what?" Drugs, no doubt. Hallucinogens, probably. LSD, mushrooms, PCP. Whatever opened the mind to enlightenment.

"Ways to achieve purity and perfection."

My scalp prickled. Those words were chilling for some reason. I nodded and gripped my blanket a little tighter. It's not that I have something against cults. To be honest, I have no experience with them, at least none I can remember. But the word makes me think of brainwashing and sex slaves. Or a bunch of hippies holding hands singing "Kumbaya."

He seemed to get the hint. "Well, I better get back to work."

He smiled politely and left, and he hasn't been back since then. I wonder if I hurt his feelings. I feel a little ashamed if I did. After all, these people graciously picked me up, brought me to their hospital, and nursed me back to health. They don't deserve to be insulted. As a guest in their house, I should be respectful. And until my memories return, I don't have anywhere else to go.

Maybe I should start practicing.

Kumbaya, my lord, kumbaya.

Kumbaya, my lord, kumbaya.

Kumbaya, my lord, kumbaya.

Oh lord, kumbaya.

Read more of Layla's introduction into the Colony! Download the free book here: **https://dl.bookfunnel.com/zlg4drlw5c**

About the Author

As a former pharmaceutical executive of 15 years, Shanon Hunt has firsthand experience with cutting edge medical advances. But it wasn't until she took an interest in CRISPR and the near future implications of genetic engineering that she became inspired to write a suspense thriller.

When she's not plotting her next story, she enjoys being tormented by her frisbee-obsessed Australian Shepherd, hiking the wilds of northern New Jersey, and canyoneering in southern Utah with her husband, Steve. She lives in New Jersey with Steve and their two sons, Nick and Ben.

Made in the USA
Las Vegas, NV
19 April 2021